D1140340

Launched in 1990 with her debut novel, *Darker Days Than Usual*, Suzannah Dunn wrote a further five critically acclaimed contemporary novels, and a short story collection, published by Flamingo, before writing her first historical novel, *The Queen of Subtleties*, which was published in 2004. She has since written a further five bestselling historical novels: *The Sixth Wife*, *The Queen's Sorrow*, *The Confession of Katherine Howard* (a Richard & Judy pick in 2011), *The May Bride* and *The Lady of Misrule*.

Praise for *The Testimony of Alys Twist*

'The question of Mary's marriage splinters English politics and these dynastic travails are the source of gossip and peril for ordinary people . . . A beautifully written portrait of the familiar Tudor court from an unfamiliar angle'

The Times

'This intriguing story is set in sixteenth-century Tudor England . . . Suzannah Dunn weaves suspense, historical detail and romance brilliantly into this tale'

Woman's Weekly

'Suzannah is known for her painstaking detail of the period and for her research and *The Testimony of Alys Twist* does not disappoint'

Woman's Way

By Su3annah Dunn

Darker Days Than Usual
Quite Contrary
Blood Sugar
Past Caring
Venus Flaring
Tenterhooks
Commencing Our Descent
The Queen of Subtleties
The Sixth Wife
The Queen's Sorrow
The Confession of Katherine Howard
The May Bride
The Lady of Misrule
The Testimony of Alys Twist

The
TESTIMONY
of
ALYS
TWIST

SUZANNAH
DUNN

ABACUS

ABACUS

First published in Great Britain in 2020 by Little, Brown
This paperback edition published in 2021 by Abacus

1 3 5 7 9 10 8 6 4 2

Typeset in Fournier by M Rules
Printed and bound in Great Britain by
Clays Ltd, Elcograf S.p.A.

Papers used by Abacus are from well-managed forests
and other responsible sources.

MIX
Paper from
responsible sources
FSC® C104740

Abacus
An imprint of
Little, Brown Book Group
Carmelite House
50 Victoria Embankment
London EC4Y 0DZ

An Hachette UK Company
www.hachette.co.uk

www.littlebrown.co.uk

For Matt Bates, my kind of muse.

Contents

[Outside the city gates] are dogs, and sorcerers, and whoremongers, and murderers, and idolators and whosoever loveth and maketh a lie.

Revelation 22:15

I

Parchment Halo

I remembered it once said, when I was small, that I would go far. Whoever had spoken over my head had been right, I thought, because just twenty or so years later here I was, arriving to work at the palace, and no servant gets further than this.

Fresh off the wherry-boat, foot in the washroom door, I was all smiles for the pair introducing themselves as my fellow laundresses: Mrs Fox – more ox-like than fox-like – and her sourpuss sidekick, Kay. I was only too aware I was no choice of theirs, but a recommendation taken up by whoever at Whitehall did the hiring and firing. And, worse, three's a crowd. So busy was I with the smiling that I didn't spare a second glance for a young woman, small and neat in periwinkle mockado, who passed us on her way to what I would later learn was the drying room.

Introductions over, I was directed to my lodgings – the Wiltons' house on Kings Street – and when I returned to the laundry a half-hour later, there was no sign of the laundresses. Instead a ruddy-faced royal-liveried man came bounding across the deserted washroom towards me: 'Mistress Twist?'

Well, there was no denying it.

He said he was Mr Hobbes, Yeoman of the Robes, and would

like to borrow me to cast my gaze over the queen's wardrobe: he'd value an expert eye, he said, and I had to stop myself from looking over my shoulder, because any eye I had was for linen, not the silks and wools of gowns. Mistress Fox had been so kind, he said, as to lend me for the day. Neither she nor the sharp-faced sidekick were in evidence to confirm or deny it, and who was I to argue with a man in uniform? So, out of my depth before I'd even started, I did my best to look competent, snatching up my pouch of fuller's earth and a couple of my flasks of flower waters: wood sorrel and celandine, if only because those had the tightest stoppers. I took no soap – gowns can't be soaped – and followed him from the laundry back to the riverside steps, which was when I queried: 'Wardrobe?'

'Baynard's.' He inclined his head downriver. 'Castle. In the city. Sorry, should have said. Queen's Wardrobe. Department of.'

That glorious mid-October morning could have been the finished article, with every previous day a mere stab at it, a muddling-through, a haphazard, half-hearted ensemble of cloud and sky, and I felt tenderly for the girl I had been, who had sometimes found life hard: if only she could have known that this was waiting for her.

A river trip in any weather, though, would beat slaving in the laundry under the sceptical eye of that Mrs Fox. 'Lend' was how Mr Hobbes had put it, but I doubted Mrs Fox felt too deprived. She had been careful to smile, but her narrowed eyes had held me at a distance, as if between finger and thumb. Done with a semblance of good humour, as if I were a joke that we were sharing rather than one of which I was the butt.

The river was crammed with luxurious barges, their flags portraying lions, bears and unicorns mid-prance among portcullises and towers: silken proclamations of the time-honoured place of each noble family at the heart of an age-old, rock-solid England. In truth, those families had been at each other's throats just a couple of months back, if only for the few chaotic days after the boy-king's death.

I could have pinched myself, not just to see this glittering new world but to be slap bang in the middle of it: me, little orphan girl, got up in glad rags. Over the years, I had laundered in ever-larger households – countesses, duchesses – but never imagined I would work for royalty. Yet here I was, laundress to the new queen, who was the first ever to rule in her own right, and if that was extraordinary to her subjects then it must be at least as marvellous to the queen herself, I thought: her day come, after a lifetime of being shunned, denied, vilified.

It took our wherry some doing to leave the palace behind; Whitehall's wall extended for miles, but I savoured the intricate brickwork, running my gaze over it as a fingertip over a weave, a welcome distraction from the pair of oarsmen to whom Mr Hobbes and I had to sit improperly close. Oar stroke by oar stroke, I urged myself to look around and breathe it in, to believe in it: mine for the taking, I told myself. I'd worked for it, I'd earned it. I'd arrived at my happy ending.

By water was from now on how I would travel, I decided, the river unspooling beneath me as if its sole purpose were to spirit me along. But at the same time, being new to it, I hardly dared breathe, sitting stock still as if trying to escape the river's notice, hoping that for it to drown me would be more trouble than it was worth. If a river could smile, this one was doing so from ear to ear, but I knew not to trust it. My mother had been a washer-woman – that much I knew – and I had been taken in by those she had worked alongside. None is as wise to water's slippery ways as a washerwoman, so my younger years were full of warnings to *keep off the bank*, *don't go onto those rocks*, *keep away from that well*. Water lay in wait for me and I would be lost to it in the blink of an eye. Drowned in a thumb's depth. Looks pretty, someone had once said to me beside a silvery stream, but never trust pretty.

What would oh-so-jolly Mr Hobbes say, I wondered, if he knew how scared I was? Have faith? Pray to St Christopher? Surely we'd be some way down the pecking order for St Chris; he would have more pressing priorities, such as men on the high seas. We two, on a wherry from Whitehall to Wardrobe, wouldn't rank. Mr Hobbes was burbling on about the Wardrobe having only just been reopened after the six years of the boy-king and no queen even of the wifely kind. Then he indicated the stretch of wall that at long last wasn't Whitehall: 'That's the Strand, behind there. New houses like palaces. Built themselves up as little kings, they did.' The noblemen, he meant: the boy-king's minders or, as most people would have it, manipulators. 'Thank God that's all over now, and Our Gracious Lady has been favoured.'

Not everyone was convinced, though: the day before, I had overheard a man saying that pious and saintly though the queen undoubtedly was, a monarch was God's representative on earth and when was God last in a skirt?

Mr Hobbes was saying that he had been making the queen's clothes for years but his eyes were no longer so good and this was the opportunity for him to step back and settle to different duties. He was now on the royal staff, salaried. 'And I can leave the tailoring to Eddie Jones. Him and his apprentices. And his girl.'

Girl? There were no female apprentices.

He clarified: 'Daughter. And I *say* "girl", but she's all grown up now. Your age, I suppose. She'll be married soon enough, I imagine, but Ed had better hope it's to one of those lads of his because I'm not sure he could do without her. Tremendous help to him, she is. Head on her shoulders. Turn her hand to anything. Lucky enough to learn at the master's knee. But still, you have to have a knack, don't you.' He grinned. 'Doesn't lack for knack, that one.'

London Bridge came into view ahead of us: a span of twenty

4

arches topped with houses, shops and inns, a city within a city. Seeing my awe, Mr Hobbes said, 'I've travelled all over the Continent in my line of work and there are bigger cities than London, but better? And that's why we get all sorts coming here. Parts of London, these days, you don't hear a word of English. Chappie who makes our needles: from Barbary.' He spoke fondly. 'Ever seen that? A black face?'

I hadn't. I wondered what colour Mr Hobbes's face could be said to be. Mine too, for that matter, wind-chafed out on the water.

Pleasantly, he said, 'I always say to him: Don't they need needles where you come from? Cocky so-and-so, charges us the earth. Says to me: No one here makes needles like I do. True, but then what about when he goes, leaving us in the lurch, no apprentices to come?'

To be fair, I thought, that was hardly his fault: the guilds forbade foreigners having apprentices. And as for all sorts coming, I had heard rumour in recent weeks of a fair few leaving. The queen was of the old religion, and those of the new who could afford to were heading to the Low Countries. To me, though, religion was all the same: priests of every persuasion calling people sinners; and surely it didn't matter to God if prayers were in Latin or English, because he must be fluent in both.

We drew alongside yet another riverside wall, of which Mr Hobbes pronounced, 'Whitefriars. Or Whitefriars as was: the old priory. Back in the day.' Back when England had priories, nunneries, monasteries. All I could see above the wall were trees. 'Blackfriars coming up and I wonder if we'll see them back now – the friars. Not if the lords have anything to do with it – it's all yes-your-Majesty and no-your-Majesty, but I can't see them voting themselves out of house and home. These old friaries have made for some very nice riverside living and there's a lot of lords sitting pretty in there.'

Still nothing but treetops.

'Lining up for Mass, though? No problem, because that doesn't cost them a penny. In fact, they'd save her Majesty a few if they attached brushes to their boots: they're in and out of chapel so much these days they could work that floor to a shine.'

Between Whitefriars and Blackfriars was the old Bridewell palace: 'The little king in his wisdom kept that one for wayward women and orphans.' A raised eyebrow – *What's the world coming to?* – but cheerfully. Wayward women and orphans were, it seemed, permissible. The uncomfortable truth was I could have been inside that building as either. I turned my back on the windows from which I might be seen gliding past on royal business as if born to it, dressed in the fine cast-offs for which every laundress by dint of her trade is first in line. I doubted anyone watching me from those windows would be fooled. Takes one to know one, and they would know me as an orphaned child, an estranged wife.

Mr Hobbes went on: 'And here comes Blackfriars, where our queen's own dear mother, God rest her soul, faced them down, and with such dignity. What a disgrace that trial was, what a pitiful injustice. Just a quarter-century ago yet you wonder how such things could ever have happened. But what could anyone do?' Against the will of the old king, he meant, who had wanted rid of an ageing wife. 'But that was probably before you were born.' A quarter of a century, give or take, and a lot of queens under the bridge: queens not of the ruling kind but the set-aside kind. Mr Hobbes said, 'First-class needlewoman, that Spanish queen. Well, first-class everything. Brilliant with the book-learning, so they say, but I wouldn't know about that. A crying shame she could never teach her own daughter. That was brutal.' Their separation, he meant. I wondered if it would have been worse to have had a mother until the age of twelve than never to have known one. Mr Hobbes pointed: 'I stood there – see? – and you should have heard the rumpus when the great lady turned up; it didn't occur to any of us that she wouldn't win her case. No one thought that Anne Boleyn could ever be queen.' He sighed. 'But wait long enough and what goes around comes around.'

The cast-aside queen's daughter was now on the throne. Anne Boleyn had had a daughter, too, but I never heard much of her.

The solid ground of Puddle Wharf came as a surprise to my new-found river-legs, and I didn't help myself by craning up at the stunning frontage of Baynard's Castle and, behind, the spire of St Paul's Cathedral. Mr Hobbes was spry up the steps, agile from all the years of sitting cross-legged: tailoring is hard on the eyes but good for the hips.

As we set off up St Andrew's Hill, I broached the subject of what might be required of me at the Wardrobe: 'The queen's clothes are kept here?'

He was amused. '*Queens*'. Centuries' worth of queens,' glancing heavenwards as if they were all up there, which in a couple of cases the old king would have disputed. 'We've been told they've been keeping them aired but I can't say we're finding much evidence of that. What we're finding, buried in those skirts, are sweet bags dried up like dead mice.'

At the top of the hill we cut across a churchyard. As a parish church, St Andrew's had been spared – unlike the private chapels, I imagined, of those grand residences we had passed. In the lee of the church was a smart square dominated by a single house: someone had done all right for himself. 'Master of the Wardrobe,' explained Mr Hobbes. '*This*,' his gesture took in the square as a whole, 'is us.' A lot of closed doors. 'Quiet since Michaelmas,' he admitted. 'Most of the men off for winter.' The same here, then, in the royal offices, as everywhere else: workers gone until Lady's Day to save on wick expense. He gestured across the square: 'Stable Supplies, whereas that' – the neighbouring building – 'is Removing Beds, which means everything that follows the court

7

around: hangings and carpets and so on.' He spoke without enthusiasm, as if those items got in the way, which they probably did. 'And that, there' – a door to one side – 'is Revels, which won't be much put upon, Our Sovereign Lady not being one for diversions, but should you find yourself in need of a parchment halo then you know where to come. And that, there, is Liveries.'

Another door on which I wouldn't be knocking: as a lady servant of the royal household, I wasn't eligible for livery.

'And last but not least, over there, our depot. And my goodness, there are some riches in there, and you'd think they know their stuff but you can still have some idiot cutting in Flemish ells when you've asked for sterling.' He sighed. 'And all this under the beady eyes of the pigeons.'

I glanced at the roof.

'Mister,' he said. 'Pigeon, and son: our bookkeepers. And aren't they just. Spend a lifetime working for yourself, as I have, and you're not used to someone looking over your shoulder and counting every hook and eye.' He added, 'Dare say I'll get used to it.'

He took me across the courtyard, saying he'd return for me at the strike of three in time for tide-turn, and his knock was answered by the self-possessed periwinkle-wearing young woman who had passed me earlier, back in the laundry: the one at whom I hadn't glanced twice. You, I thought, with some relief. I know you. She was sleek in that pale-blue damask, whereas my own sugar-tawny worsted was bulkily layered and river-damp-wrinkled. She had brought a candle with her to the door where it wasn't needed and it dazzled her, but otherwise her sky-grey gaze was steady. If she didn't quite stint with her smile, it was no more than due a stranger on her threshold.

Mr Hobbes was chuntering introductions – 'Mistress Twist, Mistress Jones' – then gone, leaving us alone together, shy as brides.

Indoors, my eyes adjusted to the gloom: shutters open but

windows high and small. It was warm in there and I was aware of a give in my shoulders, of how on the river and in the streets I must have been holding myself against the October chill. On the far wall, a fireplace housed an established low-burning fire. Coal smoke caught in my throat, and the scent of cypress wood hummed in the back of my nose. The walls were shelved from floor to ceiling, those shelves crammed with chests: some cypress, others oak, all bound with straps and hung with locks. This serene, tidy room couldn't have been more different from a laundry, with its heaps and racks, its tubs and their thuggish paddles, and the rasp of lye in the air.

'I'm Alys,' I said, tired of all the 'Mistress Twist'; I would take a chance on her being happy with first-name terms.

'Bel,' she offered in response.

'I'm new.' I got it in quick, apologetic, a plea for her to cut me some slack.

'Me too,' she said, and although I understood that she was trying to make me feel better – every royal employee was new – it had been clear to me from the way she had strolled through the laundry that she had known where she was going and what she was doing.

'My first day,' I said lightly, but insisting on it, my heart in my mouth.

'Since August,' she said of herself. Since the beginning of this queen's reign, then: she was an old hand, compared to me. Was she a silkwoman? Presumably there were treasures locked in the chests.

She said she was having a look at what was stored to see what could be used.

'And some of it needs cleaning?' I hadn't meant to sound dubious, but if clothing had been folded away then it should already be clean. If it had been stuffed dirty into those chests, then I wasn't sure what could be done about it. I wasn't someone to let

9

loose around finery. She didn't answer that. Instead, animated and purposeful, she proposed, 'Let me show you something,' and reached behind me to a row of hooks — dozens of them, each holding several key rings and each ring holding a handful of keys, none labelled. Peering down the room, she recited under her breath: a complicated reckoning, I guessed; no direct correspondence between chests and keys. With a deft swipe at a particular ring, she approached a chest on a bottom shelf, long enough to hold a body. Kneeling, she handed me the candle, indicating that I should put it up on one of the shelves. 'Careful of that,' she said, needlessly. 'Imagine this place going up.'

I stood by as she busied herself with three locks in turn before rising and hefting the lid. 'This one, in here, is new,' she said with obvious satisfaction. Unlike so much else in the room, I took her to mean: gowns left in the wake of centuries' worth of queens, theirs for the time they were queen then put aside for successors.

Whatever was inside the chest was dark and viscous. She began hauling at it while I stood awkwardly by, keen to pitch in but not knowing how and sensing that it wasn't quite my place. But then she stepped aside, made room, and from then on it was a joint endeavour.

It was leather, although I had never before touched leather so soft; it seemed as if it might still melt back into life. The smell was unmistakable, though — earthy, musty — and then I saw it for what it was: a bag, the neck of which we were dragging onto the rim of the chest, and laces that Bel set about untying. Inside it was another bag — this one mushroom-coloured and grainy, made of buckram — and she worked both back to unsheathe the contents. She said something about ermine being with the skinners — a collar, perhaps, or a lining of whatever this was — and then swimming up into her hands came velvet of the deepest, darkest blue. 'Coronation robe,' she announced, matter-of-fact.

It took me a moment. The queen, crowned at Westminster

Abbey a week ago as if she were a king. Crowned as a king, but one who just happened to be a woman. But surely this couldn't be the queen's coronation robe, here like this for a couple of girls to be dragging from its bag.

Stroking one of the whorls of gold that rose in the velvet like welts, she said, 'Less than a month, we had, to get this made. The Master Embroiderer had a whole hallful of assistants. You should've seen the size of the frame.'

To me, it didn't look as if anyone could ever have had a hand in it; it looked as if it had come intact into being. I had heard so much about the coronation, but those were stories, and now right here in front of me was something real, at my fingertips. I didn't know what to make of it: I stared, but had the oddest sensation that *it* was looking at *me*, interrogating me for a response. Cowed, I shrank from it, fell back on a jokey 'Yes, well, don't ask me to clean that.'

She took me at my word. 'Oh, all we'll ever do to this is replace the lining. And that's if it's ever reused, which I don't suppose it will be. Wedding gown next, then christening gown, and then we'll be back to kings.'

What goes around comes around, and what will come around is another king. It was what everyone said: England's crowning a queen had topped a quarter of a century of trouble, but now would come the turning of a tide, and in the nick of time. The queen was thirty-seven: time, just, for her to marry and have an heir. And God would make sure of it, people said: He hadn't brought her this far to deny her. It was what everyone said, but I, for one, was glad to have been trained as a laundress rather than a nursemaid.

When we had packed the robe away again, I braved raising the subject of how I could help. 'Mr Hobbes says I'm here to clean.' I didn't say that a laundress subjects their linens to dunking and steeping, rubbing and scrubbing with deceptively milky

11

lye, rinsing and hanging in sunshine. Silks and wools should be treated with as light a touch as possible, preferably just brushed: a mere making good and getting away with it.

'There will be things here we can use,' she said, 'which will help, because there's no money,' but seeing my look, she reassured me, 'Don't worry, you'll get paid as soon as your quarter's up, and in the new money, too.' Which was worth more, although everything also cost more. 'Queen's order,' she said, which, she explained, was the problem: everyone being paid, all of a sudden. 'The Pigeons have been sitting on wages and bills some of them going back years.' The queen had ordered that everything should be settled, in a new start.

Of the garments and fabrics uncovered in the Wardrobe so far, though, she said, not much was of any use. Tinsel and taffeta. Stuff for kings' wives. Fortunately, though, the Michaelmas warrant over at the depot was for the purchase of a great deal of crimson velvet. Proper stuff for a ruler.

Egg-white, I recalled, was best for spot-washing crimson velvet.

We set to work of a kind because it was more or less as Mr Hobbes had said: what the clothes needed was airing. Where we came across small repairs to be done, we did them then and there. Or she did. I could manage the odd hook and eye, and reattach braiding, but anything requiring any visible stitches, I passed to her. I watched her feeling for loose threads, frayings, detachments and unravellings. Hers was a gentle, ameliorative touch whereas in my daily work in the laundry I had a fight on my hands.

She said little, kept herself to herself, and asked me nothing about myself, but I didn't take her reticence as a lack of interest: on the contrary, I had a peculiar but not unpleasant sense of somehow getting known, as if she were absorbing me through her skin.

Late morning we took a break outside on the steps in the hazy sunshine, when she kindly shared her bread and cheese and beer, and then we did talk. She wasn't a silkwoman: she dismissed the suggestion with a rueful laugh: *Chance would be a fine thing.* No, she was the tailor's daughter. The one with the knack, then, according to Mr Hobbes, and I had seen plenty of it even in the small tasks of the morning. Unlike me, she had no official post at the palace and, as such, lived at home, which was a couple of streets away, with her father and his apprentices.

2

Diptych

By the end of my first week, there had been no further calls for me to the Wardrobe, and although I would have liked nothing better than to be working there alongside Bel, it wasn't as if I didn't have enough to do at the laundry. I had never seen so many clothes – being queenly seemed to involve several changes each day. I was barely keeping my head above water. I had to procure provisions: by the end of the second week my supplies of soaps and soaks were running low and it was clear that I was expected to make my own. That wasn't unusual, though, and I preferred it that way; every laundress has her own recipes.

For lye, I needed ashes, of which in my view beech is best. I needed to find burners of beech living near court, and asked the Wiltons to put word out among their neighbours. Eggs I could buy from the kitchens while they were still available before winter. The scrapings of wine barrels make a lye that's particularly good for ink stains, and since I was anticipating that a queen would be a warrant-signer, I went to talk to the clerk of a merchant who had some business with the royal cellars. He was French, so only time would tell if we had the deal that I hoped we had. As for flower waters, though, I was stuck – this was no

14

country manor house with a flower garden and a still-house – and Mrs Fox and Kay were infuriatingly elusive as to the source of their own supplies. I reminded myself that there's a lot of fuss about lotions and potions when in truth there is no substitute for clean water and elbow grease even if you'd be hard pressed to get a laundress to admit it.

We three laundresses worked in close confines, yet I made sure only ever to be properly in the company of Mrs Fox and Kay at mealtimes. In this vast household of men, we didn't dine in hall but in the privacy of the laundry, our meals delivered twice daily at the usual ten o'clock and four. I was painfully aware that whatever I did, I failed to measure up for Mrs Fox; but whenever I felt I had an inkling as to the nature of her grievance, it slipped my grasp and established new grounds. So, in her eyes I might one minute be full of myself, but in the next I was scared of my own shadow; or I was a fusspot, but then also somehow workshy. It was as if, with her eyes closed, she were stabbing at me with a pin. In fact she kept her eyes slightly averted whenever she addressed me, although not in a respectful way. I felt that when she was talking to me, she was talking to someone I didn't quite recognise, and in turn I would find myself blinking – actually physically blinking – as if to try to correct the distortion. Her animosity ran rings around me, but most wearying of all was that awful smile of hers that was anything but: the grating bonhomie, the blaring insistence that we were all friends.

She cut me down to size so that next to me she was larger than life, no-nonsense: *No flies on me. Seen everything, me.* She kept for herself and Kay the delicates – the partlets and sleeves, the hosiery and coifs, the pieces of linen and lace to cover hands, feet, throat and crown – and made sure for any blood to find its way to me: the wadding used by the ladies. Blood is the laundry's adversary, against which laundering skills count for nothing: it's merely a question of speed, of catching it at first spill, before it gets its grubby hold on the threads, after which it's a matter of brute force.

Still, my fellow laundresses' lack of curiosity about me was a relief. The most I was asked – by Kay, when Mrs Fox was elsewhere – was if I were married, and I'd anticipated that because with laundresses there's no easy way of telling: rare is the laundress who wears a ring on her finger; most wear one as I wore mine, on a thread around my neck, down inside my gown. I could claim to be a spinster, but in my experience that raised more questions than it answered – *A girl like you?* – and, leaving me open to matchmaking, wouldn't do for any length of time. And with nowhere further to go, I was at the palace for keeps. Widowhood was good for stopping people dead, but again would only get me so much grace, because the world and his wife likes to see a young widow remarried: again there was the risk of matchmaking. Whatever I offered Kay would have to hold for good. So I said I had been married but that my husband was missing. At sea, I added for good measure, which seemed the best place for him to be missing, not least in that it was unlikely to give him back up. And in truth it did capture something of my particular predicament. Kay's sorrowful glance suggested she was sympathetic to the marital purgatory in which she understood me to find myself, and which wasn't in fact so wide of the mark. 'Kids?' she asked, to which I was able to answer truthfully that I had none, before swiftly asking her in turn about herself. Widowed, she said, and I thanked my lucky stars I hadn't gone for that as my lie because I imagine it takes one to know one. She had two girls, she told me, and there came a swift but touchingly bashful recitation of names, ages and circumstances: they were small, and living in the village of Finsbury with her sister.

Over the coming days, I discovered that the new queen's marital status was a pressing concern for Kay and Mrs Fox, as indeed it was – to judge from what I'd overheard on my journey – for much of England. The queen was unmarried at thirty-seven because, before, who would have had her? Who had she been before she unexpectedly became queen? It depended on who you asked. Royal bastard, or heiress. But now it was settled: she was unequivocally and victoriously queen. That, though, raised the problem of who could marry a queen. Only a king, because no mere nobleman could be so unfairly favoured: that would be asking for trouble. A king, then: but which king? Half-Spanish as the queen was, she was unlikely to marry a Frenchman. But if she married into Spain, then England would be sucked into the Spanish empire.

Much more troubling than any of that, though, was that every wife is required to obey her husband. How could the queen be both wife and sovereign?

My fellow laundresses didn't have an answer to that; but as to whom she should marry, they were decided: the young Englishman who, as the last of the Plantagenets, could at one time have been king, which was why he had been locked up in the Tower by the old king. That young man had the very best breeding, said Mrs Fox: he'd scrub up nicely. His incarceration from boyhood – and better still, under the tutelage of a similarly imprisoned bishop – was what made him, in their eyes, the perfect gentleman. This lanky lad was stepping unsullied into the sunshine.

A Plantagenet would set the seal on a happy ending, they both felt: red and white roses entwined, peace in England for ever more. 'The two of them as they were on that day on Tower Green,' enthused Mrs Fox, one dinnertime, 'is something England will never forget. You come back in five hundred years' time and people will still be talking about it, how the queen overcame all those armed men, rode into London on the love of the common people, and went to that poor kneeling prisoner-boy and crouched in front of him, took his hands, raised him up, kissed him and set him free.' Tucking into buttered plums, she added, 'Besides, have you seen him? I wouldn't kick him out of bed.'

No, I thought, uncharitably, but if you so much as turned over in your sleep, he'd go flying.

The sole advantage of being behind with my work, of forever struggling to keep up, was that Mrs Fox and Kay would finish earlier and I would be left alone. There was no curfew at the palace; I could work as late as I needed. It's true that a laundry, and the drying room in particular, can be unsettling after dark — garments body-shaped but hanging flaccid and lifeless on the racks — and there were times in my first weeks when in my tiredness I imagined them reproachful for the drowning and wringing they had endured at my hands. Nevertheless, I welcomed any chance to work alone. Within a week or so, Mrs Fox had relented a little and let me loose on nightshirts; I had never before handled linen so fine, so elaborately embellished, and I wanted to take the work at my own tentative pace. If I did make a mistake and damage something, I could perhaps by morning find a way to repair it. Failing that, I thought, I might find somewhere to hide it. Or at the unthinkably worst, perhaps I could burn it.

During those long evenings, I would sometimes step outside into the porch for a break, and lose myself for a time in the Whitehall world going by in the lavishly lit courtyard and cloister. Arriving at the palace, I had thought that I was someone — or that I *should* be someone — but it was a relief more than a disappointment to learn that here I was a nobody. Unseen in that porch, I marvelled at all those men busy making for themselves a life at court; all men, even at this new court ruled by a queen, because just as in the court of any king, the only working women were the queen's personal attendants behind her closed doors and we three laundresses. Safe in the shadows, I was free to look at those men to my heart's desire, even if they were the kind who would never give me the time of day and whose charms in any case would be lost on me. They were grafting to move on up at court but doing their best to appear as if they could do so in their sleep. Some of them were probably, like me, only just getting by; but they swirled around themselves their hamperingly heavy cloaks – begged, borrowed and bartered for – as if they were no weight on their shoulders but might well be wings.

One evening towards the end of my second week at the palace, I was alone in the laundry when a chamberer came down from the royal apartment for a nightdress for the queen. No royal chamberer has time to wait around; she turned on her heel, leaving me to find a nightdress and take it up there. A staircase led from the royal laundry to the chamberers' room, which adjoined the queen's bedchamber, and we laundresses were required to wait with laundry at the chamberers' door, left ajar for us. If after a while no one had come, we were permitted the gentlest of prompts – a clearing of the throat, or even a knock. Before that particular evening, I hadn't dared cough or knock, but instead had lingered for as long as it had taken for me to be remembered. Loitering, I would overhear conversation a room away, too distant for me to discern actual words, but one voice was by far the most frequent and the loudest, a voice against which all others were sporadic, brief, muted. It had to be the queen's, even if it wasn't how I had imagined a queen would speak. In my first days, I had assumed that she had a bad throat; but by the end of my second week it was no better.

Nothing, though, was as I had imagined, not least that I would regularly stand at an unlocked, unguarded door to a room leading to the bedchamber of the Queen of England. Me, lye-hazed, with chapped hands, within spitting distance of a great lady who studied books and consulted with the Pope and the world's kings. Then again, any laundress knows that we are all the same underneath and there is no such thing as blue blood.

I knew a little of the queen from my daily acquaintance with the linen that lay against her bare skin, the clothing that she put on first and took off last, garments as private as prayer. She was narrow-shouldered and flat-chested. And although those smocks and shifts and stockings were in excellent condition, they weren't new: they were stalwarts, having seen her through thick and thin. In that sense, she had brought her country life with her to court: the embroidery that wreathed her neck and wrists and ran down her breastbone was of vines and tendrils, peas and cherries and peaches, lilac and lily of the valley. Incense was pungent on that linen, but there was no scent of horses, and her hosiery showed little wear. So, she wasn't often on her feet or in a saddle, but frequently on her knees in chapel.

That evening, having waited at the chamberers' door for some time, I realised I had been forgotten. A nightdress must have been rustled up from the chests in the room, and the chamberer who had come to me was now otherwise put upon and busy elsewhere. My problem was that I was forbidden to take it upon myself to leave: I had to wait to be dismissed. If I took the risk and the chamberer came looking for me, I would be in trouble. If I hung around for much longer, though, it might look as if I were lurking. I could do no right, I felt; I was trapped, cornered. Screwing up the courage, I coughed; and when that had no effect, I knocked, sharply: if I had to do it, I might as well do it properly.

Still nothing. Evidently there was no one in the chamberers' room. I could die here, I thought, and in my exhaustion that didn't seem fanciful. Then indignation like wind in my sails took me into the room and across it – eyes down as if modesty would make it less of a transgression – to the door to the queen's own room, on which I knocked.

And it worked: a lady was right there on the other side of it, a small lady of a certain age, half undressed and hair down, opening the door mid-conversation to relieve me of the proffered

20

bundle, her colourless gaze on mine as a basic courtesy while she turned, talking, back to the room. Only as the door shut did it dawn on me that the dumpy, dishevelled lady had spoken in the distinctive voice of the queen. My heart snatched at my throat. But it was done: linen taken, door closed.

The next day, I came across Bel in the laundry. I was on my way in from the well; the air outside was raw and my nose was about to drip. Bel was sitting with her head bowed over some embroidery, and my instinct was to shrink back across the threshold before I was seen.

'I'm here for Mrs Clarencieux,' she said, which had the ring of explanation but which meant nothing to me. 'Mistress of the Robes.' She inclined her head upwards: the queen's apartment. And with a flicker of amusement: 'Your boss.' One of the queen's ladies, then, the one in charge of her clothes. I hadn't thought beyond Mrs Fox, but of course there would be a chain of command. It was good to think that Mrs Fox wasn't the be all and end all of royal laundry; that she had to jump to someone else's call.

And as if jumping to Bel's, at that very moment she came banging into the room, bellowing, 'Susan White,' and to me: 'I've worked for our Missus C since she was plain little Susan White.' When she banged back out again, the room rang with her departure. Bel's response was a long look that was provocative in its blankness – *no comment* – and I was pleased to see I had an ally.

'So,' I said, 'what does she want, this Mrs . . . '

'Clarencieux,' and in answer she held up what she was stitching. A girdle: a length of beautifully stitched fabric to loop around a waist and from which would hang a pomander or prayer book.

The extravagance of the stitching drew me closer. 'For the queen?'

'Princess. But by order of the queen.'

The princess: the queen's half-sister. Anne Boleyn's daughter. She said she was just finishing up, putting her signature to it, and showed me: at one end, in gold thread, was a tiny bell. Then she said of the girdle as a whole, 'It's for hanging a . . .' but the word eluded her and having dropped the sewing into her lap she demonstrated: palms pressed together, then opened. 'Portraits,' she prompted.

'Diptych?'

She nodded, and returned her focus to her work. 'They're tiny, the paintings,' she said. 'Missus C showed me. There's one of the old king, and one of Queen Catherine.'

That didn't make sense. 'But for the sister to wear?' The half-sister.

She glanced back up at me vacantly; the whites of her eyes, I noticed, were tinted blue.

'The diptych — it's going to hang on the . . .' I gestured at the girdle.

She didn't follow.

'But, well, that's not *her* mother.' Not the princess's, but the queen's. This pairing of portraits would be an honouring of the marriage to which the princess's mother had put paid. *What goes around comes around*, and in this instance around her waist. Close to hand, I thought, should the princess ever try forgetting she's a bastard.

Bel didn't seem to have thought about it like that, and I would learn in time that her concern was always only for the job in hand. Indeed, I saw something of it later that same day, when we happened to leave the laundry at the same time to be surprised by the stars: it had been a dull day but in darkness the sky had cleared. We stopped to gaze, awed, and I swear she was only half joking when she said, 'If you were going to the trouble of putting them all up there, wouldn't you do it in some kind of order?'

3

Nest of Vipers

A week or so later, Bel was back, but long after Mrs Fox and Kay had finished for the day. She had come to measure the queen, she said, settling at the fireside. She would wait for the queen's daily business to finish, which in her experience sometimes wasn't until the small hours.

Elbow-deep in a tub, I queried, 'Measure the queen?'

Her Majesty had lost a fair bit of weight lately, she said, so her old patterns weren't much use.

'But you? You measure the queen?'

She was amused. 'Who else do you suggest? My father can't be feeling his way around her Majesty's waist while she stands there in her nightdress.'

Well, no. 'But the ladies,' I said. 'She has ladies.' Wasn't that what those ladies were for? What *were* those ladies for? 'Your Mrs . . .'

'Clarencieux.' Mrs C was good, she said, but not *that* good. 'We tailors bring a particular eye,' was her tactful way of putting it.

Nevertheless, I couldn't contemplate it. 'Not in person, though: you, measuring the queen.'

With a playful cock of her head, she said, 'There's some other way?'

Well, what did I know? Perhaps strips of parchment were passed from behind almost closed doors: the queen's ladies doing the job under Bel's instruction, then relaying back the necessary information, handing over the marked-up lengths.

She said, 'Perhaps I should pray for a visitation, an annunciation of measurements. "Blessed art thou amongst women, thou shalt work to a waist of twenty-eight inches and bring forth a gown."' Then she said, 'Come on up there with me.' Up to the queen. As if it were nothing. As if it were no more than stepping outside for a peep at the scattered stars. 'Why not?'

She knew why not. It was different for her: tailor's daughter, with no particular place, free to make it up as she went along. Tailor's daughter and, moreover, everyone's darling – even, I'd seen, Mrs Fox's.

'*Because*,' I said. My place was at the tubs and wringers and, at best, outside the chamberers' room. I had been thinking of myself as having come so far – the furthest a servant could go – but now, in front of her, it felt like nowhere much.

Perhaps she saw it, because she joked, 'You can be my assistant,' then made it worse: 'My pinholder.' If I were so lily-livered as to insist on cover, I could be her pinholder. Reclining on her cushion, she contemplated me. 'They wouldn't even see you: you know that.' I would be hiding in plain sight.

I did know it, and I had only recently seen it for myself, not that I was going to own up: the queen's eyes to mine but in passing and without actually really seeing me.

She sighed. 'But have it your way.'

That was unfair. It wasn't *my* way; it was simply how it was. My going up into the queen's apartment would be a step too far. I'd lived and worked in grand households all my life and I knew everything there was to know about just how far to go. Yet here she was, tailor's daughter with soft hands and life handed to her on a plate, dressed in silks, pretending it was perfectly possible for me to accompany her into the queen's presence. She was offering me something that wasn't in her gift, and somehow it was my fault that I couldn't take it. Of course I would want to go up into the queen's room if I could. Who was she, I thought, to know anything of me, of what I would and wouldn't do?

Perhaps that was why, a little before midnight, I did indeed accompany her up the stairs. I'd take my chances, I decided. After all, if she had misjudged this – she, for whom going to the queen was all in a day's work – then she was the one of us with more to lose. But right from the start, it was as we had both known it would be: the bone-tired chamberer who came to fetch us, who had been up with the queen for prayers at six if not also earlier at three, didn't even seem to see me.

And why shouldn't Bel have an attendant? Whitehall was a world of attendants; servants had their own servants: there was always someone a step behind, picking up after someone else, or a step ahead, putting arrangements in place. And anyway, no one knew what to expect of a tailor's girl: she was one of a kind, so who knew how she worked? Why shouldn't she, when marking strips of parchment with pins, have someone to hand her those pins?

Stay close to me, she had said. With the lackadaisical chamberer leading, we went up there as if there were nothing more natural in the world. Holding my trust in her was physical work: I recalculated it moment by moment as she moved on ahead of me, as if I were holding a brimming bowl, its depth the source of its stability but also, just as much, its potential undoing. Keeping her firmly in my sights, I felt the continuous shift of that trust in the roll of every bone in my feet; there was no time when, moving forward, I wasn't as ready to give up on her and turn and run.

But she drew me onwards in her wake. Her walk up was a

spellbinding performance, and what made it so compelling was her disregard of my presence. There was such conviction in it that she all but turned me invisible. As an orphan child I had trod a fine line: conspicuous enough to be taken account of, but not so much as to invite scrutiny. Following Bel up those stairs, I could surrender myself to invisibility, and what a novelty and relief that was. Each breath taken under cover of one of her own, I fell in with her as if I were slipping in under her skin.

When we reached the top of the stairs, I accompanied her across the chamberers' room, dragging my heart kicking and screaming. Facing us was the door behind which was a queen like the sun: to go too close would be to burn. I knew not to look at her, to make sure to see nothing of her.

With my eyes resolutely down, I couldn't see much of Bel either, and as soon as we had crossed the threshold, she vanished, or so it seemed. What she had in fact done was drop to her knees: a softening, a rendering of herself supple, and how swift, how thoroughgoing. It was clearly well practised, and I marvelled, because until then I had seen nothing of supplication in her bearing; she had been her own woman, yet now she was nothing but the queen's faithful servant. One simple motion was all it took; it was as if she had turned herself inside out. Whereas I, following her lead but a split second behind and self-conscious, my delay might well have looked like equivocation.

I kept my gaze down on the matting, which was honey-bright and nose-ticklingly fresh. The light was tangible, a sheen on the air itself. The scent was of molten beeswax, rich, runny, sticky in my throat.

The queen's voice greeted Bel, asking after her and her father and the work at the Wardrobe. *Christabel*, she called her. Bel hadn't said she was Christabel; I had assumed she was an Isobel. She – Christabel – was running through the appropriate obse-quies, as well as answering the queen's questions and offering news as if they were old friends. The mere fact of this conversation was so extraordinary that it didn't occur to me to listen for its content; the two voices remained just that: a kind of music.

In any case, the ease of the exchange told me all I needed to know, which was that there had so far been no mention of me. Nothing in the tone of those voices to suggest the question *And this? Who's this?* I was an impostor, an interloper in the presence of the Queen of England, in the most intimate setting of her bedroom late at night, and the blood-beat in my ears – harsh, hectic – wasn't about to let me forget it.

When there did come an upwards shift in tone, it was merely permission being granted for Bel to rise and start work. She was up and away from me, and I was relieved that the attention followed her even as I was scared to be left there alone on my knees.

I didn't know if I was kneeling correctly nor for how much longer I could bodily manage it. Much of my weight was on the balls of my feet and at some point I would have to shift. The more decisive a movement, I judged, the quicker. So I did it, and in doing so inadvertently glanced up beneath lowered eyelids and glimpsed something of the queen: slippers, the satin as red as red can be, and, skimming them, the hem of a nightgown of mulberry velvet so dense that it glided around her ankles like water. Beneath that gown would be the linen with which I was well acquainted.

The queen was offering up someone else to be measured: Lady Lennox, I heard; my dear cousin, she called her, to a hum of enthusiasm from Bel and from the lady herself: *Your Majesty is too kind.* And of the owner of this new voice I saw teal slippers, and – unaccountably – pictured her as raw-boned and silver-skinned with a notable bone-bright bridge to her nose.

'Daughters of queens, the pair of us.' The queen spoke fondly, but there was an edge to it that had nothing to do with happiness.

'Same age and same blood,' then something about dark times and having once wondered if they would ever see each other again.

'Oh, your Majesty, don't!' A bleat of a laugh, an audible shudder: *Too terrible*.

The queen's soothing response was that here she was, and here to stay. 'Talking of which: guess who came crawling today?'

The lady didn't need to guess; her answer was a knowing, ominous 'Ah.'

'*Actually* crawling,' said the queen, 'down on her knees as soon as she was through that door.'

For a second, I panicked – was I wrong, then, to be on my knees? – before remembering that I had copied Bel, and surely Bel would know.

'Making a show of it,' said the queen.

'Oh but when doesn't she?' said Lady Lennox.

Then this particular thread of conversation was gone under a flurry of measuring: *Here? Like this? And if my lady would permit* . . .

Christabel this, and Christabel that. But still no call for pins.

The queen and her cousin were soon back to the subject of the crawler, the showy crawler, who had been pleading for days on end for an audience, said the queen, 'As if I have nothing better to do with my time.' Then she said something about long hours of shouting at her councillors, who couldn't put their squabbles behind them. 'My so-called half-sister, though, has nothing better to do than skulk around behind my back with the French ambassador.'

So-called. Skulking. I was listening keenly now: the clamour inside me hushed, my ear cocked.

'Doe-eyed and quivery-lipped,' the queen said of the princess, 'and all because she still hasn't come to Mass. Always something keeping her away from chapel – her stomach, her head – and all pretence, and needlessly so, because if she's finding it difficult, I would rather know.'

The other lady was murmuring praise: *Oh but your Grace is so . . .*

'Am I such a monster?' The queen was affronted. 'It's the Chancellor who would have her in the Tower,' she said. 'Perhaps I should tell her that.'

She had tried to understand, she said, and prayed to God for patience, because she recognised that the princess hadn't been brought up to go to Mass and it didn't do to underestimate such an upbringing: 'Just look what they did to my brother.' They got them young, she said, and filled their heads with rubbish, and it was all very exciting and hard to shake off if you had never known better, but the point was that the princess was now free of them. 'There's no one standing over her now,' the queen said, 'telling her what to believe.' And yes, of course the princess could be provided with instruction as she requested, but really she need only come to Mass and then she'd understand. 'The sheer wonder of His presence,' the queen said. 'It's not books she needs to open, but her heart.'

'If she has one,' said Lady Lennox.

Was Bel hearing all this? Somewhere in my vicinity she gave every impression of being absorbed in her task: a litany of *if I may* and *that's perfect*, as if nothing existed for her but the parchment strips, the chalk, the pins, the ladies' hips and waists.

The queen said, 'Why I ever imagined she'd be grateful for my patience, I don't know, because when has she ever been grateful for anything?'

'Regards everything as her right, your Majesty,' said Lady Lennox. 'Chip off the old block; shades of you-know-who.'

'Yes, which is why,' said the queen, 'she makes my flesh creep.' Then she said, 'I don't know how anyone can believe there's anything of the king in her. Did you ever see that musician of her mother's?'

'Happily not,' said Lady Lennox.

'Same look,' said the queen. 'Same smirk. There's nothing of my father in that sly little face.'

Sly little face! I felt traitorous even to hear it, even if it was the queen herself who was saying it.

'You wonder,' the queen went on, 'what she herself believes. What she's grown up being told. Various people filling her head with lies, for their own ends. She's certainly grown up thinking herself a princess. Acts like one – pitching up at her convenience with a couple of thousand soldiers in tow. An army that, lest we forget, she was careful to keep to herself in my hour of need.'

Lady Lennox said, 'But God was on your side, your Grace.'

'And now here she is, at my court, with that household of hers. Name me one of them, Margaret, who isn't a heretic.'

Lady Lennox couldn't.

Yet they had to be accommodated, the queen complained, to be given house room, with the whole world watching and laughing up its sleeve. 'But if I don't keep them here, they'll disappear back off to the countryside.'

'Nest of vipers,' said Lady Lennox.

A shift in the air signified Bel bowing, stepping back, returning to my side, and my heart leapt at the prospect of imminent freedom.

The queen continued, 'I said to Elizabeth: Come to Mass. We'll go together.'

'Oh your Grace is so very—'

'But when you do, I said, make an effort. All this black – prim and proper, high and mighty – it's mere posturing, Margaret, because God made rubies and pearls just as He made everything else. Our Lord made beauty and magnificence in His image, and for her to be turning her back on that . . .' but in the same breath she said, 'Thank you, ladies,' and I realised that Bel and I were being dismissed. Bel had finished her work.

'"Princess"!' the queen said disparagingly to her cousin. 'How can anyone think that I'd have as my heir the bastard of a trollop and her lute-boy?'

As soon as we were across the chamberers' room, I hissed, incredulous, to Bel, 'Did you hear that?'

'Hear what?' She reached around me to close the door.

'That!' I couldn't even articulate. 'That! That!' I was practically jumping up and down.

She glanced distractedly at me; she was preoccupied with the parchment strips. 'What?'

'About the princess!'

'Oh, *that*.' She started off down the stairs.

That?

'I've heard it all before,' she called back cheerfully. 'Everyone has. Lady Lennox can probably recite it word for word.'

'But . . .'

'But what?' She turned, smiled. 'She's queen, she can say whatever she likes.'

True.

'At least she doesn't keep secrets.'

Well, that was one way of looking at it. England had had enough of plotting. Better, perhaps, a monarch who made her views known. I clattered down the stairs to draw alongside her. 'Still,' I ventured, 'it was all rather personal.'

'Ah, but nothing's personal when you're queen.' And that, too, I supposed, was true.

But still. This was a queen who, it was said, had forgiven just about everyone. A queen for whom bygones were bygones, although it was true that if she had persecuted the traitors to her cause then she would have had to put just about every nobleman in England in the Tower. Anyway: she had forgiven, and magnanimously, making something of it. But then this, in the privacy of her room: this harping and carping, this casting aspersions on her half-sister's paternity. It had me recall that diptych of the queen's own parents: her gifting it to her hapless half-sister made which of them the more pitiable?

Back in the laundry, as Bel tidied her parchment strips, I considered what I knew of the half-sister who was young enough to be the queen's daughter. Next to nothing, I concluded, and doubted that I was unusual in that. No one much did, it seemed to me, although those at the coronation might have caught a glimpse. Looks just like her father, I had heard it said, and has his bearing, but the eyes are her mother's, and no one had needed to add that the eyes tell you everything.

Her mother – Queen Anne – had been a mistake, the traces of which had been kicked over. No one was left of the Boleyn family. The princess was on her own. Nevertheless, she must have had it easy, comfortably far down the line of succession: the third of the three children. No one had been looking too closely at her. A fair-weather princess, and fair weather was all she had known because she had found it easy to be her brother's sister in a way that the lady who was now queen hadn't. And the brother had been going to grow up and marry and have heirs and then there would be no looking back: a reformed England. But suddenly he hadn't, and England had had to look behind him for a monarch and found the unfavoured older sister holed up in the east with her priests. And in she had come, turning the tide so that the princess was the one on the rocks.

Bel had intended to bed down in the drying room – always did, she said, when she had been working late for the queen, and had an eiderdown stashed away for the purpose – but I protested, although for my own sake as much as hers: I would have felt bad leaving her there and swanning off to my lodgings. It would have been kinder of me, though, because my lodgings – where she would have at most half a mattress – were a fair walk away and would be stone cold by this late an hour.

I was persuasive and we set off, well wrapped up and rehearsed for any challenges from watchmen and porters. We hurried down the cloister that had long since been hollowed of its friars, and across Old Court in the lee of Cardinal Wolsey's old Great Hall, which was by now great simply in bulk, scuppered like the cardinal himself. Out of puff, hard-breathing the black air, we passed through the scrutiny of successive watchmen, falling under suspicion but within the blink of an eye identified as mere ladies and reprieved time and again until we were giddy with it, convinced we could get away with anything.

That was, until the Wiltons' dog. I'd forgotten about Lamb. Lamb had been the runt of a litter, Mrs Wilton had told me, but had clearly been making up for it ever since and would now need to be reassured and placated. *It's only me, it's only me*: there I was, insisting on my identity and my good intentions as I unlocked the door, which rather brought us down to earth with a bump.

My two roommates slept like the dead, but in any case Bel and I kept to a minimum our preparations for bed: a swift removal of outermost garments, a garbled prayer, and then we settled alongside each other, top to tail.

Before I knew it, morning came crashing in and we were up and away, on with the work of the day, and it was as if that night had never happened, except for one thing: from then on, I could ask her if she needed an assistant. I could come right out with it: *Need a pinholder over at the Wardrobe?* Our little joke, but she always said yes and I made sure to take her at her word.

I asked every four or five days or so. If I worked all hours at the laundry for four or five days then I could usually leave Mrs Fox's jovial hostility and Kay's sidelong glances for a day downriver with Bel in the Wardrobe. Not that Bel actually needed any help. There wasn't much use for those old clothes, but we kept busy enough scavenging lace and braid from the various extravagant silks and satins that had been stuffed into bags and boxes for a future royal consort. Queens had forever been turning up in the wake of kings: some fine-bred girl sailed in from overseas or supplied by an old English family, to be taken up by a king as his wife. England's finest silk and satin altered to her size and shape, turning her head so that she forgot where she had come from and considered those gowns her own. But the day she became dowager or was disgraced or died, back they went into their boxes, under lock and key.

After we had picked clean those old garments, it seemed wrong to leave them as we'd found them, bundled away and rotting beneath stains inflicted by dining, dancing, hunting, the particular grind of queen consorts' lives. I cleaned wherever I could and Bel cut away whatever I couldn't; and then, having aired and pressed them, we packed them away in a kind of laying to rest.

Bel's working methods were so different from the dunking, rubbing and wringing that I undertook daily in the laundry, and I loved watching her edge along seams by touch. As a laundress I had to peer into warp and weft even if discretion demanded that when faced with a blemish I would somehow at the same time turn a blind eye. Laundresses see everything but at the same time make sure to notice nothing. Bel would hold her work in her lap, head bowed over it, and biting her lip, the lower of which was unequal to the top like a baby's. She was glad of any faults she found because then she had work to do. Her skills were a stitch here and there, a coaxing back to form, a making good, whereas in the laundry I would have to throw myself into my work and it was only ever trial and error as to a stain's resistance.

I loved listening to her talk about what she was up to. *Look at this*, she'd say, awed: perfection, she meant, and she would stroke her thumb pad lingeringly across it. But imperfections, it seemed, she loved at least as much: *Look what they've done, here* – a tender indulgence of whatever had been managed, of knots and slips and surreptitious makings-do.

She liked to say of the Wardrobe: *They could lock me in here and throw away the key.* But for all her love for the finest fabrics, she herself dressed plainly, bringing to mind a pebble that I had had during childhood and how its smoothness in my pocket had comforted me.

One day when I got a splinter from an oak chest, I became Bel's task in hand. 'If you have to have someone coming at you with a needle,' she said, 'you want that person to be me,' and as she set to it, I was left looking down on her crown, the pinprick precision of each hair in her scalp.

4

Normal Girls and Women

By mid-October, summer had shrunk back with, it seemed to me, an air of rebuke, the accusation that we had taken it for granted. *You've had your fun.* England was revealed in its true, murky colours, and it might only have been in our imagination that it had ever been any different. Cold mornings left us to warm our rooms for ourselves, and afternoons succumbed to ever-earlier, harder-pressing dusks.

It was chilly to be sitting on the steps with our bread and cheese, so one day Bel invited me back to her house, a few minutes' walk away in St Thomas Apostle Street, not far from St Paul's. And after that, it was what we always did at dinnertime.

Her father was often away, usually elsewhere in the city but sometimes further afield, either on business or charitable work for Barts Hospital and the new Christ's Hospital orphanage. Even when he was physically present at dinner, he was barely there: he was tiny, apart from his ears, which – red raw – appeared to bear the brunt of the world. His gentle voice held the promise of a smile even if it never quite surfaced. Being widowed was no bar to him having apprentices because Bel was of an age to step up to be lady of the house; and before that, they had had housekeepers. Privately, I felt Bel could be tougher with the apprentices. In the absence of his boss at the table, the senior of the trio – Matt – would hitch up his long limbs and sit cross-legged on the bench: an elbowing-out of his fellow apprentices but with knees. His chalky fingers were everywhere across the table – first dibs, last dibs, all dibs in between – in a provocation to which the rest of us tacitly refused to rise. He relished the current unrest, insisting that no one wanted the old ways back. The queen was mistaken, he said, if she thought that was why people had lined the streets back in the summer to cheer her into the city; it was simply that everyone had been happy to see her given her due. He made much of the troubles, amplifying tales and regaling us with accounts of harassed and assaulted priests.

He was tedious and tiresome but Bel mostly left him unchallenged, although once when he referred to priests as holier-than-thou she did point out that that was the very definition of a priest. And once when he claimed the queen was going to marry the Spanish king and we'd be a Spanish dominion like practically everywhere else in the world, the padres scuttling into our country with their thumbscrews, Bel spoke up to say that ours was a queen who listened to her councillors and her people – every last one of whom, she didn't need to add, was dead set against a Spanish marriage.

Generally, though, we suffered it all from Matt, not least because had we wanted to argue the toss, we wouldn't have got a word in edgeways. *Girls*, he addressed Bel and me, emphatically and, it seemed to me, unpleasantly. His two fellow apprentices looked no more comfortable in his company. Rob affected a weariness, head inclined as if the barrage of words might thereby slide off him, and his smile lopsided as if a part of him were making a run for it. But, then, I supposed, a troubled complexion probably had him well practised at turning the other cheek. I felt sorry for him. He even managed to eat as if that were a bit of a joke, wary of committing to proper portions but taking small, infrequent, casually executed spoonfuls and slices as if hoping we wouldn't catch him at it.

The youngest of the three lads was Ollie, all of eighteen, an outsized Adam's apple lodged in his girlish throat and his gaze burning its way up through his unruly fringe and switching beseechingly between me and Bel: *Don't leave me alone with the other two.* Not that he was in fact ever on his own because he was flanked by the Joneses' faithful old hound, Kit. Whenever Ollie returned from work, Kit rose unsteadily but ceremoniously from his cushion, so narrow-hipped that he looked likely to collapse sideways with each precarious step, and positioned himself to be claimed by Ollie's hand on his sleek head, which was incongruously bony for such a furry animal. They even looked a little alike, the shambolically furred hound and floppy-fringed Ollie who hadn't yet quite grown into his face, his jaw still too large for him, muzzle-shaped.

Strange to think of this bunch as the depository of their families' ambitions: families that had cultivated contacts, solicited interviews and bartered payments so that their gormless sons could be here in the St Thomas Apostle Street house to learn a good living.

Bel had grown up with apprentices and it seemed to me that she treated these three as if they were her brothers. She seemed oblivious to or at least tolerant of their various idiosyncrasies. Away from the table she never mentioned them, as if they were no more than household furnishings.

Mr Hobbes, the Yeoman of the Robes, had hoped she would marry one of them, I remembered. Not overbearing Matt, surely; but then Rob's diffidence was grating, and Ollie – sweet-natured though he seemed, and sweet-faced – was a boy. If any of them held any aspirations in Bel's direction, I saw no evidence of that, although it was possible my presence there at the table put a dampener on things.

After dinner, the route that Bel and I usually took back to St Andrew's Square was down Trinity Lane then Huggin Lane, across Bread Street – inhaling the fragrance of the Mermaid's famous fish dinners – into Friday Street, where we skirted the notably less salubrious Saracen's Head, then along Pissing Alley and into Maidenhead Lane. Occasionally, though, we sauntered up to St Paul's, eschewing the hubbub inside in favour of the bookstalls between the buttresses in the churchyard. Bel said books were a growing business and a draper of her father's acquaintance owned one of the presses in Paternoster Row. St Paul's churchyard had been a wreck, she told me, before the charnel house was demolished and the bones carted away; she didn't know where those bones had gone, but the stones had been reused to build Somerset House, one of the grand residences that I passed on my river journeys. Sometimes we wandered eastwards to the gorgeous little frippery shops beneath the Mercers' Hall before treating ourselves to yeasty, spicy buns at the Blossom Inn in St Laurence Lane, then strolled into the broad market street of Cheapside, where a great cross honoured some long-dead queen consort who had been Spanish. The stone saints at its base – because they were outside any church – had been spared.

Bel was also a frequent visitor to Whitehall, accompanying her father on visits to clients. Late one afternoon she dropped in at the laundry after Mrs Fox and Kay had already dined and gone to chapel. I hadn't had time to stop, and some supper had been set aside for me, which I offered to share. She wasn't keen – she and her father had been plied with delicacies all afternoon – but joined me at the fireside, and I was pouring beer when the door opened and in came a staggeringly well-dressed gentleman. He couldn't possibly have any business in a laundry, but with one swift action he had admitted himself and closed the door neatly behind him. His stepping into the laundry was clearly no mistake. My breath snapped off in my throat. There he stood in his iris-dark velvets amid the pallid linens that were lolling on our racks, their necks slack and cuffs cluttered with the close stitching of ladies passing long days on the same motifs their grandmothers would have favoured: perky peapods and bright-eyed daisies. Staid old faithfuls. There he stood, and the wearing of his elaborate clothes would have been a job in itself, the layers tucked and belted and hoisted, the fabrics fluffed, buffed, brushed, pinked and primped. Here was a nobleman in the queen's laundry, and every fibre of me stiffened in anticipation of calamity. But his nod to us wasn't so far from a wink and his touch of gloved hand to jewelled cap gave the impression of a doffing and held the suggestion that we understood one another: *Don't get up*. And with that, he was across the room, his absence of entourage almost as startling as his being there at all, as remarkable as if he were bare-legged.

He was heading for the door to the stairs: a stray nobleman broken loose and about to breach the queen's apartment while I was standing by – sitting by – doing nothing. He opened the far door and was gone nattily into the stairwell beyond it, his footfall ever lighter, higher, and in no time he would be at the chamberers' door.

Even before I could muster the words, Bel was reassuring me: 'No, it's fine, he's fine. He's Spain's man and we've been making him some clothes – we made him that jacket, actually, and what do you think? Would've been better in a damask, I think, and I did say, but ... ' A roll of her eyes: *Who listens to me?* 'And we've got Rob making him—'

'Bel.' I had to get her to stop. 'Bel. Bel.'

She did stop, but only to sip her beer.

'He's gone up the stairs.' I felt ashamed even to be saying it. We had let him go up there; the admission almost made me cry.

But she leaned towards me, playful, mock-confiding. 'He *does*.' She grinned. 'That's *what he does*,' and then she was saying again about him being from Spain although he had just come from Brussels, something about his family still being there and more to the point his money too, and if her father hadn't extended him credit—

'*Bel*. Bel, Bel—'

She cut across me, 'He's gone to see the queen,' and something came to mind, or came close: a fairy tale or rhyme that I couldn't quite remember, something fantastical involving cats or mice. But this was real. *He's gone to see the queen*.

'Like *that*?' Unannounced, unaccompanied through our laundry, past the queen's laundered smocks and up the unguarded stairs to her bedroom. 'What, and who's next? The Bishop of Winchester? Just . . . ' I flung a gesture at the room to mark the route from one door to the other, the absurdity and audacity of it.

Unperturbed, she said, 'It's because he's Spanish. He has to go in secret, at least some of the time – can't be seen to be favoured.'

'And is he?'

She gazed at me, perplexed: *Is he . . . ?*

'Favoured.'

'Oh.' She considered. 'Well, he's there a fair bit, as I understand it.'

Secret. Favoured. Was she telling me what I thought she was telling me? That it was worse even than people feared, because not only was the queen going to marry a Spaniard, but one who wasn't even king: that fastidiously bearded little man, whoever he was, a mere duke or lord. And Bel knew?

She said, 'Think about it: she's always been alone; the emperor is all she has.'

'That wasn't the emperor.'

'No,' she said, 'but he's bringing letters from the emperor.'

And at last the penny dropped. 'That man's a messenger?'

A sceptical wrinkle of her nose suggested he was rather more than that. 'The emperor's man.' Standing and stretching to release the small of her back, she said, 'She calls him Father: that's what she says to Missus C: *Father has written, Father says, Father would like ...*' She offered me some more beer before topping up her own cup. 'And I doubt she'd do that if she were going to marry him.'

She was probably right. I marvelled at how much she knew.

At the end of October, the queen was unwell for a week or so – nothing serious, apparently, which was borne out by the state of the laundry, but whatever was wrong was bad enough to keep her to her apartment and declining all visitors, which meant far fewer changes of clothes and table linen. As a consequence, I managed two days downriver with Bel, and my first overnight stay at her house.

That evening, I met Mrs Wilkinson, the queen's silkwoman, purveyor of beautiful things: she supplied ribbon and lace, tassels and buttons to the queen and the queen's ladies. She lived around the corner from Bel, in Budge Row, and, widowed, was a regular visitor at Bel's house, inviting herself along irrespective of whether the master of the house was home to receive her. She didn't let a small matter like that get in the way of having what she wanted, which was an audience.

Bel and I had had to take a longer route back from the Wardrobe that afternoon because of a protest at the reinstatement of the Mass, and when we arrived, Mrs Wilkinson was noisily concerned for us. 'It's lethal out there!' She was a good-looking woman, and flying the flag for old-fashioned frippery. Rising from her chair in the parlour, she greeted Bel with a kiss. 'Do these people have nothing better to do? Some of us have a living to make. Some of us have silk to deliver to the queen. Truth be told, today's was only stuff from Mr Hart, and frankly they'd be welcome to it, horrible stuff even by his standards and I did say to him: Is this really the best you can do? Still, Missus C loves it, and what Missus C wants, she shall have. If our sovereign lady wants to go around dressed like a performing monkey and pays me handsomely for doing the honours, then who am I to object?'

As if none of that had been said, Bel said warmly, 'It's lovely to see you, Mrs Wilkinson,' and introduced me.

'And for you and your little friend here,' Mrs Wilkinson said, 'I've some good stuff just in, some samples; have a rummage when you're ready and help yourself to what you fancy,' and when Bel demurred, she batted away her qualms with 'Good for business.'

What wasn't good for business, she said, was reformism. 'At least we now have a monarch who likes a bit of fun in the wardrobe – only place she does like a little fun, but that's fine by us, isn't it. Just think: we had a narrow escape, because if the little king had lived and married, we'd have got some misery-guts wife, head to toe in black, and, really, I ask you – does St Peter have a dress code? Come on, live a little,' she urged, as if addressing the reformists en masse. 'God's not going to be fussing about ribbons. Me, I've always liked a bit of ribbon – a lot of ribbon – and if I've incurred God's displeasure then He's been kind enough to keep it to Himself.' She added, 'I don't see Jesus wearing black.'

She had done well from the reforms, though, she admitted to me. 'That's where I started: unpicking clerical robes. Rich pickings – or should I say *un*pickings – teasing out all that gold and silver thread and ermine and aiglets. Bishops' robes are lovely for linings. Waste not, want not. There's a lot of us stinking of incense when we lift our skirts. From bishops' shoulders to ladies' thighs, but that's nothing new.' To Bel, she said, 'If I'd known you were out there on the streets with that rabble, I'd've sent my boys.'

I had yet to be acquainted with her boys, who were in the

kitchen, but later, when I went to fetch some more beer, I came across a posse of five, six or more – I didn't dare stop to count, was in and out of there in a flash, but they were quite a presence, poured over the benches like a colony of cats; and, like cats, affecting disinterest. Unlike their mistress, in their dress they were the picture of restraint, although the plain damson velvet looked to me to be of extraordinary quality and the lack of adornment made clear how they didn't need it. No doubt they had their uses, but street brawling wouldn't be one of them: a sight though they would be to behold on any street, they didn't inspire confidence as bodyguards.

If her boys were like cats, apprentice Matt was a puppy in her presence. The pair spent the evening playing cards, which he took seriously but pleasurably, his outbursts limited to an occasional good-humoured exclamation of exasperation. She should come over more often, I thought. At the same time as regaling Bel and me as to the state of silkwomanly business, she would be joshing Matt: *Oh, you'd give an old lady the runaround, would you. Chuck this lad in the Fleet and he'd bob up in a new doublet.*

It was past the strike of nine when she said, 'Better be getting these old bones of mine home to bed.' Laying a hand on Matt's head, she ordered, 'Haircut.'

On Mrs Wilkinson's departure, Bel and I headed up to Bel's room, and I was unprepared for how shy I felt on the stairs despite the two of us having already spent so much time alone together. The mere fact of the room acted as some distraction, though – a whole room to herself! – and then to see it, from the threshold, bowled me over. Not for Bel the usual fruits and vines embroidered onto the bed hangings, the leaves and petals, the stuff of the daytime sunlit world bold and bright, intricately and faithfully rendered; instead she had moons and stars on midnight blue. Not the moon as it really is, though: not blotchy. These moons of hers were made of silver thread. They were depicted at different stages of waxing and waning. Her remark that time in the courtyard about the stars made more sense in the light of the embroidered stars, which had been given the care that in her opinion God hadn't given the real ones. I liked how her hangings didn't ape nature's beauty but made it beautiful in its own right. I asked her if the embroidery was her work, but all she said was no, and my guess was that it had been the work of her mother.

Putting on a borrowed nightdress, it occurred to me that Bel might see the ring I wore around my neck. If she asked, I decided, I would say it was my mother's, although I didn't know why I was going to lie, because it wasn't as if it would matter to her. We were chatting about Mrs Wilkinson; Bel told me she was widowed, years back, and when I remarked that she would have no shortage of suitors – such a handsome and wealthy woman – she said, 'I doubt she'll ever remarry; she's fine as she is.'

And you? Was Bel fine as she was? She gave that impression, but I doubted that could be true of a woman of her age. Of my age. Of marriageable age. So far, she had never mentioned marriage or romance in respect of herself, nor even passed personal comment on any man. Little did she know it, but it suited me to steer our conversations clear of such matters. Nevertheless, now that our friendship had grown, the omission was beginning to feel awkward.

Of Mrs Wilkinson I said quickly, 'She has her boys,' and we shared a laugh. I went on to wonder aloud why anyone would need so many boys, however decorative, even if they were, as we spoke, being glorified link boys, escorting the curfew-flouting Mrs Wilkinson through Blunderbuss Alley back to her home .

Bel brushed it off. 'Well, I don't know, but they're just ... her boys.'

Equally lightly, I said, 'And everyone should have boys,' before I had quite thought how that would sound.

This was my chance, though, to push her just a little on matters of the heart. How come she and I never talked about men and marriage? All girls and women do. All normal girls and women. Indeed, some of my acquaintances over the years had talked about nothing else, even if it was often a roundabout and undercover way of talking about everything else. And Bel and I were much more than acquaintances. We were friends. Weren't we? The best of friends, even.

Turning to wash her face at the bowl, she said that Mrs Wilkinson was keeping a hope chest for her, filling it with finery for her dowry, and although this was what I had been waiting to hear – Bel one day a married woman – my heart lurched. A married Bel would be lost to me; there would be no more moments such as these, the two of us alone together at the end of the day. To cover my dismay, I joked that a hope chest instigated by Mrs Wilkinson would alone be worth getting married for.

To which Bel said, into her linen towel, 'I'm in no hurry.'

Did that mean that no one suitable had yet come along? I should ask: why couldn't I just come out with it and ask? It was ridiculous to feel so uncomfortable.

She indicated that I should get up into her bed, and, doing so, I noticed a book on an adjacent stool. Knowing that she could read but probably not well enough to tackle a book, I remarked on it.

'Oh, that's Ollie's,' she said, blithely, looping the towel over a rail to dry. 'He sleeps in here sometimes. He has nightmares.'

I recovered myself in an instant, smiling, careful to take it exactly as given, as if it were nothing, as if it were natural. In truth, I couldn't tell what astounded me first and foremost: her frankness – she could have made an excuse, said she'd borrowed it – or the matter-of-fact manner in which she'd relayed the information, or the actual fact of it. What *was* the fact of it? Did he sleep in here on a truckle? But I'd seen no truckle tucked beneath the bed, and apparently I wouldn't be sleeping on one. Did he sleep – as I was about to do – in her bed? Top to toe?

Or – as we were going to do – alongside each other? Did the pair of them, in fact, sleep at all? Ollie might well have nightmares, I thought, but that might not be why he slept in her room; and, oddly, it came as a relief to think it. I had been regarding myself as the reprobate and Bel as whiter than white, but now I saw that perhaps it wasn't that simple.

I expected her to say more, but she didn't; and then, when prayers had been whispered and the flame put out, I lay there and let this new knowledge – if it was indeed as much as that – settle over me.

It wasn't as if I didn't have my own secrets, I reminded myself. I, for one, *had* been in a hurry to marry; or as soon as I'd met Francis, I had. Before that, I had never expected a conventional life and had never hankered after one. Why on earth had I married Francis? A youthful mistake was how I had made sure to think of him in the past handful of years, if I thought of him at all. But as I lay there in the darkness of Bel's room, I thought how I didn't make mistakes, not even back when I was young, and perhaps particularly then. I had always been cautious in all things – I couldn't afford to be otherwise – and I should have known better. And hadn't I been warned? *Never trust pretty.* The truth about Francis was that I'd had my head turned, pure and simple. Or not so pure. Perhaps it would have been different had I had a mother to warn me.

Blond and blue-eyed, Francis had been a travelling player in a troupe that came on high days and holy days to the household where I was working. So, it was party time whenever he turned up, which could only have acted in his favour: professional raiser of spirits, pretty-boy bringer of cheer. The first time I ever saw him, he was tucking into refreshments in hall but looked up as I came in and smiled as if I were the one to be welcomed. I was struck by how nice a smile he had; what I missed was that he knew it. I was flattered to be singled out by someone who could have had anyone. No need to dwell on what I missed there.

For his part, I'd learned in time, he had an eye for the main chance. A lady's laundress – dressed in ladies' cast-offs and privy to their intimate lives – is a cut above.

That smile of his began the protracted dance that is in truth a stopping still and stepping back from the world to stand shoulder to shoulder, so that before long we were sweethearts. Back then, I was no stranger to that particular dance. The mystery was why within months I had married him.

It had felt to me that he was the answer; but to what, I'd soon enough forgotten. For him there had been the attraction, perhaps, of a different version of himself – married man, family man – as if dressing in new clothes, which was something he did whenever he could. In a sense, for him I was an unlikely choice – goody two-shoes and, I'd say, a mere buttonhole onwards from plain – but several of his troupe had already married, each sporting his new status like a shiny badge, and by choosing me, Francis could top them all, because a lady's laundress is a catch, although no doubt that wasn't what he'd meant when he said I was almost a lady but not quite.

5

Burning a River

I made sure to be well and truly taken up by Bel that autumn, working all hours at the laundry so that every fourth or fifth day I was well enough ahead to go downriver and assist her at the Wardrobe, and sometimes stay the night. Despite all the toing and froing on the river, it seemed to me that I was coming to a rest after a lifetime on the move: in the St Thomas Apostle Street house I felt for the first time in my life that I had a home of a kind. With Bel herself I felt at home in a way that I had never experienced with anyone nor had imagined I could; and whenever we were together, daily life seemed to perform itself solely for our intrigue and entertainment.

One afternoon in November, I arrived late at St Andrew's Square, Bel and I having agreed that I would stay that night at hers for an early start the following day. I looked for her at the Wardrobe but she wasn't there, and eventually I found her alone at a bench in the main tailoring workshop. As I closed the door behind me, she sat back in a kind of stretch but also to show what she had been working on, and took no small pleasure in the revelation. What she said – not much above a whisper – was pitched between admission and announcement: 'The kirtle.' From her reverence, I understood – even though I hadn't until then known of its existence – that it was the kirtle to be worn beneath the queen's wedding gown.

So, the queen was going to be married. And Bel had known it for long enough for all this work to have been done, the beautiful, painstaking embroidery on which wick-light eddied as I neared the bench: weeks of work during which, dismayingly, she hadn't breathed a word to me. All those nights when I had lain alongside her beneath the silver-thread celestial bodies, chatting over the day's events. Never once had she let slip. And I had thought *I* was good at keeping secrets.

She still hadn't told me who: who was going to be our king? She wouldn't have had to know in order for her to have been able to do that work, but I bet she did.

I braved it: 'Who?'

She didn't miss a beat. 'The heir,' and the speed and calm with which she said it held the hint of a plea: *Don't* . . .

And she was right to cringe, because how on earth could she have kept this from me? The Spanish heir: he was the only heir anyone ever talked about. Not the emperor, then, as people feared, but his son. So, we would have a Spanish king, whose sons would be our future kings.

Don't give me 'Don't', Bel.

Did she not understand? England would be part of an empire where people were herded in their hundreds into public squares, gagged and hooded and shackled to stakes to burn for what they believed or didn't believe or what they thought they believed but the priests in their wisdom had decided they didn't. Bel knew this. She *knew*. Everyone did. It had been talked about for years in the houses up and down the land; there was no one in England who was unaware of what the Spanish were like, and everyone knew about that heir, riding around the pyres to check that the burning was done to his satisfaction, once telling a pleading

50

figure, 'Were you my own son, it would give me the greatest pleasure to be the one to set you alight.'

Their women, Bel: they stone their women. *That's us, Bel*: women. The women are veiled to keep them pure but then when the priests decide the veil has failed, they belt them with bricks until the brains run through. *You know this, Bel, you know all this, so how can you sit there looking up at me with your oh-so-blue eyes, asking me to admire your oh-so-careful stitching?*

She said, 'We're making his, too,' and gestured across the workshop. 'The queen is the one in charge. She's even dressing him; he isn't allowed to dress himself for his own wedding,' and she spelt it out for me: 'He's coming here on her terms.'

I was the one, she meant, who was naïve.

'And no veil for her,' she said, 'no bridal veil, because this is England. He's coming to live in England and he'll live as an Englishman. Everything that people are saying: it's lies,' she said, 'it's ignorance, it's just to cause trouble; it comes from people who have no faith in her, who don't want her on her throne.' She said, 'Alys, this queen has fought her corner all her life. She's scared of no one. She wasn't even scared of the old king – remember? – and she must've been the only person in England who wasn't.'

True.

'That week when she was ill?' She shook her head. 'She'd shut herself away to think and pray. A whole week of it, every God-given hour.'

Again, I marvelled at how much Bel knew.

'She has thought it all through, from every side. She's going in with her eyes wide open.' Then, lighter, 'Besides, she's a woman as well as a queen, and why shouldn't she have a chance at happiness?'

I stood there, shaking, confused as to what to make of it. *Trust me*, Bel was saying. Should I? Level-headed Bel, who had known the queen for years. And this was a queen who had promised her people to be unlike all other monarchs, not in that she was a woman but because she was forgiving and peace-loving. It was true that ours was a queen – a woman – who knew more than most about being denied and silenced.

'Now,' Bel said, offering an olive branch, 'come, see.'

And I did as she said, came closer, to stand beside her, and there it was, slick and lucent on the workbench, like a natural wonder. A milky bone-white, secreted skin, the waxy carapace of some magnificent mythical creature. Insensible, unknowing of its own power. The sheen demanded to be stroked, but at the same time repelled me. Its shape was indiscernible – it could have been anything. If she hadn't told me, I would never have known. She could've got away with it, had she wanted.

Her fleeting sideways glance was like a touch to my shoulder. 'You should try it on.'

Very funny.

'I mean it.' She was cheerful – as she always was, about everything. 'It'd be a help. You're her size, give or take. I could see how it hangs.'

I tried to laugh it off. *Here we go.* Pinholding all over again. 'I am *not* going to try that on.' Nor even touch it. Nor even, if I could help it, *breathe* on it. '*You* try it on.' We were roughly the same size.

Her perfectly reasonable response was 'But then I wouldn't be able to see it.'

'Well, someone else, then: make someone *else* put it on.' Meanly, Ollie came to mind – pretty little Ollie-boy – and I almost said so.

But she wasn't having my refusal; she said, 'No one will know.'

Since when was this about what anyone else would or wouldn't know? 'I'd dirty it,' I tried.

'You're a laundress,' she countered, which was disingenuous and she knew it. This could never be cleaned. It was only ever to be worn once: that was the whole idea.

'I'll help you put it on.' Calmly practical. 'It'll just drop down over your shift, and we'll loose-lace it at the side.'

How come we were already discussing practicalities? I said nothing and didn't move, but somehow that was an offering up of myself for unpinning as I did whenever I stayed over at her house, although then it was reciprocal. This time, though, I alone would be down to my shift.

She was brisk, making small talk – how was my journey? – in a vain attempt to distract me from the slide of every pin through the fabric and its release into her possession. With each one, I thought of a different way in which what we were doing was wrong. I didn't want her to see – to feel – how I was shaking.

When I was unpinned, she stepped back for me to do my bit, to unwrap myself and step free of my gown, which she took from me to lay somewhere safely out of the way. Next was my kirtle, which was back-laced; I had to turn my back on her. Without my gown, I was cold, with shivers added to my shakes.

Her touch was light, her fingertips untrackable. I was thinking I should come clean about having been married. But why did I think she would want to know? A youthful mistake: that was all it was. And anyway, I had a sense she already knew. She must have seen the ring.

She took my kirtle, tidied it away, and I stood there in my underlinen just as the queen had in front of all her ladies. Was mine as clean as it should be? It was on its second day of wearing. With so much laundering to do for others, I was sometimes neglectful of my own.

'You're cold.' She was concerned.

'No,' I lied. I didn't want fuss; I badly wanted to get this done.

She lifted the wedding kirtle off the workbench, candle-glow streaking and spilling the length of the fabric like something disturbed and making a dash for it. I raised my arms so that she could begin to hang it around me, arrange it, ease its falling; and she was right, it was easy. Saying something about not pinning it into place – this would do, was as far as she needed to go – she stepped back, the better to focus, and in turn I watched her appraising her creation. She paced around me, frowning in concentration. Uncomfortable under her detached scrutiny, eventually I spread my arms to assert my own physical presence. *Well? What's the verdict?*

Her reverie came to a halt in an apologetic smile and she took me in, eyes widening. She smiled again, but properly, if with a shyness as if to concede something, and, nodding her approval, pronounced, 'Very lovely,' with an amused lilt, as if I were a child to be humoured. Nervously, I reciprocated in kind with something short of a bow: *Credit where it's due*. Then we both laughed at our mannered solicitude, and laughed at our laughing at it, and there was a shared sense of having got away with something. I said I should get out of it and she said yes and moved to help me, and that was it, the moment gone.

Except that it hadn't, and we both knew it. I busied myself retrieving my layers and doing my best to put myself back into them as she bustled about, putting under lock and key the kirtle that should never be worn by anyone but the queen, and it was clear between us that we had a secret to keep.

When we stepped outside together, the cold rushed at us and I was glad of it; we sparked against it, our blood and breath pumping and pulsing to give that autumn chill a run for its money. We called in on the card-playing, hearth-hugging pages for an escort, recruiting them as cut-price link boys, and there were several who were happy to oblige, as much for the chance of a sanctioned foray through the dark streets as for the tip.

So there we were, a ragbag little procession with Bel and me at the hub of it. Along the unpeopled lanes, the shutters were fastened, London done with the day and leaving us to the night.

We pitched in, sink or swim. The dark air drifted and massed, banked. It towered over us. Night makes no claims as the day does to busyness, transparency, balance; night spins no line, but just *is*. As we rushed along, Bel and I were all clatter: there was too much of us, too present, we were too physical and I found I was saying anything to distract from that. 'The moon,' I said, as if I'd never seen one before; and 'It's cold,' as if the chill had before then been kept from us.

At the house, supper had been left for us and we set about retrieving platters and serving ourselves, and all the time I felt like laughing because *look at us*: giving the impression of everything being as usual. I knew from the light in her eye that Bel felt the same. We could get away with anything. She had dressed me in the queen's wedding underdress; candlelit, I had worn it for her. We were untethered.

The house seemed smaller and our pattering around the kitchen a mere humouring of the everyday. The respectable workaday world had had of me all that it could reasonably expect. Something was going to happen: I didn't know what, but something.

After we had eaten, we climbed the stairs to her room, changed into our nightdresses, knelt as usual and separately said our prayers and got into bed with clean consciences. And then when the wick was extinguished and the hangings drawn around us, the night didn't close over us but opened, upended like a bowl, and drew me up onto an elbow as if to do some thinking or talking, but instead I found myself leaning over Bel and lowering my lips to hers as if there were nothing more natural. And hers came to mine, and on them I detected a smile. Because no one need know. No one would ever know. This was something that didn't exist: a kiss as between a man and a woman, but between two women. There was no word for it because it was impossible, like singing a tree, burning a river.

I pictured her mouth, its tantalising modesty. No crowd-pleaser, that mouth, little more than a pleat, but it had confidence. *Take me as I am* was what that modest mouth said, and it didn't have to ask twice. Never before had I wanted to kiss anyone like her, anyone sober and self-composed. And female. The mouths I had kissed on May Days and at Christmases were male, every last one of them, their tongues like something springing from a trap. Bel's mouth was mindful: she kissed as if she were working something out; her lips as tentative on mine as fingertips. That mouth was in no rush to give itself up to me, which I found attraction enough. Untouched, untested, untried, it seemed to me, although I suspected that probably wasn't the truth.

Every time our mouths lifted apart, for a breath, I expected one or both of us to stop and say something, if only *Well* . . . Saying something – anything – would bring us to our senses and put a stop to it. We would laugh it off. But it didn't happen. We kept going. Anyone placing an ear against that bedroom door would have heard silence roaring as in a seashell.

It was madness to be doing what we were doing. Yet it couldn't have been more natural. Two mouths together. We didn't do anything else, we didn't have to, because two women together make a better fit than a man and a woman. Our kissing held us slotted against each other, one of her thighs between mine and one of mine between hers – the best way for two bodies to lie together – and the slow rotation of our tongues took with it the rest of us, our nightdresses riding up a little as nightdresses do.

Gently, I reassembled her through her linen in the palm of one hand – neck, backbone, hips, bottom, breasts – uncovering bit by bit what I had known to be there beneath the much heavier daytime folds and drapes. So familiar to me yet somehow still a surprise. I was accustomed in bed to the compact hips of a man; the generous span of Bel's, neat though they were for a woman, was at least as odd for me as anything else. The more I uncovered of her, the more I saw how good a job she had done of seeming ordinary. She had almost had me fooled. There was no getting it past me now, though: the truth was that she was perfect. Neither of us mentioned the ring, which pressed against my breastbone.

When I woke in the morning, the world might have been subject to a visitation, a light but transformative touch like snowfall, and like snowfall both capricious and solemn. Bel turned her head to me on the pillow and said, 'Well . . .' and we laughed, because there really was nothing more to say.

I went into that day with the tang of her on my hands and my thigh puckered by her wetness, and from then on it would have taken something to stop what we were doing. I let it go on like a wherry gliding fast when the oars are raised, my face turned to the sun. Until then, I had had a story – a story that I told myself even if sometimes I had to lie to others – about where I had come from and where I was going. I had been patching together a life, making do, working hard and hoping for the best. Mine had been a hope chest of a life. But Bel had stopped me in my tracks. It was as if she had opened a door and taken me through to where I was supposed to be, then reached around me to close that door on the rest of the world. Isn't any story supposed to turn on such a moment? But this, with Bel, was done before I knew it. None of it was anything until it happened – my lips to hers – but then it was already done, pitching me into my future. Had I known, beforehand? Only as it's possible to guess at snow before opening the shutters, from a distinctive ring to the silence.

Luckily for us, that autumn, no one was interested in what Bel and I were up to; no one was in the least bothered about anything beyond the queen's intention to marry the Spanish heir, news of which broke a few days after I had been dressed in that kirtle. Mrs Wilkinson could be relied upon to be refreshingly direct on the subject. 'I thought she was better than this. She needs to buck her ideas up.' We were getting Spain's cast-off, she said;

indeed, Europe's, because 'they've been touting him around the Continent for years but no one wants him and no wonder with his tart and idiot son in tow'.

It was from Mrs Wilkinson that Bel bought the beautiful silk garters that she began embroidering for her wedding gift to the queen before discovering that a pair of Mrs C's own garters were to be the 'something borrowed'. Bel's garters would hardly go to waste – because who in the world doesn't need spares? – but with her original plan scuppered, and being not too far on with the work, she lost interest and decided on another project, a pair of gloves. She tried to give the garters to me and was amused when I couldn't be persuaded that it wouldn't be some kind of treason to be wearing the conjoined emblems of the queen and her prospective husband in the crook of my knee.

Protests against the marriage now made for daily skirmishes in the city's streets, and one morning when I was returning to Whitehall the barge had to idle at a distance while the Bishop of Winchester's household was unloaded at the palace steps. He had scarpered from Southwark, seeking refuge from the people of London even though it was said he had tried his best to dissuade the queen from the betrothal. But even witnessing England's Chancellor running for his life, I wasn't worried, because it seemed to me that all the difficulties of the world, its privations and persecutions, were happening to others. Bel's presence in my life was a balm and at her touch I had shucked off the cramped, cringing existence that I had assumed was bred in the bone. I would weather anything, I felt. For the first time in my life, I was resting easy while everyone else was running scared.

Then out of the blue everything changed again, and fast. Or more accurately, out of the grey: an early December morning on St Paul's wharf, autumn down to the dregs, sunk to sludge and swilling away, while detectable in the distance to a cocked ear was winter's howl. Amid a dozen or so others, I was waiting for a barge to take me back to Whitehall. The wind was making flutes of my bones, and my sleep-puddled head was empty of thoughts. I held a vestige of Bel's warmth inside my cloak.

A barge moored, and as the crowd shuffled in anticipation of boarding, I recognised one among the clenched faces: Rob, queuing there in his apprentice blue. Rob, the middle of Bel's unholy trinity of apprentices and the one to whom I paid least mind. The permanent shrug that was Rob.

Having seen me before I'd seen him, his half-hearted smile was at the ready. Suddenly, disarmingly, we were equals in the outside world as we went about our separate business, although strictly speaking he as an apprentice was permitted none to take him beyond his master's beck and call. With a sinking heart, I realised we would have to make small talk on the journey.

I did what had to be done, held back so that the crowd could file on before us and we could then fall into step and board together, but at that point he stepped in front of me, barred my passage, raising a placatory hand to the boatman to send him on his way – *Don't mind us* – and told me, 'You're needed.' His business, then, was to fetch me back to Bel, but why hadn't he said?

Softly, he said, 'The Lady Elizabeth's been granted leave, she's back off home,' and at first I didn't understand who he meant, then wondered why on earth he would think me interested in the half-sister princess. What did she have to do with anything? He said, 'You'll be joining the laundry there for a couple of weeks – keep your eyes open, your ear to the ground.' It dawned on me that he hadn't come from Bel, and then I was furious at having been made to miss that barge; I had waited in the freezing cold for nothing, and would have to wait all over again and then spend the day catching up, and all for some madness of this ridiculous apprentice. I was hardly less angry with myself for letting him waylay me. And with Bel, even – for not being harder on the boys, for failing to keep them in line, so that they thought this was an acceptable way to behave. As if mouthy Matt wasn't bad enough, now reticent Rob was acting all cloak-and-dagger. '*Rob*,' I remonstrated, 'I needed to get that barge.'

He continued, 'She's trouble,' but speaking even-handedly, as if the princess's troublesomeness might have been an affliction as much for herself as those whom she troubled. 'She needs watching, and needs to know she's being watched, and the plan is that you join the—'

'*Whose* plan?' There was no plan; this whispering dreamer wasn't going to be in on any plan. Had he really nothing better to do than come up with this kind of rubbish?

'The queen's plan.' He was mildly amused, as if my ignorance were cute – *The queen's, silly* – then detailed a fantastical chain of command, rattling off names that meant nothing to me.

I had no time for this nonsense. 'I need to get to work,' I said, pointedly craning over his shoulder for sight of the next barge. *I have a life to be getting on with. Unlike some people.* 'But good luck with finding someone else.'

'A week or two,' he said, 'just to keep an eye, and you're perfect: no family and new at the palace, and anyway you're barely ever there so who'll miss you? Except . . .'

Bel: her name unspoken there between us, and it was probably nothing. Bel and I were known to everyone as close friends. Yet it was as though he had flourished her from behind his back to have me make a grab for her.

Which I didn't, I wouldn't. She was mine, and I didn't need to prove it.

And anyway it was nothing, I reminded myself. Still, I couldn't help scrambling back over the days and weeks for whatever he might have seen or heard, for whatever she and I might have unwittingly laid bare. At the same time, I knew that even if this gawky idiot-boy had spent those nights sitting at the end of her bed, he was incapable of understanding anything of what

60

she and I had between us. *Whatever it is you think you know, I can tell you, Rob, you definitely don't.*

'The princess is going up in the world, or so she thinks,' he said, 'and it wasn't hard to persuade her ladies that she needs another laundress.'

'I'm not a spy,' I said, not that it needed saying.

'No one's a spy. But you have eyes, you have ears.' Spoken merrily, as if this were some party game, *eyes, ears and bumpsa-daisy*. 'And in your line of work more than most.'

He really did have no idea: discretion runs deep in every laundress, ingrained from the first smock she soaks. Our eyes are only for the traces, and averted from the bodies that leave them. We mind no one's business but our own.

He said, 'We are all going to have to do whatever we can in our own ways, in any way we can, just to keep the peace, and never more than now, with the wedding coming. You've seen the riots.'

'Yes, well,' I countered, 'and can you blame people?'

He shrugged. 'What do they expect? She's a woman, she needs a husband, and what do people want? That she choose from one of our own great families? Choose some nobleman who'll then lord it over the others until there's civil war? Or that she settle for a nobody, a count from some miserable little province somewhere overseas? Our Majesty has aimed for the top; it's a bold move, but she's nothing if not bold.' This was the most I had ever heard him say. He had clearly been untouched by mouthy Matt's tirades. I had taken his silence at the dinner table as acquiescence; I had mistakenly assumed the three apprentices were of a piece when it came to the royal marriage.

He sniffed and hunched against the wind, which brought him closer to me, and I took a step back, trusting blindly to the platform. 'The princess has about as much claim to the throne as you or I do,' he said, 'and they know it, her entourage, they know it but they don't care; they appeal to her vanity – no shortage of that – but it's for their own ends. They're just using her. Just as they did with the last one.'

The nine-day impostor, he meant, the little girl cousin locked in the Tower.

'And when they're done with her ...' He relinquished me, glancing around the deserted wharf. 'People have short memories. All these years of the nobles making little kings of themselves and ruling every corner of our lives.' He spoke wistfully: 'We can't even pray for our dead. Even that; they've taken everything from us, even our dead. And even you, Alys,' he said to the sky, 'will have dead.'

Gulls scythed overhead.

He blew on his cold hands. 'But now we have a chance. We have a queen who was born to the throne and who lives for her people, has dedicated her life to us, risked her life for us, upheld the truth, kept the faith. She's decent and dignified and merciful. Do it for the queen,' he said. 'Do your bit. This is your chance to do something good and it's for just a week or two. Come Christmas, the princess will be back here at court.'

That I should tell no one was impressed upon me by the three gentlemen in the warm office to which Rob ushered me when we arrived at the palace, and where I was plied with marzipan confections. Assuring me that I faced no danger – the princess would accept as par for the course that there were informers among her staff – the gentlemen explained that I would be placed in her household on the recommendation of a lady, and a name was cited. Everyone in the palace laundry would be given to understand that I was going home, that I had to drop everything and leave because of a family problem.

'It *is* a family problem,' quipped one of the gentlemen. 'Just not yours.'

The story would be that I had a relative who was gravely ill. I nodded and smiled, cramming in as much marzipan as I reasonably could. I didn't doubt those gentlemen — they looked like men of influence in their plush office in the heart of the palace and with a platter of dainty cakes. But I was the wrong person, I knew, for this job. They'd realise it soon enough, I thought, and certainly before my scheduled departure the next day.

I went straight from there back to Bel and told her everything. What amazed her most — as it had me — was that Rob had been the one to approach me: take-it-or-leave-it but most often leave-it Rob. It was almost funny in the telling, if I kept to myself how he had evoked her name but not voiced it, and how he had said this was my chance to do something good as if I were usually doing the contrary. In keeping that from her, I told myself it was she whom I was sparing, but in truth I flinched to recall how — for all his mild manner — I had felt he had me over a barrel.

I told Bel I had come to say goodbye, but in truth I was thinking she would save me. I was hoping she knew those gentlemen at the palace and could intervene on my behalf. But despite looking anxious, she was dismayingly accepting of the plan, and so I came to understand that I was just going to have to do it.

6

The Great and the Good and Bishop Gardiner

Despite my reluctance, had I been offered the chance to turn around when I eventually arrived at Ashridge, I doubt I'd have taken it. By then, even the prospect of being back on the road in a few weeks' time, before Christmas, was bad enough. Thirty miles, I had been told before we set off, which had meant nothing to me; what I'd wanted to know was how many days. Depends, came the answer: good weather, an early start and enough hours in the day, and at a push a rider could do it before dark. But a wagon, midwinter? Three or four days.

Five, as it happened; five long days, which the driver complained were too short because we were leaving as late as eight on those dark mornings and the horses were stabled again by three. The few hours we did have each day on the road were stop-start, one calamity after another, most involving mud: we seemed to be dragging half of England along in our spokes, one tortuous wheel-turn at a time, and if it was torture for us inside the wagon then I hated to think how it was for the horses.

Every hoof-thud drove it home to me that I'd been cast to the wilds, although I tried to think of it rather as something like a dive for pearls – a touch to the riverbed and a shooting back to the surface. Sometimes I persuaded myself that the whole escapade was one long homecoming, of which the outward journey was just a brief, necessary inconvenience. I knew, though, in my heart of hearts, that I had been living an enchanted life since October, as if finding coins anew each dawn in a fairy-tale purse; and girls like me, I thought, don't get something for nothing.

My only company on the journey was my minder: a different man each day, dressed in different livery. The shrieking axles and the roar of rain on the canvas made conversation difficult, and anyway it took all we had in that lurching wagon to hold ourselves apart. It was exhausting to be braced all day, yet at night I never slept the better for it, the strain burning in my long bones like fever.

Our staging posts were manor houses or their principal farmhouses, and if I had hauled back the wind-racked canvas and peered through the teeming rain on our approach each dusk, I would have seen mill house, dairy, still-house and orchard all empty, bare and shut for winter as if the household had turned its face to a wall. Inside, the houses were comfortable enough, but I couldn't bed down in the ember-warmed hall with the working men, and almost all the female servants were back in their villages until spring. The exception, the lady's maid, would make room on her mattress for me, except for the night I slept alongside a nurserymaid and three small children, which meant that I didn't.

Our hosts were tenants of one noble family or another, with corresponding loyalties. Some might have been told they were welcoming the queen's informant; others would have thought they were taking in a new servant for the princess. I never knew which I was, so I played safe, said little, and smiled. It was possible that they had been told nothing at all, nor even wondered, accustomed as they would be in their comfortable homes to sheltering travellers on the road.

And my minders: what did they know of me? Of them, I knew nothing but names, Mister This and Mister That, and even those, in the mayhem of the journey, I didn't always retain. It was a good plan – if that was what it was – to have me handed over each morning from one to another; it made neat work of the deception so that it happened almost by itself, almost but not quite by accident, so that I had left London as Alys Twist, laundress to the queen, but would arrive at Ashridge as someone else altogether.

The put-upon air of my first three minders suggested short straws, but the fourth was different and he was the one to greet me by my new name. There on the sleet-slick cobbles I became Annie Turner, laundress promoted from some princess-sympathetic household into the service of the princess herself. Or so the story would go. My fifth and final minder was no Mister anything but a simple, cheery Mike; and we, Annie and Mike, would make it to Ashridge by sundown, he said.

At Ashridge, I was welcomed into the laundry by Mrs Smith, a pillowy lady whose face was a vein-threaded patchwork of blotches and pouches; had such a thing been possible, the whites of her eyes could have done with a scrub. She shooed the cold from behind me as if it were a bothersome dog, ushering me into the drying room, where supper had been put aside for me: a loaf – white – with a dish of spiced apple and a chunk of matured cheese. Cheese! In this respect, then, at least, my stay might not be such a hardship: this, clearly, was a non-observant household, and it was my job to fit in, so if they ate dairy in Advent then I was just going to have to do the same.

We were joined by someone called Brigid, as amply proportioned as Mrs Smith but of far fewer years: a luminous blonde with amber eyes broad-set like lamps. While I settled down to the delicacies on the tray, the pair of them chatted away, pleased to have help now that they were laundering for the heir to the throne. Strictly speaking, they weren't: Rob had explained me, on our barge journey to those marzipan-touting gentlemen at the palace, that the monarch nowadays had to choose a successor. That change of law had been the old king's doing, and, like much else, had been done to get him out of a corner of his own making. For so many years the king had said that his daughters had no right to the throne because their mothers hadn't – in his view – been queens; but then at the end of his life he'd made succession his gift and given it to his daughters anyway so that they were second and third in line behind their young half-brother as they always should have been. It then hadn't gone so well when that brother, on his own deathbed, had chosen his little cousin, but the people of England had risen up just enough to line the roads from the east into London so that we could have our rightful queen. That queen would now have to be thinking about her choice, and Rob hadn't needed to tell me that it was unlikely to be her half-sister.

Yet here they were, these servants of the princess's household, talking of her as heir to the throne, and I wondered if such talk was of interest to those gentlemen back in that office at the palace. I had no idea what they wanted from me. Keep your eyes open, was all they had said, and your ears pricked. One of them said I should think of myself as a candle in a corner for them to pick up if and when they needed to look into something.

I bet they had considered themselves clever to install a laundress at Ashridge, but clearly they hadn't known the place, because, I soon discovered, the princess's laundry was in the inner courtyard, far from the life of the household, the comings and goings, the gossip and speculation. And we laundresses largely stayed put, eating and sleeping in the drying room, and using a well and privy of our own in our back yard. The furthest we would go, it seemed, was chapel, and then the only person talking was the priest. There was scant chance of me uncovering much of interest, I realised, and I can't say I was sorry. I wanted no trouble, and this battle wasn't mine. By being at Ashridge, I was doing what I had been told to do, but I was merely marking time until the household's return to Whitehall for Christmas.

'Funny old place,' Mrs Smith said of Ashridge on my first morning: an odd choice for the time of the year, she said, because Hatfield was where they usually went for Christmas, which was much more comfortable. 'Oh, we laundry ladies are comfy in here with our cauldrons' – she and Brigid hot-washed, which was new to me – 'but most of the rooms in this place are huge, and while I'm sure that was fine for monks' – Ashridge had been a religious house, apparently, before the trouble – 'it's miserable this time of year for mere mortals. I honestly can't think what we're doing here.'

Brigid said the princess could hardly be blamed, though, for wanting to put Whitehall as far as possible behind her, which prompted a scandalised Mrs Smith to tell me about the most recent stay at the palace. 'Everything we sent into her rooms was searched. The princess's delicates! All rummaged through, and flung about. All!' She threw up her hands. 'And who knows why. Who knows what they thought they were looking for.'

They almost certainly weren't looking for anything, I thought, remembering that Rob had said the princess should know she was being watched. Few better ways to impress it upon her than to have her undies tossed around by officials. She would guess she was being watched at Ashridge, although she wouldn't know by whom. Well, she wasn't alone in that. The gentlemen had implied there were other candles in other corners, but hadn't been forth-coming with names.

'And Mrs Ashley, you know what Mrs Ashley's like,' Mrs Smith said, which obviously I didn't: I didn't know any Mrs Ashley. 'Not someone to let anything go, not where the princess is concerned, so every time she was straight round there to have it out with the lords, dangling those stockings in their faces . . . '

Brigid lowered her gaze, but not before I'd glimpsed a smirk.

' . . . and yelling at them, "Would you like *your* stockings delivered in this state? What do you think you're playing at?" And you know what they said?' She was aghast. '"You can't be too careful." Said it of the queen's own sister!'

The queen's own sister: I'd heard from the queen herself that that wasn't how she thought of her.

'You can bet,' Mrs Smith crowed, 'that no one messes about with Lady Lennox's delicates.'

I remembered Lady Lennox in the queen's room: *Oh your Grace is so . . .*

'Lady Lennox,' she accused, 'lodging right next door to the queen, all cosy.'

'And her a Scot,' added Brigid dolefully.

'Invited every evening to dine with the queen when the queen's own sister was left in some poky room in the back of beyond.'

Skulking, I recalled, was the word the queen had used.

Mrs Smith huffed. 'You're right, Bridge: why stay where you're not wanted? Our Lady's Grace is best off out of it.'

My first morning, the garment I took from the top of the pile was a nightdress embroidered not in the usual black or white but the colour of a blackbird's beak. Glancing over, Brigid said, 'Miss Parry's. Anything that colour is hers. Whereas the princess's . . . ' she held up what she was ironing, 'you can always tell what's the princess's because there's a tiny acorn and sprig of honeysuckle tucked away somewhere.' She turned back a cuff to reveal some stitching. 'Look, see? Acorn and honeysuckle.'

Bel's tiny signature bell flashed through my mind.

'These stand for her parents,' Brigid said. I remembered that the queen believed a lutenist was the princess's true father, which was something I'd never heard before, although it was true that most of the world denied the old king had been properly married to her mother. I thought of the diptych that the queen had given the princess, the miniature paintings of the old king and the old Spanish queen. So this, hidden away on her underthings, was the princess's own version. I remarked that the stitching was beautiful, which was enough to please Brigid. 'Doesn't settle for second best, our princess.'

Which was what she was, though.

'But to think,' Mrs Smith chimed in from across the room, 'there was a time when our Lady's Grace had nothing. Back when she was a tot. Left with nothing. Because men only think about the big problems, don't they. They'd had a big problem in the shape of her mother and dealt with it by way of the axe, and then that was that. Don't stop to think about who's left at home, do they. Don't stop to think about babies.' She was working a salve into her hands. 'Had to be reminded there was a little mite needing clothing. The old Lady Bryan, God rest her soul, had to write to Lord Cromwell and say we needed clothes. "We've a princess here, needs a winter cloak." Everyone goes on about how the queen had it hard, and no doubt that was so, but it wasn't exactly plain sailing for the princess.'

'Funny to think of her ever having been a little mite,' mused Brigid.

'Of course we lost Lady Bryan,' said Mrs Smith, 'when the prince came along – new royal baby for her to tend to – but for most of us,' she continued with obvious pride, 'once we're here, we stay.'

Brigid dimpled at me. 'Yes, this is you, now, for life.'

Smiles all round. I didn't consider myself to be doing the dirty on them, because even if I had wanted to play the part of informer, there was little possibility, here in the laundry, of me discovering anything. Instead, I would work hard in the brief time I was here, pull my weight and thus repay them for their kind welcome. All my life the trust and goodwill of others had kept a roof over my head, food in my belly, boots on my feet, and I always did my best to play fair in return. When my time was up, in a couple of weeks, and we arrived back at Whitehall, I'd slip away from them, back to where I'd come from, under cover of some other story, and they'd be none the wiser.

I encountered Miss Parry of the vibrant underwear the following day, when Brigid and I were fetching water. Striding across our yard in a yew-green cloak came a lady as tall as any man, peeling off her riding gloves, snatching at her hood and shaking loose an abundance of grey hair before nodding amiably to us.

'Miss Parry,' Brigid said admiringly, as the lady disappeared down a passageway; 'Blanche,' as we lumbered back across the cobbles with our pails, and then, shouldering our door, 'Such a pretty name, don't you think? If I ever have a daughter, that's what I'm going to call her.'

From the washroom, Mrs Smith said, 'And will your husband – when you get one – have a say in that?'

Brigid confided to me, 'I'm having a bit of a rest from men.'

You and me both, Bridge. As far as she and Mrs Smith knew, I was a widow. I wasn't staying long at Ashridge; the lie would do for the duration.

Brigid persisted. 'My husband – *when I get one* – can name the boys,' she told Mrs Smith.

But Mrs Smith was unconvinced. 'Some fathers like to name the first daughter for their own mother.'

Brigid plonked her pail down beside her tub, and said, as if in refutation, 'My husband isn't likely to have a mother named Blanche, is he. More likely some Ann or Mary or Katherine.'

I said, 'Unless . . . ' and gestured to the door.

It took her a moment. 'Miss Parry? Oh, no.' She rolled up her sleeves. 'No sons. No children. Never married. No time, what with bringing up the princess.'

'Mrs Ashley, too,' chipped in Mrs Smith. 'Married only a couple of years back, too late for children. As for Miss Parry, she started here as a rocker,' and she demonstrated, shifting her weight to one hip and pivoting her foot. 'Princess's cradle. That's how long she's been here. Kat Ashley came a few years later, not that you'd guess it from how she rules the roost.'

My appointment was thanks to Mrs Ashley, they told me. No mean feat, they said, in that I would have had to have been sneaked – as Mrs Smith put it – past the other resident member of the Parry clan, who was holder of the household purse strings, keeper of keys to the coffers. 'Chief bill-payer,' Brigid called him – 'Chief bill-quibbler,' Mrs Smith corrected – and I resolved to avoid this Mr Parry looking too closely at me, or, if I could help it, at all.

Even within a day or two, I had the sense that had it not been for Bel, I would have been as happy to work at Ashridge as anywhere, and certainly happier than at the palace. And it was liberating to live a lie that wasn't of my own making. But despite the company of big-hearted Mrs Smith and beguilingly bashful Brigid, I longed for Bel, and longing was exactly the word for it: into the vast distance between us, I poured my love like a libation. Missing her was, I found, a work of its own: I took it on and kept at it, diligently and rigorously, in the knowledge that I would soon be on my way back and telling myself that it might feel even better to be arriving back than if I had never gone away in the first place.

A week or so into my stay at Ashridge, though, when I made passing mention to Brigid of what I took to be our forthcoming trip to Whitehall, she paused, puzzled, her red-hot iron held aloft. 'But we're not going, are we.' Hers was a face that didn't lend itself to solemnity: bug-eyed, biting her lip, she looked contrite. 'We'd be busy packing, if we were.' And even as she was still speaking, I knew it for the truth. Mrs Smith came banging through the door, burdened with bed sheets, adding with grim satisfaction, 'Everyone's sending gifts but sitting tight. Court's no place to be if you're not of the queen's persuasion. This is no time to stand up and be counted.'

All I could think was that those gentlemen had promised me, as it dawned on me that actually they hadn't. There had been no promise.

Brigid was concerned for me – 'You were hoping we'd have Christmas at the palace' – and her sympathy almost undid me; I busied myself folding tablecloths. I felt as if my lifeline had just been severed: I had actually felt, inside, somewhere, a snap and the sting of a whiplash. I had no way of getting back. I didn't even really know where I was: up the Great North Road, then somewhere across country,

'Annie?' Brigid hovered. 'Are you all right?'

Hot, I said, just hot. It was simply something to say. I did feel bad but it might just as well have been that I was cold; I couldn't at that moment have told the difference. Mrs Smith weighed in with her own sympathies, wittering about how the room was stuffy, and then we were all nodding and clucking, united in our disapproval of December, but inside I was urging myself to take my home-going into my own hands. I could take care of myself: it wasn't as if that was anything new. Those gentlemen at the palace hadn't kept their side of the bargain. I had trusted them that I would be home for Christmas but I'd been duped – and didn't that mean that I owed them nothing and was free to go? I had already done what they had asked of me: I had spent a week or so here in the Ashridge laundry. I reasoned that there would be someone, soon – someone from here or nearby – who would be travelling to London before Christmas; I would come up with some story to get myself into his wagon. A road's a road, I told myself, wildly: a road's a road. I'd come up it; I'd get myself back down it.

As is the way of things, that same day – the day I downed tools, determined that I had already done more than enough for those palace gentlemen – word reached the laundry that Mrs Ashley required help choosing New Year presents for the princess's companions. One of us would have to go up to the royal apartment, and because Mrs Smith avoided stairs and Brigid had begun mixing a vat of lye, the job fell to me.

In no mood for it, I stomped up there to be met at the door by a sloe-eyed, snub-nosed slip of a woman in rosehip velvet, whose first words were, '*She* should be doing this.'

She?

'But Mr Cecil's here, so they're going over the books. Best get this done while the girls are off dining with Mr Cecil's gentlemen.'

The girls: Mrs Smith liked to joke that any call for 'Elizabeth' in the princess's apartment would cause a stampede. All of an age, they had been named for the princess in the two years when it had looked as if England would one day be hers, which was when statues of the Virgin, for whom the firstborn royal had been named, were being smashed and thrown onto rubbish heaps.

'Chop chop.' Mrs Ashley swaggered ahead, drawing me with her to a table littered with luxuries: ribbon, lace, silk; buttons, bags, gloves. My own New Year's gift to Bel – which I now had no chance of getting to her in time – was rather different: a velvet and leather collar for Kit. Mrs Ashley slid her own exquisitely gloved hands into the small of her back, which she arched in a stretch, letting loose a breath of rose perfume that was incongruously light and simple. 'Still, Mr Cecil makes us the money that pays for all this, he's the one who keeps Mr Parry in business: it's all very well being clever at coin-counting, but you need those coins in your coffers in the first place. That's the way to look at it. The queen could do with her own Mr Cecil, but of course that woman can't leave anything to anyone else.'

74

That woman?

'Oh, she *involves* everyone else,' she said, as if I had begged to differ, 'but then thinks she knew best all along and just does what she was going to do anyway. This marriage of hers – they've all implored her to call it off, the great and the good and Bishop Gardiner.'

I might as well not be there, I thought; or, rather, I could have been anyone. She had things to say and it didn't matter who heard, which in a trice made me the informer I should have been all along, ears pricked. *Palace gentlemen*, I thought, *come and get it*; and then pay me, please, with safe passage back to the palace.

'Priests, though,' she continued disparagingly, 'she hangs on their every word, just as her mother did, and look how that turned out.' Barely drawing breath, she held up a length of silk ribbon, 'Will this fray?' and before I could consider a response, she said, 'Well, if it does, by then it'll be someone else's problem, won't it,' and added it to a pile. 'She should be doing this, but it's impossible to get her to do something she doesn't want to do. And speak of the devil . . . '

I hadn't heard the door, but across the room towards us came a young woman, top to toe in black. Long-waisted, long-limbed, long everything: face, nose. No long look, though: she took me in and passed over me in a glance of dark eyes within invisible lashes before addressing Mrs Ashley: 'Here you are.'

This was the princess herself. I couldn't help but gawp.

'Where did you think I was?' Mrs Ashley made a play at being offended; she was flushed with pleasure. 'Someone's got to do your dirty work.'

The princess merely said that one of Mr Cecil's men had a bad head; she was after some rose water. I was trying to get a good look at her, but everywhere my gaze went, from beneath my dutifully lowered eyelids, it slid off her. How did she do that – evade me like that? She picked up some lace from the table: long hands, long fingers, but her smile was full of teeth as small as a child's. Mrs Ashley made a performance of slapping it from her hands back into the pile. 'Not for you. I'll be down in a minute with that rose water.'

Then, as abruptly as she had appeared, the princess was gone, but my heart took longer to settle, beating furiously for a few more moments, and perhaps it was indeed fury, because if it weren't for her, I thought, I wouldn't be stuck at Ashridge. If it weren't for her and the problems she caused. If it weren't for her, lodged in the world like a bit of grit.

There had been never been a realistic chance that I could travel to London so late into December, but I had dreamt of it because I had so badly not wanted to be at Ashridge for Christmas. And then when it came to it, I barely was, because on St Lucy's Eve I went down with a cold which in a day or two worsened into a fever. I missed the entire twelve days of the season – which was in any case unprecedentedly subdued, lamented my fellow laundresses, with no guests, no one daring to visit a household so out of favour with the queen. The only excitement was a rumour that the Spanish prince's negotiators, arriving in London, had been pelted with snowballs.

'Quaint English custom,' said Brigid, with a glint in her eye.

'And one we should enjoy while we still can,' said Mrs Smith, 'because once the rest of them are here, we'll be burned and beheaded and buried alive for less.'

Brigid agreed that probably no one had thrown a snowball in Spain for a long time and not just because there was no snow.

I stayed in the laundry, often in bed, half dreaming of how lovely the St Thomas Apostle Street house would be at Christmas. It was a monstrous injustice that I was marooned at Ashridge. It was bad enough that I couldn't now get Bel's gift to her in time, but far worse that I couldn't even send word. I fretted about what she would make of my absence, even though I knew the absence of the princess's household as a whole would be clue enough: Bel would understand that something had happened and arrangements had changed. Still, I was tormented that my own non-appearance could be misconstrued and taken as a dereliction on my part.

My sickness made me sore all over, tender to the touch, my marrow turned to milk. Absolutely everything was too much — particularly my fellow laundresses, looming large as they did in the little world of the laundry. I rattled with every sound they made, of which there were plenty. Poor Brigid developed a sniff at which, inwardly, I raged.

I lay in my bed day after day in a stew, vowing to myself that when I did eventually get away, I'd never look back. There would be few reminders: this whole escapade would all have been for nothing because before too long the princess would be no trouble, nothing more than someone's wife, the wife of no one much because no one who was anyone would want a wife of dubious lineage and under suspicion of disloyalty.

My longing for Bel was no exquisite ache as before, but deep-rooted and chafing, drawing hot and heavy on me. Mostly I left it to run its course, but in rare moments of privacy, first and last thing, I probed it, tried to determine its advance or otherwise, what it might have in store for me that particular day or night.

In my sickbed, I concocted the story that I hoped would see me out of the door, which wasn't so different from the one that had brought me in there. As soon I was well enough I said that usually I visited a relative in the new year: would that, I wondered, be possible? That was when I discovered that Mrs Smith visited her cherished nephew every January. 'Not the best time of year for travelling,' she admitted, 'but the best time to leave the laundry,' when, with no drying weather to be had, we laundresses do the bare minimum. She was too nice to lay claim to it, but she didn't have to; duly, I backed off. The sooner she could get going, she said, the sooner she would be back and I could be on my way: indeed, she'd get a move on, have a word with Mrs Ashley to see if she could be off by the end of the week.

But later, when I came back into the washroom from the drying room, Brigid slid me a look that was ominous, and in an exaggerated whisper told me that Mrs Smith's leave had been cancelled. She looked disconcerted to hear herself say it, and I too didn't much like the sound of it. I asked the reason but she didn't know, and just then Mrs Smith came in, avoiding our eyes. 'You'll have heard,' she said, bustling, trying to look displeased rather than upset. 'All leave cancelled until further notice.'

All leave.

I asked why, but the response was a tight-lipped 'Your guess is as good as mine,' before she burst out, anguished, 'She knows I always go at this time of year! All these years I've worked for her!'

She: Mrs Ashley, I presumed, roost-ruling.

'And it's to suit her! It's to make it easy for her!' Furious, she recited the confrontation she hadn't been able to have with Mrs Ashley: '"Oh, so shall I go instead in"' – the most absurd scenario – '"June? *July?*"' Near tears: 'I *said* to her, it's for *you* that I choose January. But all she can say to that is "What if we decide to move?"'

I asked, 'Move?'

'Move!' She poured scorn on the idea. 'In January! This whole household on the road in January?' Her eyes narrowed. 'I'll tell you what it is,' and the explanation came like a threat. 'She hates it that the princess can't be at court, she hates it that we're all stuck here, and she's taking it out on everyone else. We're all of us going nowhere.' Finally, damningly, 'You know what she's like,' but in case there was any doubt, she mimicked her on her high horse: '"Well, I'm sorry, Mrs Smith, but my word is final."'

The knockback made her ill, and for days the ailment roved

fugitive around her body: head, guts, eyes, joints, chest, back. Brigid and I pursued it with various ointments and balms, while we tiptoed around Mrs Smith's actual bulk on the cushions at the fireside. It grieved her to have been treated by Mrs Ashley in so cavalier a fashion ('Barely civil, she was!') after years of unstinting service, and often she wiped distractedly at tears on her face as if they had nothing to do with her but were a natural phenomenon, like rain. In those long, bleak days, I took on her anger towards Mrs Ashley. Just who did this woman think she was? I had seen in the princess's room, that time, that she thought she was quite something. She was headed for a fall, I decided. She had it coming. I wouldn't be around to see it, more was the pity, but I didn't doubt she'd get what was coming to her.

While Mrs Smith was incapacitated, I could go nowhere even if I did somehow find the means. I wouldn't have the heart to leave Brigid doing all the work, and anyway, it wouldn't harm to hang on for a little longer to see if there was any truth in that talk of a move, a move that would solve my problem of how to get back to London.

In the second week of January, when I was close to the end of my tether, after prayers one evening there was a shove of our door and the cry of 'Visitors!' No word as to who, nor how many. All round us we heard the opening and closing of other doors, as if we were under siege. Brigid dashed off somewhere and was back in minutes with news: a pair of lords. Well, lords dine and sleep in a certain style, so napery would need to be dispatched and bed linen retrieved from storage; and these lords, whoever they were, would have riders with them who would be equally damp and cold.

'At this hour?' queried Mrs Smith.

She didn't question that they were lords. Lords are the queen's men, or should be. This particular pair, though? Belting up to the princess's gatehouse under cover of darkness?

Catching her breath, Brigid managed more. 'Doctors with them – the queen's physicians.'

Nothing untoward, then: they were indeed from the queen, these late-riding lords. But why the physicians? The princess was in fine fettle, as far as we knew. Only an hour or so earlier, there had been the strains of music and dancing from her apartment. That was no sickroom up there. Something was happening, I realised, or was about to happen, and actually I didn't care if it was good or bad: what mattered to me was that something was, at long last, happening. And those visitors, those people against whom this household would dearly love to lock its gate even as it was careful to give every appearance to the contrary: they were palace people. My people. For an instant I wondered if they had come for me or were at least bringing word for me alongside their business, whatever that business was, although really I knew they were unlikely to be aware of my existence. But I would remedy that, I thought: I could put them straight. Not then and there, when they were cold, hungry, exhausted, their skulls ringing with hoof-strike, but in the morning.

As it happened, though, we were woken well before dawn by Miss Parry, glimmering among our racks in a rich glaucous velvet. Dressed for the company of lords even at such an hour, I thought, groggily, but perhaps she had never been to bed, because she looked exhausted, her face a grey to match that gown. She had come to tell us that the princess was about to leave for Whitehall, if with a small retinue rather than the entire household. An opportunity for Mrs Smith to visit her nephew, she said with forced brightness. Which meant that either Brigid or I would be the one to go. 'I'll go,' I said, quick off the mark, and Miss Parry moved on to the subject of what needed packing, which was, she said, anything and everything white.

'White?' Brigid, blinking, spoke up.

Brigid wouldn't have wanted to go to the palace, I was sure; nevertheless, I'd outmanoeuvred her, and my blood thwacked in my ears as if I'd run a race.

Mrs Smith — perky — said that Miss Parry had come to the right place, because no one did white better than we did, but Miss Parry said that she meant gowns: we were to pack as many white gowns as the princess had, whatever the fabrics.

'Miss Parry?' Brigid again, insistent, as if tugging her sleeve. 'Is the princess getting married?'

No, said Miss Parry, grim-faced, and explained: 'They won't hear that she's too ill to travel, but that's what everyone along the way is going to see: the princess, deathly pale, being dragged mercilessly from her sickbed.'

7

Enceinte

Laundresses are hard to place at the best of times, and in the hastily assembled entourage I was put with three girls luxuriating in what looked like London russet. Too young to be ladies-in-waiting, they were perhaps attendants to ladies-in-waiting: hangers-on, wranglers of positions, from the ragbag of relatives that every successfully placed lady hauls along with her. Hard to imagine, though, what these gawky, preening girls had been doing at Ashridge other than getting in the way, and harder still to imagine what use they would be in the cut-and-thrust of Whitehall. The girls, though, were the least of it. This was the first royal entourage I'd encountered, and it was breathtaking. Word had somehow gone in a flash to every supportive household for miles, and hundreds of men wearing the princess's livery had shown up in force.

The girls seemed to regard me as crashing their party, although who knew quite what kind of party they were hoping for in a wagon in February. Their luggage took pride of place; we all arranged ourselves around it. Cooped up under that canvas, we were mere minutes into the journey when the smallest complained she felt sick, only to be slammed down by a second

('Don't you dare chuck up in here'), who was put in her place by the third ('Marcella!'). The sickly girl sat back, arms folded, eyes closed, white-lipped, resisting the urge to vomit, which at least kept her occupied. The rest of us were left with the job of not staring at one another, although even in the gloom I detected an interrogative light in the eyes of the one called Marcella: she was itching to ask me who – or what – I was. I pretended to doze. In truth, I was nursing a lump in my throat: it had been hard to say goodbye to Mrs Smith and Brigid, all the more so because I knew we wouldn't meet again.

I was anxious about the practicalities of returning to my old life back in the palace laundry. A lot of planning had gone into getting me to Ashridge, but all I had ever known about my return – all that I had wanted to know – was that I would travel back with the princess's household. But then what? Would I sort of fall off the back of the procession and sneak away to take up where I'd left off? I had told Mrs Fox and Kay a story of a sick relative; that relative would just have to have been sick for two months. As for the princess's people, I didn't like to think of leaving Miss Parry without a laundress, but it was she who had made the choice to travel with just the one of us. She would have to find someone else to do their laundry, or send back to Ashridge for Brigid. As for me, once I was back in the royal laundry, no one from the princess's household – relegated to some back courtyard – was likely to come across me; and even if they did, well, it was none of their business. If they put two and two together and realised I had been at Ashridge as an informer, then so what? I had had no say in the matter; I had been following orders, working for the queen.

Little did I know that the journey back to Whitehall would end up taking twice as long as the journey up. Each new morning we cowered under canvas in wind-strafed courtyards while hundreds of other carts and wagons were corralled around us, and never would we so much as glimpse the princess's litter at the head of the procession. After each protracted departure, we travelled for barely any time before the first stop, and these visits to houses or inns were solely for the supposedly unwell princess while we, way down the line, had to wait in our wagon, uncatered-for. And these comings and goings of the day were nothing compared to the billeting at the overnight stops. From under our canvas, we'd overhear an exchange with our driver, and a decision reached – we were for, say, the Boar – but then other riders swooped by to confer or revise or retract and in the end it would be onwards for us to the Three Keys in the next village, or a backtrack to the Seven Stars that we had passed an hour or so ago, or a trek off route across country to be hosted in someone's residence. By the end of the journey, we would have spent ten nights in inns, hunting lodges, manor farmhouses and once in a manor house itself, but at least we had been spared the mill houses and barns that many of the men had had to endure.

During our first long day on the road, eyes closed, I let the girls' chatter pour over me. Subdued at first by my presence, they soon forgot I was there. They often talked of what they imagined as their future lives: they would or wouldn't have a house like this or that, and they'd have an old or a new one near a river or on a hillside; they would or wouldn't have their daughters at court, and would or wouldn't winter outside London. They played at making decisions even though they knew these would be matters for their future husbands and in-laws.

On the second day, the girl who had felt sick at the beginning of the journey – Lina – wondered aloud at our frequent stops, to which button-nosed Marcella said something about talk at court. She used a foreign word, which had Lina protest that the princess wasn't married. Pregnant, then, I guessed: that was the rumour? That the princess was pregnant? The third girl, no-nonsense

Rose, sounded her contempt for the notion, to which Marcella insisted she was merely repeating what she'd heard. Then she said, 'There *are* some ladies, Lina-Lou, who can't wait until they're married for a bit of jiggery-pokery,' shaking off Rose's habitual warning ('Marcella!') with 'We could name a few, couldn't we, if pressed.' *Pr-essed*, she enunciated, evidently keen for her companions to do just that. When they didn't, she carried on regardless. 'Problem is, once you know what it's all about, Leeny-Lee, you can't stop. Even you, Lini-Lou, will be unstoppable.'

I found myself struggling to keep a straight face.

'Marcella,' blared Rose. 'Whatever's the matter with you?'

'I'm bored,' she said, then levelled with them. 'Men don't want to marry virgins and anyone who tells you otherwise is lying. Because think about it – what fun is a virgin on your wedding night? You don't want to spend the whole night saying, "Sorry, darling, is that sore?"'

Lina squealed, whether with terror or glee wasn't clear.

I had been a virgin on my wedding night, and not only had it hurt, but the mess had astounded me. It wasn't as if I hadn't seen it all before – the stained sheet is my stock in trade – but anything of that kind encountered by a laundress has given up the ghost and lies on linen like a shed skin, whereas what I had to deal with as a wife came in a rush, slick, with a life of its own. But in time I toughened up and what had at first been painful and fraught with misadventure became as easy as falling off a log but a great deal more pleasurable; it became an excellent way to pass the time, and indeed we did it almost in passing. It was like working some silly toy from a pedlar, a trick so simple that you are compelled to do it again and again, the same thing happening every time but that being the thrill of it.

Marcella offered, 'In one of the households I used to be in – naming no names – the girls all practised with a broom handle.'

85

She had gone too far; Rose was stern. 'That is *not true*.'

'Oh, just the tip of it. Just the tippy-wippy little end of it, Lini-Lee, don't you worry. Just eased in—'

Lina shrieked, 'Make her stop!'

I hoped no one could see me laughing; I had a horrid suspicion Marcella might be playing to me.

She said, 'They took it in turns. Or so I was told. I don't know the ins and outs. Left them to it. Intact, me.' That protracted enunciation again: *In-tact*. 'But they were all married within the year, those girls, and had babies the following year, so I reckon it must've done some good, must've got them going, got them good and ready.'

Thoroughly disgusted, Rose pronounced her ungodly.

'Nothing ungodly about it, Rosie; quite the contrary, because God made us for a purpose, remember?' and she added, 'Bless 'im.'

There was a pause before she said, 'You do wonder about the queen, though, don't you.'

If anyone did, they weren't owning up.

'It'll be the shock of her life on her wedding night, and being queen won't help her. You know what they're like, the Spaniards, and a man who's already had most of the known world roll over for him – he's not going to take no for an answer from his good lady wife, is he. Once she's got that ring on her finger, she might as well be Molly Milkmaid.'

If I had been looking forward to more of the same the following day, it was clear when I climbed up into the wagon that I would be disappointed. There was an atmosphere; Marcella in particular was transformed, sitting small and catching no one's eye. Something was going on. Wasn't it always, with these girls, I thought; but on this occasion, unusually, it was wordless. I wouldn't have predicted that strained silence could be more tedious than some of the chatter I had had to suffer, but only minutes into the journey I was thinking how it was going to be a long day if they kept this up.

It was Marcella who broke the silence, and with a question, as if mid-conversation, although gravely asked: 'Will it happen to all of them?'

By the sounds of it she was after reassurance, but Rose rebuffed her. 'We just don't know, do we. No one knows anything. We just have to . . . ' A flap of the hand: *carry on regardless.*

So quietly that I almost missed it, Lina said, 'What about the princess?'

But that got similar treatment. 'She had nothing to do with it.'

Marcella emitted a sceptical-sounding sigh, which had Rose rounding on her to repeat, 'It was nothing to do with her. She knew nothing about it.'

Marcella muttered, 'And if you believe *that* . . . '

To which, notably, no one said anything.

Then she added, 'It was done in her name. She might not have wanted it, but it was in her name.'

Rose persisted. 'You don't know that, and even if it was – which it wasn't, but even if it was – it doesn't matter. She did nothing, which is what matters. We're not Spanish, yet – you can't get in trouble for what you think. You have to *do* something. Treason's something you *do*.'

Or preferably don't.

What treason hadn't the princess done?

Marcella said, 'If we keep as slow as this, it might've blown over by the time we get there.'

Lina muttered something about how the princess should have gone to Whitehall when she was first asked, instead of feigning illness, but Marcella was incredulous. 'What, and walked into the lion's mouth?'

First asked? Had the princess had been hiding away, of late, at Ashridge? *Skulking.*

Lina faltered. 'The queen said it was for her own safety.'

Marcella hooted. 'Oh, and if you believe *that* . . .'

I had no idea what had happened, nor did I feel I could ask them. So who else could I ask? Me: part of no crowd. These girls had ample connections. This was just as true, though, I supposed, if in a different way, of those at the bottom of the pile, who were working at close quarters with the staff at the various inns and houses along our route, and my being separate and singular did give me the advantage of being able to go up to anyone. I had a hunch about who I could try.

Just the day before, I had taken the opportunity at one of the stops to stretch my legs, and rounding a corner I had come across a boy leaning back against a wall, his face tipped to the ghost of a sun. He was a scrap of a kid, half my height and probably half my age: a kitchen boy, to judge from his pallor and his clothes, or what I could see of them beneath the blanket he held around himself. None of the windburn and swagger and fustian breeches of a stable lad. I was about to back away and leave him to it when his eyes snapped open and he slid his gaze to mine with a blankness that was both a welcome and a warning: I could join him for my own moment of peace and solitude as long as I respected his.

There was, then, an understanding of a small kind between us as we stood side by side before he took his leave with a heartfelt sigh: *On with the day* . . . I didn't know for sure that he was one of ours – he might have been a servant at that inn – but if he was on the road with us and I could find him in the entourage, something told me he wouldn't be a bad bet.

At the evening stop, I found him unloading supplies. I had to pretend to some business with him ('A word, please'), which wasn't all that credible – what would a laundress want with a kitchen boy? – but nor was much else in a procession of thousands in February behind a play-acting princess. And anyway, everyone was too tired to object, or even suspect.

As soon as we were out of anyone's earshot, I spoke without preamble. 'What's happened?' I couldn't think how else to start; I'd see if that made sense to him.

And it did. 'You mean the executions?' Seeing my eyes widen, he informed me, 'Lady Jane and the hubby.'

The pair who had been pretenders to the throne by no fault of their own. That couldn't be right, though, because Lady Jane was the queen's own cousin, and anyway, she and that husband of hers were barely of age.

'Why?'

If the boy was surprised that I had to ask, he didn't show it, although there was a pause while he considered his approach.

'Well ...' He was going to run through the basic facts, to check we were in agreement on them, but the first – 'London was attacked' – clearly came as a shock to me, so he paused to reconsider.

Attacked? London? London, where Bel was. In one held breath I saw her street in ruins, windows smashed and doors wrenched open, smoke and fire, people running and screaming. But the boy read my thoughts and was quick to dismiss my fears with a shake of his head: no big problem, no one hurt. Kentish men, he told me. There were going to have been others, from elsewhere, from all over, but the lords had got wind of it and it had stopped before it started except that no one told them down in Kent, or perhaps they didn't want to hear it and they just kept on coming. 'Thousands,' he said.

Thousands. How many was that? How big? I glanced around: bigger than this entourage?

They did well, he said, those men, along the way. Got handed all the guns from the Medway ships. So then the lords decided they'd better do something about it and asked the city for men, and then off went the city men, butchers and bakers and so on: volunteers, kitted out in city whites. 'But when they reached the

Kentish lot, they decided Tommy-boy was the one talking sense, which means he ends up with twice as many men and into the bargain the new ones had brought their own weapons.'

Turncoats, then.

I had to ask. 'Tommy-boy?'

Wyatt, he said. Thomas. Sir. 'Good sort. No trouble. Queen's man.'

Funny way of showing it, I said.

He shrugged. 'Didn't want her handing herself over to the Spanish. He's on her side, really, if you think about it.'

Well, at a stretch. But what had this Wyatt been intending to do?

'To ask her to step down.'

'Step down?' *Ask* her? As if this were a conversation he might have with the queen. And then I understood why this was so very bad for the princess; I knew why she was dragging her heels. Because if the queen had stepped down, then who would have been there behind her to step up into her place? Not Lady Jane: she'd failed the first time around. Which left only the one candidate. Even if the princess had played no part in this, and whether she liked it or not, it was clear that it had been done in no one's name but hers. This was no homecoming for her at the warm invitation of her sister; rather, she was being hauled in front of the queen to account for herself. In my mind's eye I saw her swinging into that room at Ashridge, when I had stood there with Mrs Ashley. *Try swinging your way out of this.*

The boy said that the queen had ridden along to Guildhall to speak to the people. 'Calm as you like, standing there in all her robes and saying we should trust her: her people come first, she says, like we're her children, and no husband is going to tell her what to do.'

That, I remembered, was what Bel had said. Had Bel been there? Had she got those robes out for the queen, dusted them off?

And all the time Sir Thomas just across the bridge, said the boy, but the drawbridge up and all the boats city-side. So, he was stuck in Southwark, but on best behaviour, paying his way, buying his suppers for himself and his men and popping by at the Marshalsea to let the bishops out although they said thanks but no thanks because they wanted their day in court. Three days in Southwark was enough so off he went with his men towards the next bridge but that road is bad at the best of times, said the boy, which February definitely isn't, so it took all day – Wandsworth, Putney, Wimbledon, Richmond – and then, after all that, at Kingston the bridge was down.

Just a little bridge, though, he told me, and not hard to put back together again when you've the locals on hand. They crossed in the night, he said, and on the London side the going was easier. Kensington at dawn, then Westbourne, which was where one of the queen's lords turned up and said to stop: stop now and fair enough, no harm done. The boy gave me a look: why would anyone stop then? So very close and everyone on your side.

'So,' he said, 'on to the palace.'

Armed men marching on the palace.

One better. '*Past* the palace and on to the city.'

Had Bel been there at the palace?

He said, 'But panic at the palace with everyone locked in and armed, even the ladies, all of them running around with' – he considered – 'rolling pins.'

Spoken like a true kitchen boy.

With what did Bel arm herself? A needle? *If you have to have someone coming at you with a needle . . .*

All this had happened while I was kicking my heels at Ashridge, feeling hard done by and never doubting that the world would be waiting for me unchanged when I got back.

There was a bit of argy-bargy, as the boy put it, with the lords' men at Hyde Park and St James's and St Giles, but not enough to stop the marchers coming up Fleet Street, where people just stood in their doorways and let them pass. 'And then they were right up to Ludgate and it was wide open, but just as they got there' – he shrugged – 'someone closed it.' He nodded to himself, *Yep, shut*. 'Sir Thomas knocks on it, it doesn't open, knocks again, still doesn't open, and there's the lords' men coming up behind him, so . . .'

So?

'Game's up: sits himself down outside the inn there, takes off his hat and waits for them to come for him.'

The final night of the journey, we stayed just outside London, up the hill in the village of Highgate. The princess was to lodge in the house of a senior judge not long out of prison for having been on the wrong side the previous year. This was his chance to demonstrate his new-found loyalty to the queen, timely now that she was the victor twice over. Then again, this second victory had been slimmer. Because in all the time those Kentish men were on the move, no one had lifted a finger in the queen's defence – or, if the kitchen boy had the story straight, a finger was all that had been lifted, a single finger at the very last minute to drop a latch. I wondered if the judge, in the privacy of his own home, wouldn't be too hard on the half-sister who was still, despite everything, the queen's most likely successor.

Alighting at Highgate, I saw there was money up here: new houses near the city but in the fresh air, the peace and quiet, above it. Clever move. The girls were excited to see London in the distance, but I barely glanced; the sleet-laced sky was so low that it was hard to make out much, and I'd had enough of the day, indeed of the whole ten days. All I wanted was to get my head down, to crawl into whatever was to make do as a bed and pull the blankets around me as much as my bedfellows would allow.

We ended up passing a surprisingly comfortable night in the Swan, though, and in the morning I felt almost fond of the girls as they fussed over their hair. The mood was celebratory: we'd come through something together; we'd survived. I left them to it and went for a breather, and, indeed, Highgate air seemed airier than usual. The sky itself was higher and brighter, and had me lift my head for what felt like the first time in months. Adventure over, I thought, which was what it had been. Adventure well and truly over and already mostly forgotten, as if I'd been away not for a couple of months but a mere week or two.

What, though, was I returning to? The hundreds of men who had spent the night under canvas on the Green were cooking over fires and tending their horses, while down the hill was the city of London with its back turned to us, gloating over its prized possession, the river. Our fate was not its concern. The city had a life of its own regardless of who was on the throne. A monarch had been brought to the brink and Londoners had had the inconvenience of having to shut up shop for a day, but this day like every other was business as usual. I couldn't help wondering, though, if it was a little short-sighted for the city to keep its back turned on us, because these men who were about to descend weren't dressed in borrowed clothes and marching on foot as those Kentish men had been. These were gentlemen, the crowd of whom had grown along the way to – word had it – more than a thousand strong. Scratch the surface – damp and muddy though it currently was – to find confidence of a kind up here, I felt.

For all that, the atmosphere turned circumspect as we loaded up. Because who were we, as we approached Whitehall palace? Rabble, or rebels, or self-righteous reformists? Having had so long to prepare, the procession seemed oddly caught on the hop. In the wagon I watched the girls remembering themselves, turning themselves back after ten days on the hoof into the ladies of the princess's ladies, or whatever it was that they were. Steeling themselves for the return to a different kind of slog, but slog nonetheless: sewing, singing, dancing, amusing their seniors. They were rising to their return, actually sitting up straighter. Even Marcie the Minx behaved herself. Well, up to a point. She knew full well we were too numerous for the city streets and would instead shy west across Smithfield, but when the baying from the dogs' home told us we were near Moorgate she said with a mannered recoil and a wrinkling of her little nose, 'Let's hope we don't go too close to the gate.' Because nailed up there would be what was left of Kentish men who would never see Kent again.

8

A Filching

Back at Whitehall, I was dispatched to the King's Head for
lodgings, but found it deserted. Everyone was at Tower
Hill for the execution of Lord Grey, father of the luckless Lady
Jane, or so said the elderly lady who limped from a neighbouring
building to direct me to a third-floor room of which, it seemed,
for the time being, I had sole occupancy.

Luggage lugged and porter tipped with a few coins from my
dwindling cache, I stood in my room at a loss, reeling from ten
days on the move. Bel was likely to be in London, either in St
Andrew's Square or at home. I would have to head into the city;
and if I stopped to rest I might never get going again.

My intention was to return to the King's Head for the night.
This initial dash to Bel was just that, because I'd decided to stay
in the service of the princess until told otherwise. If I heard nothing by the end of the following day, I'd go in search of word as
to what to do.

I was sorely tempted to close the door and sink into that bed.
Never in my life had I had a bed to myself, let alone a room, and
this one was so peaceful. It had actual walls: sliding my hand
behind a hanging, I tapped on wattle and daub rather than a

mere partition of cloth or board. There was a window, too — a casement, glazed and hinged. With a view, no less. Of rooftops and trees. I should have been able to tell where I was but couldn't quite get my bearings. I did know I was on the park side of Kings Street rather than the river side; not having gone through the Kings Street gatehouse, I was outside the palace proper.

I should eat, but I wasn't hungry, and anyway there was nothing on offer and no one to ask. I should freshen up, too, but there was no way to warm the jug of water — the hearth was swept — and, so tired, I couldn't face a cold wash. As for a change of clothes: my luggage squatted by the door, but for days on end I had been stuffing things in there and hauling on the drawstring, pretending that somehow I'd be saved from ever having to deal with the contents.

Footfall on the stairs brought Miss Parry into the doorway, and suddenly the room seemed nothing much and I didn't dare invite her in, fine lady that she was, although for all her eye-blue velvet and mink she too looked far from her best. Ten days of travel had taken its toll on her. She had come to check on me, she said, and I guessed she had gone first to the girls, who had been sent to lodge in the gatehouse. She would be doing the rounds, to see that we were properly accommodated. I felt bad, standing there smiling at her, every inch the loyal servant, when I knew I'd be gone by the following day. Little did she know, poor lady, that she was going to be deserted by her sole laundress. She was sweetly concerned that there was nothing for me to eat — she'd try to find someone, she said, and have something sent over — and apologetic that she couldn't yet tell me anything of laundry arrangements. What she did tell me was that the princess had an apartment over by the kitchens, across the courtyard from the old Great Hall, and I expressed sympathy, although actually this was good news for me because after my move back into my life at the palace, our paths were unlikely ever to cross.

'Still,' she said, 'we might not know where to do our laundry, but at least we know where we can cook.'

The kitchen boy would already be busy, I thought: not for him a room of his own and time to loll around gazing at rooftops.

It beggared belief, she said, but Lady Lennox had a kitchen over there, too, despite her dining every day with the queen, and this kitchen of Lady Lennox's just happened to be directly above the princess's rooms.

I was perplexed – 'Above?' – and she confirmed, 'Upstairs.'

An odd place for a kitchen, I said: how would all the water and firewood get upstairs?

'Noisily,' she said, 'which will be the idea. There's an awful lot of coming and going; she's making sure we know our place' – *as she sees it*. 'You're best off out of it,' she said, and with a nod towards my window, 'You, with your view of the tennis courts. You've the best of it over here.'

After she had gone, I just upped and went. No eating, nor washing, and my bulging bag remained untackled. It was the only way: I had to get going and see how far I got. As luck would have it, the tide was in my favour. On the journey into the city, the various landmarks were familiar but the familiarity itself was the surprise, as if the landscape were sneaking up behind me and tapping on my shoulder: *Remember me?*

I disembarked onto Puddle Wharf in the dregs of daylight, into a rush of people heading homeward; no one was hanging around in the February twilight. Hoping Bel would leave work alone, I was going to wait discreetly at the square's entrance. As I trudged up the hill from the wharf, street life drained away around me: Londoners, well wrapped against the chill, rushing past. I tried to keep up, but that meant pretending to a sense of purpose that I didn't have, and anyway, walking at all was hard enough. For weeks I'd gone no further than across a laundry room or courtyard, and for the last ten days had been cooped up in a wagon. The wind coming off the river scooped the breath from me and my feet were an unequal match for my boots, sliding around inside them so that I felt I had to lunge with each step to keep my legs with me.

Standing still at the square was no easier, with the wind bowling at me, its force redoubled by a corner. My cloak was well lined – close at hand for cast-offs, laundresses don't lack for linings – but nothing is sufficient against a riverside dusk in February. I stood shivering like a dog. I hadn't thought about how long I should give it, how long to stand there in that short, sharp deep-winter dusk before cutting my losses, but after a few minutes a solitary someone left one of the buildings and I knew, with the pulling taut of some core fibre I hadn't even known I had, that the cloak-clad figure was Bel.

I stepped from the shadows to a jolting realisation that I hadn't any notion of what to do or say to her. But time was on my side because, as she wrapped herself up, gathered herself against the chill, she was still unaware of me, and my advantage over her was intoxicating because this, here, was Bel as I'd never seen her, deep in her own life with no thought of me in her head. It was as if I were granted a glimpse of her before we'd ever met. In a second, she would see me and everything would be as it had been, everything would resume and go forward and of course I wouldn't have it any other way and couldn't ask for more. But here she was as she had once been, before I'd ever known her, and how she would have stayed had we never met, and only my step forward would save us from our former solitary selves. I wanted just a taste more of it, wanted my tongue to skim the poison the better to know how close I had come to the fate of never having known her. This was my last chance to savour my good fortune, and then, even better, when she saw me, to have it granted all over again.

But somehow it had already happened: the crucial step forward had already been taken and was swilled behind me into an under-tow of similar steps. And I was discovered, because instinct had had her glance over. Her face sparked with recognition, her expression lightened, and for that instant, dismayingly, I didn't quite know her. All the pieces of her were there as I'd known them on that face but as if worn by someone else.

We were no more than a pace apart and I knew I should offer an account of myself as I loomed from the shadows to crash in on her small sphere of cloak-fastening and end-of-day weariness. Now that it came to it, though, all I could manage was a tentative apologetic 'Hello,' and it didn't feel right.

Not that she seemed to notice. Her eyes widened, hopeful, and she started, 'When ... ?'

No, stop, listen. 'I shouldn't be here, I'm still ...' with the princess's household.

'Till when?'

I shook my head: I don't know, don't ask.

She looked tired, her features indistinct but at the same time stark: lips chapped and one eyebrow left askew by a rub at her face. She was smaller than I'd remembered and I was at a loss as to how to – whether to – approach her, to touch her. And what, I wondered, did she see, gaping at me? I didn't want her looking at me like that: guileless, clueless. I hadn't anticipated feeling awkward like this at our reunion. She seemed unfazed, reaching for me, her fingertips on my forearm. 'But you're coming ... ?' Coming along as usual, she meant, to her house.

'I can't,' I said, and my relief at being able to say it, at having an excuse, disconcerted me. Across the square a couple of men were leaving one of the workshops, loping off into their uncomplicated lives, and just then I would have given anything to join them.

She said, 'But you can't go back.' On the river, in the dark, she meant, and although I knew she said it from concern for me, I was exasperated. 'I can't *not*.' A short journey on a river in the dark would be nothing compared to what I'd endured of late, if only she knew. But what *did* she know – she with the comforts of a day spent indoors rising off her like steam? My throat ached: why was I angry with her? This wasn't how it was supposed to be. This was all wrong already but I didn't understand why, nor how to put it right.

She persisted, gently: 'Come back with me.' She would take care of it, she meant: she would get me into and out of the house unnoticed or otherwise explain away or excuse my presence, just as she always had. But I still wasn't having it, because didn't she see? This was different, this was serious, this was no simple matter of trusting to smiles and nods from others, which was how she lived her life. And anyway, it wasn't for her to decide: she had to leave it to me to get clear of the situation I was in, and I knew that my return to the palace for the night was the only way to get it properly done.

She capitulated gracefully, with a rueful smile – *if you say so, because there's always another time* – which brought me to my senses and I began to backtrack. 'Well . . .' Perhaps I should take the chance, I thought, not that it was even much of a chance, because this particular evening was surely the one on which to absent myself, when the princess's household hadn't yet caught its breath or found its feet: her ladies still unpacking and preoccupied by privations, grumbling among themselves and arguing with various officials. I wouldn't be missed. No one was going to be looking for me: no laundry would need doing until the following day. And at the St Thomas Apostle Street house no one would see me, because Bel would be able to smuggle me in and I could leave at first light.

And anyway, she was right, it was just practical: famished and exhausted, I didn't have the wherewithal to get back upriver before nightfall. 'But I need to sleep,' I blurted out, even as I cringed at the allusion to bed when we had never once acknowledged what we did in it. Worse, I was repeating it, 'Sleep and sleep and sleep,' but the crack in my voice wasn't so far from laughter because for all those weeks at Ashridge I'd longed to be in bed with her, and now that my chance was here, I could think only of her bed linen and bolster.

Bel, though, was untroubled and cheerful, 'No better place for sleep than my house.' Taking hold of my arm, she drew me to her side and we pitched ourselves together against the wind and sleet, inching along as a pair if deep inside our respective hoods. Our linked arms were a hindrance, though; we tottered on the icy cobbles as if encumbered with a third person and eventually I extricated myself, the awkwardness of the move unmitigated by my utterance of regret and her dismissal of it with a shake of her head: *No, you're right.* Actually, I felt, I was wrong: I should've kept us mincing conjoined across the cobbles for the sake of appearances, for a keeping of the peace, because from then onwards there was a physical distance between us as we picked our way along, and a lump in my throat.

And, worse, polite conversation: How was my journey?

Well, where to start – which in any case I was too weary to do. 'Long' would have to cover it, but actually its glaring inadequacy lightened the mood and there was warmth in her voice when she said, 'But now you're here.'

Not quite, I thought. I asked after everyone back at the house and she said they were fine. The siege, though, I reminded her: there had been a siege, of a kind. All I got was a knowing, 'Oh, yes, well, *that*.' No, she hadn't heard the queen's appeal in the Guildhall but she'd been there later that evening to help fit the men into their whites – the tabards that the city kept for its volunteers – and she enthused about the send-off: like a party, she said, what with all the drink being ladled out.

It had continued a bit like that, too, I said, from what I'd heard, and to a quizzical turn of the hood beside me, I said, 'Turncoats and deserters.' That was what those men had become. But she shrugged, and fair enough, because ultimately that turning of coats had been of no consequence. The rebellion was over, as if it had never been.

At St Thomas Apostle Street, getting into the house couldn't have been easier. She had a key to the back gate, and then, after some careful listening, we made it undetected, as far as we could tell, across the yard and into the house and up to her room, where a fire had already been lit. I assumed she would go off to dine downstairs, but she said she'd bring food up for us both. In truth I wouldn't have minded some time to myself, but she wouldn't be persuaded otherwise.

Thinking how strange it had been, back at St Andrew's Square, to lay eyes on her after so long, I remembered how when I had been married, absence had made my heart grow fonder, but then my fonder heart had had a hard job of reconciling the man I'd been missing with the one who would reappear. The memory of him had been inflated to keep pace – he was funnier, sweeter – but when he walked back through the doorway those memories were cut down to size and my heart was left flailing.

Bel locked the door and I clambered up onto the bed, and there all around me were those stars, those moons. How I loved that room. 'Happy New Year,' she said, chucking a linen-wrapped and ribbon-tied handful across the room at me, which was when I realised I'd forgotten to bring my gift for her, although that seemed to please her: something to look forward to, she said, jovially. Inside the gift-wrapping was the pair of garters that she had originally intended to be her wedding gift to the queen. Not only had she finished embroidering the conjoined royal insignia on one of them, but – 'See?' – adjoining it was a crest of her own invention: a letter T twisted around an A and entwined with her signature bell. I laughed aloud: it was ingenious and beautiful and – putting us on a par with the queen and her husband-to-be – scandalous. I didn't need telling that I would be safest keeping it hidden beneath my skirts.

Then she took a nightgown from a chest. 'Here.'

I breathed in the soap scent and, without thinking, said, 'You have a good laundress.'

That amused her. 'The best,' she said, coming to me and chancing a hand over mine. I turned my own to meet it and then there was nowhere for our fingers to go but between each other's, and there we were, holding hands. Then there was a touch of her lips to mine, the levity at odds with the persistence, and my physical response was as unequivocal as it had ever been for any man. With her lips still on mine, she enjoyed reminding me, 'But you need to sleep.' Oh, don't worry, I said, I would sleep like a dream. Afterwards.

We undressed, and her tang, released from her clothing, was as particular as an endearment. Everything was all right again, and perhaps I was overcome with relief as much as passion. As ever, I felt conspicuously bony and sinewy at her side, and conscious of that ring on the cord, but I fitted myself to her so that I and the ring disappeared, and my skin was hers and hers mine. We lay as close together as is possible and then somehow even closer; and it was a filching of pleasure, a slow pressing of pleasure into and from ourselves, and her stickiness when it came was like a spoonful of syrup.

In the morning, she had to do most of my waking for me – getting me into my clothes, brushing and fixing my hair, then smuggling me out of the house – but half an hour later, on the wharf, tucking into a bread roll from one of the vendors licensed for the earliest sales, I felt up to anything that fate could throw at me. Which was just as well, because at the King's Head a man was waiting for me. This was it, then: the end of my Ashridge episode.

He took me to a room similar to the office in which the

Ashridge plan had been hatched, but in which there were just two men rather than three: a nobleman at a desk, busy with papers, and a clerk in attendance. I wasn't cowed; I felt fortified by the time spent with Bel. Invincible, even. Ashridge was over: I was back, had my life back. They shouldn't have sent me there – it was a poor plan – and they certainly shouldn't have left me there. It was gratifying that I had nothing to tell them.

The clerk announced me – 'Mistress Twist' – and the nobleman repeated my name but only to commit it to memory: an act of filing rather than greeting. No cakes. No niceties, either, when he asked me if, at Ashridge, any household move had been prepared for. Only when he had finished the question did he stop scratching away with his nib and look up at me, but the look was empty, a mere receptacle for my answer. His eyes were like some colourless, formless matter to be avoided on a path.

No word of thanks for the time I'd spent at Ashridge, nor even any recognition of it. Certainly no excuses or apology for how I'd been left stranded.

No, I told him. No preparations.

This was not the right answer, it seemed, because his pause was clearly a rebuke. Then, 'You're sure about that?' It was an invitation for me to reconsider .

I confirmed it. We were stuck there, I said pointedly. No plans. Our setting off, the week before last, had come as a complete surprise.

'Oh, I don't doubt that,' he said to himself, before doublechecking. 'But before? No plans?'

If only there had been, I thought. And I wished that the man who had been responsible for sending me there was in the room; I would have liked to look him in the eye. And I wanted cakes, although not anything like as much as I wanted an apology.

'No activity – either your own or of others that you observed or knew of – that at the time or might now upon reflection

104

suggest to you that there was an impending move?' Then he barked, 'Think,' which made me jump.

No, I said: nothing.

He made a note, his free hand raised to still the shifting clerk: 'Just . . .' *let me finish writing.*

I was on the cusp of dismissal.

And that was when something came to mind: that inexplicable cancellation of Mrs Smith's leave, which Mrs Ashley had said was in case the household should move. Was that important? Probably not. Neither Mrs Smith nor Brigid had set any store by it; it had seemed to be something between Mrs Smith and Mrs Ashley, some peculiar locking of horns. I wondered if I should mention it, though. The nobleman's head was down over his notes. I looked to the clerk, but he was gazing at the floor. It was probably too late for me to speak up, and anyway it was probably nothing.

And how exactly would I break the silence? *Well, actually, now that I come to think of it . . .*

How stupid would that sound? I had only just said no and no and no, confirmed it time and again. That rude nobleman would be even ruder to me, and for what? For nothing. Because I was quite sure it was nothing. And he had asked about preparations, and there had been none.

In that instant, he glanced up, and must have detected something of my predicament. 'Yes?' It was voiced like an insult, though, which hardened my resolve. Nothing, I said again. And so then the moment was gone, beyond retrieval, and good riddance. It might have been otherwise if he had been doing his job properly. He could have made it easy for me: *Mistress Twist? Perhaps there's something after all? Something now that you've had time to think . . . ?*

Even then, though, what could I have told him? And whatever I might have said would have necessitated a lot more questioning, but really I knew nothing. No, it was done, I told myself; I was done with it. I did need to check, though, and have it confirmed that it was over. *Ask*, I urged myself: *just ask*.

'Sir?' I said it to the top of his fancy cap.

He paused mid-scribble and looked up.

'Sir, may I ask what happens now?' It sounded to me like a whisper, but that might have been because my blood was roiling in my ears.

He stared at me. 'Now?'

I was going to have to say it: 'To' — and I resented how small it would sound – 'me.'

His stare stayed empty, as if he couldn't think for the life of him what 'me', when voiced by the young woman in front of him, might mean.

I would have to press on. 'Do I . . .'

Still no help.

'Well, where do I go, now, sir? Am I finished?' And I contrived a shrug, as if to make it a trifling matter. 'Should I just . . . ?'

He snapped back to writing. 'Stay,' he said, as if it were a given, beyond question, although I suspected he hadn't before then afforded it any consideration. 'Stay where you are and see it through until it's done. It won't take much longer.' This interview, I took him to mean, but then he said, 'A day or two, and then just see yourself back.' *Back into your little life*.

Little though my life is, I thought as I left that room, I bet I had one more happy young lady beside me in bed at night than he did.

I couldn't get away fast enough, which brought me into near-collision with Mrs Ashley, who was emerging at speed from the Holbein gatehouse. Her head barely covered and curls unruly, she could have been a farmer's wife about to upbraid a farmhand, but she swooped on me, took up my arm and hauled me close, unnervingly chummy.

'You too, then,' she said, with some satisfaction. 'You too, in for questioning. They're having *everyone* in.' She was breathless, puffed up, relishing her indignation. 'Who did *you* have? Who was yours?'

What was she talking about?

She suggested a name I'd never heard. 'Piece of work, him. I always want to say to him, "You damn well look me in the eye when you talk to me," but then when he does, I have second thoughts.' She shuddered. 'God preserve us, did you ever see such a cold fish. And what a waste of time this is,' she went on, 'because what do they think we're going to say? That we were planning a runner and going to sit somewhere nice and pretty until She Herself was turfed off the throne and then – whoosh! – sweep down into London, victorious?' She took a breath. 'Did he ask about Donnington? No? Good girl: that's because he knew he was getting nowhere with you.' She had me by the elbow, marching me along.

Donnington? Who or where was that?

'Thank goodness it was you in there instead of Mrs Smith or Brigid – they'd probably have drawn him a map.'

Map? And talking of maps, where was she taking me – and at such a pace, flying in the face of scrutiny from the porters?

Across Old Court we rushed, and up some stairs, and all the time she was harping on about intolerable conditions and lack of respect and it wasn't until she had opened a door and ushered me ahead of her across the threshold that I saw I was in the presence of the princess. I halted, which had Mrs Ashley bump into me, shoving me forwards but pushing past at the same time.

The princess was in the far corner of the tight-panelled room, in a window seat: long-bodied and fine-boned, with her red hair loose. There was none of the swagger that I had seen that time at Ashridge, and not just because she was seated. She looked every inch the mere girl she still was, collarbones stark and splayed, painful-looking in their protuberance. The room was sweltering – a fire boisterous in the grate – and I fought an urge to rush and open the casement.

The princess's turn in our direction had been reluctant; she looked full of dread, as if it were pooled in her veins. I dropped to my knees but Mrs Ashley yanked me up as if I were being tediously conventional. I was careful to keep my gaze down, though; I wouldn't look up unless spoken to, which was unlikely because Mrs Ashley was in full flow at the princess.

'This one,' she crowed, 'this one's the latest, but they got nowhere with her.' I felt the scorch of the princess's gaze. 'She denied all knowledge, and they didn't even ask about Donnington, didn't even bother, and that's because they know they're on a hiding to nothing.' My downcast gaze was on a level with the princess's be-ringed hands; she was gripping her seat. 'They're second-guessing, Bette, and they'll never prove it: nothing said, nothing written down, no preparations made.' She sounded so pleased with herself. 'No one ever actually knew, not even our laundress lady here.'

I glanced up, by mistake, right into the princess's eyes, which were like knots in timber: resinous, dense, durable.

Drily, she said, 'Well, she does now.'

Did I? All I knew, now, was that I had missed something: there was something specific those palace men were after, and I'd missed it. I was far from alone in that, though, it seemed, and my fleeting unease gave way to grudging admiration. Not for an instant did I consider going back to the cold-eyed gentleman with this, because, really, what did I know? Nothing, apparently, that he didn't already know. And anyway, I had no interest in assisting him, and, most importantly, he'd said I was nearly done. I was going to keep my head down until this was over.

Mrs Ashley sent me off, telling me to return in a quarter of an hour to take delivery of some laundry from Miss Parry. Crossing the courtyard on my way to the King's Head, I felt anxiously as if I were dodging my cold-eyed interrogator. Back in my room, I dithered before retracing my steps. Mrs Ashley was the one to answer my knock, flushed and dishevelled, with not a jot of recognition in her stare.

I prompted, 'Laundry,' which no doubt confused her because I wasn't carrying any. 'I've come for—'

She snatched me into the room, in which were four noblemen, caps absurdly plumed, but no Miss Parry nor princess.

'Laundress,' she hissed at the noblemen with such vehemence that I feared this was my uncovering, but then she was commanding them, 'Add her to the list, she comes with us.'

So, they were being taken somewhere. That, then, was what my questioner must have meant by something being done: *Until it's done*. That was when I would step away, and see myself back to the palace laundry.

An intake of breath from one of the men signalled an objection, but Mrs Ashley was straight in on the attack. 'No, because with all due respect' – said with a notable absence of any – 'her Grace is the daughter of a king, and if you think she should sit around in dirty linen . . . But then you don't, do you, my lords, you don't think; you've not given it a moment's thought. Well, let me tell you that the queen will intend her Lady Sister's Grace to have her own laundress and would confirm it if actually granting her Lady Sister's Grace an audience as promised and not suddenly busy elsewhere as you insist.'

I risked a glance at them: four weary faces under all that plumage.

'The problem with you, my lords, is that you never have to think; you suit yourselves and everything just gets done for you. Well, it's the likes of this lady here who slave away to keep my Lady's Grace pure and safe in a world full of danger. We will take kitchen staff because we're wise to some people's murdering ways – oh yes, my lords, you know full well this is no time to trust anyone – and we will take this laundress.'

I made sure to look biddable, to play the part, keep up the pretence.

'One laundress,' allowed one of the noblemen, which brought Mrs Ashley up sharp, although she recovered herself sufficiently to take offence even at that.

'One is quite enough,' she said, 'for our Grace's needs.' Then she marched me out of there and back down the staircase. All I would have to do, I reminded myself, was make sure I was nowhere to be found when it was time for them to be moved. At the foot of the stairs, she stopped and said, 'I don't know ...' but the rest was clawed back on a rasp that had my own breath catch in my throat, because I saw she was crying and I knew she wouldn't thank me for seeing it.

I should do something, I thought, panicking: I should stop gawping and do something, or someone should; someone, from somewhere, who knew what to do, should step in and do something. But as I cast helplessly around, it was she herself who turned practical, fussing with a handkerchief and allowing me to fall back on the simple, time-honoured suggestion that she sit down, although there was nowhere to do so except on the stairs. She demurred even as she did so, and I pictured damp stone dust sticking to her gown.

I was left in the awkward position of standing over her, and she was small enough as it was.

'All the things,' she said, desolate, to the floor, 'over all the years. The worries and the fears.'

I was unsure if she were actually talking to me, and didn't dare even acknowledge that she'd spoken. She pressed the handkerchief to her eyes; the skin there, I noticed, was slack. Too old for children, I remembered Mrs Smith and Brigid saying, but I had had to be this close up to see it.

'All that's ever happened,' she said, 'we've come through it.'

No note of triumph; she sounded bereft.

'There were times when I doubted we would, but we did.' And now she did look up at me. 'But now the Tower . . . '

'Tower?' It was shock that had had me repeat it, as if it wasn't bad enough to have it voiced the once. The Tower: something, then, must have come to light, something drastic had been unearthed. Whatever it was that they'd been hiding, presumably. *Donnington*: whatever – wherever – that was. Someone, somewhere did know something specific, and had spoken up.

Mrs Ashley rallied. 'Well, they have nothing on her and they won't get away with this,' and then, full of malice, she said, 'That witch has been waiting so many years for this,' and it took me a full, deep breath to accept that she meant the queen. I didn't dare look around to see if there was anyone who could have heard. 'Now she can do anything to anyone, or so she thinks, but if I were her I'd be careful, because it didn't look so clever for her, did it, a couple of weeks back.'

It was all I could do not to clap a hand over her mouth: I wanted no part in this – not even to hear it.

'She thinks she can swill the princess away downriver like rubbish, but just let her try, because this is England, and the people won't stand for it.' Then that ire was gone as if it had never been. 'We need to pack up the bedclothes,' she said, listlessly. 'Go back to your room, pack your bag and return here to help me.' Rising, she batted the stone dust from her behind. 'What this queen of ours is doing, it's the wrong move, because the people love the princess, not least because she's English, whereas *she*' – a curt nod towards the heart of the palace – 'has never looked as Spanish as she does now.' She sniffed. 'Our princess isn't so very different from the rest of us. Think what she came from. Look at it one way, and yes: daughter of a king. But from the other?' We moved off together. 'And that's her strength. The princess doesn't shout about her origins – of course she doesn't – but nor does she pretend to be something she isn't, and the people respect her for that. She has no family, no emperors to go whining to. She's alone and always will be, whatever Blanche and I try to do for her, but I'll tell you this: she'll never go hitching her wagon to anyone else's procession. You'll never catch her kneeling to some pope and marrying a tyrant. Because she knows her own mind.' For the first time, she looked me properly in the eye. 'She was three when I came to look after her, and she used to say to me, so pleased, like she had the answer to something, '*You* won't go, will you, Kat. We can stay together. We can be buried together.'

This had me wondering, on my way back over to the King's Head, how the princess had been told about her mother: when, and by whom. And what exactly she had been told.

I remembered being told that my own mother had died. I had no memory of what was said, nor of how old I was, nor where, nor of the lady, whoever she was, who had had the job of telling me. I didn't know if my mother had been ill. I remembered nothing of her, or not so there is anything to tell; just a memory of someone having at some time been there – of there having *been* someone – if that counts as a memory.

I had never known anything of any father.

The lady who told me about my mother had crouched down to me and her eyes had been bright with tears, which was something I had never seen of any adult. She was trying hard not to cry and, in an effort to spare her, I kept my gaze politely over her shoulder and on a laundry rack, on the bone-coloured linen dried and inflexible there on the frets, as yet unsoftened by body warmth.

Years later I had overheard a passing remark of my having been in a particular household since I was six. If that was the first household in which I lived alone, then perhaps I was six when I was orphaned and taken in. But then who's to say that the speaker hadn't misremembered or been misinformed. The truth of it, I felt, was long gone.

I never asked anyone. Children don't ask questions of adults, especially not adults to whom they are beholden. I was never in any rush to remind anyone that I didn't quite belong. It took years for it to dawn on me that I didn't know how old I was, and by then I couldn't own up to such fundamental ignorance about myself. And anyway, it was too late: I'd been passed on, hand over hand, always someone else's problem, or protégée, depending on how you saw it.

9

Neither Here nor There

I did go back to the princess's room with my bag, hoping to be intercepted on the way and dismissed from my duties. No such luck. Evidently it was going to be left to me to step aside at some point and bow out.

This time in the princess's room there were two new noblemen, who clearly hadn't expected to be hanging around; they were dressed for outdoors and in that stifling room were suffering for it, their faces boiled. Firelight toyed with their arsenal of buckles and buttons. The princess and Miss Parry stood across the room from them, in some kind of stand-off. The princess looked stretched so thin as to thrum with the slightest shifts in atmosphere; and although I didn't see her face, I knew that her eyes were swallowing light, taking it in and turning it dark.

Mrs Ashley's poppy-bright silk spilled across the room ahead of me, flowed into the bedchamber, and by the time I joined her she was already vigorously dismantling the bed hangings. I had to work hard to keep up, and it was even hotter in there; my scalp was instantly damp, and my heart pounded meatily.

Back in the main room, the princess was saying something about the queen having given her word: a complaint, but carefully done, fairly pleasantly, as if offering up information that might be of use to the noblemen. As if he hadn't even heard, one of them said, 'We need to get on, we have to get you there.'

Now Miss Parry spoke up, her tone not dissimilar to the princess's, querying why they were travelling by water.

'Safer all round,' came the response. 'We need to get you there nice and quick. There's plenty of people ready to cause trouble.'

At this, Mrs Ashley slammed a fistful of linen onto the bed – making me jump – and hollered through, 'That's because the people of London know what you're doing!'

The embarrassment in the ensuing silence was as much at her having yelled like a fishwife as at the accusation itself.

I, for one, though, was impressed.

The nobleman pointedly responded only to Miss Parry. 'Our orders from the queen—'

'I had her Majesty's word,' interrupted the princess, 'that she would hear me out.' It was said calmly enough, but her breath fluttered in her throat when she added, 'If and when it should come to this.' *This*: the Tower. Her mother had been killed there, as – only days ago – had her girl-cousin. Sometimes a prisoner will walk free from the Tower, but it's better to keep on the other side of Traitors' Gate.

Mrs Ashley was looking daggers at the doorway as if to intimidate time itself into standing still until the princess was given an adequate answer. The nobleman, though, was exasperated. 'Hear *what* from you? We've all heard that you *don't know* how a copy of your letter to the queen, making your excuses, was found in the French ambassador's bag; and how you *don't know* those traitors—'

'But I *do* know them!' She screamed it and my scalp contracted, ducking for cover of its own accord. 'I never said I didn't!'

Mrs Ashley was stock-still, staring into nothing.

'Of course I know them!' The princess's fury and indignation rose but disappeared in a puff of despair. '*You* know them. We *all* know them.' In my mind's eye I saw her hands flung, in confrontation and supplication, her fingers splayed: *I am hiding nothing.*

Mrs Ashley was primed, rapt, seeming to listen for something beyond my range. The princess was keening a roll call of names, followed by a cry of protest: 'Who *doesn't* know them?' Beneath the rage and self-righteousness, she was crying like a child abandoned in the cold who knows there is someone who should come to the rescue but can't or won't. '*Yes* I know them, because how could I *not*?' I imagined her pacing this way and that, the panels of her gown failing to keep up and swinging dumbly around her. 'But this *plot*?' She let the word hang in the air as a glaring absurdity. 'I knew nothing before you did. *Yes* they sent word, but only when it was under way, and I sent it straight back: *Thank you but no thank you.*'

Pausing to draw breath, she must have heard herself, because now her tone changed so that she was no longer railing at them, but reasoning with them. 'All this, my lords, I've told you. And what could I have done better? Locked the gate?'

Mrs Ashley raised her eyebrows: *Quite so.*

'Sir William,' the princess impressed upon them, 'sweet Sir William at your gate, late on a January evening. You'd have locked him out?'

There came no response that I could hear.

She said, 'I didn't know what he'd come to say, didn't know that he'd come to say anything at all. So we let him in, and in he came but bringing word from Sir Thomas, which was – as you know – that I should move away to Donnington because there was trouble starting, and I should stay safe there until it was over. And you know what I said to him because I've told you.' But she repeated it anyway, everything above board. 'I thanked him for his concern but said I would make my own decision. Which

116

was why, when you came looking for me, you found me still at Ashridge.'

This, though, I knew, was disingenuous: leave had been cancelled; the household had, I now realised, been held in readiness to move. If I stepped through the doorway, I thought, and unburdened myself of the little I knew, perhaps it would be enough to tip the balance, to shut the princess up and bring all this to a close, and then I could go free, and, with luck, step clear of any suspicion that I had withheld information. But what I was hearing, next door, was those noblemen being spun a line, and I was riveted.

They weren't convinced, though. 'And the letter? The French ambassador informed of your decision?'

It seemed the princess didn't have an answer for that, but she didn't pretend otherwise. 'I don't know. I can't explain that. All I can tell you is that I didn't send him any copy of any letter I'd written. You have my word. The queen has my word. I have no idea how that ended up in his bag.'

If she had done wrong, wouldn't she have been ready with some story?

'What I do know,' she said, evenly, 'is that certain people, for their own ends, are keen to present me in the worst possible light.'

Mrs Ashley couldn't resist catching my eye and – unnecessarily – mouthing *Spaniards*.

'I'm guilty of nothing, my lords,' the princess said, 'and it's in the interests of no one in England to say otherwise.' She added, 'And far be it for me of all people to countenance disloyalty to a queen,' which at first I took as no more than the conventional expression of loyalty to the sovereign before I realised she had said *a* queen, not *the* queen. *A* queen: queens in general, of which potentially she was one. And *of all people*: a deft reminder of whom they were dealing with. Point made, she returned to her original complaint. 'I need to see my sister.'

And that too was a reminder: *sister*. Sisters together in the will of the old king.

There was some bluster – the claim, repeated, that the queen was away – but the princess merely said she would write to her, and then the nobleman from whom we hadn't so far heard said, grudgingly, 'Just quickly.'

Even at my distance, I felt the disapproval coming off his colleague. But this wasn't the time or place for disunity, so he bit his tongue. The letter-writing was permitted. Mrs Ashley held my gaze in hers and emphatically widened her eyes to share her elation, and in the circumstances I couldn't help but feel similarly.

'Thank you, my lords.' The princess was both gracious and businesslike: grateful, but clear that this was no more than her due.

Mrs Ashley took this as her cue to go barging in, avowedly to sort out writing materials for the princess, as if that were beyond the princess herself or indeed Miss Parry. Her appearance did nothing to ease the tension, and indeed inflamed it, undoing all the princess's good work and provoking an incendiary exchange as to whether the lords should leave while the letter was written. Initially, they refused, but Mrs Ashley was insistent that the letter needed doing properly – would they have her Grace dashing off some mere *note* to the queen? They were a distraction, she said, and as such would bear responsibility for the letter lacking due respect. They in turn demanded to know just how long she needed in order to plead for mercy. The princess said that she wasn't pleading for mercy but asserting her innocence and her loyalty. To which one of them retorted that she would be better off pleading for mercy.

I stood amid the disarrayed bed hangings, wondering what she would write. She had what she wanted – permission to write the letter – but now had to make the most of that opportunity. Had she any plan in mind for this letter, or had she been thinking on her feet? Was it merely a ruse to delay the inevitable journey to the Tower? I couldn't read or write, had never written a letter nor received one. Instructions and lists and bills and orders I could imagine putting together. But she had talked of the queen hearing her out. She had points to make, then, with which she hoped the queen would credit her. Not so unlike a bill, perhaps, except that no one bills the queen.

Miss Parry stepped in, conciliatory: for how long would they be prepared to grant the princess some privacy?

There followed some talk of the tide before an agreement was reached. No doubt those lords were desperate for a break. Their parting shot was that no one – *no one* – should leave the room.

As soon as they had gone, Mrs Ashley turned her fussing to the subject of sustenance: the princess should have something to eat. The princess declined, which had Mrs Ashley insist, which in turn had Miss Parry appealing, 'Kat—' and Mrs Ashley flaring, 'Don't you Kat me!' and ranting about a river journey this late in the day at this time of year.

Miss Parry said to the princess, 'Just a little frumenty?'

But then the problem was how to fetch it, seeing as no one could leave the room. Except me, perhaps. But no one mentioned me and I didn't offer.

I stayed in the bedchamber to finish my job, which didn't take long, then had to remind them of my presence by going into the doorway but stopping shy of the threshold and standing there, waiting to be noticed. The princess was at a desk, Mrs Ashley was at the window, Miss Parry at the fireside. Miss Parry was the one to catch my eye; she indicated a fireside cushion, but she couldn't be thinking straight because surely I wasn't to go and sit with them. Instead, I prompted, 'Shall I . . . ?' with a nod towards the door to the stairwell.

'No one's to leave the room,' she reminded me.

That didn't apply to me, surely. In fact, no one was precisely who I was, in this room. An odd position in which to find myself, keen to insist on my own irrelevance. I didn't dare speak up, though, and had to take my place – or *a* place – among them. There I sat, sweltering, my gaze anchored to my hands.

There was something like grief in that room, a sob caught in a collective throat. Soon they would be gone: the noblemen would take them away and then who knew what would happen. Not me, though: this was as far as I would go. My time with them was coming to an end.

It was so hot in there that it was as if I were drugged, but outside was gusty, and a fistful of icy rain was flung at the window, from which Mrs Ashley recoiled, turning to the room but for once meeting no one's eye. The princess didn't falter in her writing: impervious, absorbed, dipping her nib and writing, then pausing to let it dry, and to think. Her air of concentration was familiar to me; it was, I realised, as if she were assembling a garment: considering if it would hold, and what impression it might make, and what might be needed next.

The fire alone in that room was ebullient and a memory came to me of a fire in the middle of a vast room and of all of us – whoever we were – around it. A household. The smoke, I did remember: on its way up to the roof, where there must have been an opening in the rafters, but dallying in my eyes and throat. I had sometimes seen scorch marks on the floors of old halls, but it was hard to believe it ever happened, that there had ever been a time before fireplaces, let alone in my own lifetime. Now fires are confined to their own domain like dogs in kennels, where they fossick over kindling as if it were bones.

When the lords reappeared, the princess merely said over her shoulder that she hadn't quite finished. No apology or appeal, nor any defiance: she was merely informing them. To which they informed her that it was time to be going. She rose, and there was something startling in how she did it, the ease and speed, and then there she was, standing, facing them, and it was unclear whether this was capitulation or provocation. Was she falling in with them, or standing up to them? Her pale lips parted – a hint of those small sharp teeth – and she looked about to say something, but whatever it was, it was left unsaid and she remained there, suspended. What, I wondered, were those noblemen going to do? Lay hands on her? Bundle her through the doorway down the stairs and into the barge?

One of them gestured at the desk – *Get on with it, then, but be quick* – and she accepted with the same ease, sitting back down. Mrs Ashley and Miss Parry guardedly exchanged a glance I couldn't read, and the lords shifted, unsettled.

She wrote on, and as the minutes passed I felt the lords' irritation veer towards disquiet, because how many ways were left in which to say that she had to get a move on? Then she moved briefly into a different rhythm, the nib held in contact longer with the paper: her signature, perhaps. The men recovered themselves, stood to attention, and she stopped and sat back, shoulders dropped as if after physical exertion. The men closed in, keen to conclude the whole unsatisfactory business, but then she was at it again, in what looked alarmingly like an act of destruction – long strikes of the nib – but what she was doing, I supposed, was scoring through the blank space so that no one could add anything either in their own hand or a forgery of hers. When she had left no corner for fraud, she handed it over.

At once, both nobles were off through the doorway, down the stairs, conferring, officious, their agitation echoing in the stairwell, while we four ladies barely dared to breathe; then within a couple of minutes they came crashing back with an about-turn: no departure now, too late, too close to the turn of the tide, the next of which was not until midnight and too risky. They made as if the princess were the recipient of their favour and this delay an artful revision of their plan, whereas we all knew it was its unravelling. Again, under no circumstances was anyone to leave the room, and this time the sweep of the speaker's gaze definitely included me.

Well, so be it: I would have to spend the night there. Uneasy though I was, at the same time I was past caring. I would have found it hard to get myself back over to the King's Head, exhausted as I was and overpowered by the heat of the princess's room; I had no wish to go outside into that weather and over to the alehouse, to that solitary room of mine with its cold hearth. Anyway, I too had missed the tide and wouldn't be going to Bel that night. And after the separation we'd endured, one more night was neither here nor there. She would guess I had been held up. And just think, I told myself, what a story I would have for her.

Yet every moment longer that I stayed would make it harder for me to extricate myself when the time did at last come.

The noblemen left us alone, but poor were the circumstances in which a night of house arrest before the Tower could be considered a victory. Mrs Ashley and Miss Parry did what they did best, if with an edge of desperation: they turned to practical considerations, of which on this occasion, unfortunately, I was the focus. I was the one who needed to be accommodated: there was discussion, in which it wasn't my place to participate, of where I should sleep.

The princess took no part in it, her attention averted to the dark but as yet unshuttered window, perhaps picturing the passage of her letter from the gloved hands of those noblemen to the queen. I imagined she was willing it speedily on its way, and praying for a swift and favourable response.

It was decided to put me in the bedroom, which upon reflection probably wasn't the trusting move that at first I presumed, because in there a closer eye could be kept on me. Safer to have me in there with the princess than close to the door, because no one knew for whom I might, in the dead of night, open it, unwittingly or otherwise.

The room had to be made comfortable enough for that one last night, which necessitated undoing some of our earlier work: unpacking and re-hanging furnishings. At least this gave us something to do. Heavy work, though, again, in that stuffy room, and in time my head felt as if it were bound in cloth.

That was one reason why, when some supper was delivered, I ate almost nothing despite the novelty and luxury of the food. Mrs Ashley had refused to accept it until the princess's personal cook was escorted to the top of the stairs to vouch for it, laboriously, dish by dish. Even if I had been starving, though, I wouldn't have been brave enough to dig into those dishes, for fear not of poison but of showing myself up: a laundress dining with two grand ladies and the heir to the throne. Watching what they did, I then did the same but as little, as lightly as possible.

Fortunately, I wasn't the exception: no one ate much, despite Mrs Ashley hectoring the princess that she needed her strength. Even though I hadn't wanted it, I was irked to see so much handed back untouched: dishes that I would no doubt never again in my life have a chance to taste.

Afterwards, Miss Parry came to the rescue with some sewing tasks, which were startlingly easy in such abundant candlelight. This was scant compensation, though, for the miseries of the evening. Mrs Ashley was reduced to occasional inarticulate expressions of frustration and despair. Perhaps I should have spoken up earlier, when I had been in the bedroom overhearing the princess hoodwink the noblemen: I was sorry that these ladies didn't have the chance of freedom, but I did. I had a life waiting for me and I longed to be in it.

I didn't feel safe, in that room: it was as if the building itself were quaking on the bank and about to pitch us down into the river. What of the entourage, those hundreds of wagons, and that team of Elizabeths? How could that whole household have come down to this? These three ladies alone were the subject of the queen's suspicion. Three ladies would be so easy to get rid of. A mishap on the barge, say.

Would no one come sweeping up the stairs to the door before morning to voice reason and put a stop to this? A pall of future lordly regret hung in that room: *Oh, well yes, that was a sad story, but really, under the circumstances, what could any of us have done?* The absence of footfall boomed in the stairwell, and the silence pressed so that I had to resist an urge to clear my ears, to hold my nose and blow. There was no sound beyond Mrs Ashley's sighs, and the purr of thread through fabric. The fire, subdued, sulked in the grate. The queen had just killed her cousin, who was barely a woman and further than the princess from the throne – and of whom, it was said, she had been fond. And when all was said and done, that cousin had been innocent of any plotting. None of that had stopped her being taken in front of a crowd and asked to turn her back on a canvas-aproned man, fall to her knees and bare her nape for the blade.

A high-minded little thing, I remembered Mrs Smith had said of that little cousin – Mrs Smith had known someone who had worked in the Grey household – and there had been mention of puppy fat. Whereas the princess was skin and bone, and she made sure everyone knew it. That apparent fragility of hers was a conspiracy of collarbones. Easy to forget how hard bones are. Easy to forget to look up from those collarbones to the eyes, where there was something not so far from insolence.

No need, though, to look into the eyes for that. It was visible across a room, whenever she came swinging through a doorway. Certainly she was bright, sharp – that was obvious – but to see her, to hear her, 'high-minded' wasn't what came to mind. The word was 'tough'. It wouldn't be so hard, if you had decided she couldn't be trusted with your life, to think of her as a weed leeching your patch – the slender wand of tough stalk, the casting of seeds – and then it might not trouble you that much to cut her down.

Into the silence, Mrs Ashley said, 'Well, if ever we needed a musician . . . ' a conversation opener to which the princess put paid by saying she had a headache, which was a misjudgement, as she probably realised as soon as she voiced it, because Mrs Ashley was unleashed on the subject of physicians, apothecaries, medicines and potions. An attempt by the princess to bring that to a close by saying that she was tired only served to switch Mrs Ashley to the necessities of sleep. And then when the princess snapped that she wouldn't sleep, Mrs Ashley's talk was of sleeping draughts until the princess insisted, 'I don't *want* to sleep,' which finally, mercifully, had Mrs Ashley lost for words.

I understood, though: this was a night to be vigilant. Also, for the princess to close her eyes would be to surrender. Her fate was coming for her and there was nothing left to her but to stare it down.

She took herself off to the bedroom but didn't close the door or draw the hangings, and I saw her cross-legged on the bed, partially undressed, head bared and hair loose, intent on her sewing.

At the strike of ten, Mrs Ashley announced that she was ready to turn in, and I became the recipient of a flurry of concern: 'Come on, then, you: let's sort out that bed of yours.'

I assumed that if the princess was going to stay up, she would move back through to sit with Miss Parry, but she stayed sewing as Mrs Ashley climbed into one side of the bed. Across the room from them, I lay on the truckle. The central light, above the bed, wasn't extinguished, and for that reason as much as propriety, I turned my back to them. I wondered where in the Tower they would be held. A room would have been adequately furnished for the cousin, and recently vacated: a quick sweep-through would

125

have it do for the princess, leaving the ghost of her cousin's fingertips like a breath on a window pane, perhaps, and a strand of her hair fled beneath the bed. I lay resolutely turned from the girl up there on the bed with the sewing slung across her lap, but my backbone picked up the heat of her as a kind of ache.

When I woke, the princess was dead to the world while Mrs Ashley was at the ewer, washing her face and drying it with linen, which would have to be packed damp. In the main room, Miss Parry was tending the fire. I was mindful that I should set about the business of getting myself free, which first and foremost meant watching for the right moment.

Mrs Ashley oversaw waking the princess, which took some doing and meant Miss Parry had to do the honours with breakfast – the interrogation of the cook who accompanied it, supervised, like a hostage. In the event, though, and without consultation, she turned him and his trays back on the threshold. More waste, I thought, although of no consequence for me personally because, I reminded myself, I'd be eating soon back at the inn. I hadn't caught Miss Parry's reason for the refusal beyond mention of the river: not before a river journey, was probably what she said. She had spoken even more softly than usual, perhaps to hide her betrayal of the princess's hope of a favourable response to her letter and a reprieve at the eleventh hour.

The princess came through, pallid and creased as if part of her were left behind in the bed, which in a sense it was, because a little later, when stowing the bed linen, I found her body warmth in it. Then the lords arrived, gruffly defensive, brisk and too big for that room. The outdoor air was all over them like smuts, and they had been flattened by the elements like drenched cats. They looked no more rested than we did; their night, too, had been a mere gap into which they had fallen and from which they were now dragging themselves up to be slapped around by daybreak.

They showed no recognition of me, and I saw that I couldn't turn to them for help in getting free. To them, the ladies were cargo, and their eyes were busy with calculations as how best to get them onto the barge, and a hankering for the whole distasteful business to be over. Their demeanour made clear there was no word from the queen, and the princess had to swallow it – folding dejection away down that long, soft girlish white throat. Determination in the set of her jaw showed, though, that she refused to take it as a setback. Early days, yet, I could see she was telling herself, and everything still to play for.

In the meantime, there was nothing for it but for them to get going. I stood by with a suitably respectful and regretful stance, but then, as they were ushered towards the open door, I did what I had to do and stepped back. Mrs Ashley, though, swooped, scooped me up, bountiful, as if rescuing me. It was as if I were merely being bashful, relinquishing a rightful claim to be included. I had forgotten how difficult she was to shake off: resistance would only bolster her resolve. So I went down the stairs as one of the party. There was nothing else I could do.

Outside, the air was gritty like smoke and as sour as ale. Mrs Ashley drew me to her, kept me close. In my favour, though, was that there would be different arrangements for the transporting of servants. The ladies' barge was no place for the likes of me. That would be my last chance: I'd be stopped by one of the dozens upon dozens of royal-liveried men who seemed to have some role in getting the princess's departure under way. To them, I would be due to follow, in time, with laundry; but for now, I would be sent packing. Scanning the faces of those men, I didn't see myself in their eyes: I was no one, didn't figure. Yet still I was being ushered towards that barge. This was going too far. A siren of protest rose in my throat, but what I needed to say was something about my luggage, about not having it with me. Purposely, I hadn't picked up my bag. Luggage, Mrs Ashley would understand: so much of her life was about luggage; it was, to her, a legitimate concern.

'My bag . . . '

But she flapped her free hand at the ranks of liveried men – *Let them see to it* – and there was vindictive glee in the gesture: *Let them worry about it*.

There must be something else for me to say, I thought, that would do the trick of giving her pause, but I couldn't for the life of me think of it. Trying to grasp it was like delving into a pail of water in pursuit of a sunbeam, and before I knew it, the soles of my boots were sounding gruff on the boards of the barge. Frantically I told myself that it didn't matter, that the gates of the Tower are hard and fast only for its prisoners: only the prisoners, there, are prisoners. And I was no prisoner. I would be just one among the multitude of servants and tradespeople free to come and go. And as soon as I was there, and the ladies were escorted away, that was what I'd do: go. I'd simply turn around and go.

The princess, though, ahead of me, ducking under the canvas awning: even if she did in time leave the Tower, it would probably only be to go abroad, to be married off. She was unlikely ever again to come back up these riverside steps, to turn her face unobserved to the sun before leaving in her litter for Ashridge or Hatfield or whichever of her homes she chose as mistress of her household.

The four of us were crowded under the awning, ostensibly sheltered although the elements nonetheless made themselves felt. It was no longer raining, but the wind was on the canvas like a dog on a rat. We were sitting on cushions, the princess clasping her knees, eyelids lowered to give the impression that she was lost in thought, but this keeping of herself to herself might have been a keeping of the rest of us at bay. I resigned myself to the journey. I'd failed to stand up for myself, but at the Tower, when the ladies were being dealt with by officials, I would declare my mistake.

The cushions were made from exquisite fabrics, and surreptitiously I felt my way along redundant seams and over repairs to try to guess at the garment of which mine had once been a part. And whose barge was this? Not the queen's own, the royal barge, which I had seen moored a stone's throw upstream at the palace's private royal steps. I hadn't thought to look for an insignia, but probably wouldn't have known it anyway – and that was if it hadn't hastily been lowered, because it was hard to imagine which nobleman would go so far as to fly his flag for this particular journey.

There was a guard at the opening of the awning but he might not be enough to stop Mrs Ashley from making our presence known to Londoners. She had a big voice for a small lady, and no shame where the princess's welfare was concerned. I didn't put it past her to shove aside that solitary guard and raise the alarm to those on other boats and on the banks. For the time being, she sat composed, holding herself notably straight and still, as if her dignity were something to balance on her head. To see her, it was as if an inconvenience had been visited upon us, which she bore as if doing our captors a favour. Her gaze, though, darted around the rest of us, as if to shore up a conspiracy.

The princess remained at a remove, as did Miss Parry, if differently, her head tilted back, giving the impression of openness even as her eyes were closed. She swayed with each oar stroke, the motion of the barge moving her in a way that didn't budge the resolute Mrs Ashley or the hunched princess. She rode each stroke but it was impossible to know if she found relief in the sway or if it was a kind of nauseous swooning. There had after all been that hushed refusal of breakfast, on behalf of us all but perhaps she was the one who felt it most. Or possibly it was tiredness: I wondered if she had sat up with the princess while Mrs Ashley and I had slept.

Each dip and haul on the oars stitched us further into our journey. Rain started up, the first strikes sounding petulant on the canvas but then like one long ripping of it. And under that awning there was nothing to do but listen to it. The journey stripped of its landmarks was baffling: I had no sense of how far we had travelled. The ladies probably wouldn't know Puddle Wharf even if they saw it, and there had been a time when I myself hadn't known it, which now seemed ludicrous to me. Before I had met Bel, life had merely been idling with me, playing catch-me-if-you-can.

Other boats were detectable nearby – once too near, because outside our awning came a brief, unpleasant exchange, the contesting of a right of way. This animated Mrs Ashley: to none of us in particular she said, 'I hope they're not going to take us beneath the bridge,' her tone implying they would do exactly that. But why wouldn't they? How else would we reach the Tower, downstream? The princess raised her eyes to her guardian's with a studied blankness to imply this was the least of her worries. Miss Parry opened hers and frowned, puzzled and pained in equal measure. Mrs Ashley addressed the princess as if she were the one about to transgress: '*No*. No heir to the throne gets knocked about beneath that bridge, not on *my* watch,' and then to Miss Parry, as if ordering her, 'We get off, as everyone always does, and walk to the other side.'

Knocked about? Then she was up and seeing to the matter, tapping the hapless guard on the shoulder, demanding of him where we were – I didn't catch the reply – before insisting she speak with the earls.

Miss Parry murmured something about Mrs Ashley being right, about the tide being low, but she sounded apologetic; and the princess sighed with disgust, although at what or whom – tides, earls, guardians, orders, or just life in general – was impossible to know.

130

Mrs Ashley reappeared unmollified. 'Water all the way,' she announced, 'because should we alight, would you believe, there's a risk that Londoners might spirit us away.'

'Ridiculous,' said Miss Parry, faintly.

Plonking herself back down, defeated, Mrs Ashley was furious. 'Tell that to the earls.'

The princess said, insincerely, 'We'll just have to pray for safe passage, then, won't we.' Whatever the problem was, it didn't bother her. And so, I decided, I wouldn't let it bother me, either. I was sick of Mrs Ashley's fusses. Surely bridges were for going under as much as for going over.

'How dare they,' hissed Mrs Ashley, 'that pathetic pair. When you're queen, Bette, you can . . . ' but her voice broke on a sob and we'd all reached for her before we knew it but not before she'd reined herself in and flapped us away. She drew herself up again – grim, resigned – to await our fate.

Or so it seemed, but she couldn't resist, and in a heartbeat or two she was off again, at top speed. 'I've never liked them, I've always said, I always knew, and talk about true colours . . . '

She wasn't talking to me, but there I was, feeling beholden to respond, nodding like an idiot.

' . . . two-faced cowards, which the queen herself would do well to bear in mind . . . '

I smiled genially as she bandied about accusations that were tantamount to treason. Then as suddenly as she had started, she stopped, and deflated herself with a hefty sigh.

Nothing could have prepared me for the slam of the barge into the bridge. All I knew at first was the ramming of my neck into the base of my skull, and a surge of my blood through my body as if making a break for it. *This is it*, I thought. Mrs Ashley shrieked an oath and we all lunged in a catch-all attempt to steady not just ourselves but the barge as a whole, and perhaps even the water itself. Outside on deck, men were shouting and

131

running, a whirl as chaotic as any in the actual water. A second blow came as if something dying had lashed out at us: more vicious than effective. And then, although we wouldn't know it for a moment, it was over: we were through, we had coursed the rapids, the churning water between the piers, and been spat out the other side.

Those men now had to face the wrath of Mrs Ashley. An absence of anyone at the opening of the awning was telling, but there was only so long they could avoid her. She was trained gimlet-eyed on that absence, even as she groped for the princess's hand, arm, shoulder, to check she was intact. Miss Parry was babbling reassurances – *Goodness me, Bessie* – over the princess's own shaky attempt to make light of it: *Phew!* Then Miss Parry checked, 'Annie?' and oddly it was her use of the name that wasn't mine that brought tears to my eyes. I was saved by the appearance at the awning opening of one of the noblemen, who didn't stand a cat's hope in hell of facing up to Mrs Ashley and lost the fight within a heartbeat of her drawing breath.

We hadn't pulled up short of the bridge when we should have, but in a move so inexplicable as to leave Mrs Ashley speechless, the barge moored upstream of the Tower so that we would have to walk across a drawbridge in the downpour. I was thankful for a hiatus, though: shaken to the core as I had just been, and sodden and wretched, I needed to dredge up the resolve to resist being swallowed up by whatever awaited the ladies.

Rain seethed on the surface of the river like a life form, and the oarsmen looked inhuman: dumbstruck, heads hung and noses dripping, each torso imprinted with a weird, extravagant configuration of dampness. The deck of the barge was awash, the riverside steps treacherous.

We made a pitiful little procession, hoping in vain that our herding together would afford us shelter, and had only just assembled on the wharf when the princess lost her footing, or so it appeared: down she went, hood back and head almost bared to the elements, her lace coif so fragile that it might dissolve. What was exposed of her hair smarted under the hammering rain. Everyone was reaching for her, to help her back to her feet, but she shrugged them off, head held high, and I understood that it hadn't been a fall: she was kneeling, and enacting some kind of resistance.

The kneeling was without humility; it was a pose to put her beyond the reach of any of our party and show that she answered only to a higher calling. She held us there while the rain threw itself at us as if these were the dismal last moments of our lives. Her ladies and the lords together were reduced to pleading – *Your Grace, please* – unable to hide that this was for their own sodden sakes at least as much as for hers, but she merely tipped her face to the heavens to be anointed, then took no small pleasure in telling the earls loudly enough for everyone to hear – oarsmen, guards, the meagre, shamefaced reception party of officialdom that had assembled at the wharf – that they were making a prisoner of an innocent. Then she got to her feet like a braid whipped in the fingertips of the Almighty.

10

Blood and Bone and Marrow

My reprieve came in the blink of an eye: the princess and her two ladies escorted away by jailers, leaving me with the porters, none of whom had been expecting a laundress nor had a clue as to what to do with me. There I was, washed up in the porters' lodge, a fish out of water. I didn't plan on staying, but the porters didn't know that, and, in no rush to be back on the water, I kept quiet and let them fuss about where to accommodate me. When I had warmed up, and with luck been given some food, I would slip away, head back to the palace and my old life in the laundry. It would make for a long day, but I'd had worse.

A merry key-jangling redhead took up my case and, in a daze of exhaustion, I played along. Off we went in a lull in the rain to search for lodgings in which I had no intention of staying. We splashed down an alleyway that looked rarely visited: a storage area, perhaps. Even my guide seemed doubtful: for him, too, it was unfamiliar territory. Eventually he had me wait in a stairwell while he sprang up several steps at a time to open and close various doors before galloping back down with an apologetic wince – nothing doing – and this was then repeated at a series of what appeared to me to be identical stairwells. I knew I should say something to let him off the hook, but the further we went along, the harder it was to own up.

Half a dozen or so staircases along, he practically flew down to fetch me, and took me back up with him to the third floor, the top, to show me his find: a small lime-washed room, clean-swept, with a shuttered window and – he demonstrated – a lockable door, to which he proffered his copy of the key. The room was furnished with a bed frame for which he seemed to think I'd have my own hangings, which I didn't deny but had to stop myself joking that I'd have my servants bring them up. Who on earth did he think I was? He said he happened to know the whereabouts of a couple of new mattresses – replacements, he called them, which, seeing as we were at the Tower, didn't strike me as the recommendation he perhaps intended – and one of these would be brought up. A couple of rush lights, too, and a pail, he said, and then you're set. I made all the right noises and he was somehow already halfway down those stairs, calling back that he'd have everything rustled up in a trice.

I was left with the first moment I'd had to myself since I'd stood gormlessly in that room at the King's Head – which was only the previous day but felt as if it was a month back – and I was relieved not to have to trudge all the way back to the lodge and stand smiling at various busybody porters. The mention of the pail, though, had made me aware of an increasingly pressing need; I hoped the redhead wouldn't be too long. In the wake of his departure, I unfastened the shutter; the air hung at the window like a blade, lulled and mutedly bright but still keen and sharp. The courtyard below was deserted, although there was a telling gleam to the cobbles around the well.

I had no idea where I was within the Tower, but the Tower itself was, I guessed, a half-hour at most away from Bel. All I'd have to do, it occurred to me, was find Eastcheap, head down west into Cheapside proper, and from there I would know my way. The thought perked me up, and I changed my plan: before the barge back to Whitehall, a walk through the city to Bel. After those weeks away from the Whitehall laundry, a few more hours wouldn't hurt. And the later back to the laundry, the better: I was too weary, after the night I'd had and then that awful river journey, to do much work. I'd see myself back there as instructed, but I'd take my time about it. No one was expecting me.

The princess, though, would be going nowhere. She would be released if no case was found against her; but otherwise, I thought, I might be the last outsider to have seen her alive. Several dozen guards with fire-wattled faces, runny noses and sleep in their eyes had bumbled off with her in their midst, she taller than most of them. I pictured her narrow shoulders and long back, her cloak in a wool too fine to shine.

For all that she acted as if she herself were made of rare stuff, I bet that when she was taken away by those slipshod-liveried nobodies, the blood was roaring in her ears the same as it would for any new prisoner. And should the unthinkable happen, the blood swamping the straw and soaking the boards beneath her would be the usual sticky stuff for the servants to clean up. What a waste it would be, I thought, to take an axe to a perfectly healthy body, to shovel perfectly fine blood and bone and marrow into the soil.

Down in the alleyway were men's voices – raised, disoriented – and I supposed they were searching for me. Perhaps the redhead had forgotten exactly where I was, or had delegated but not properly explained, or they hadn't listened to him or couldn't quite recall, but whatever the reason, they sounded as if they were in a muddle, so I was going to have to show my face.

And there in the sodden passageway was a pair of men burdened with a mattress, and behind them another pair heaped with bed linen. It wasn't until they crowded into my room that I recognised the linen as belonging to the princess: not her best by a long chalk, but still. And not only had they plundered the princess's chests, they'd then carted their spoils around in the rain. One of the men stepped up as spokesman, keen to placate: I would have to have this bed linen because there was nothing at the Tower prepared for me. And it wasn't as if her Grace didn't have loads more, he said.

Oh, do me a favour, I thought: a few spare sheets nowhere to be found in the whole of the Tower? This was a message from the powers-that-be: they weren't going to put themselves out for the princess's people. But I wanted rid of those men, and in any case, I wasn't going to use the linen, so I simpered and they clattered off back to their porterly duties, leaving me with a treasure trove that almost filled the room. Brigid had laundered one of the quilts when I was at Ashridge, and the memory of her clutched my heart. I sifted the pile, and none of it was as damp as I'd feared.

The promised pail, though, hadn't appeared, so I had to go asking for one, but at the lodge I was nabbed by someone who claimed to have been looking for me. He whisked me into an office where I sat with my legs firmly crossed as he, wall-eyed, decreed that laundry services for the princess would not be permitted. No deliveries of any kind, he insisted, which included laundry. The incarcerated ladies would do whatever they could do by themselves, in their suite of rooms, and everything else would be dealt with by the Tower laundry.

He took me for the princess's bona fide laundress, and I didn't feel like enlightening him. The ladies had enough laundry with them to see them through for a while, but thereafter they would definitely need a laundress: it wasn't going to be me, but he didn't have to know that. I tried to explain: at the very least they would need their own soap, made for them by someone they trusted.

He said, 'They can take their chances with our soap. There's no need to be silly about it.'

I didn't know whether he meant me or them, but anyway it was he who was silly. Any laundress could have told that man a thing or two about how a body can suffer from a genuine mistake, a misjudgement or mismeasurement that results in too harsh a soak. An undergarment has a hold on a person, has its wearer in its grip from dawn to dusk, or dusk to dawn, by which time the damage has been done, and God only knew how bad it could be if someone actually intended harm. Just as the cook was to vouch for the food for the princess, a laundress was essential. A trusted laundress would buy the ingredients for soap from suppliers whom she in turn trusted, and would alone see to the washing, drying, pressing and storage of the linen. No one but a laundress of the princess's own household should touch the linen that would touch the princess's bare skin. I tried to explain, but he wouldn't listen. He didn't actually dismiss me, just insisted that I wasn't needed.

No one had told the porters, though, because when I went back to the lodge, not only was there a pail for me but some rush lights. And a little later, when I passed back through on my way to Bel, I was waylaid with a tray of food from the princess's kitchen that the men had been keeping aside for me because, they admitted cheerfully, none of them knew exactly where I was.

Once I'd eaten, I ventured city-side of the Middle Tower gate and – hey presto – I was back to being Alys Twist. Never had I been so glad to be me. The Ashridge episode was well and truly over, and relief had me halt in the narrow Petty Wales lane amid the bustling water-carriers to take a deep breath and lift my eyes to the sky to give thanks.

I was off the hook. I was pretty sure I couldn't be blamed for disregarding what had been no more than rumour and insinuation when what the queen's men needed was proof. Which presumably they now had, seeing as the princess was locked away, awaiting trial. I didn't like to think of her possible fate – but if it did come to that, then at least I would have had no hand in it.

When I found Bel at St Andrew's Square she was entranced to hear of my cell-like room bizarrely stuffed with splendour. 'This I have to see,' she said, and insisted I turn around then and there so we could retrace my steps. And back at the Tower, it was as easy as she had said it would be – we chanced it through the porters' lodge and for the purpose of the deception she was my silkwoman, although the porters didn't ask, too busy admiring the braids and buttons we gave them for their lady wives. In any case, we were no risk: we weren't going on through Coldharbour Gate into the main body of the Tower; we were going no further than any of the suppliers or labourers who came and went all day every day. The porters already knew me, and what was one more fresh-faced, clean-pressed, well-scrubbed young lady?

Taking Bel back there with me, I saw how my room – within the moat yet still city-side of the central Coldharbour Gate – was neither in London nor in the Tower proper but in a kind of nowhere. No one was looking for me either, because the princess and her ladies had been told I had been turned away, and the queen's gentlemen would assume I'd done as instructed and seen my way back to the palace laundry. I had slipped from view, I realised, down a fold between city and fortress, between the princess's household and the queen's. Perhaps just the one night, then, I dared myself when Bel had exclaimed approvingly over my little room and left, and exhaustion had come for me anew: for just one night I could sleep like a princess in my absurdly opulent cell and no one would be any the wiser.

The next morning, well refreshed, I came across a tray left for me at the lodge: I could dine like royalty, too. I decided then and there to stay for that day, just the one day, for the supper tray at five. After Ashridge, I reckoned, I was owed.

I crossed the city again to Bel that day, and brought her back with me for the afternoon, for lolling around in my wonderful room. My intention was to take a barge to Whitehall in the late afternoon; but when she had gone and it was time for me to pack up and leave, I wondered what was to be gained by arriving at the laundry in the evening. I reckoned it would be better done in the morning.

And then in the morning, emboldened by that second night, I allowed myself to wonder whether I had misunderstood the gentleman at the palace when he said I should stay with the princess's household until it was done. Perhaps this hadn't meant the princess being taken to the Tower; perhaps he had wanted me to hang around until her fate was decided, her release or her committal to trial. And despite speculation everywhere in the streets, there was still no official word on that. A day or two, the man had said.

Later, when I met up with Bel, I told her there had been a change of plan but didn't specify who had made the decision, which she didn't question because she was too busy voicing her incredulity: what use was I – nowhere near the princess? I shrugged, reminding her that it had made no sense, either, to send me to Ashridge.

Everyone, everywhere, agreed that the princess couldn't be held much longer without trial, but a day or two had become three, then four, and I was in too deep, dependent on the princess's release or condemnation to set me on my way back into my old life.

Well, I was in no rush. At the Tower, I was a kept woman but in no one's keeping. I was answerable to no one: my lifelong dream, granted without ceremony and in the last place I would ever have expected to find it.

As luck would have it, Bel too had time on her hands: the wedding preparations were done, but no good Catholic marries in Lent. So she came each day to the lodge. At the strike of one I would find her there, bestowing samples and sequins, and I could see from how the porters chatted to her about their children and grandchildren that they took her on trust. There was none of how they might have regarded any other woman, furtive and appraising. They looked her happily in the eye and, reflected there, saw their own best selves. There were the same readily bared heads and broad smiles for me, but hidden within those greetings I felt there was a nod and a wink. Skulking through the gates at Bel's skirts, I was running scared, convinced I was seen through: me, trailing her with my wolfish smile, as if I were the interloper.

We would get through the lodge, and then we were up the stairs and into my room and down to our shifts, then, in all that sumptuous bed linen, down to our bare skin. My wedding ring was just another layer, which surreptitiously I removed and slid beneath the pillows. Before Bel, I'd never seen a naked body, not even my own, because – raised in crowded but respectable households – I had been taught to preserve my modesty by undressing at the same time as dressing in something else, slipping on one garment as another was shed. The habit had persisted after the move from several girls innocently top to toe in a bed to just the one man, my husband, when it had become part of the fun. Bel's naked body could not have been more different from mine: hers was a perfect fit for her, it seemed to me, whereas mine, as I saw it, was make-do and mend, toughened by the lugging and pounding of laundry, and my hands in particular were rough, scalded, iron-burned. I wasn't all of a piece as she was, I felt, although she always gathered me to her as if I were.

A week turned into two, but still no decision about the princess, and I was trapped by my lie. March was colder even than February, the light merely wiping through the grimy sky before the day was bundled up and chucked westwards on the wind. In my bed I sank into the winning warmth of Bel, which was everywhere on my skin all at once, somehow surface and depth equally there and endlessly re-forming around me like a body of water.

141

After she'd gone, I would head to the porters' lodge to benefit from the fireside in return for sewing jobs and small talk. I was surprised how I hankered for the company of those men, and disconcerted how after an afternoon of Bel's lavender scent I would draw deep on their reek as if somewhere inside me twitched a hungering snout. At the end of an evening I'd leave with only a rush light for company, declining an escort because – I'd joke – where could be safer?

Annie Turner had been written off by those who had created her but I hadn't yet gone back to being Alys Twist, and in truth I suppose I was hoping by then that perhaps I never quite would. After all, I had only worked at the palace for a couple of months, and much of that time I had in fact spent at Bel's. With any luck, by the time I returned to the palace, no one in the laundry would remember exactly what it was I was supposed to do, and I'd be free to make it up as I went along. My aim was to end up with a life something like Bel's.

For three weeks I got away without crossing paths with anyone who had a clue who I was, before coming down to earth with a bump to see the kitchen boy in the porters' lodge, although the shock of the encounter at the time was his split lip. My recoil had him grin before he could think better of it, and we winced in unison. The cheerful response to my concerned enquiry was '*Some* people don't want us here,' and when I asked which people, he said none of them did. Clearly his dignity depended on making light of whatever had happened to him, so I let it be and he left me with a breezy 'Best watch your step.'

That was when I started leaving the Tower for the daylight hours when Bel wasn't with me. I had nothing else to do, and if I kept up a pace, I was warmer outside than in: striding past the water-carriers, sidestepping livestock and their drivers, dodging the nifty but precarious two-wheeled wagons, with no concern other than the toll on the soles of my boots. Beneath St

Magnus's clock in Thames Street were the steps to the bridge, and often I went up there to browse the shops although never all the way across, because no one respectable would go to the south bank. My favourite area of the city was towards the north, Bucklesbury, its grocers stocked with every last thing that anyone could ever want, its self-important apothecaries dealing less in medicines than in scents, their walls jewelled with jars and doorways hectic with delivery boys. Sometimes I went along Cheapside and up St Martin's Le Grand, where foreigners were allowed to trade – shoemakers, hat-makers – and it was a good job I had no money to spare or I would never have stopped shopping.

Usually I was careful to stay east of St Paul's, keeping my distance from Bel's house, avoiding being seen by anyone to whom I would feel obliged to give an account myself, but sometimes when it rained I did duck into the cathedral to shelter in the nave among the crowds of Londoners conducting business there. Once when the heavens opened I didn't quite make it, and slipped instead into the porch of All Hallows on the corner of Bread Street to find it already occupied by a boy still young enough to have the bow lips of a baby. He had with him a horn slate, which, before I had drawn breath, he angled so that I could see, asking me without preamble, 'Is this right? It's my name. See? Samuel Saunders.' A tiny fingertip guided me reverently through the shapes he had made.

His seriousness was touching, and although I couldn't be of any use to him – I knew the two Ss but the rest was beyond me – I felt I should rise to it in any way I could, so I frowned over the words and murmured approvingly.

But he wasn't for fobbing off. 'Is it right?'

'It looks it,' I said, adding pointlessly, 'You're very good at it.'

He returned his attention to it as if it had nothing to do with him – as if it had somehow just ended up there in his lap – then looking back up at me with his great grave eyes informed me, 'My daddy's the rector here.'

'Oh,' I said, with no better idea of how to respond, but hoping again to have struck the right – appreciative – note.

He chirped, 'What's *your* name?' and for a second he had me, because who was I supposed to be here, not in the Tower and not at Bel's house but outside All Hallows in Bread Street? In my confusion, I rushed at it, trusting myself to come up with the correct answer but falling for something in between: 'Anis.'

Just then we were joined by a young woman whose face lit up at the sight of him, so that I felt awkward and shuffled to one side to relinquish him. She gave me a look that was somewhere between apology and conspiracy, and I realised with a jolt that she considered me an equal: she mistook me for a wife and mother, and not only did I feel a fraud but I was struck as to how much I would now likely never have. The little boy displayed his writing to her with exaggerated care, as if the letters risked sliding from the slate. 'Look, Mummy.'

She crouched, a black frizado skirt visible beneath her cloak. 'Nearly,' was her judgement on his efforts, and spoken like a promise. 'Just here, you forgot . . .' but she didn't need to say, because he exclaimed in recognition of his omission, perhaps one that he had previously or habitually made. Clearly he was glad of the opportunity for the pair of them to put it right. With a smile, she excused them both from my company, saying to him, 'Let's run through this rain and get home before Daddy.'

With nowhere in particular to go, I hung around for the rain to let up, peering dejectedly up and down the lane, which was when I spotted Bel and my heart gave a glad little clap to see her crossing Bread Street with Ollie and gone in a flash into Pissing Alley.

I mentioned it that afternoon when we were together in my room, and she took me to task for not having made myself known. Casting her bag across my bed, she said I shouldn't worry about Ollie. 'He's not going to say anything. Or even *think* anything.' Settling on the bed, she smiled up at me. '*He* doesn't know where you're supposed to be. Or where *any*one's supposed to be. Not even himself, half the time.'

It wasn't that, I told her – I'd been too far away, up on the corner of Watling Street. Picturing her hurrying along side by side with Ollie, I remembered Mr Hobbes once saying she should marry one of the apprentices. That would amuse her, I knew, so I told her, but she was retrieving her bag and delving into it, and didn't respond. I teased, 'Don't you *want* to get married?'

She glanced up at me as she had once at the night sky to advocate a tidying of the stars. 'Don't *you*?' A tilt of her head, an expression of concern. 'Don't you want children?'

My heart flared into my throat but her attention was back inside that bag, leaving me securing the shutter and wondering how she wanted me to be, there at the window. Who she took me for. I'd been a joker, moments ago, so I fell back on that. 'And who's going to be daddy, do you think, of those little Bels?'

She found what she had been hunting – a handkerchief – and blew her nose, concluding nasally, 'I've no plans.' With her clear blue gaze on mine, she said, 'But some things just have to be done, don't they.'

Do they? Which things?

Marriage, children.

My heart was blasting my throat but I came up with a smile: no trouble.

She extended a hand to me. 'If we *do* end up having to do all that, so what?' Practical Bel, capable Bel: *If you have to have someone coming at you with a needle, then you want that person to be me*. My hand found its way into hers. 'Because nothing will ever stop this, will it.' She didn't mean this particular room, I knew, but somewhere – anywhere – we two could be alone together.

There would always be somewhere for us to be alone together, for some of the time.

I didn't dare ask questions because I couldn't bear the answers. And anyway, I told myself, give her time. Everything that had happened between us had come fast from nowhere, and she had yet to catch up. It was easy for me – I had no appearances to keep up, nothing to live up to and nothing to lose. I had no idea how we would live our lives together – but not with her married to someone else: of that, I was sure. And if I stuck around, she too would see it.

Sometimes, though, I feared that I was making a habit of wandering up blind alleys. Because look at how I had deserted my husband without thinking about where it would leave me.

He had been a travelling player, and whenever he had gone off to work, I had waited for him. At first that had been hard, but in time it was harder when he came back. Perhaps I resented him crashing in, requiring me to turn on my heel and be a wife. Or perhaps it was that I didn't know how to be a wife, or not the wife he wanted. Nor was he, though, the man I'd taken him to be, and by the end of that year of our marriage he was morose, petty-minded, selfish, even vindictive, although he probably would have said the same of me. The truth was that we were both unhappy.

He was away so much over that year and in time was coming back less often and not for so long, and then he came back with the pox. Saddle sore, he claimed, but a laundress knows pus when she smells it. Saddle sore: it happens sometimes, he said.

Yes, when you've slept with a whore, I thought.

But a nice girl doesn't voice suspicions of her husband, so I said nothing and planned my escape. When he next left, I didn't for once ask him when he would be back, and he didn't say. My monthly bleed came as no disappointment, and three weeks later

I took an opportunity to move households but didn't leave word of where I had gone. When another chance of promotion came up within a couple of months, I took it and did the same; then again later that year. And so I covered my tracks. Not that he would come looking, I knew. The pair of us backed away from that marriage, which made neat work of its abandonment.

I hadn't run, nor lied; I just hadn't told the truth. And I had considered myself to have done well. Too well, though, it dawned on me in time, because although I was free of a husband, I was still married, and even a widowing wouldn't help because I had taken myself beyond anywhere I could hear of it.

London should have been turning towards spring, but if anything it was colder, as unforgiving a March as I could recall, and then April was no better. The Tower, on the banks of the river and windward of the city wall, was no place to be. The wind cut under doors and roof tiles, down chimneys, and made a mockery of mortar to find me wherever I was and rattle my bones. The porters' fireside conjured only a superficial flush, and the warmth of Bel in the afternoons was now no more than skin deep, and oddly tight on me like a scald.

I kept up the walking, but was growing wary of the various city gates, the displays of Kentish remains to which I should by then have been inured. I developed the strangest sense that from their vantage point those hacked hips and shoulders were waiting for me. Perhaps it was the steadiness of their hanging there: the suggestion of expectation. And in time I came to feel they were waiting to ask something of me, or would if they could, those bits of flesh dumbstruck by the atrocities that had been inflicted on them.

During that desolate April I began wondering about the men they had been and what they had been thinking to risk their lives. They must have believed they had right on their side, that they had the people on their side, that the people would see them right, and I recalled from what the kitchen boy had told me that it had indeed been so — the surrender of the Medway ships, the bridge rebuilt in the dead of night — until the very last minute.

I understood why they were up there on the gates: I did understand that men can't go marching through the streets of London while a queen cowers behind a door armed only with a rolling pin. The kitchen boy had told me that the queen had said she was mother to the people of England. But surely no mother would see done to her child what she had ordered to be done to those men. She could choose, it seemed, who was and wasn't her child, just as she seemed to think she could choose who was or wasn't her sister.

Mid-April, Thomas Wyatt swore at his execution that the princess had known nothing about his rebellion. Her release would come, Bel said, as soon as the queen was married. Which was when? That, Bel didn't know. No one did, she said. Not even the queen herself, it seemed. But the delay was nothing, as far as Bel was aware; just more of the same: negotiations, stipulations as to who and what the Spaniards could bring into the country, and what backing would or wouldn't be given for Spain's latest war. Oh, and sailing conditions, she said: could be that, because remember he's coming from Spain.

As if anyone could forget.

If the sea was rough, it was barely better ashore. Nearly May, but still so gusty, chilly, damp. I was careful to go nowhere near any city gate, but some of what was rotting up there would be carried on the wind, I knew, and if I tried to brush it off my cloak then it was on my gloves, and anyway there were specks in my eyes and on my lips. This was nothing I knew how to clean away.

It would be all over Bel, too, not that anyone would have believed it to see her step blithely up my stairs. We never spoke about the bodies up on the gates, but then we never spoke about much, and anyway what would there have been to say about those tar-cauterised lumps? And to have said it so long after the executions would suggest that we had simply grown sick of the sight of them. It would have been worse to voice it so late, it seemed to me, than to stay silent.

During those afternoons with Bel in my room, I was the closest I had ever been to anyone in my life, but the heart of our encounters began to elude me like running water, going and gone in the same instant, beaching me high and dry beside her. Something was wrong, or at least not right, or not for me; but from her came no sign of anything amiss, which might have perturbed me had it not also been something of a relief, a reprieve. I didn't want her questioning me.

On May Day she brought me a pearl folded for safe keeping into a handkerchief, and I knew, without her owning up, where it had come from. She had spent weeks sewing thousands all over the queen's wedding dress. 'Look what turned up in a corner,' was all she said, mischievously, and I acted properly impressed, remarked how beautiful it was, this treasure, but in truth its pallid pinkish sheen put me in mind of a nail or a just-lost tooth or the surface of an eye, something bodily but bloodless.

As soon as she had gone, I was back to thinking of those Kentish men who were no longer men. I tried not to dwell on the last moments of their lives on scrubbed gallows-boards in front of a crowd keen to get it done and go back home. Those men had marched and it had seemed fine but then it wasn't and suddenly they had had their day before they had known there was a day to be had.

None of them would have anticipated that it would end in front of a restless crowd in February rain, and until the very last minute each would have been expecting someone from somewhere to come pushing through that crowd with word to save them. *Not me*, they must have been thinking: *I am not someone to end like this, dropped half dead from a noose and my britches yanked down for the mutilating knife.*

Not you, I thought, who once upon a time, in a moment turned up like a penny in the grass, must have lain peering at a sun-spangled hair on your forearm and narrowed your eyes, shifted your gaze and shuffled the beam to make your own tiny private rainbow.

II

Amongst Wolves

One day in mid-May I woke before first light to shouting in the alley: someone urging me to pack up and get down to the wharf. Sleep-fuddled, I did as I was told, abandoning the bed linen but stuffing my belongings into my bag and dealing with the pail, and I arrived at the riverside as an ornate barge slid away upstream behind a tug of a dozen rowers. Still moored was a second, plainer, scantily canopied one, onto which were clambering a man I recognised to be the cook, an assistant and the kitchen boy.

So this was it, at long last, I thought: the princess's return upriver to Whitehall. No trial, then, in the end, and no execution. Just a rap across the knuckles, a shot across her bows. This grudging release in the early hours with a distinct lack of fanfare was the queen's climbdown.

And for me, an awakening from the weird enchantment that had been my time in the Tower. I should be relieved, I knew, even as I was apprehensive as to how my excuse, back at the laundry, would wash. Sleep-sozzled on that quayside, though, I felt nothing. Getting myself back into my old life was just a job to be done.

Clearly I had been demoted from the princess's barge to the company of the kitchen staff, but they would be easier travelling companions than Mrs Ashley, and anyway what mattered was that we survive the bridge.

Aboard, beneath the tatty awning, were two benches, on one of which the three kitchen staff aligned themselves so that I took the facing one. We exchanged nods of acknowledgement but not a word, not this early. Tall and limber though the cook was, he folded himself down, retracted his pot-stirring arms and closed his eyes to hover somewhere between slumber and wakefulness like a hoodwinked bird of prey. His stocky assistant would be the one to look to, I suspected, if we hit trouble beneath the bridge: he'd be the one chucking us driftwood and bellowing instructions while his boss struck out for the bank with long, measured strokes.

The tide was low, though, and we were beneath the bridge before we knew it, although a mere few oar strokes onwards came some booms from the bank that sounded like battle but which the assistant cook claimed was a salute. He craned around the awning to confirm it: 'Steelyard. Hansas.' The depot for the Hansas, the merchants from the Low Countries. 'Word's out, then, that we're out,' and he grinned. 'Bet Mrs Ashley's . . .' and there on the bench he demonstrated a stunted version of what in actuality would be her exuberant waving. Later, as we drew alongside Whitehall, he was the one who said, 'Not Whitehall, then,' while I was under the impression that we were on the approach to the steps but rather speedily. He said it as a matter of fact, as if it were nothing of note.

Not Whitehall?

The kitchen boy spoke up for the first time, just as casually. 'Where then?'

None of them had an answer nor were willing to speculate, but they seemed accepting, as if this were half expected. Cook sat back, crossing his long legs at the ankle, settling down for the duration, which could have been defeat but was as likely relief at not having to try to cook in the dank old kitchen in Outer Court.

I was doing my utmost best to look as nonchalant as they did – but if not Whitehall, then where? For me, anywhere other than the palace was complicated: a longer journey back, potentially expensive and, not having been paid for months, my savings were low. Hampton Court was all I knew of the Thames upriver, but if the court had moved there then Bel would have mentioned it – her main source of business relocated a couple of hours upstream – and anyway, it had looked to me as we passed Whitehall that the queen was still in residence there. Whatever this was, the princess's release from the Tower, it wasn't her welcome back to court.

My own predicament deepened with each oar stroke. Bel would be trusting to see me later in the day and everything she was doing, even at this hour, would be shot through with that expectation. Waking, she would be calculating what work to take on that could be finished or put aside just after midday, when she would set off through the streets for the porters' lodge, only to be told that I had gone. *Gone, Miss, first thing; didn't you know?* This would bring a mere scratch of dismay to her heart, though, because she would assume – as no doubt had those cannon-happy Hansas – that we had merely gone to Whitehall. She would expect me to turn up, this evening or tomorrow, at St Thomas Apostle Street, and it was odd how my already knowing different felt like treachery.

People gawped from the banks as we passed. In their eyes, we must be quite a spectacle: a pair of glossily painted, banner-bright barges. And no doubt our oarsmen had us looking purposeful. The royal-liveried attendants on the other barge probably looked as if they were there for the passengers' protection, but in fact they were the princess's jailers.

If the princess being hauled blinking into the light wasn't so much the granting of her freedom, it could yet be an easing of restrictions. She could be bound for some halfway house. Or perhaps it was simply that she was no longer important enough for the Tower, and destined instead for some backwater.

Just as the people on the bank looked at us and wondered, I now looked at my travelling companions. Who were these people, the ladies in the barge ahead of us and the cooks on the bench across from me? Were they the schemers, traitors, heretics that the queen seemed to think they were? Or hapless innocents, harried and persecuted? Almost half a year I had lived alongside them, but I was nowhere nearer knowing. If anything, I felt, I knew less than when I'd arrived.

But it didn't matter, I reminded myself, it didn't matter what they were because I wasn't one of them, I didn't belong with them, these people with whom somehow I had fallen in. Their fate wasn't mine. For me, this was a mere inconvenience, a detour, and as soon as possible I would about-turn and take myself back to Whitehall. My time between two households was at an end.

The sky was clearing – mere smudges here and there of cloud. For almost three seasons I had been in the palace or the city or the Tower or shut away at Ashridge, and although it wasn't so, I felt as if I hadn't in all that time seen the sky. For a moment I allowed myself to imagine that it might have been different out here: sunshine for all that time, not a touch of winter, and the people living their merry lives unaware of what had happened in the city, of what was hung on the gates and the set of Londoners' faces as they passed beneath. I hadn't known the Thames could be anything but cold-blooded and full of itself, shouldering the city aside as it bullied its way to the sea, but here it was in lazy splendour, the reflection of clouds like fingerprints on its sheen.

We passed a manor house tucked into a bend of the river, its blush brick rising here and there with captivating precision into chimneys, and its orchard crazed with blossom. At the riverside steps basked a barge painted all over with lilies, amid several other busybody service boats. The house itself shied away from the river under long hoods of roofing, and subjected us to a glassy gaze. One casement was open, though, in the balmy mid-morning air, and suddenly it was as if I were there, inside that room, intimately acquainted with the give of its floorboards and beguiled by dust motes and lilac scent.

It was dairy season: the laundry in that house would be besieged by aprons and muslins. As we were towed past, it was close to dinnertime: hall being graced with tablecloths and ewer bowls. *Home*: the word came to me with a pang, although I had never had a home, or not that I knew or remembered. Nevertheless that house seemed to call across the water to me as if it knew me and it was true that I had had a life like those being lived in there and, slipped down the back of all those days, many moments like the one I had imagined for myself on the inside of that window.

Despite our awning, the kitchen men with their prisoners' pallor were beginning to burn, so it was a relief when the oars-men pulled into the shade of some alders to take a break. They unwrapped packages and passed a flagon between them while our assistant cook rummaged in boxes and bags – from the look of it, the kitchen had had no more time to pack than I had. He rustled up an acceptable spread with which the cook loped off to the barge ahead while we in our barge made do with day-old bread. What, I wondered, was the mood in the ladies' barge? How much did they know or could they guess about where we were headed?

After a stint back on the water, we glided round a long bend towards a cluster of a dozen or so linen-coloured towers topped with silvery domes. The ladies' barge was already moored in isolation in front of those towers and looked to be empty, everyone disembarked. 'Richmond Palace it is, then,' said the cook.

It didn't look to me like a palace. It was grand enough to be one — tapering silvery domes, golden weathervanes — but in the manner of those long-ago gowns that Bel and I had unearthed in the Queen's Wardrobe. Whitehall was the only palace I had known, and it sprawled, laying claim to miles of bank to make a small city of its own, the buildings of so many different styles, some tumbledown and others bright and brash, all under a pall of smoke. Richmond Palace's sole province was the sky, towards which it rose all of a piece, although when we drew alongside I saw there was more to it than the dozen or so slender towers, because nestled between them were lower buildings with large windows, apartments with river views.

It looked deserted. No queue of boats and barges and wherries at the steps. The queen wasn't here, court wasn't here, no one save the motley crew of blue-liveried guards who had travelled in the other barge from the Tower and who insisted when we moored that we unload nothing. No need, we were told, because we weren't staying long; this was a mere break. Naturally the cooks objected, and then the guards seemed at a loss, glancing up at the many blank windows for someone to come to their aid. This wasn't right, I thought. Anything could happen to the princess here, and no one would know.

Eventually one of the guards sloped off and came back behind a tall, fair, purse-lipped and apparently put-out gentleman, elegantly dressed, excessively so for the May sunshine. The cook ambled over and appeared to confide in him while his assistant puffed and paced to make clear that he wouldn't be anything like so conciliatory. But the cook's tactic paid off, because the gentleman flapped a hand at a swathe of guards — *Look sharp, what are you waiting for?* — and in a flurry a contingent was on its way somewhere with the kitchen three, who lugged their various bags and boxes.

One of the guards who hadn't been quick enough on the

156

uptake caught the gentleman's attention and gestured to me: 'Sir?' And although I had been there all along, the gentleman stared at me down his long nose as if he couldn't believe his eyes. I saw that I was going to have to help him out: 'Laundress, sir.'

The response – addressed to the guard – was 'Gatehouse.'

'Gatehouse,' the guard repeated into the void left by the gentleman turning on his heel, and again, 'Gatehouse,' as if it might come to mean something the more he said it, but this time it was barked at a fellow guard, who simply passed it to a third: 'Gatehouse!'

It struck me that this might be my moment to get going: I could ask for a few coins to help see me on my way back to London and do them the favour of disappearing. Hesitating, I found myself led by the trio to a door in a wall – its only recommendation, as far as I could gather, that it wasn't the one through which the others had gone. Chastened by that gentleman's glare, these men were under pressure to show some initiative, to strike out on their own.

The door opened onto a vast kitchen garden, immaculately maintained: a garden that meant business, of which there was none to be had with our sorry shower. Behind the far wall, beyond the elevated slatted roof of what must be a kitchen, were some low roofs suggestive of an outer courtyard, which would be the place for a gatehouse. We made our way along the paths, but when leaving the garden took a series of wrong turns into blind alleys and stark yards. We needed a porter to give us directions – however deserted a place, there is always a porter – but of course any porter would be at the gatehouse.

When eventually we did come across a gatehouse, there was no answer to a knock on the closed door, which opened to a push. And that, as far as my keepers were concerned, was the job done. The gentleman in charge had specified a gatehouse but not that the gatehouse be staffed.

It looked as if no one had been inside it for some time, but the guards were already retreating and it wouldn't harm to get shot of them for a while, not least so that I could relieve myself behind a bush. They would be back soon enough, I thought, either with provisions or with instructions as to where I should go to dine; and after I'd eaten, I would turn my attention to the tricky business of bailing out, of getting myself back to Whitehall. My cursory exploration of the gatehouse confirmed that no one was around and I nipped over to the gate itself and gave it a try, although quite what I was thinking I would do if it was open, I don't know. It was locked.

Distant clock-strike confirmed that the useless guards had been gone for more than half an hour, and I was parched. I ventured off and found a conduit which smelled fresh enough – a laundress is a good judge of water – so I chanced it. Back at the gatehouse, I heard the strike of one but still no food had been delivered. If I went in search of people, I might miss them and end up stranded because, I remembered, we weren't staying, although it hadn't been clear what that meant: a break of an hour or two, or perhaps an overnight stay. My only visitor was a cat, pretending friendliness. Just you and me, I thought. And some warring crows, overhead.

I thought about the house downstream that had been so like those in which I had been raised and for which I had felt a pang as we had passed. *She'll go far*: I had indeed, I thought, but what choice had that been of mine? I had only ever been able to ask so much of people who owed me nothing, before moving on. It was mere chance that onwards had, so far, been upwards. All my life I had been careful to be no more than second best, because although no fine lady will admit it, she keeps for herself the best laundress and it's only the second best she recommends to someone else, even to the queen.

Giddy with hunger and solitude as the day turned to dusk, I

slipped into a dream of staying lost, of making a life of a kind there, of lying low and troubling no one, helping myself with impunity to that abundant kitchen garden. I could walk to the nearest town and take in laundry, wash it in the river and like any ordinary washerwoman hang it on bushes to dry. I had lived my life on the move, but what if I now stopped? It seemed to me, as I sat there on that doorstep in the shadows, that a simple life was perhaps all I had ever wanted.

It would be a life without Bel, though. The shadows were so long that they weren't shadows any more but darkness, and in my mind's eye I pictured Bel, hours away downriver, making good use of my absence: ratcheting up stitches as she listened and at the same time didn't listen to the apprentices, a practised half-smile holding them at arm's length. An evening much like any other, for her. She would soon give up on me for the night and go upstairs into her room of placid linens to comb the day from her hair, each stroke singing down the length of it, then get into her bed, where those moons and stars would hold her in their steady regard, blank but attentive like the best servants. She would give up on me for the night but would wait for me, I knew, in the coming day; it would never occur to her to doubt me.

And just as for Bel the darkness was no more than the sun coming down for a polish before going back up in the morning with a shine, so it would be in the St Thomas Apostle Street house: lights extinguished, doors locked, fire left grumbling, to make the night a mere tidying away of the day.

It was strange to be in the doorway of a deserted gatehouse thinking of the St Thomas Apostle Street house, spick and span, with its place for everything and everything in its place: that house, lulled by its ballast of treasures and moored at the Land of Nod, shutters shut and bolts slid home, its inhabitants as snug as bugs, their consciences clean as laundered sheets, while here I was, beyond the pale, with nothing but the clothes I stood up in and a door jamb against which to rest my head.

Bel would soon be sound asleep, safe in her belief that I would set off back to her at break of day. Hunkered wide awake on that doorstep, I thought back to my first-ever glimpse of her, remembered how when I had first seen her, I hadn't, quite. I hadn't afforded her a second glance. Well, there was all the time in the world for that in the deep Richmond darkness, and I found that my first sight of her had burned itself onto the back of my eyes. There she was, poised at the drying room door: a small span of shoulder blades, and how straight she stood but with such ease, unlike how I had ever stood at any door.

In Bel's house, the dark would lie like a hound at the hearth, but at Richmond it came rolling in, teeming with animal eyes; a few streets away from Bel's window, the Thames would be supine and moon-dazzled, but in the hush at Richmond I heard it churning and gurgling, working on bodies that had one way or another ended up in it, a long gut sluicing skin from bone.

I rose and turned to the desolate little room – time for sleep – with the solace of my return to the St Thomas Apostle Street house, even as I had to shake off the old unease that I wasn't quite up to scratch. I was not clean as a new pin, as Bel was. I was not whiter than white, good as gold, a keeper of the faith, a stayer for the course, ask no questions and tell no lies, cross my heart and hope to die. I was none of that. I was no one: I had grown up being all things to all people and was nothing but a ragbag from which to rustle up a good impression. All that had ever mattered to me was that I get taken up, taken in, fed and watered. Respectability for me had only ever hung by a thread.

Pulling-to the stubborn gatehouse door, I thought how mine had been a life of side doors and back gates because I was a servant, but how at Bel's house I had been spared the formality of the porch because I was family, or as good as. But then, in the dense Richmond darkness, all of a sudden I understood that for the dream it was. Bel would one day be someone's wife. I might have always known it, I thought, but now here it was, no longer merely tapping me on the shoulder but placing a hand on my arm. To stay with her, I would have to pretend to be her close companion, her spinster friend, and that was the one lie I wasn't prepared to live. Because I might as well be buried alive. I knew then and there that I wouldn't be going back. I couldn't go back. A voice in my head – my voice – laid claim to me, laid waste to the life I had naïvely been hoping to have: *You're on your own now.*

Eventually I must have slept, because I woke to the grunt of the gate in its housing, to footfall, to an exchange as desultory as a kick of gravel: someone was around, something was happening. I opened the door of the gatehouse to a haze of horse scent and not so much the coming of light as a weakening of the dark. Tiptoeing to the main gate, I tried it, and now it opened on an extraordinary sight. As far as I could see were wagons and carts, parked up; and among them, blearily tending to horses and repairing wheels and securing luggage, were hundreds of men in the red livery of the princess. What on earth were they doing here, in the middle of nowhere, at this hour?

Not one of them looked my way. A lady did, though: a noble lady, standing unattended among the campfires and horse muck. She was of a similar age to me, but wearing an extraordinarily beautiful gown of a bramble-blossom blush in what I guessed was Bruges satin. She stood expectant, although it couldn't have been me she was awaiting. Her fine-boned face held eyes that appeared violet in colour, their focus on me as tight as a tripwire. Despite my dishevelment and confusion, I edged forward as I knew I must.

She tilted her blond head on a neck bred for just such a gesture – *And you are ... ?* – and the unvoiced enquiry was like a blade-tip under my chin, implying that for me to be anyone or anything would be presumptuous.

'Miss Turner,' I managed. Remember, I told my sleep-groggy self, remember, remember: Turner, Turner, Turner. Among these red-liveried followers of the princess, I was still Annie Turner.

A tilt of her head to the other side commanded me to elucidate.

'Laundress.' I knew I wouldn't look like much of one, having slept in my clothes. 'The Lady Elizabeth's.'

She said, 'Well, at least there's *that*,' snapping each word as if crunching small bones. Then, 'Which cook is with you?' I hadn't known there was more than one cook in the princess's household, but she prompted, 'Tall, thin? Or bald?'

'Tall, thin,' I said, but there was something wrong with my answer because she uttered an oath and flicked heavenward those fabulous eyes and took some pleasure in claiming, 'He practically *poisoned* me.' It was said as a joke but I knew not to laugh. 'I've never been so ill.' She sighed. 'Still, let's hope he's been baking, because we've been on the road half the night.'

But no one travelled anywhere at night and especially not wearing the gems she had at her throat. What was going on? An usher came barrelling up, portly and pleased with himself, and executed a few bizarre knee bends with a comically pained expression to imply he was stiff from the saddle. 'My lady,' he greeted her.

She indicated me. 'We have a laundress.'

He enacted a minor bow for me but was straight back to her. 'Of course we do: our marvellous Mister P makes sure we have everything and everyone we need.'

'Fats is the cook, though,' she complained to him, 'and I swear . . .'

' . . . he poisoned you. Yes, yes, I know' – jauntily sceptical – 'but you bounced back, Bluebell; you're looking good on it, and you have to admit the man . . .'

'. . . makes a good fishcake.' Another sigh. 'I know.'

I took a surreptitious step backwards – I had to get out of there – as she was asking the usher where they were going.

'No idea.' He spoke pleasantly. 'By road is the most we know. But wherever our Lady's Grace goes, we'll all follow.'

This, then, in the small hours, in the middle of nowhere, was a show of strength on behalf of the princess.

The usher surprised me with a question – 'Were you in the Tower?' – but luckily for me as he spoke the gate was opening, and through it came a dozen or so guards, and with them the princess and Miss Parry. The lady and the usher dropped the double act, and had they been able to reach for the princess through those guards, they would have done. She, too: as soon as she laid eyes on them, her pallid face lit up, and as she was led away she called softly to them, two or three foreign words. On hearing them, the usher gave an appalled yelp, but the bluebell lady brought him up sharp with a tap to his forearm. 'Not "to the slaughter",' she corrected. 'She means "amongst wolves". We need to be like lambs amongst wolves,' and, sing-song, she quoted: '"Be wise as serpents and innocent as doves."' With a light to her eyes that stood for a smile, she added, 'And I dare say we can manage that.'

12

Sitting Pretty

She'll go far: not a benediction, then, after all, but a curse. I'd come too far and would never again find work back in any house like the one downstream, because recommendations are everything and after my time in the Tower, no one but Bel knew who I was. To avoid destitution in Richmond, I would have to move on. That morning, a possibility had presented itself on my doorstep. And I had decided that I preferred the look of that rogue lot to the princess's jailers. So I stuck close to the princess's entourage when it in turn set off to trail the princess and her jailers. I made sure to be swept up – and, for the first time in my life, into a litter: Bluebell took me on trust and into her own litter. So there I was, unable to believe my luck, along for the ride.

But after four days that ride had come to an end and Mr Parry – kinsman of unspecified degree to Miss Parry, and in charge of the retinue – had turned up to look in on Bluebell. I'd heard plenty from him during the days of journey: instructions and exhortations bellowed down the procession in an accent that was a mystery to me until I overheard one of the passing riders joke that we should watch out for the Welsh. Now here was the Welshman himself, peering up into our litter: a squat man in a cloak so short on him that he must have gone to special lengths, as it were, for a look that, given his girth, wasn't flattering.

If anyone would know who should or shouldn't be in that retinue, surely it was he. But if he was wondering who I was, he didn't ask, and Bluebell didn't say, and I did my utmost best to look as if he should expect to find me there. Luckily, he had a distraction: Bluebell indicated the heaps of cloth-wrapped and be-ribboned delicacies on the floor between us. 'Queen of cake,' she said to him, 'if nothing else.'

The spices were heady, and he reeled to comic effect. In every village we'd had to relieve locals of their offerings: cake-wielding multitudes diverted down by Miss Parry from the princess's litter to ours. Often we'd been surrounded – once, alarmingly, on a bridge, when I'd found myself praying aloud for the horses to stay calm.

Cake reception from hordes of common people wasn't a duty any attendant of the princess expected to be assigned, I imagined, but Bluebell had risen to the challenge, dispensing gracious smiles and platitudes. It had cost her, though: I saw how it was hard work for her to hold herself against recoil from all those dirty hands and all that sour breath. After the first day, she had changed her gown of Bruges satin for one of a more service-able fustian.

Between villages, we were left alone in our litter, and she kept herself to herself. Once, she opened a locket, held aloft two wisps of hair of indiscriminate shade and told me, 'Sons number one and two,' but then clicked the locket shut and settled back, eyes closed, before I could respond.

Now, though, for Mr Parry, she was charm itself, and it was as if the cake escapades had been unrelenting fun and games. 'We won't starve,' she said, 'wherever we're kept, if they don't feed us.'

'*We're* feeding us,' he said, in his funny little growl. 'We're feeding *them*, because we're footing the bill, would you believe, for this whole tawdry little exercise. At her Majesty's pleasure, but not at her expense.'

She glanced past him, dubious. 'Where *are* we?'

'Woodstock.'

'*Where*stock?'

'Half-hour ride from Oxford.'

Her look suggested this was no recommendation, but he said, 'You mightn't believe it, but there's no love lost around here for Oxford. Reformist country, this, when you get your feet on the ground, which luckily for us our lords and masters at court rarely do.'

She remained doubtful. 'Still.'

He sighed. 'I know: it doesn't look much, it's seen better days; but, well, who hasn't, and I'm told it used to be quite something. Leopards.'

'Leopards?' She folded her arms and fixed him with a sceptical gaze.

'Park-load of 'em,' he said, 'back in the day, with a few descendants still around to cause trouble.'

She smirked. 'Someone's been having you on, Mr Parry.'

'Brought here for the mistress of some king or other, one of yer Henrys; don't ask me, I'm no historian, but we all know kings like to impress the ladies, and back then, I'm reliably informed, the ladies liked leopards. Problem is, kings come and go, but leopards? No such luck: breed like rabbits.' He winked at me, and – taken unawares, noticed – I jumped and blushed.

Bluebell turned serious. 'Forget your leopards; just tell me how long *we're* going to be here.'

He shrugged. 'When there's something to know, you'll know it, and that's the best I can do you.' And with that, and a parting slap to our litter as if dispatching us, he was off.

He, like Bluebell, had resisted making too much of the cake. I supposed they didn't dare set too much store by it, because it

166

didn't necessarily speak of people's support for the princess: it might well be no more than a celebration of her physical presence, a passing princess – any princess, of any persuasion – being big news. On the other hand, we had been quite lavishly accommodated on each of the four nights of our journey, and it seemed to me that just because our hosts were the queen's men didn't mean they weren't also the princess's. Just because the queen saw her half-sister as her enemy didn't mean that everyone else did.

Bluebell was adept at getting down from a litter, and, light on her feet, disappeared into the crowd, leaving me in the sights of the lofty gentleman whose stipulation of 'Gatehouse' at Richmond had condemned me to that loneliest of nights. No gatehouse for me this time around, I vowed, and as Mr Parry was mired in an exchange close by, I sidled towards him in hope of shelter. A bad move, because it was he whom the gatehouse man was after. 'Mr Parry?' He came stalking over. 'Mr Parry, what is all this?'

Mr Parry paused pointedly mid-conversation. 'This, Sir Henry?'

'This,' the man insisted, reddening. 'These . . .'

Mr Parry followed the man's gesticulations as if they themselves were of interest. 'Well, *this*, Sir Henry, *these* are gentlemen of the household of my Lady's Grace.'

Sir Henry squared his shoulders. 'No, sir. This little game of yours is over. Two ladies, the Lady Elizabeth is allowed, and one gentleman usher. Those are my instructions.'

'Well, and kitchen staff,' Mr Parry added, which Sir Henry then had to concede. 'And laundry, too.' He smiled at me. He did, then, know who I was. I made sure to give nothing away, as if it were the most natural thing in the world for me to be standing there.

'So, we've kitchen staff,' Mr Parry recapped, 'three—'

'Two.'

'Three, because the two cooks need a boy; and laundry, one,' which I was glad to hear, but then he pushed it too far with a cheeky cock of his head. 'And me, of course.'

'On your way, Mr Parry,' snapped Sir Henry. 'Two lady attendants, one gentleman usher, three kitchen and one laundry staff' – I was in – 'and that's your lot. Now, kindly make yourself scarce and leave me to get on with my duties in setting up this household.'

'Duties for which you will be paid from my Lady Grace's coffers and' – nice as pie – 'I'm her cofferer. You'll appreciate that no bill can be paid without my signature.'

'Oh don't worry, I shall be sending you the bills.'

Mr Parry looked regretful. 'This household, Sir Henry, is royal.' His accent resounded in 'royal'. 'As such, it is administered with the utmost vigilance and attention to detail. Not from afar, nor on any old body's say-so.'

Before Sir Henry could respond, Bluebell's usher friend came bumbling up, indignant, saying something I didn't catch but which had Mr Parry exclaim, '*Gatehouse?*'

Oh please, no, I thought: save me from another gatehouse.

Sir Henry countered primly, 'It's four good rooms . . . '

'Good God, man, it's a *gatehouse*.' Mr Parry was aghast, hands on hips, bobbing in his tiny boots.

Sir Henry tried again. 'It's by far the most secure—'

'*Most secure?*' There couldn't have been anyone within a mile who hadn't heard that. 'The most secure place in this residence is its *gatehouse?*'

Sir Henry said, 'I am not answerable to you, Mr Parry.'

'No, but you're answerable to queen and Council, and I bet it's not on her Majesty's or Council's orders that my Lady's Grace is kept in a gatehouse.'

'My orders,' he said, 'are to keep the lady secure.'

'Your duty,' Mr Parry closed in on him, which, given their

168

difference in stature, should have disadvantaged him but somehow did the opposite, 'is to keep England's heiress presumptive
safe in this time of great unrest.'

Unrrrest.

Sir Henry tried to laugh this off.

Mr Parry turned conversational. 'When were you last in
London? I was there a couple of days ago and I saw a monk on
a gallows ... '

Sir Henry looked as if someone had slapped his face.

' ... although on closer inspection, it was a cat, some poor ol'
moggy strung up there, all got up as a monk and fur shaved.' A
circling of his head with his fingertips to show he meant tonsured.

I shuddered, unsure which was worse: a monk, or a cat mocked
up as a monk.

'And just around the corner, a wall with a hole in it, about so
big. Call the queen's name into that hole' – he said it pleasantly,
as if it were something anyone would do – 'and nothing. But call
the princess's, and the wall calls back Amen.'

I had no idea of the truth of this – the hole in the wall, the
gullible spectators – but I couldn't see how it was helping his case.

Sir Henry was flustered. 'Yes, but that's just ... people.'

'Indeed so, Sir Henry, and there's a lot of 'em about.' Mr Parry
stared up into Sir Henry's face. 'This country is full of unstable
elements at present and my Lady's Grace is in as much danger
from them as is the queen. And you're the one charged with her
safety.' There was a hardness to his mouth that had Sir Henry
back off, albeit in high dudgeon.

Mr Parry watched him go as if letting out a leash before turning to me and commenting, jauntily, 'No manners, some people.'

Four rooms meant no room for me, so Mr Parry said I was to
go with him into Woodstock to the Bull. I was happy to do so:
I could think of worse company. After four days and nights of
Bluebell, he was a breath of fresh air.

The Bull was quite something, he'd bragged, and at first sight across Market Square it was indeed impressive.

'Commodious,' he said, as we crossed to the porch. 'Capacious. This is where we set up camp, where we dig in for the duration, and in no time we'll fill this place to the rafters.' To my perplexed look he said, 'Well, it's a free country – just – and if friends of the princess fancy a bit of Chiltern air? Well, that's up to them, isn't it, and if they can afford the Bull, then so much the better for them.'

He was going to be good for business, he said, and the proprietor knew it; they understood each other very well was how he put it, which was why, among other favours, a cottage across the courtyard behind the inn had been vacated for the retinue's use and which he now decided would be mine, as a makeshift laundry. 'And as long as the princess's own tenants don't get it into their heads that she's a lost cause – as long as every last one of our farmers knows it's business as usual and keeps paying us his rent – then we in turn can pay ours, here,' he said, 'and we're sitting pretty. Sir Henry can huff and puff all he likes but we're going nowhere.'

He left me at the threshold of the cottage with a small advance against wages. I had just got myself a home of a kind and a job, it seemed, and on no one's recommendation. The cottage was a fair-sized room, with a ladder leading to a loft, and I started on a clean-up, relieved to be able to lose myself in some brisk activity after that journey: those interminable days when I had dwelled on everything I had just left behind.

After a half-hour or so, there was a knock at the door from a fresh-faced, curly-haired lad smart in the princess's livery but wearing it in a way that made it his own. He'd been sent to ask if I would be joining the household at dinner, and although I demurred – I was in no fit state, I needed a wash – I found myself crossing the courtyard in his wake, amused by that saunter cultivated by snake-hipped, long-legged boys probably the world over and for all time.

The dining hall held three tables of a dozen men who had ridden hard all day and were now tucking in and slacking off in some style, heads bare and boots kicked off. Most households in which I'd lived had stipulated silence at dinner, but the opposite might have been ordered of these garrulous men. This was no place for me. Sensing my loss of nerve, the boy turned on the threshold to bestow his sweet smile, and again I found I couldn't disappoint him, so in we went, my gaze fixed on his back with the intensity of prayer; and as if a prayer had been answered, the miracle was granted whereby none of those men so much as glanced up as we passed.

The boy delivered me directly to Mr Parry, who was in the thick of it at top table, before he ducked away to join a table of younger faces. Mr Parry's companions, like Mr Parry himself, were men of substance, with the weight of the world on their jowls, and the talk coming from each and every one of them at once was of business: ... *agent's a crook* ... *consignment's the best* ... Without drawing breath, Mr Parry patted the bench beside him, his hand smaller and softer than my own and bright with Welsh gold and gemstones. Then he drew a platter towards me, which came trailing such a delicious fragrance that I forgot myself and, famished, dived in with my spoon.

No sooner had I started serving myself than we were joined by another newcomer, dusted with tangy evening air, who jubilantly mimicked Mr Parry – 'Nice place you've got 'ere' – so that Mr Parry seized him, clapping him on the shoulder, laughing that it was best at top table but you needed to keep in with the cofferer for that. He asked after the man's journey as we all budged up to make room for him. 'So, so, *so* ... ' he crooned in greedy expectation of information, as the man took his place at the table.

But the answer – 'Norfolk man' – caused a collective groan.

171

There was more. 'His father was jailer of the queen's mother at her last place.' He checked with Mr Parry. 'Kimbolton?'

A sharp inhalation, 'Kimbolton, yes,' and then they were all at it, sucking their teeth in a kind of keening.

Mr Parry said, 'Well, he'll be wanting to redeem the family name, then, which means we're dealing with a yes man, and we've already seen a bit of that, haven't we.'

Belatedly I realised that this was addressed to me, and concerned the long-nosed advocate of the gatehouse, Sir Henry.

'And more fool Council,' he said, 'because a yes man only ever wants to know what he should do, and frankly Council hasn't a clue.'

The following morning, I learned what my job was to be: I was to see the princess every few days, when I was picking up and dropping off laundry, and report back to Mr Parry. I had to ask: report back what? 'That she's alive,' he said. 'I'll settle for that, and as to anything more, in time: well, we'll see.' Fats, the cook, would be seeing the princess several times each day but only ever for the handing-over of a tray or two at a door, and anyway, he was Fats: no one's choice for an informant (nor, if Bluebell were to be believed, much else). Fats as a source of information would have been better than nothing, Mr Parry said, but much better was me.

It was his guess that Sir Henry Bedingfield – 'Bedders', as he was calling him – would regard laundry as treacherous: the layers and folds, seams and toes and pockets would be the stuff of his nightmares. 'Considerable sifter of ladies' wear, that one,' Mr Parry said, 'I'll bet you,' and it was to be during these thorough, pointless searches that I would observe the health and welfare of the princess.

Leaving Bel had had me wanting to crawl into a hole; but like it or not, I'd fallen on my feet, taken in by a rebel household.

13

Girl Like You

When I first turned up at the gatehouse, Sir Henry himself fetched me and accompanied me up the stairs, expounding, 'The whole purpose of this detention of the great lady is to ensure there are no unauthorised communications. In this way, we protect her from further scurrilous attempts to implicate her in treason. To leave her at liberty would be to leave her vulnerable to allegations of complicity that she can't disprove.'

From the room at the top of the stairs came an answering voice, which I recognised as that of the princess. 'Why don't you just put everybody in prison and have done with it?'

I felt like a collaborator there with him on the stairs.

'And silly me,' the princess continued, 'to think I'm being shut up here to break my spirit and have me confess to something I didn't do.'

Sir Henry pressed on with an explanation of the arrangements. It had been brought to his attention, he said, that his searching of the laundry would leave him open to accusations of planting evidence, and because neither party could agree on an independent witness, his search would be conducted each time in the presence of both parties: 'Everything in the open. Everyone present.'

173

Which was exactly as Mr Parry had hoped.

At the top of the stairs, behind the half-open door, he said that the princess had agreed to refrain from speaking directly to me. 'The purpose of our great lady's stay here is to keep our business within these four walls, not bandy it about, willy-nilly.'

'For the record,' she said, as we entered the room, 'and I mean yours, Sir Henry – I am in fact addressing you, not this lady here – I have agreed to nothing.'

This lady here.

My sight was slow to adjust and my gaze was properly lowered; her physical presence was grainy and indistinct as if stamped on the gloom. Sir Henry knelt, as did I alongside him. 'These are difficult circumstances, my lady,' he said, cheerfully.

'Unlawful,' she said, 'is the word.'

I kept my eyes down but her presence was as insistent as that of my own heart. Of Miss Parry and Bluebell, I detected nothing, although at least one of them, I knew, would have to be in attendance.

'And as for your "unauthorised communications", Sir Henry, I'm unaware that any communication *is* authorised. Not even with Mrs Ashley, who is like a mother to me.' The princess began pacing, linen hissing against her shins, rushes rasping underfoot. 'And is that acceptable, do you think, sir – to be deprived of one's mother? My sister, the queen, was deprived of her own mother. But – oh!' – she made a deliberately poor play of just having remembered – 'you *know* that.' A dig at his father having been jailer of the queen's mother. 'Well, well, well,' she said, 'how the tide turns.'

'If I might respond, my lady,' which he did before permission was granted, 'that was different.'

'Yes,' she said, 'because my sister was in open defiance of the sovereign. Whereas I . . . ' She must have raised her hands, because they slapped down onto her gown. 'I haven't defied my

174

sovereign, have I, Sir Henry.' Whenever she addressed him, he was required to answer, which she reminded him: '*Have I, Sir Henry?*'

He tried to make a joke of it. 'Well, there's the matter of your Grace's preference for the English Bible. Your Grace is quite the scholar, I'm told, so I doubt it's the deciphering of the Latin that's the problem.'

She ignored that, and stepped closer; patterned black velvet danced in front of my eyes. 'You suspect me,' she said, in an even, detached tone, standing over him as if examining an insect on a pin.

I was shaking, although perhaps only because it's never easy to kneel for long.

Her tone was one of mild interest. 'You are searching my laundry because you suspect me. Or my servants, which amounts to the same.'

My servants. Me.

'Your Grace,' he said, with a deliberate weariness to suggest this was old ground, 'it's merely a precaution.'

'One that you yourself have devised, unless I'm wrong and there is in fact a specific order from Council about rifling through my intimate garments.'

I couldn't resist a sideways glance. A blush rode high in his skin as if slapped there. Clearly there had been no such order.

Then, as if she were bored, 'Well, get on with it. This lady doesn't have all day.'

He took himself to be off the hook, I sensed, and was anticipating permission to rise, but she stared him down and I felt it sink in that no such permission would come and he would have to do his searching there on the floor at her feet.

Afterwards, I was taken straight to Mr Parry, and although it had been good to get out of there, it then didn't feel quite right to be taking along the dirty laundry. His door opened on fug and disarray; he was reclining in a chair, stockinged feet up on a stool. My escort bowed out on the threshold, leaving me unchaperoned; nevertheless, Mr Parry indicated that I should close the door behind me.

We weren't quite alone, though: a sleek brindled hound lay beside his chair, with a thoroughgoing devotion to the floor, back half tucked away and front half long-throated across the matting. It raised its eyelids to give me the obligatory once-over. Mr Parry motioned for me to draw up a stool.

'So,' down to business, 'you've been there.'

I confirmed I had.

'And you saw her.'

Her. No *my Lady's Grace*, then, here, between the two of us. Down to business indeed.

He cut to the chase. 'And how was she?'

This was awkward. What could I say? She had been high-handed and vindictive – even if Sir Henry had deserved it – but no one was going to catch me saying that about a princess.

He prompted, 'Dressed?'

Dressed? Well, at least that was easy to answer.

'And? And, and, and?'

'Cross,' I plumped for, pathetically, then made it worse with 'Very,' but at least it had started me off and from then on it was easier. I reported what she'd said, keeping to her own words. He nodded me onwards with no clue as to what he made of any of it until I told how Sir Henry had had to stay kneeling while he searched. At this, he laughed, which had the dog raise its head, swan-like, disdainful.

'And how did our Bedders manage that?'

I didn't intend it as a joke when I said, 'With difficulty,' but that got another laugh.

Later, back in my cottage, I felt there was more that I could have told him. I had reported what she had said but I could have described how she had moved, how she had paced, although that seemed the wrong word because pacing is something that caged animals do, helpless and doomed, whereas she in that room had been calculated and predatory.

He hadn't asked, either, about the princess's two attendants. Of Miss Parry, there was nothing to say except that she was there. I recalled my first sight of her, at Ashridge, striding across the yard and shaking loose her lovely hair on her way back indoors after a ride. The time she had spent with the princess in the Tower meant that it was six months since she had ridden a horse. This incarceration was hers as much as it was the princess's, and it was showing on her. Bluebell, though: whereas Miss Parry had kept her gaze averted, refusing to dignify Sir Henry with her attention, Bluebell had watched him with avid interest and infinite patience, as if what he was doing there on his knees with their undergarments were a truly commendable course of action, which served to emphasise that it wasn't.

My Woodstock work was easy, the load light, coming from a mere three ladies with nowhere to go, nothing to do, no one to see, although sometimes – I could tell – they had walked outside; the feet of their stockings had been inside boots. The bed linen I'd used at the Tower had been retrieved and sent along as if never plundered from the princess's chests and marooned in that lime-washed room near the moat. I washed it first, that linen in which I had slept with Bel, keeping it at arm's length as if it were just anything else. In general, I stayed as busy as I could, but reminders of Bel were at every turn, scattered through the days: down the table came words and phrases she habitually used; on the platters were dishes to which she was partial or averse; and any room, courtyard or lane was a blur of colours and fabrics she favoured and disdained. These shards of her stuck in the corners of my eyes, lodged in my gullet and my gut, yet I couldn't stop myself trawling my waking moments for them, and hoarded them. I rattled with her observations and inclinations as if I had been scooped from my own skin and she had stowed away in my place.

Nevertheless, it was proving easy enough to make a life of a kind at Woodstock. Mr Parry's men rigged up drying racks in the cottage, and the water in the Bull's well had a decent mineral bloom to it. From a local vintner I got wine lees, and even found something of a friend, too, in his wife, Letty, whom I first encountered on their doorstep with a babe in arms. 'My brother's,' she had said in response to my admiring gaze, grimacing to confirm the loss of a sister-in-law. She was due her own baby – her first – in November, she said as she took me into her parlour, where the black-haired baby boy – Alban – settled placidly in her lap. She herself was so fair that it was as if she'd been tipped upside down and her mere sprinkling of colour had spilled like pollen from her lips and cheeks to line the rims of her nostrils and eyes. She enthused about having the princess at Woodstock, spoke of it as an honour – I didn't quite know how to respond – and said that should her own baby be a girl, the name would be Elizabeth. 'I was going for Rosamund,' she said, 'after the mistress,' then laughed to see my face. 'No! The royal one, I mean, the long-ago one, up at the old palace, not *my husband's*,' and then her laughter leapt in pitch. 'I mean, he doesn't *have* one. Or not as far as I know,' and despite everything, I, too, laughed.

When I left, brimful of biscuits, she said to drop by again any time, and after a respectable interval of several days I took her at her word, ostensibly to request a lend of her still – I might as well be using my free time at Woodstock to make flower waters. 'Perfect timing,' she said conspiratorially when she answered the door. 'Because Alban's in town with Dam.' Damascin was their help – perhaps fourteen or fifteen years old – whom Letty had described to me as her sister-in-law's sister-in-law.

My offer of some laundering in return for the use of the still was politely declined because, Letty said, Dam should do it, Dam had to learn, which seemed a little harsh to me, although admittedly I knew nothing of having a sister-in-law's young sister-in-law under my roof to supervise. On my first visit, I'd glimpsed how the girl's eagerness to be seen to earn her keep only invited Letty's derision, enacted playfully for me in long looks and winces that I had felt uncomfortable in humouring.

Mr Parry's laundry, too, I offered to do, having so often seen his stockings rinsed and steaming over the back of his chair. He was only rubbing them through, which merely ingrained the dirt, and never hanging them properly to dry, which was asking for trouble.

'Very kind of you, Mistress T,' he said, 'but a bundle of laundry gives me an excuse to nip home from time to time.' His home, I knew by then, was about an hour's ride to the east. His wife would have him back for every meal, he said, if she could, although God knew he was hardly wasting away at the Bull, and this was said with a pat of his gut, to which my smile was carefully non-committal. 'It's good to get home to see the kiddies,' he said, 'although Mim's only interested in what I've got for her in my saddlebag.' Mim – Muriel, *Myrrh-iel* – was eleven, he had told me. 'It's not as if I'm away anywhere special,' he complained, adding, 'although there's the gloves.' Woodstock prided itself on being a place for gloves: there were several glove-makers around the square. 'But how many pairs of gloves does a girl need?'

Don't ask, Mister P.

I recalled Bel's embroidering of a pair of gloves as her wedding present to the queen.

Mr Parry went on. 'Whereas Tommy . . . ' a year Mim's junior, 'serious-minded little chap, night skies, that's his latest, and all he wants from me is that I'm outside with him after dark with a crick in my neck.'

*If you were going to the trouble of putting them all up there,
wouldn't you do it in some kind of order?*

'Knows all the names – bears, belts, what-have-you – but none
of it sticks with me. Feet of clay, me,' he said ruefully, raising
them and letting them drop back down with a thud.

Mr Parry liked to say that I was crucial to what he was doing at
Woodstock. 'We're making it difficult for them,' he said. 'We're
getting in the way.' The princess had been sent to the middle of
nowhere to fade from view. 'But we're watching,' he said, 'and
they know it.'

He always wanted to hear from me in person and always had
treats laid out for me: marzipan-stuffed dates, sugared almonds,
candied orange slices, and hazelnuts baked hard in honey ('With
added teeth,' he said, 'if you're not careful'). And there was
Maud, the hound, as faithful servant in that room but also at
the same time queen. I marvelled how Mr Parry was the perfect
host despite never-ending demands on his time and attention, the
daily business of running a royal household in exile and defiance:
mayhem on his desk and a stream of queries and requests at his
door. He could hold several conversations at once, like a kind
of choir, yet no one ever got short shrift and for me he gave the
impression that there was nothing better than my company in
which to put his little feet up and set the world to rights. I was
keen to do my best for him; here was where I wanted to stay.

He liked the sound of his own voice, but I liked it, too. It was
a relief to go to his room and be looked after and lose myself for
a while. He'd rattle on to me about his wife or the children or
various relatives (No-Panic Parry was what he admiringly called
his distant cousin Miss Parry). He did once ask if I had family and
gave a fair impression of being interested, but I suspected that
like all men he had asked because he felt he should and he took
it without question when I said I didn't.

Letty, though, did have questions, as I knew she would, and I

180

wasn't confident of pulling the wool over her eyes. One midsummer dusk we braved the garden with a platter of cherries between us on the bench. The evening had kept us waiting all dismal day long but then arrived with a certain wide-eyed sheen and jaunty with birdsong as if to deny any part in the lacklustre performance of the earlier hours. Letty asked me if I'd ever been married, and I surprised myself by going on the spur of the moment for a simple no; I'd chanced it before I knew.

She said, 'You've been close, though.' It wasn't a question. 'Girl like you.'

I let that pass, saying only that there had been no one for a long time – more credible, I judged, than an out-and-out denial – and bolstered it with something about having been so often on the move with work. I wondered what she made of me, who came from nowhere and had lived a life on the move. Born and raised nearby, she was lady of her own little house: she was – despite the glint in her eye – a conventional girl; and determinedly so, it seemed to me.

'Stuck here now, though, aren't you.' She tipped her sugaring of freckles to the last of the sun. 'And is there no one you've got your eye on? Because that inn is full of men.'

Old men, I protested before I'd thought better of it, and she liked that; she laughed, because we were supposed to value prospects, prosperity, respectability. Her own husband – she called him by his surname, Locke – was barely more than a boy: Lanky Locke, who earlier had stumbled upon us and retreated, apologetic.

'Those men at the inn are all married,' I said.

'Potential widowers.' Alarmingly cheerful for someone recently bereaved of a sister-in-law and herself facing childbirth. Sucking cherry flesh from its stone, she mused, 'I always say to Locke: Not Dam.' If she died, she meant. 'Just not Dam.'

My turn to laugh, if uneasily.

She flashed me a mischievous glance. 'But doesn't that sound reasonable to you? Not someone from under your own roof,' and with a mock-weary sigh she lamented of husbands in general, 'But of course that's what they always do.'

Yes, and not only husbands, I thought.

I couldn't quite believe that Mr Parry never questioned where I'd come from. Head in a ledger, he liked to say of himself, but he protested too much: I suspected he was all eyes and ears. Surely he would know that I was relatively new to the household, and, in the circumstances, wouldn't he have asked his right-hand man, Fram, to do some digging? *Fram's yer man*, he liked to say of this wonder whom I had yet to meet. *There's nothing and no one that Fram doesn't know.*

I began to wonder whether even if Mr Parry did know where I'd come from it would matter to him. He was a pragmatist. He could find a use for anyone, perhaps even a traitor to his cause, and, it occurred to me, perhaps especially so: friends close, enemies closer. And anyway, everything had shifted in the past year so that the old loyalties no longer held. If I were uncovered and cornered, I could talk my way to safety. That I had come from the queen's household said nothing of my opinion of the princess. I myself, even, wasn't sure of my opinion of the princess.

What mattered to Mr Parry was that everything go to plan, and the plan was that I see the princess every few days and report back. And that I was doing. Even if I were an informer, what harm could I do? I could cover up for the princess being moved elsewhere, but any such move would soon enough be rumbled. As for planting anything to incriminate her, that would be foiled by Bedders himself with his zealous and openly conducted laundry-sifting. And all I could report back to the queen's men of the princess's people, if I were so inclined, was that they were in Woodstock in some force, but the queen and her men already knew that, which was the whole point.

14

Knife, Throat

It was no easier as the days went by to be in that room in the gatehouse, not so much because of the conditions of the ladies' confinement – airless, despite the open window – but because of how the princess spoke to Sir Henry. She could dress up her verbal parrying and feinting however she liked, but we all knew it for what it was: a demonstration of the upper hand that her breeding gave her. That breeding was all she had now, the precise degree of which was keeping her from the block as it hadn't the other royal girl. A queen can kill a cousin, it seemed, but perhaps not a sister, although admittedly this one was only a half.

We three ladies of the princess's were, I sensed, supposed to be impressed by her cutting asides, rustled up under such trying circumstances, but to me it only served to show how scared she was. And short-sighted. She was picking fights, but she would be the one to come off worse. Sir Henry and I, on our knees, had little further to fall, but if the princess did lose her composure – she seemed so often on the brink – and lunged, if she took a swing at him, then she would be the one to tumble. While she harped on at him, I would think, *Nail, coffin, your own*, although if she continued like this, an actual coffin was a luxury she would be denied.

If I had said any of this to Mr Parry, I knew what he would say back: what else was there left for her to do? She had to do something, he'd say, or she might as well lie down and die.

One afternoon towards the end of the second week, I was barely inside the room before the princess said to Sir Henry, 'Life for you is going to be that bit emptier, isn't it, without Mrs Sandes' underwear to play with.'

Mrs Sandes: Bluebell, who was standing benignly beside the princess. Sir Henry closed his eyes in a display of weariness but the princess said with disinterest, as if remarking on the weather, 'No permission to close your eyes,' so he opened them, if to a deliberate deadness. *Nail*, I thought, *coffin*, but this time his, should the princess ever become queen, although his skin-deep compliance – his obvious contempt – had me wonder if he knew more on that count than we did.

The princess had obliged him to enlighten me, which he did with fake solicitude. 'Mrs Sandes is to leave us.'

Bluebell, leaving? But no one could leave here: surely that was the point. I glanced at Bluebell and, mock-rueful, she stuck out her lower lip: bulbous, glistening, grotesque.

'For no reason,' added the princess mildly.

'By order of the queen,' Sir Henry countered.

Bluebell spoke up. 'Perhaps I'm a troublemaker.' She sounded hopeful.

The princess said, 'But that's what *I* am – or so I'm told – and *I'm* not getting sent home.'

When I told Mr Parry, he was disappointed but unsurprised. 'Can't win 'em all. And we did well to get Mrs Sandes in there in the first place.'

What, I wondered aloud, could she have possibly done?

'Just been herself, I imagine,' he said. 'Not the meekest and

184

mildest of ladies, as you'll have noticed. Which is why I wanted her in there. No disrespect to my dear cousin Blanche – quite the contrary – but we needed someone to complement her.' He said that the wheels of court turned slowly, and anyway Bluebell didn't move in the queen's circles: she would have been unknown to the royal advisers and it had probably taken this long for them to ask around and learn how much of a mischief-maker they had by oversight permitted in there. 'And this, now,' he said, 'this dismissal of her is just a flexing of monarch muscle. It's just a slap in the face for the princess.'

As with Mrs Ashley, then, who with no official explanation had been detained, I'd learned, in the household of the Highgate-residing judge: presumably to hit the princess where it hurt. 'Mind you,' Mr Parry had confided, back when he'd told me that Woodstock was one roost that Mrs Ashley wouldn't be ruling, 'let's face it, we've all in our time wanted to lock a door on that woman.' Now he said of Bluebell that he hoped she wouldn't be going the way of Mrs Ashley, under lock and key somewhere, so I reminded him: home. What the princess had said was '*I'm* not getting sent home.'

He was pleased with that: nicely made clear by the princess, he said, and well spotted by me. And good for Bluebell but just as good for us, because, he said, Fram could pay her a visit when he was back. 'Over to Fram, to find out what he can.' *Fram's yer man*, although I still hadn't had the pleasure because this Fram was back at home for the birth of his son.

A week or so later, heading into Mr Parry's room, I heard from outside that he wasn't alone, but that wasn't unusual, and any visitor would probably take his leave when I turned up, so in I went, only for shock to smack me full square in the face. A set-up, I thought: I'd walked right into it. My life flashed before me and a taste like blood came into my mouth. I'd come a long way and so nearly got away with it, but hadn't

I always known, deep down, that my husband would be the end of me?

Because there he was: there was Francis, if five years older than the Francis I had known, five years fleshier and that flesh now turning puce because the one thing as bad as laying eyes on your renegade husband, as I had just done, was coming face to face with your runaway wife.

The shock on his face showed that he hadn't in fact known I was here in the household. Mr Parry, too, in his own way appeared oblivious, embarking merrily upon introductions – 'Mister Francis Verney' – and praising each of us to the other.

Instinct had me smiling and nodding to keep that one dreadful moment going because I had no idea what could possibly come next. *Yes, Mr Parry, no, Mr Parry, three bags full, Mr Parry*: there I was, simpering for the life of me, and as if working myself with strings I moved across that room, sat down. Inside my smile, my teeth were chattering, but then rising through my terror like steam came a marvelling, because here, right in front of me in this room, was Francis. This 'Fram' was merely Francis, and then, in spite of everything, I found I was trying hard not to laugh: because *Francis*? Oh, but I knew a thing or two about Mister Francis Verney, and what I knew without any doubt was that he was no better than I was. How on earth had he done it – got himself here, right-hand man to the princess's right-hand man? Francis, sitting across the room from me in beautifully cut best-quality broadcloth. He'd come a long, long way in five years. But then he was probably thinking the same of me, although my own haphazard little pitching-up and hanging-on in this household was nothing, compared.

Back when I'd known him, he hadn't seemed ambitious. He'd liked the finer things in life, but who doesn't? He'd just been one of the boys, if the one – blue-eyed blond – who had stood out from the crowd.

It occurred to me that all I had to do was lean forward from my stool, pause Mr Parry with a touch to his arm and say, 'This man here in his fancy clothes, eating your dates: I know a thing or two about this man, or three or four. He is – beg your pardon, *was* – a wanderer, a hanger-on, a chancer; and to top it all, to put no finer point on it, he is – *is* – a bigamist.'

But then Francis could say all but the last of me.

And then miraculously it was over, or at least for the time being, because somehow I'd smiled my way back across that room to the door and, with a promise to pop back later, had put myself on the other side of it and was pelting down the staircase with a single notion in my head: *Francis knows that I am not who Mr Parry thinks I am.*

Slamming the cottage door behind me, I pressed back against it, to bar it, and only then did I catch my breath and make myself think it through. Because, yes, Francis knew that I was living here under a different name – 'Miss Annie Turner,' Mr Parry had said – but then so what? I could be living under a different name for any number of reasons. Many people did, and running out on a marriage was as good a reason as any. And yes, he knew I had worked in a Catholic household, back in the day, but, well, I had been a servant: nothing of my allegiance or otherwise to this household could be inferred from where I had once worked. Anyway, he himself had worked there too, on and off. I reminded myself that the age-old allegiances no longer held: not all Catholic families were for this Spanish-marrying queen, and, I remembered, not all reformists trusted the princess.

So it didn't matter – surely it didn't – that I had worked for Catholics: that was something Francis couldn't hang on me. It didn't follow that – here, now – I was an informer. I was pretty sure that if he told Mr Parry what he knew of me, I wouldn't be in so much trouble that I couldn't wriggle out of it. Now that I was thinking more clearly about it, I saw that Francis was the one in trouble. I didn't have a fancy new spouse and child. I wouldn't have dared; I'd made my bed and been lying in it for five years, catching no man's eye, resigned to the life of a spinster.

Kind of.

Fram, family man. Six years ago he had married me, and I wasn't dead yet, which meant that I was still his wife. Which meant that his new wife wasn't, and the baby everyone believed to be his son and heir might well be his son but could never be his heir. That poor baby was a bastard. If I spoke up about us having been married, everything Francis had secured for himself in the last five years would come to nothing, or worse than nothing, a disgrace that would be impossible to live down. If I spoke up about his past, he would go crashing to the ground, and with him that so-called wife and their baby son.

Francis couldn't expose me as an impostor without exposing himself as worse, and he was the one with everything to lose. Which must mean I was safe. My existence – as his wife – was a knife to his throat. Then again, no one is ever safe around knives. He might well wrest that knife from me, as it were, and turn it against me. And knowing him for the chancer, the devil-may-care fly-by-night that he was, knowing how far he had come and just how much he stood to lose, I imagined he might well have a go. Because how could we both live in this household, with what we knew about each other? And if it was him or me, I didn't rate my chances. The door against which I laid my full weight was all that stood between us, and if anything it was, I felt, a provocation, inviting a shouldering, a kicking-down. I felt that I could detect his ill-intent already pouring from the inn across the cobbles, the courtyard brimming with it.

A few polite excuses to Mr Parry and he could be on his way. What story had he been telling, I wondered, in these five years? No first wife? Or a dead wife? Either way, I didn't exist. Yet here I was, alive and kicking.

Going to ground in the cottage would offer me no refuge: I was backed down a hole. Standing there at that door, I was listening through a clamour of heartbeats for the swinging of a distant door, for boots on cobbles; I listened so hard that it was weirdly as if I were willing him.

And before too long I was indeed willing him to come, but with an idea, a deal, a solution to this mess that didn't involve him somehow making sure that I was unable to tell anyone that he was married to me and not to the mother of his son. Only after a clock strike had marked the passing of a quarter of an hour did I leave that door, but to dither, shaking; and by suppertime I was in the peculiar position of longing for him to arrive just so that this dread would end. I bit my nails and skipped supper. By then, dusk was gathering in the corners of my room, not descending but instead rising like smoke and finding the cracks as smoke does, while the sky over the rooftops was still pale, perhaps paler than it had been during the day, to bely the coming of darkness like the turning of a great blind eye.

Eventually I realised that if he wasn't turning up by the light of day then it probably wouldn't be him who would come under cover of darkness. He was a man to have contacts and connections, not all of them good. Someone else might well come to do his dirty work for him, whatever that was, which would deny me the satisfaction of looking him in the eye.

No one was going to get into the cottage after dark, I vowed, and in the last of the daylight I barricaded the door with whatever I could marshal, despairing at what a girl's effort it was, a higgledy-piggledy heap that proclaimed its uselessness and mine. After the barricade-building came a clock strike that I was too tired to count, and it occurred to me that I couldn't recall hearing the previous one, and suddenly I was defeated, I no longer cared: if I was going to fall asleep, then I was going to do it in my own bed. I had worked myself up into fearing for my life, but, exhausted as I was, I'd be damned if I was also going to give him my sleep.

I scuttled off to bed and lay there feeling doomed. I had considered myself used to loneliness, but this was different: there was no one to whom I could turn, to whom I could tell the truth of my predicament. And not only was there no one to miss me more than in passing, neither was there anyone who would think to ask the questions that should be asked if I were found murdered in my bed.

My body in that bed was my own worst enemy, I felt: my heart beating and lungs billowing regardless, quite possibly taking me hale and hearty to my bitter end. Outside, the Bull was awash with a flotsam of night sounds: footfall dropped in passageways and washed on a swell of hush into the courtyard. Coughs and throat-clearings: the innocuous indistinguishable from the ominous.

Don't hide from me, I thought: step out of the shadows, come into the open, whoever you are and whatever you want. But night worked its spell and then I woke unassailed, intact, and obliged to start another living day.

Calmer in the morning, I came up with a plan; not much of a plan, but I needed to feel safer in the cottage and my idea was better than nothing. Before dinner, I took a deep breath and broke cover, emerged into the everyday world that – incredibly – looked to all intents and purposes just as I had left it. I went to Mr Parry and lied, said I found it difficult to sleep alone in the cottage, said I knew it was silly but I just didn't feel safe. I had hoped to get used to it, I told him, but hadn't, and I was wondering if he would consider lending me Maud at night. He was surprised but sympathetic and the deal was done.

I spent that day as much as possible in or near the company of others; I was only ever fleetingly and nervously alone. Then, at dinner, Francis and I were seated only a few places apart at the top table. Every fibre of my being tightened at the sound of his voice, although like me he didn't say much – just enough to head off any concern from our fellow diners. During that long meal, I contemplated his largely silent presence for any clue as to why I had ever had anything to do with him, let alone married him, but by the end I was none the wiser. A mistake was all he had been. Depressingly, I seemed to be making a habit of those.

That evening, if Maud was at all put out by the new arrangement, she was polite enough to keep it to herself and entered the cottage with good grace. In turn I steeled myself against her moulting fur, the prospect of fleas, and her smell – like the inside of an old boot – to make up a bed downstairs into which she poured herself, serpentine, one foreleg tucked completely beneath her so that it vanished. I was under no illusions as to how much she could do for me if it came to it: I had never even heard her bark. Mute and mild-mannered as she was, though, she was an obstacle – a sharp-toothed one – in the path of anybody attempting to make life difficult for me. I congratulated myself to see her ears tracking every sound, her eyes – barely open, unfocused – seemingly latched to them.

The first night passed in this way, then another, and a third. During the days my door was propped open and I kept myself as much as possible in view of everyone at the Bull. Francis didn't come. Then I discovered he was away again, although that didn't mean someone else wouldn't turn up on his behalf. Five nights, six, seven and still nothing, and somehow one week became two, and it dawned on me that we were just going to ignore each other, to pretend that there never had been anything between us. Well, it wasn't as if we weren't practised at that, and it hadn't failed us so far. And really, I supposed, what else could we do? So we were – it seemed – to carry on doing what we had always done, but better, harder, to keep up our peculiar pact.

191

15

Our Bedridden Grace

That summer, Francis was forever coming and going, but whenever he was back at the Bull we circled each other like floodwater around a sinkhole. Avoiding each other was hard work — actual physical work — and if we were unlucky enough to find ourselves in mutual company it was as hard to avoid each other's eyes. It was exhausting to maintain the pretence that we had never known each other, let alone been married. We did it, though, and this secret of ours held us tighter than our marriage vows ever had.

It so happened that he was in Mr Parry's room when I first had something tangible to report, and my heart sank to find him there. I sat feeling horribly conspicuous, determined not to catch his eye. My news was that there had been a splodge of ink on the cuff of one of the princess's shifts. 'The princess,' I told Mr Parry, 'has been writing.'

Mr Parry exclaimed, but Francis — whose opinion hadn't been solicited — was sceptical. 'Could be an old stain.' This was addressed to Mr Parry rather than to me.

But Mr Parry backed me up — 'Annie would know' — before even checking with me: 'You'd know if this was new, yes?'

Yes, I said: none of the princess's shifts had had an ink stain on the cuff.

But from Francis, 'And you're sure about that?' As if I had no right to be. What did he think I spent my days doing, if not inspecting her garments? To Mr Parry he said, 'Perhaps the princess has been studying.'

That, admittedly, I hadn't considered: she might have been writing for herself as opposed to writing to someone. I didn't think that was the case, though. I insisted, 'She looked at me.' She had caught my eye and held it. Sir Henry had been shaking out the shift and I had glimpsed the ink on the cuff, and then when I glanced at the princess she was looking directly at me. 'And she never does that,' I said. She had made sure that I'd seen it, and would she have wanted me to know if she had merely been studying?

Mr Parry checked, 'And did Sir Henry see it – this stain?'

I couldn't say for sure; there seemed to have been no attempt to hide it from him, and the princess hadn't seemed anxious when it was lifted from the pile. He could easily have seen it, but I couldn't be certain that he had.

Mr Parry concluded for Francis, 'Sanctioned, then, presumably, by our Bedders: this writing, whatever it was. Ink provided for it.'

Gaining in confidence, I suggested, 'Mrs Ashley?' I had recalled the princess's outburst, the first day, at being forbidden to write to her. Maybe she had persuaded Bedders to relent.

Mr Parry said, 'Well, Fram here can do a bit of poking around for us, find out if Mrs Ashley receives any letter.'

And the loathsomely self-important Francis gave him the nod: *Consider it done.*

About a week later, Sir Henry met me on the gatehouse stairs and in an effort to make light of the matter informed me, 'We are not graced, today, by the great lady's presence.'

This was new. The princess had never before been absent. Stepping into the room, I looked to Miss Parry but, as usual, drew a blank, which was almost enough to have me miss Mrs Ashley; I wasn't going to learn anything from No-Panic Parry. It wasn't as if the princess had anything else to be doing, and she would be well aware that Mr Parry wanted sightings of her, so why wasn't she here? Her absence meant that Sir Henry wouldn't have to kneel, which was probably why he was cock-a-hoop.

Then Miss Parry surprised me by speaking up. 'My lady is sorry that she can't be here.' She hadn't spoken directly to me, but still, there it definitely was: the word *can't*.

Sir Henry, too, picked up on that, but to dismiss it. 'Chooses not to.' Jaunty, as if this were a joke between them. Keen, though, not to have the blame for the princess's non-appearance laid at his feet. 'And it's probably for the best,' he continued, 'if she rests up. I'm sure Miss Turner here can get by with the pair of us.'

The pair of us: he and Miss Parry. All very pally, although I sensed Miss Parry baulk at it.

Later, when I relayed this to Mr Parry, he asked me how Miss Parry had seemed. Tired and tense, I said, but she always did, in there. A far cry, I thought, from when I had first seen her, striding across a courtyard and shaking loose her hair.

'Sounds like a spat of some sort,' Mr Parry decided, 'and our lady is refusing to come out to play. Spats with the princess,' he said knowingly to Maud. 'Two a penny.'

But that made no sense. 'If there was a spat with the princess,' I said, 'he wouldn't consider himself all cosy with Miss Parry; she'd be on the princess's side.'

'*Been* a spat,' he revised, 'over and done with, and now he's making up, or trying to, and starting with Blanche, as anyone would.'

Whatever was wrong, it hadn't blown over when I next visited — once again the princess wasn't there — but this time Sir

Henry was subdued. 'Our great lady prefers to keep to her bed,' was how he put it.

'The Lady Elizabeth is unwell,' Miss Parry corrected. She couldn't have spoken more bluntly and I was braced for him to pull her up for passing information, but instead he took issue with what she had said. 'The lady has experienced a setback,' he said to her, as if I weren't there, 'for which she has only herself to blame.'

I had a sense of having pitched up in the middle of something that was moving fast over and above my head.

Miss Parry's response sounded somewhere between appeal and outrage. 'My Lady's Grace is held without charge——'

'Oh, Miss Parry, spare me!' A stocking was balled in his fist. 'Why would she make things harder for herself?'

Miss Parry tried, 'My Lady's Grace is angry——'

'Yes, and now she isn't the only one!' It was almost a howl. 'What, precisely, did our bedridden Grace think was to be gained by disrespecting her Majesty?' He began jabbing a finger at Miss Parry. 'You, you, you,' he barked. 'I'd like to see how she would react if *I* used such a form of address to *her*.'

So, that ink had been for her to write to the queen – she had at last been permitted to write to the queen – whom she had then addressed as 'you'?

'I just don't understand,' he wailed, 'why on earth you let her do it.'

Miss Parry said, primly, 'I don't read her letters.'

He sighed and laid down the stocking as if relinquishing a weapon. 'Well, might I suggest that in future – if any of us still *have* a future – that you do.' Then to me: 'And no word of this to Parry; I don't need him on my back. Her Grace has taken to her bed, feeling sorry for herself: that's the long and the short of it. You bring that man strutting to my door with his accusations and insinuations, then this carry-on' – he struck petulantly at the pile of laundry – 'will end and frankly your great lady can go naked for all I care.'

That afternoon, conveying the gist to Mr Parry, I omitted both the references to mere 'Parry' and the word 'strutting'; I didn't want to voice either to his face, and oddly I was embarrassed for Sir Henry, who prided himself on his sangfroid but had on this occasion lost his rag. I did, however, feel duty-bound to report the 'naked'. All this I had to do in front of Francis, just back from wherever he had been via – I could smell it on him – a nip into Woodstock's best bakery. When I had repeated Sir Henry's accusation that the princess had disrespected the queen, Mr Parry inhaled as if he'd accidentally done himself an injury, and Francis snapped shut his eyes. Not for the first time, I wondered why they stuck around; the princess was sometimes her own worst enemy and if she went down then so did they. She hadn't tried to escape in the sense of rushing the door, but the writing of that letter was as bungled a bid for freedom as a banging on that door, which in response had now been harder bolted.

Mr Parry recovered himself and managed to sound amused when he said: 'You were told not to tell me.' This was either admiration at my loyalty or a ribbing at the ease with which I'd passed the buck.

'I work for you,' I said, 'not for him.'

He sat back, to take stock. 'So . . .'

Francis, though, sat forward, avid. 'No time to waste. The princess is sick and he's denying her a physician. This is dangerous.'

Mr Parry said, 'As is our being shut out of that gatehouse for the foreseeable. We need to tread carefully.'

Francis frowned, evidently thinking there might not be any kind of future, let alone a foreseeable one. 'Tom,' he urged, 'this is it, it's here, it's happening exactly as we feared: lock her up and do away with her bit by bit. A little too late with the doctor, to let something get a grip on her.'

It came as a shock to me to hear it baldly stated. I wasn't sure I'd understood that was what Mr Parry had meant by fading from view.

'We can't allow this to happen,' Francis said. 'That's why we're here.'

Mr Parry cautioned, 'It's delicate. This has to be Blanche's decision; she's the one stuck in there and she's the only one who knows the truth of the situation. If she wants us wading in, then of course we will, but . . . ' He turned to me. 'She said the princess is unwell. Did she say this *to you*?'

He knew she couldn't speak directly to me. 'Well, no, because she can't.'

'Yes, but was it said *for* you?'

No, I decided, it wasn't. It had been said between the pair of them.

'And what *did* she say to you?' A flicker in his gaze added the qualifier: insofar as she could communicate anything to me.

Nothing, really, I said. Or I didn't think so, anyway. I hoped I was right.

He turned to Francis. 'Blanche wants us to know, but she doesn't want us in there kicking up a fuss. If she did, she'd make that clear.'

Francis was unconvinced, I could see, and I cringed to have their strategy dependent on me, on my interpretation.

But Mr Parry was confident. 'Trust to Blanche,' he told Francis. 'Anything she wants to tell us, she'll make sure Annie gets it.' It was a neat sidestep, for which I was thankful, to make it Blanche's call rather than mine. 'I vote we hang fire,' he said conclusively, there in fact being no vote, and turned with unusual curtness to some papers on his desk to suggest we should go.

So Francis and I found ourselves leaving together and alone however fleetingly in each other's company, which so far we had contrived to avoid. All that happened, though, was that when

197

he'd closed the door behind us, he said over my head, 'You don't work for him: you work for her.'

Speak for yourself, I thought as he stalked off ahead of me down the stairs; speak for your own deluded self. He thought of himself as a knight in shining armour, but a leopard doesn't change its spots and I knew him to be vain, faithless, callow, self-regarding. How pathetic he was: I doubted he had ever even actually been in the princess's presence. I might not know much about her, but I knew more than he did, and I suspected that given half the chance she would chew him up and spit him out.

16

Happy Ending

Francis wasn't around much in July; and whenever he was, he had had the shine knocked off him by the weather. It was the same everywhere, he told Mr Parry: we were no longer in the wetter west, because everywhere was wet and indeed becoming more so. Rivers were breaking their banks, which made his comings and goings slower, circumlocutious, as he edged around misplaced bodies of water. I remembered when he had claimed to be saddle sore: well, he probably really was now. He arrived back looking dejected: it's hard to play the hero with your hair plastered to your head.

Summer seemed to have taken fright and scarpered. At least in my line of work I had a fire in my hearth, but crossing the courtyard some mornings I glimpsed my breath. The sky was steeped in cloud, and those clouds were filthy, overburdened and rupturing so that we were forever dodging downpours. There was no outrunning the rain, though: it was always there before us, underfoot and grabbing at our ankles, at least as much of a menace on the ground as overhead.

'Wetstock' was what Mr Parry's long-legged usher-boy, Dominic, took to calling Woodstock. Even Maud was down in the muzzle: lying on her bed in my makeshift laundry, slotting her snout between her stick-thin, implausibly rigid forelegs and regarding me mournfully. Maudlin Maud. Whenever I fetched her from Mr Parry, I rushed to rub her down before she could shake herself, which she would do with such vigour as to lose her footing. Despite my best efforts, muck came in on her paws, in the whorls and seams and folds of pads and fur tufts and nails. The smell of her damp fur was like dried peas on the boil, almost fabric in its density, like a wadding up my nostrils.

At least I was kept busier. A bad summer makes more work for a laundress than any winter because the days are so much longer and busier, and the fabrics – of light, open weaves – vulnerable. Even the poorest summer teems with foliage, flora and seed heads, much of it smashed from stems and branches, a tide of it to wash up onto hems.

A week or two of rain we could weather; we weren't English for nothing. Well practised, we all huddled in doorways, grumbling as if the rain were a bad sport, but after several weeks the concern became the harvest rotting in the fields, the suppers of the forthcoming year turning to slime. Every day I sensed everyone waking with the same thought, the foreboding chiming across the courtyard and through the town and further away: could the harvest be brought in today? But there again was the rain, outside, pulsing like an airborne pestilence.

By mid-July there was only so much anyone could say, and nothing that could be said would make it better. Nobody quite met anyone else's eye, because there was no comfort to be found there, only a reflection of fear. And shame, too, perhaps, because what fools we had been, how naïve to have made a song-and-dance about the rain as if our disapproval would bring it up sharp.

How resilient, I began to wonder, was the princess's household? I had jumped ship, but was this ship now sinking? Rent from tenant farmers kept the Bull's roofs over our heads. If those farmers were going under and this household's funds ran short, it would almost certainly be a case of last in, first out. And I had been last in. I always was. I had made a life of being last in and it hadn't yet failed me, but there was a first time for everything. These might be my final days at Woodstock, I thought, which filled me with dread.

This isn't July, I would find myself thinking, stupidly, as I stood on my threshold each new morning. It couldn't be. But, well, no one had told it, so it kept turning up, every day, with its rain and gales in tow.

One day on my way to the old palace I saw that an expanse of water lay in place of the river, smooth and bright as if it was the sky there on the ground. Its claim thoroughgoing, its conquest complete, there was no trace of the land that had been there, as if I – bystander – were mistaken to remember it differently.

Francis's returns were heralded by Mr Parry – *The man himself!* – but I was beginning to wonder how useful he really was. He worked with hearsay and conjecture. If the information he brought back to us then proved unreliable, he could blame his sources. Mr Parry once said to me, 'You confirm for us that the princess still exists, then Fram takes that out into the world.' It made us two sides of the same coin, he said, and I smiled as I was supposed to do but privately bridled at the pairing until it occurred to me that held fast and diametrically opposed to Francis was the safest place for me to be.

According to Mr Parry, Francis was bringing back news of the preparation of London for the return of the royal couple from their Winchester wedding: pavilions being built, platforms erected, acrobats trained, all in the pouring rain. But we already knew all this, I felt, or could have guessed. And Francis was probably aware of that: returning, he was no longer riding high. He sloped back, having been given the brush-off, I suspected, by those he'd been to see, whose ears he had intended to bend. My guess was those fair-weather friends of his were now too busy for misgivings about the marriage. Misgivings were not to be afforded by those required to pavilion-build for the forthcoming festivities and whose neighbours were doing similar but better and faster. Francis, turning up at their gates, would be in the way of favours being called in and deals struck. Those old friends of his – if that was what they were, for which we only had his word – might now barely have the time of day for him, at most sparing him a raised eyebrow, a shrug, a grimace to say: *If you can't beat 'em, join 'em.*

And he himself didn't say much whenever he returned; merely related his findings and observations, such as they were. What else was there to say? That people had short memories? That they didn't know what was coming to them?

God only knew what he would make of my garter embroidered with the insignia of the queen and her chosen king.

Everybody loves a wedding: that was the substance of what Francis brought back, but he didn't need to have left Woodstock to have learned that. You can keep your ear to the ground where you stand. This was no longer a prospective marriage, its merits or otherwise to be picked over; it was an imminent wedding, and, well, everybody loves a wedding, or so it seemed, or so they said, and especially when there isn't much else to celebrate.

Letty was excited to tell me that she'd heard the queen would have for her wedding ring a plain gold band, as would any ordinary woman. We were in her kitchen, making up a tray of treats for ourselves. This marriage, she said, for which the queen had longed and from which she had not been dissuaded even by an armed revolt: she was choosing to honour it with a plain gold band. All the riches in the world, she enthused, but the queen wanted nothing more than the wish of the women of Woodstock and anywhere else in her realm: a helpmeet and bedfellow, and a chance of children. In the back of my head, I heard Bel: *Don't you want children?* I kept to myself that there was nothing ordinary about the dress or the kirtle beneath it. Bel would be airing those, it occurred to me. Incredibly, I had worn that kirtle in secret, and then even more extraordinarily, Bel and I had gone from there to her bed. Just as incredibly, try as I might to regret it, in view of how it had all turned out, I didn't.

I asked Letty how she knew about the ring. She turned and dumped Alban on me – suddenly in my arms was the odd mix of softness and solidity that is a baby and which there is no other way to hold but tight and close – and gave me a look to imply I was a contrarian. Because why wouldn't I want to believe it? Surely this was the happy ending to a story of a woman who'd been misunderstood, maligned, denied but now had the chance of a late-flowering happiness. Why would anyone with a heart begrudge her?

But for all the talk in town of ordinariness, in the next breath would come an account of splendour and spectacle: the same stories that Francis was bringing back, but told approvingly, admiringly. In this, too, then, in the eyes of her people, the queen excelled – no cutting corners for her. No appointing committees of mealy-mouthed men, with their back-rubbing and back-stabbing. The queen knew what she wanted for her wedding celebrations; she had the guts and balls for magnificence and wouldn't take no for an answer as she had had to do for the past quarter of a century. No more hiding away. And the skies could chuck it down, but what, to the English, was a little rain?

I wondered what the princess, shut away in that gatehouse, knew of any of the wedding preparations. She had no news unless it came from Sir Henry. If she didn't know of the wedding before it happened, she would know afterwards because the prayer offered daily for the queen's health would then include her new husband, and the princess would be expected to say Amen to that. But what would she make – if she could know – of the sea change on the streets? I myself didn't know what to make of it. Back when the princess had been at liberty, the talk wherever you cocked an ear was at the very least of reservations about the marriage and often of resistance; and, if word was to be believed, those conversations hadn't been confined to street corners but had been had in the country's cathedrals and castles, too. No one had favoured that marriage. Now, everywhere was happy chatter about wedding rings.

The princess's continued absence at the laundry handover should have made it easier for me: no performance, no baiting of Bedders for me to have to witness; simply the job of laundry exchange. But my real task was to bring back sight of her, or at least news, and for weeks I had been unable to do that. Give me a job and I'd do it: that was all I ever asked. Making myself useful was all I had ever known how to do. My life had depended on it.

I was failing Mr Parry, even if he was at pains to reassure me otherwise. 'Still nothing?' he would ask, strenuously nonchalant, perhaps peeling an apple. And I'd have to confirm: nothing, or not that I'd seen. No princess, and Miss Parry kept her eyes down, her fingers interlaced: No-Panic Parry, although I worried that she was in fact hoping against hope, willing me to wake up to whatever was going on and fetch help. Nothing, I would say to Mr Parry, and he would tell me that the nothing I was bringing him was in fact something; that I was bringing him my observations even if we didn't yet know what to make of them. He gave the impression of holding his nerve and keeping faith with me, but I couldn't help but suspect I was being humoured.

By the third week of this, I was miserably convinced that I was missing something, and what worried me at least as much as the princess's fate was that I was failing Mr Parry. To say nothing of how Francis would make a meal of it if the princess's life drained away in that derelict palace while I was in the gatehouse fiddling with collars and cuffs.

Day by day, I willed her to appear – *Come out, come out, wherever you are* – and my disquiet turned to frustration, sometimes even to anger. But I should have been careful what I wished for. I suppose I was expecting that if and when she did appear, she'd be frail, hesitant, perhaps even apologetic. Well, I should have known better. One day, weeks into her absence, our sorry little laundry-sifting band was assembled as usual when the princess came barging in as if shouldering through a crowd, and delivered herself into her chair. There she was, at long last, arms folded high and gaze resolutely down. I had caught a glimpse of those eyes, though: forgetting myself, I'd stared as she had come stalking into the room, and I'd seen how they were an encumbrance – over-large and heavy, damaged-looking, whereas before they'd been alive and scything through the world ahead of her. She was undressed, too, in her nightgown, her hair down and fingers bare of rings. Her demeanour screamed: *Happy now?*

For all her habitual high-handedness, she had always had charm of a kind, I realised, and baffling though that charm had been – tricky, uneasy, unpredictable – it had been at the heart of her like the redness of her hair. For her to storm into the room like that, she had had to tear herself free of that charm; and even just to look at her – even to be in her presence – was, I felt, to be doing her further injury.

But somehow we stumbled through and did what we had come to do, completing the laundry handover. Next time, the scenario was repeated, and then every time I visited, day after day, for a week, two weeks. But in all that time I didn't tell Mr Parry. This was something more, then, that I was keeping from him. I did tell him the facts – that she was undressed and she limited her participation to presenting herself slumped in that chair – but I was covering for her. Because what was unnerving wasn't what she neglected or refused to do – get dressed, look anyone in the eye, speak. *Or she might as well lie down and die*, I had once imagined Mr Parry saying, back in our early days at Woodstock, and this, now, it seemed to me, was what she was doing.

17

Dog Days

The turn towards autumn felt like a sleight of hand, because we hadn't yet had a summer; and by mid-October hopes of even a St Luke's little summer were dashed. Letty was soon to go into confinement at her mother's, an hour's ride away: she would leave sooner than necessary, ahead of the winter weather, then wait for winter's retreat before – God willing – she would return.

She was suffering from aches in her hands. 'My feet, I'd understand,' she complained to me one day, mock-trudging a couple of steps to portray a vastly increased weight, which was something of an exaggeration, 'but hands? Am I walking on them in my sleep?'

I told her I had over the years come across laundresses similarly incapacitated during pregnancy, although I agreed it made no sense.

'Nice to know I'm in good company.' She kicked off her shoes and sat in her husband's chair. 'And you, too – I bet it won't be long before you're waddling like a house.'

Houses don't waddle, I pointed out.

She ignored that. 'We need to get your fancy man to step up.' This imaginary man she insisted I have. Denial was futile, I'd learned, and ran the risk of fanning the flames. ('You're just shy! It's always the quiet ones.') I didn't know if she suspected me of holding something back from her or simply holding out on her, declining to lend my weight to the state of wifedom. Letting the side down. Well, she didn't know the half of it, and thank goodness. Sometimes it pained me that she didn't, because I would have loved to reciprocate in trading confidences, and there had even been moments when I felt that if anyone could ever know how much Bel had been to me, then Letty could. In another sense, though, Letty least of all, because it was a point of pride for her that we were ordinary girls: we two rather than the simpering specimens around town, the pair of us with our shoes off and feet up, feeding our faces, bad-mouthing whomever we pleased. But there was nothing ordinary about what I had felt for Bel.

Returning from Letty's one dreary October day, I ran into Mr Parry, who said he had just been paid a call by 'our friendly leopard-tamer'.

I was taken aback. 'Here?'

He quoted, '"Business matters",' then elaborated. 'There he was, in my room, warming his toes and drying his cloak, because it turns out there's not a lot of firewood up there at the palace, and he asks me for a loan so he can pay the guards. Honestly, you couldn't make it up. He tells me Council's being slow and I said there's nothing he can tell me about Council shutting its eyes and clapping its hands over its ears; we, ourselves, here, I said, are pretty well acquainted with it pretending we don't exist. I said, Tell you what: I'll lend you some money if you lend me a princess.'

I accompanied him across the courtyard.

He said, 'Council wants to forget about the princess being out here, because they know she shouldn't be. Most of them served her father and they know what a dim view he'd take of one daughter locking up the other. I said to our friend Bedders, This is hardly what we were promised, is it – the bringer of peace and reconciliation.'

The queen, he meant, because that was how she had presented herself when she had ridden into London to claim the throne.

'But our dear Bedders says, "I just follow orders." Yes, and his problem is that he hasn't had many of those, of late. And, you know, I do feel sorry for him, I truly do' – clearly he didn't – 'because back there at Whitehall they've stuck their heads in the sand. He's been petitioning Council about a damn sight more than the guards' wages, you know; he's been angling to get shot of his duties here.'

I was startled. 'He told you that?'

He laughed. 'Of course he didn't tell me that! He's not going to say that, is he. Because it's *an honour*, remember, to serve the queen.' He went on his way, chuckling at the thought: 'No, of course he didn't tell me that.'

Which must have meant that this had been one of Francis's finds.

As if the princess knew something was afoot, a couple of days later everything changed again. There came a snapping-to, a shaking-off, so that she no longer sat there in that room like a weeping wound, a raw and bloodied socket, a crimson nail bed. Nor, though, was she back to her previous ways of coil and strike. Instead, she took on a practical air, even though there was nothing in that stifling room to be practical about, and if anything this was the time if there ever was one – all these months in and no prospect of freedom – for her to be furious. But no: she sat up, forward, and focused. A demeanour not unlike the donning of an apron, had she possessed such a thing. And in none of this did I detect anything like the provocation that Bluebell had perfected. The princess wasn't playing at this – it looked to me to be a genuine effort to be biddable and amenable, and, oddly, put me in mind of myself. What was she up to?

She was making a pair of sleeves as her New Year's gift for the queen, which I reported back to Mr Parry in the surly presence of Francis. Mr Parry said, 'Well, a little stitching won't go amiss, although for our Majesty her Christmas has already come; in fact all her Christmases have come at once, because her old friend Reggie Pole is on his way.'

The name meant nothing to me.

'Papal legate,' he told me. 'Twenty years of exile in Rome, but he's sailing up the Thames as we speak – am I right, Fram?'

I braved a glance at Francis, who didn't return it but nodded, disgusted.

Mr Parry said, 'He's on his way to forgive us our heretical ways and embrace us back into Rome, and this – Reggie's return, with his hocus-pocus – is our Majesty's New Year's gift to her subjects. Because it's just what we always wanted, yes? To shut up and put up and pay a pretty penny to your priest for your every sin: that's why the common folk lined the streets, she thinks, when she rode into London to claim the throne. Not because she'd been wrenched from her mother and bullied by her father and his witch of a new wife and shut away for most of her life in Norfolk. Not because we, the English people, wanted to be fair to someone who'd endured the rough end of the stick. Nope, we were cheering her on because we wanted the clock turning back twenty years.' He rolled his eyes. 'That's what our Majesty, in her infinite wisdom, thinks. As far as she's concerned, her people have spoken, cheering her into London, and that's what she thinks we said. So now he comes, her beloved Reggie, decked out in his robes, and I'm surprised she's sent a barge down to Gravesend for him because you'd think she'd expect him to walk on water.'

I recalled how bishops' robes twenty years ago had been made into cushion covers. Now clerics were going to have to be kitted out again. Good for business would be Mrs Wilkinson's view. What goes around comes around.

Mr Parry continued, 'Off he sped, twenty years back, to sanctuary in Rome, for which his mother and brother paid the price, and I tell you I haven't been to an execution since his mother's. You wouldn't put an animal through what that axeman did to her. To live your full three score and ten and then die like that, crawling around in the straw while some kid bashes at you with an axe. I suspect it was the kid's first and I certainly hope it was his last.' He spoke directly to me. '*You* could have done better.' Then, 'Makes you wonder how much our Reggie knows about it – safely stowed away over there. I wouldn't have been the one to tell him. To know your dear old mother had suffered like that because of something you'd done: I wouldn't inflict that on my own worst enemy.'

'Which is what he is,' said Fram, drily.

Mr Parry said, 'To be fair, we don't know that. He might be so pleased to be back on home soil that all is forgiven and the worst we get is some smells and bells. We can but hope. Of course, it's just as likely he sees we've gone to rack and ruin, we're heathens and heretics, and he starts piling up the faggots.'

The following week, my mention of the princess being busy with the sleeves for the queen had Mr Parry mutter that she should get a move on because she needed to make a start on baby clothes. He was dispensing dried apple slices to Maud as he spoke, and for an instant he'd lost me: baby? I could think only of Letty's newborn – mother and baby doing well, according to Damascin – but the princess wouldn't know about her newest namesake let alone be expected to stitch for her. Who else was expecting a baby? Bluebell? Or Mr Parry's own wife? But Mr Parry – down in the mouth and admonishing Maud even as he indulged her – didn't look to be bearing glad tidings.

I did wonder if he meant the queen, but I had seen her with my own eyes and she hadn't looked capable of carrying so much as a kitten. And if there was even a rumour of a princeling, surely Mr Parry would have come right out with it; he would have been bursting with it, not stewing until we had already swapped what passed for news and commiserated with each other about the weather and consoled ourselves the whole way through a dish of spiced figs.

But when he looked at me, I saw his affected nonchalance was a warning that we shouldn't admit to consternation, not even here, to each other. That look said it was true, then, but that we were to pretend even to each other that this was nothing that we hadn't expected – the point of the marriage being to produce an heir – and nothing for which we weren't prepared. Then he did allow me a little more: 'Quickened the second she clapped eyes on Reggie Pole, if you can believe it. That man is the Angel Gabriel now, as well as pope-in-waiting.' He informed Maud, 'Man of many talents, that one.'

My heart hovered in my throat. 'Will the princess know?' Because a baby prince would mean that in no one's eyes would the princess any longer be heir to the throne. That, though, Mr Parry slammed down by throwing up his hands – *Don't ask me* – which seemed a little unfair, because who else could I ask? This much he deigned to speculate: 'If *he* knows' – Sir Henry, he meant – 'then so will she.' Bedders wouldn't pass up an opportunity to crow about this miracle as he – and no doubt so many others – would see it. Beyond that, it was apparent, Mr Parry was in no mood to be drawn, and a fuss over the state of Maud's breath indicated the subject was closed.

After a perfunctory leave-taking, I paused on the other side of the door, fighting an urge to go back and demand he tell me that everything was going to be all right, but I'd already seen that he wasn't going to oblige on that count. What confounded me at least as much as the news itself had been his blank-eyed bravado, his insistence that we keep our qualms from each other.

Back in the cottage, I mulled over what this might mean for us at Woodstock. The queen was at the end of her fourth decade and had never been in the best of health. In her eyes, this unlikely pregnancy would be God's blessing, which might mean she would be in the mood to put the past behind her, to forgive and forget and allow the princess her freedom. Equally, though, if the pregnancy continued well she might be off into her glorious future without a backward glance and we would be left here to languish.

But that was if she were blessed and a glorious future was to be had. Twice thus far in my life I had been faced with the bed linen of a woman who had died in childbirth, and there had been nothing to do but burn it. All that blood, cooking in the flames. The one piece of linen that never comes to a laundress is a shroud. If the queen were to die, what then? Would the princess become queen? Or would she be taken prisoner by the Spanish?

Over the following few days, Mr Parry made himself scarce, and, try as I might, I gleaned nothing more at the Bull or around town. When I was next at the gatehouse, Miss Parry let me know that they had heard the news, by poking into the princess's pouch of silk threads and remarking to her, 'You'll need more peach; I always think peach is nice for a baby.' The princess was quick to agree: peach stitching, definitely. This holding of nerve was different from Mr Parry's, and the determined cheerfulness had Bedders chiming in, fond and indulgent: *you ladies* this, *you ladies* that.

The pregnancy was made public just before Christmas. The news would have made for quite a festive season at the palace, but in the wilds of Woodstock we merely went through the motions. The Bull did its best by us and laid on various feasts, but no one felt like dancing. As good as any gift I was given was Francis's absence for the two weeks.

213

Bel was facing a second Christmas without me. The first, I had been stuck at Ashridge, and back then nothing had been more important to me than that I spend every future Christmas with her. Yet here I was, just a year later, most of which I had lived without her, and the separation had been my own doing, even if it had left me reeling.

After that one tense and unsettling exchange with Mr Parry, any mention of the prospective prince elicited no more from him than an incredulous, good-humoured rolling of his eyes. He had pulled himself together, it seemed, and the princeling was relegated, one more problem amongst many. I didn't forget how thrown he had been, though, and it brought home to me how diminished he was from when we had arrived in May. We had been at Woodstock for more than six months and the princess's prospects were only worse.

After a half-cock Christmas came the slap in the face that is January. One bleak day Mr Parry intercepted me on my way through the Bull, saying something about a favour and guiding me by the elbow into the empty dining hall, where he gestured for me to sit before doing the same. He was Maud-less; Maud had the sense not to stray from a fireside if she could help it. For dogs, these were the dog days of the year.

'It's Fram,' Mr Parry said, his apologetic tone an admission that he was aware we didn't get on. No love lost, was probably how he thought of it. 'Laundry,' he said, which made it easier: there was only one possible response to that, a biddable incline of my head: *At your service*. I refrained from asking what had happened to Francis's own laundress, back at his fancy family home.

'He's just back.'

Well, so be it. All I cared was that he kept his distance from me.

'There was a burning,' Mr Parry said, 'in London,' and into my mind's eye came a thatch in flames, 'and this time of year everything's damp, nothing burns, so people do whatever they can to help it along.'

This I took as it was offered – solemn, grave – but I didn't follow.

'And it all turned a bit ... ' but he bowed out with a half-hearted twirl of one chubby little hand. 'And Fram got caught up in it all. With the gunpowder. Got too close.'

Francis is dead.

Mr Parry's eyes sparked at something he saw in mine, which in turn had me freeze, but then he blinked, let it go, set about reassuring me – 'Oh, no, no, he's fine' – and I thought he might cover one of my hands there on the tabletop between us with his own, but he sat back and cast around for how to explain. 'It's just that he's a mess, what with the smoke, and the ... ' and before I knew it, his gaze was on mine and entirely without niceties, 'fat.'

Human fat: somehow I knew that this was what he meant – a person had been burned – and so unequal was I to anything like an adequate response that, shamefully, I blushed.

He was saying that Francis had just ridden in and we should help him clean up and I was saying yes, of course, as if this were manageable, this washing from someone's clothes the spattered fat of someone else. I didn't know what else to say. Never before in my lifetime had a person been burned, or not that I knew of. My head swam. Across the tabletop lay my forearms in sleeves so clean and crisp, stitched with a pattern of daisies, and I couldn't recall if I had ever noticed before now that they were specifically daisies.

'Clerics,' Mr Parry said from the corner of his mouth, and I understood that he was telling me who had been burned, although there was no need for this hush, surely, because there is nothing secret about a burning; quite the contrary, which was presumably the point of it. 'Couple of clerics. John Rogers, from St Paul's, and, well' – he grimaced, remorseful – 'I never could stand that man, but ... '

'Yes,' I offered up, quickly.

'And the other one I don't know – some chap Saunders.' He was saying he would have Dominic bring me the clothes, but I rose, telling him that I would go myself, now, and fetch them.

Saunders: I knew that name, although it took me until the foot of the staircase to remember it had been the name of the little boy alongside whom I'd sheltered from the icy rain in the porch of All Hallows, back on one of those days when I'd gone from the Tower to traipse around the city. A little boy with a slate, practising his writing. Hadn't he said his daddy was rector? And then his mother had come along – elegant in black – and she and I had been grown-ups smiling conspiratorially over his little head. 'Let's run through the rain,' she had said to him, 'and get home before Daddy.'

There would be other Saunderses in London, I told myself, and quite possibly one of them would be a rector. It wasn't that I wished this particular fate on any other Saunders, but the man who had burned didn't have to be the father of that little boy and the husband of that lady.

I paced around the courtyard in the drizzle to work up my nerve before my thumping heart propelled me up to Francis's room. Coming to a halt at his door, I was dizzy to the roots of my hair. I would have chosen to be knocking on just about any other door in the world, but I had to ask about this Reverend Saunders.

Francis was as surprised by my visit as I was. He took a couple of steps backwards and I took one forwards but keeping the door open behind me. It was unimaginable to me that we had ever been closer than we were on that threshold, and I noted how no thread of me held any memory of it and how liberating that was. For all the effect he had on me, he honestly could have been a tree stump there in that doorway.

He glowered as if I were trying my luck, but I stood my ground because I was there neither to extend the hand of friendship nor to cause trouble. I made to look him in the eye but didn't quite succeed, and found I needed to clear my throat before I could say, 'Mr Parry says you have some laundry.'

At that, he relaxed his stance and dismissed it almost pleasantly. 'Oh . . . ' *No, you can forget that.* He thought he was doing me a favour, which riled me, because this wasn't about favours, his or mine. He should just hand over the laundry. I didn't want a song-and-dance about it.

He said, 'I take my laundry home,' before realising his mistake, because his mention of home – the allusion to the new wife – took us both aback, but I snapped to my senses, knowing that laundry of this kind, laundry in this state, didn't go home to any nice lady wife and her lady laundress.

'We'll do that laundry here,' I said, although why I had said *we* when I meant me alone, I didn't know. *This household* was perhaps what I meant: it would stay in this household, was a matter for this household.

He didn't argue, retreating into his room – which was as cold as iron – to return with a bundle at which we both scrupulously avoided looking, and muttering thanks, which annoyed me because I was merely doing my job. Taking the laundry from him, I made myself broach it: 'Saunders – from All Hallows?'

He was surprised. 'You know him?' and corrected himself: 'Knew him?'

Saunders, then, from All Hallows: yes, it had indeed been him. But no, I didn't know – hadn't known – him. Francis was saying that he himself hadn't. 'Wife and kid,' he added, quietly.

'Samuel.' The small boy, the name on that slate, and I found myself asking, 'Was she there – the wife?' At the burning.

He said yes as if I shouldn't have had to ask. But I could think of good reason for keeping away, if I were the wife, because surely for a man to die like that would be all the harder for having your loved one witness it. I wondered if she had gone

217

alone in that crowd, and where she had gone since and what she had done with her husband's clothes, those he hadn't worn to the stake, and I heard myself asking Francis, 'Have you bathed?' Because a change of clothes was all very well, but he would feel better for a bath. 'It's good water here,' I said, 'and we can heat it.' Heat it easily enough, I meant, even as I despaired at myself for having started on this and for persisting; I could see it was too much for him. But as my breath stopped dead in my throat, he collected himself and told me, 'It's something I'd never seen before,' and for a second I thought he meant a bath until I realised he was talking about the burning. Peculiarly politely, he asked, 'You?'

I said no, but he had already thought better of it – 'But of course not' – because no one in our time had, and then I felt able to ask, 'Why? Why did it happen?'

'Heretics,' he said, in that same conversational tone, voicing it emptily to imply that it wasn't his word, wasn't *a* word, to him, or not a meaningful one.

To me, it sounded like a word from another world, one of black-robed figures bowed under an enormous sun like beetles under a rock.

I said, 'Is it because we have a Spanish king?' but then answered before he could. 'It's the Church, though, that decides you're a heretic: it's for the Church to decide.'

'The queen signs, though,' he said, turning back into his chilly room. 'Has to sign. For each and every one.'

Back in the cottage, his laundry offered up nothing: there was nothing untoward on those clothes and I wondered if he hadn't been as close as he had told Mr Parry, or perhaps even there at all, before it occurred to me that he might just have handed over other, relatively unsoiled clothes to spare me.

18

The Face of the Deep

Before the end of that week, we knew that the London burning wasn't a one-off. There had been several more, in different places. I fretted that having taken Francis's laundry once, I should probably offer again, although I didn't know whether he had been to any of these burnings — Mr Parry hadn't said, and I hadn't dared ask — or, if he had, he had known better this time than to get too close. I resented finding myself in the ridiculous position of wondering just how close he would need to be to qualify for laundry services.

Mr Parry told me that one of the burnings was that of a bishop. Actually, it was Maud whom he told, fondling her ears. It was easier to tell Maud, in a slightly sing-song manner to demonstrate his incredulity.

I asked him what this bishop had done wrong.

'Married,' he said.

I flinched, but I knew what he meant: the law had not long ago changed again — changed back — so that clergymen should be unmarried.

'Got to be above all that now,' Mr Parry sang to Maud. 'Got a flock to attend to; no time for a wife and kids.' Then to me, 'They

219

can be as rich as princes and lord it over swathes of the country and somehow that's no distraction from their godly work . . . but to head a household? Heaven forbid.'

To burn merely for being married, though?

'The problem with her Majesty,' he said, 'is that if you're not with her, you're against her. Simple as that. And I don't care what she believes – she can believe what she likes. But this is no way to run a country. Because today it's priests marrying, but one day soon it'll be black's white.'

In the end I did decide to go to Francis for his laundry, only to be met by the same magnanimous demurral, which infuriated me because the offer hadn't come from any goodness of my heart. His job was to ride around England bending ears, but what had him welcomed into those households was, in no small part, a clean shirt. His job now was to bear witness, and mine, whether I liked it or not, I realised, was to clean up after him. He messed about with gunpowder and I made good. We had to work together. So when he tried to fob me off, I refused to have that merry dance but stood my ground, dug my heels in, obstinate as the mule I felt I must look like there on that threshold. Reduced, I knew, in his eyes, to a woman fussing over mere details. Or, as he would probably have it, a woman. A wife, near as damn it.

Eventually he acquiesced, but handed over a bundle that looked fine and smelled clean. Back in the cottage, as I prepared the soak, my thoughts turned to what a person would wear to his own burning. Only buttons and buckles would survive into the ashes. Clothing is no protection from a burning; on the contrary, it will fuel the fire, wick the flames. But then, in any case, no one would want protecting; no one would want it protracted. I pulled myself up sharp, wondering what on earth it had come to for me to be thinking like this. Back to the task in hand, I unfurled Francis's shirt for the soak, and as I did so, a wingbeat of memory clipped the back of my mind, gone before I knew it. Not so much a memory, perhaps, as a sense, of a place: a house I had once known, I felt, but that was now beyond my recall.

Later that same week, Sir Henry remarked jovially to the princess and Miss Parry that they would no doubt be stitching the finishing touches to their baby shawl right up until they were unpacking at the palace. My heart leapt to hear it — *palace* — but at the same time my head cautioned against a jump to conclusions, because this could well be wishful thinking on his part: he was, we knew, desperate to leave Woodstock. He would want to believe the royal half-sisters could be reconciled over a baby. Women: all they need to put them right, he'd think, is a newborn in the house. (*Don't you want children?* And that tilt of her head.) I looked to the ladies for a reaction, but as usual there was nothing, or no more than a cursory, polite acknowledgement that he had spoken. If they were surprised by what he had said, they didn't show it. *Steady as she goes.* They had become so good at this. The Elizabeth of old would have been unable to resist making a caustic remark about house arrest doing wonders for her needlework.

Taking it to Mr Parry, I didn't know if this mention of a return to the palace was something or nothing; he would be the one to weigh it up. When I told him, though, his eyes met mine but there was an enamel shine to the gaze that then slid away as if what I had just tried to hand him had dropped between the floorboards. He made no effort to retrieve it, didn't ask me to repeat myself or speculate, but instead reached across his desk for a toothpick, with which he then busied himself, pausing in his probing to remark, 'We've been told to expect the queen to summon her.' The off-hand delivery implied he didn't believe it, but it was clear that he wasn't going to elaborate, and after some desultory conversation, I returned nonplussed to the cottage.

I hadn't long been back when usher-boy Dominic knocked, curls veiled with raindrops, a pair of boots in one hand and Maud at his side. Chief dog-walker and boot-polisher.

He said, 'Thin-air diet for you again?'

Dinner. I'd forgotten. I was late but – thanks to him – not too late: I could still make second sitting. Grateful, I reciprocated with a reminder of my own, a bit of fuss in his direction: 'Cloak?' Because this was no weather for no cloak.

He said that Mr Parry had his cloak, and when I suggested he go back and get it, he clarified: 'Mister P's *borrowed* it.'

Assuming this to be a joke that I didn't quite get, I laughed, and he did the same but protested, '*And* my spare doublet *and* my spare jerkin.' The umbrage seemed genuine: Mr Parry really did have his clothes, then. 'Mister P moves in mysterious ways,' he said.

I said, 'He'll need a fair few thin-air dinners before they'll fit.' It was nothing that Mr Parry wouldn't say of himself. 'Still' – I gestured at the boots – 'you'll have dry feet.'

He pulled a face. 'Mr Verney's.'

Francis's.

He proffered them as if for inspection, which had me venture an exploratory fingertip. He sighed, complained, 'I can't even nip home and get my *spare* spares, what with all leave being cancelled.'

Watching him saunter off with Maud, I pondered. *All leave cancelled?* But perhaps it always was and I was never aware of it. It wasn't as if I was ever planning on going anywhere.

I was uneasy, though. If Mr Parry truly hadn't believed what he had been told – that the princess would soon be summoned to court – he would have ridiculed it, I felt. *I won't be rushing to get the horses shod.* But he'd let it go without comment. Perhaps he had been too weary to rise to it. In any case, if he gave it any credence at all, he would have to tell me, because I wasn't obligated to keep the princess's laundry in a state of readiness. Laundry needs to be washed, dried, pressed and packed before it can travel. If there was any prospect of the princess going somewhere, Mr Parry would have to tell me.

The disquiet stayed with me when I went to bed that night, although it wasn't so much the readiness or otherwise of laundry that was keeping me awake but the prospect of a return to court. Because where did that leave me, jumper of ships?

This odd little household had become a home of a kind, but if the princess left Woodstock, I would come to the end of this particular journey as surely I had known one day I would. I had been treading water here; I had been washed up a backwater and now the turn of the tide would, I feared, cast me onto the rocks. As the hours crept by, I tossed and turned, despairing of myself because way back I should have stayed put somewhere and made a life. A simple life. The house I had remembered – or almost remembered – the other day: I should have stayed somewhere like that. Nestled in a nook. Destined in the end for the churchyard down the lane, but, God willing, before that married at that church's door, with spring flowers in my hair, and then my babies baptised at the font.

Memories of houses rattled around inside my head: a chapel bell, a dinner bell, a litany of latch fall. A threadbare patch on some matting, and a particular finish to that scuffing that spoke of the heft and gait of a particular few old faithful servants. The smell of salt on the breeze: that, I remembered of one house. That house, wherever it was, had been close to the sea. A memory of the briny breeze sparked inside my nose, just as it had done earlier in the week, I realised, when I'd shaken out Francis's shirt.

Had Francis been to the coast, then? Not London, this time, but the coast? His boots, too, which Dominic had lobbed at me with a look on his face because only so much could be done for

223

them: hadn't I reached for them in consternation? What I had noticed on those boots, without quite registering I'd seen it, was every laundress's dread: salt-water damage.

Francis had been to the coast. Not fire, this time, this trip, but seawater.

I recalled Dominic cloakless in my doorway, and not only his cloak commandeered but everything else required to attire a young man: Dominic, good-naturedly resigned, robbed of the clothes on his back. *Mister P moves in mysterious ways*. He certainly does, I thought. This household looked likely to be going back to court but he had said nothing to me of laundry. These days, he wanted garments from Dominic, not from me. His concern was with boys' clothes, not the princess's. There must be a lad somewhere whom he needed to dress, whereas the princess, if and when summoned, would have to go to the queen in the clothes she stood up in.

Unless those boy-clothes were for her. Which meant she wouldn't be headed for the palace.

I remembered a story that her half-sister – the queen before she was queen – had once planned to escape England disguised as a milkmaid. She could probably have got away with it: she would have made a good milkmaid; a frumpy, grumpy milkmaid, with that put-upon, achy-hipped waddle that they get from their milking stools. When everything had been unbearable for her in England, the story went, she had been going to flee to Spain as a milkmaid. Now that the tide had turned, was the princess going to escape as a boy? A perfect boy in her cloak and breeches, shrug-shouldered and snake-hipped, slipping away across the sea to France.

I was right, I knew I was. I threw on some clothes and told Maud to stay. It wasn't late by some standards: I didn't know that Mr Parry would be up, but I suspected so. I had no idea what I'd say, but I would trust it to come to me. What mattered was that

I get to his room. It was a physical imperative that I stand there in front of him.

I bolted across the courtyard in the dark and didn't stop until Mr Parry's door gave me pause, but even then I pushed on and he answered my knock with an invitation to enter.

That was when I faltered: standing there on that landing, half-dressed and hard-breathing and full of what struck me as a stupid notion. Because who on earth did I think I was? No way could I compel him to tell me what he was up to. He called again, impatient, and I half opened the door just to stop him – to stop it escalating, to let him see there was indeed someone there and that the someone was merely me.

'Annie?' He wasn't alarmed, but alert.

I preoccupied myself with closing the door quietly behind me, which allowed us to compose ourselves before we faced each other. I cut to the chase. 'Mr Parry, if there's any chance of a move, you'll need laundry.' He could take this however he wished, but I was pretty sure he recognised it for the accusation it was: *Why keep this from me?*

And indeed there was a missed beat before the crestfallen admission: 'You're right.' He rubbed at his eyes. He still hadn't asked me to sit. 'Laundry,' he said, 'yes,' with one of his half-hearted twirls of a hand: go ahead and do it, he meant. Prepare the laundry. I saw he meant that I should play along. Cover our tracks. Then he lowered his voice to confide, explain, apologise. 'Annie, we just don't know what this summons is, what it's for. We don't know what's in store for our Lady's Grace. We've no way of knowing what the queen's thinking, now she's in her confinement.' He grimaced. 'Fram's good, but he's not *that* good.'

Not good enough to get behind closed doors into that locked, ladies-only room. That was somewhere Francis couldn't have his ear to the ground.

'We don't know what it's about, and we can't wait to find out. This could be our only chance.'

To run.

So, when the princess was released from Woodstock to travel to Whitehall, she was going to make a run for it. She herself probably didn't even yet know it – stuck in the gatehouse, how could she? – but that was what Mr Parry and Francis and whoever else had planned for her.

'We do whatever we can,' he said, adding, 'It's nothing that can't be undone.'

And that, incredibly, was it. Interview over. Dismissed.

Back in the cottage, lying in my bed with Maud dreaming twitchingly on the floor below, I thought how the end was coming. When, exactly, I didn't know, but soon, perhaps as soon as a week or two. The princess, dressed as a boy, bundled onto a boat and borne away overseas. Saving her own skin. That silvery skin stolen away across the sea to France. Like a story; and, like a story, to be handed down the years: a princess on a far shore, but if one day we need her, she'll return.

The queen before she was queen would have gone as a milkmaid, sturdy-skirted, clogs belting the planks as she lugged on board the dead weight of her desperate, dreadful years, with the waves – so she would have thought – keening at her departure. The boy-princess, though, would turn her face to the sun: boy-moody, yet still – in the way of boys – buoyant.

There was nothing I could do about it, so I tried to sleep. In my shallow dreams the princess was borne away on a small craft, flitting from sun-spangled wave to wave to a ship. Then came the ship's bewitching glide over the tumult, and on the horizon a flash of sails, sparks showering from oars, and, impossible though it was to see from the shore, an imperfection in the weave of her servant's cloak that made for a parting wink.

In my dream there was nothing for it but to turn and trudge up dunes, shale sliding underfoot and at my back the breeze that had been playful in the company of the sun but was now – gale in its tail – boisterous, picking up the scent of my solitude. Darkness was coming, and I was wondering how it had got so late with me so far from shelter.

Waking in the small hours, I consoled myself that the princess might not be so great a loss. Who was she anyway? Skinny half-bastard with a cosseted life. Insolent, vain and unreadable. Without her, we people of England could still speak up: we could still say white's white and black's black.

Our voices would be lost, though, I feared, on a chill wind.

I didn't have to like the princess to recognise that she knew how to be all things to all people whilst at the same time she was more herself than anyone I had ever encountered. Nothing like the queen, hoarsened by a lifetime of telling herself her own story.

Now Mr Parry was telling a story: the princess's readiness to return in England's hour of need. A story was all it was, because I knew all there was to know about running and I knew that once you've run, there's no going back.

Something else I was pretty sure of: this, already, was our hour of need.

I lay there in my bed as if playing dead and in time more dreams came, of water: a rising tide, its liquid slip onto the shore and into every crevice. I had never been in the sea but in these dreams I knew it as if I had: brutish like a fist but at the same time a palm pressed over mouth and nose; a colour that is no colour but dirt and dark, muck and murk. And below the dead-eye surface it froths with life, cold-blooded. I knew in my dream as I did in my waking life that it is impossible to outrun water. It never goes away but pools and sinks and rains to join up the whole world, and even fire won't survive it. Water, though, will survive fire; it's the only thing on God's earth that does. This, I witnessed every day in my little Letty-borrowed distillery and on the walls of my laundry: burn water away but it flies and settles elsewhere, somehow even fresher. Water is everywhere, snaking below the surface, its cold breath on the underside of every stone in the land; it was everywhere even before time itself, when darkness was — the priests say — on the face of the deep, and, I imagined, it would rise up everywhere as soon as we were gone.

19

Someone

Not even Fram is that good; not even Francis could get himself inside a locked room. But I knew someone who probably could, and in the half-light before I was fully awake I recalled her falling to her knees as if her bones had unhooked themselves. Bel could pour herself beneath a locked door, it seemed to me, but in any case she would know what was going on in that room; she would know the ladies who were locked away in there, a captive audience to the queen's hot air, of which there was plenty because this was a queen with time on her hands and a lot on her mind. Bel might well know if there was any need for the princess to run. Or no need. She knew more than she knew. It was simply the air she breathed. For a time I had breathed that same air. Once, I had slid myself inside each breath of hers and walked in her footsteps into the queen's room.

In the cold light of day I knew I was too late, because the queen's baby was due and the princess's summons imminent: it was only a matter of time, probably less time than it would take me to reach London. The summons would come and this household would go trundling towards the city but then at nightfall turn towards the coast.

But even if I had all the time in the world, I still probably wouldn't reach Whitehall. Francis would see to it that I didn't. Me, leaving behind some cock-and-bull story, some red herring, something that might be believable of the spinster laundress Mr Parry believed me to be but whom Francis knew I wasn't: he would smell a rat. He would think me an informer returning to the fold. If he didn't yet know that Mr Parry had let slip to me their plan to smuggle the princess to France, undoubtedly he soon would – Francis being Francis, being *yer man* – and, thinking me a traitor to his cause, he would make sure I didn't reach court with what I knew. I could run from Francis but I couldn't hide. Which meant that my only chance was to go and face him down.

First, I went to Letty's house to find Dam and said I had a favour to ask, at which she was all smiles as I had known she would be. I said I knew she was good at keeping secrets, and the smile froze on her flushed face as I knew it would, but I didn't care what secrets she had or thought she had; I hadn't come for her secrets but for her attention, which I now had. I was going to have to go away, I told her with a look she could take if she wished as woman to woman. A matter of the heart, I might have meant, and duly her flush became one of warmth for me: sisters under the skin. I said that I would be back within perhaps a couple of weeks but if for any reason I wasn't, I owed something to Mr Parry and would need her to return it to him. She knew who Mr Parry was; everyone in Woodstock did. I had to have a date, something she couldn't possibly forget, so I asked her when the next big Woodstock fair was.

St Mary Magdalene.

Perfect. So if I wasn't back by St Mary Magdalene – which I almost certainly would be, and probably with a month or two to spare – then she was to take something to Mr Parry, and him alone, and tell him it was from me. Tell no one else, I stressed: she should tell no one at the Bull until she was alone with Mr Parry in his room. I didn't tell her that this was to protect her from Francis. I didn't want Francis bumping into her on Mr Parry's stairs and putting two and two together and coming up with her as the bearer of what, in terms of consequences for him, would be the worst possible news. In her favour was that Francis didn't bother himself with locals and certainly not with their servants. He almost certainly wouldn't know she existed. Still, I knew better than to put anything past him.

I handed her my wedding ring, which was engraved with lettering that Mr Parry would detect if he turned it over in his fingertips, and which, if he turned it to the light to investigate, would reveal itself as a date, a place name and two sets of initials, AT and FRAVV.

I went to find Francis just before dinner, when he was likely to be alone in his room; I knocked but then let myself in and sat down on his bed: cards on the table. He made something of being startled. I could see that he assumed I had cracked under the strain and was coming crawling to make peace. Thinking himself to have the upper hand, he drew up a stool and sat with elbows on knees, chin on knuckles, all ears, to ask me, 'So, where've you been, Alys, these past few years?' He was clearly looking forward to pleas and excuses.

I was fairly sure he knew where I had last been – the surprise would have been if he hadn't – but anyway I listed the various households of the past few years, finishing with Whitehall, an admission I hoped would take the wind out of his sails. 'They sent me here,' into the princess's household, 'but then forgot about me and I chose to stay.'

He recovered himself enough to flourish an empty smile: *You don't get away with it that easily.* 'If it suits them to remember, they will.'

That almost made me laugh, and I said, 'I think you'll find

I'm easily forgettable,' before moving swiftly on to why I'd come: I was returning to Whitehall, I said, because no one in the princess's household seemed to know what her summons signified, but I knew someone who probably did. Someone I had worked with.

On the back foot, he bolstered himself by repeating it, flatly, to ridicule it: 'Someone.'

I had a fleeting recollection of being on St Paul's wharf and the apprentice, Rob, not saying her name.

He sneered, 'And this someone will tell you; this confidante of the queen, with whom you happen to be acquainted, will tell you whatever you want to know. You, gone for a year into the princess's household but suddenly back. Your someone will trust in you and tell you what you want to know.'

He had more of a point than he knew but I said, 'You have a better idea?' and told him that I needed my safety assured. If I didn't turn up back from Whitehall in good health, I'd made arrangements so that everything there was to know about him and me would reach those who would want to know. 'And I mean the when and the where of it.' He knew very well that the church had had a register and we had had witnesses.

All posturing dropped, blank-faced with disbelief, he accused, 'You've told someone.'

Did I look that stupid? 'No.'

It was all he could do to repeat it. 'You've told someone.'

He had forgotten the existence of the ring he'd given me, and under any other circumstances I might have been wounded by that. 'No one knows,' I said, 'nor will they unless I'm not back here by a certain date.' I was impressed to hear myself; inside, I was shaking enough to break.

'What date?' And when he realised I judged it safest to keep that to myself, 'You can't write! You've had to *tell* somebody.' I could have sworn he was close to tears of fury.

I didn't have time for this. I stood up. 'If you don't believe me, you can always chance it.' But I was worried, now, that he might. Push had come to shove, and he just might tell on me even if it meant giving himself up as a bigamist; he might think it a price worth paying. It sickened me to be suspected when, in truth, going back and involving myself again with Bel was the very last thing I would choose to do. Nevertheless, it looked as if I would somehow have to prove to him that I wasn't returning to the queen's service.

He blanched when I started lifting my skirt. He should be so lucky. Yanking the garter down my leg, I offered it up. 'Look.'

He recoiled.

Oh spare me. 'Just look. This was supposed to have been for the wedding. For the queen.'

It seemed I had him now. Wide-eyed: 'You took this?'

'No, I was given it. By the tailor's assistant.'

Now he thought he was on to something. 'The "someone".'

If only you knew. But then he was going to have to know; I was going to have to tell him. So I showed him. 'That's me' – the letter T twisted around the A – 'and this,' the little bell, 'that's the tailor's assistant.'

He sat back. 'You're married,' he said, wondrous, and I hoped he hadn't seen me flinch. He would love me to be married, I reminded myself, because that would make us quits.

Well, sorry to disappoint you. 'Bel can't marry me.'

Even better, then. 'Your Mr Bell is already married.'

This was my chance, and I steeled myself to say it. 'Mistress Bel,' I corrected, briskly. 'Christabel Jones. And no, she isn't.' Well, *wasn't*, last I knew.

Comprehension dawned on him incrementally, like a key turning several times in a stiff lock. Or comprehension of a kind, and enough to suit my purposes, but I hated that he thought he had the measure of me. *You think you understand, but you don't and you never will.*

'That little bell,' I continued, 'is on a lot of the queen's clothes, so they'll recognise it. They'll know it's hers. Keep this,' I passed him the garter, 'until I get back. And if you think I'm not coming back, then give it to the queen's people.' Because, as he would appreciate, that was enough to put paid to any chance for me of a welcome back to court, to say the very least. And now for the tallest order. 'Tell Mr Parry something to keep him happy, and make sure the princess doesn't move until you've heard from me.'

This was the last straw. He laughed, incredulous and outraged. 'Who do you think you are?'

From the doorway, I reminded him. 'You know who I am.'

20

Black's White

'I've come from Woodstock,' was all I managed when Bel came unsuspecting around the corner into St Thomas Apostle Street. I knew to get it said before anything else; but as to what I should say next, I had no idea. Sink or swim. By the sound of my heart, I could in fact have *run* all the way from Woodstock.

You, my heart clamoured, in a spin: *You, you, you*, because there she was, despite everything, at long last, and just as I had left her, as if she had been standing around that corner the whole time I had been away. I had to make fists of my hands to stop myself reaching to touch her, test her: Bel, in the flesh. And, I noticed, no wedding ring.

It was no lie that I had come from Woodstock: the truth, pure and simple. I had been nowhere else, I meant, but into those words sneaked the pretence that there was nothing more to my absence, that I had merely been doing my job as informer if for rather longer than she and I had envisaged.

She'll go far, all those years back, and in it I had heard the hint that for me to go far would be to go further than my due, which I had resented because I relied on the goodwill of others and it mattered to me that I honour that. And now look, I thought. And

235

for me to be deceiving Bel of all people: Bel, who had taken me to her heart and into her home.

But then on the other hand, she hadn't been entirely straight with me, had she.

I knew she didn't see it that way, though, and sure enough, after a tight-lipped pause, she said, 'It's been a year.'

A year and no word, she meant. Well, yes. No denying that. What had I expected from her? In her eyes, I had run out on her. I had known – hadn't I? – that she wouldn't be welcoming me back with open arms.

'Yes,' I said, although it hadn't been a year, not quite a year, but this was no time to nitpick. Whatever she wanted, I'd give her. If she was claiming abandonment and a whole year's worth of it, then it was hers.

No, but, 'It's been a year,' hushed, vicious, as if she herself couldn't quite believe it even though she had been waiting a long time – almost a year – to say it to me. It wasn't enough – not nearly enough – for me to concede it. Her face, and her tone, made it clear: *Oh no you don't; you don't just say 'yes' to that. You don't just turn up here like this.*

She was right: I should have stayed and had it out with her. I shouldn't have run, leaving a year of silence behind me. Almost a year: I did still want to say 'almost', even as I knew that on no account should I do so. I should take what I had coming to me, shut up and take it. It had to be done. I could have piped up that she had said she might marry Ollie; I could have reminded her that she had had him in her bed, sometimes. Sometimes me, sometimes him. But I made myself say nothing and just stand there – heart dropping to my boots even as it sparked with indignation – and take it in anticipation of more to come.

She didn't so much as hold open the gate for me, but nor did she shut it in my face. She was allowing me to follow her, if only because she didn't know what else to do: it was late afternoon and the tide was against me. If she wanted rid of me, she would have to kick me away, and she wouldn't do that. So there I was, scampering after her like a stray.

She took our old secretive route to that room of hers, which at least at first sight was unchanged and as lovely as ever. Life at St Thomas Apostle Street had clearly carried on fine without me, as I had known it would. Seeing that room ahead of me through the doorway was like looking into a tub of water but finding no reflection.

I followed her in, bracing myself for sign of Ollie even as I told myself not to look, and she shut the door behind us. She stood with her arms emphatically folded, a show of not giving an inch, and I felt for her because I knew that making a show didn't come naturally to her.

If she was begrudging me the air I breathed, she certainly wasn't going to grant me an audience, and suddenly it was all too much: I was overwhelmed and exhausted, not only by the journey but by all of it, the past year or more, the unfairness of it, of being judged to be in the wrong when I wasn't. How had I ever thought this return of mine would work? *Have it your way, Bel.* Peculiarly, though, this was enough to have me rally: she wasn't going to give me a moment of tenderness, but that wasn't what I'd come for. I had a job to do, I reminded myself.

She asked: 'Why did you go?'

It was the obvious question, yet it threw me, because did she really not know? I had anticipated *Where have you been? Where did you go?* and I had already covered that. And I had imagined her asking why I was here. But as for why I had gone, I stuck to the simple explanation: 'The household went, and I went along too.'

She dismissed that with a laugh that was nothing of the sort, and I didn't blame her. Best, though, I felt, to stand my ground and insist that I had merely been doing my job. 'I saw the princess most days.' I kept to myself that for much of the time I had seen nothing of note.

This, unfortunately, was a red rag to a bull. She gestured towards the door. 'Oh well ...' *Get back to it, then, if it's so very important; don't let me stand in your way*; and in the face of this dismissal I lost my composure, heard myself plead, '*Bel.*' She wanted the truth? I'd give her the truth. 'You think I should have hung around to be guest of honour at your wedding?'

She slammed that back at me – 'Don't be *ridiculous*' – but then turned away, snapping that she was busy, the new priest of St Andrew's was coming round for supper; he had invited himself, and although only she and Ollie were at home, he wouldn't be put off.

Just her and Ollie. Playing at house.

'Join us,' she said, unpleasantly. 'Make yourself useful.' *Sing for your supper.*

So that was how, on my first evening back, I was stuck with Bel and Ollie, and no distractions bar a priest. Begrimed and bone-weary, I was part of an unlikely threesome, a motley crew welcoming that new parish priest to the house. Bel's father was away – a royal christening meant brisk business; his customers didn't have the luxury of waiting to see how the birth went before they placed their orders. He had taken the other two apprentices with him, but that favour hadn't been extended to the junior. Hand on heart, if I were her dad I would have chosen Ollie over those other two.

When we arrived downstairs, Ollie was in the parlour and I glimpsed him before he was aware of me. He was gazing into the embers, lost in thought, and I was struck by how much of a kid he still was. If Bel did marry him, I thought, he would suffer as much as I would. Seeing me in the doorway, his little face lit up and I realised that he was the only one there that evening whom I was genuinely pleased to see.

The new vicar was an affable enough man of middle years, broad-shouldered and clean-shaven, his face of folds and pleats like a good-quality garment – at your service but without servility; on the contrary, durable, deceptively strong. Bel had said he was new, and I didn't dare ask what had happened to the previous incumbent. Who, I wondered, had replaced Saunders at All Hallows? This one was happy with small talk (his move from Suffolk, the spring weather in London, the food on his plate), during which Bel never once looked my way – nor indeed Ollie's, as far as I could see. She did the talking for the three of us; Ollie said nothing, and I didn't take in much of the conversation but – shattered – let it roll over me.

Not until we had finished dining and were in the parlour did the vicar remark that Ollie hadn't taken Communion the previous week. His tone was kindly: could he be of any help?

Ollie looked awkward, but that was nothing new. I saw in Bel's glance that the vicar's observation had registered as news. She would have been elsewhere, then, at the time: probably at chapel at the palace. And now here was the vicar doing his rounds, gathering a lost lamb to return him to the fold. Bel nudged a plate of dates in his direction; smiling in gratitude, he shook his head, patted his gut, although to me he looked perfectly trim. And now the smile was for Ollie, along with an inclining of the head to offer a listening ear. Ollie, being Ollie, didn't instantly accept, so we sat there in silence, and somewhere in the fog of my exhaustion I felt a twinge of annoyance that he couldn't do the simplest thing without being ushered like a child. *Just say something*, I snapped at him, inside. *That's how it is – someone speaks and you speak back.*

And then he did. 'Seems weird,' he ventured, doubtful,

shooting the vicar a wary but intense glance like a fingertip laid on a forearm: his demeanour earnest, confiding: *You with me?*

By the look of it, the vicar wasn't. Nor, for that matter, was I. The vicar inclined his head in the opposite direction: he was here to lend an ear, and if the first one hadn't worked, he had another.

Ollie swallowed his Adam's apple. 'Because I read in the Bible—'

'You've been reading the Bible?' The vicar was impressed, as if Ollie were a star pupil.

Ollie didn't deny or qualify it, which probably meant yes.

The vicar asked, 'Here?'

'Oh no,' Bel piped up, amused, as if it barely needed saying that this wasn't a house of books. This was a house of learning for its three apprentices, but not book-learning.

The vicar turned back to Ollie for clarification, which duly he provided: 'When it was in the church.'

'That would be the *English* Bible, then?'

Presumably yes, although in the absence of any affirmation there was merely a mumble. 'Sometimes I'd go into the church to try to help my reading ...'

I felt faintly irked: he wasn't in this household to read.

'We have a reader,' the vicar announced, smiling expansively, bestowing approval.

But Ollie fought shy of that claim. 'Try to be.' He was shrinking, shaking it off, and I felt a little ashamed of my unkindness, my impatience with him.

'A reader of the Bible, no less.'

Ollie sniffed. He seemed unsure of what exactly he was being asked to confirm or deny, or why.

I wondered how much longer this had to go on. I was tired; it was late.

The vicar mused, 'Pattern books, Oliver, I'd understand – but the Bible? That's for men of the cloth – a different kind of cloth,

I mean.' He twinkled. 'Whenever you want to know what's in the Bible, come and ask me,' and with a sly, merry glance at Bel, 'And whenever I want a jacket, I'll come to you.'

Ollie looked mortified at being talked to like a five-year-old, and Bel's smile was fixed because there was now no mistaking that this was a reprimand. Ollie was being put in his place – or his place as the vicar deemed it – and my hackles rose in his defence.

The vicar returned to the original matter. 'But "weird", you say?'

Ollie blinked. 'In the' – as if he shouldn't say it – 'Bible.' He wasn't sure he should cite the Bible, which had been established as the vicar's domain, but the vicar was confirming it and encouraging him: 'Bible, yes,' *happy to be of help.*

'About the bread.'

'Bread, yes.' A smile. *Go on.*

'He – Christ – said, "This is my body."' Bashful to be quoting Christ, or perhaps mentioning a body.

'That's right.'

Probably rather impolitely, I reached for the dates and helped myself. If I was going to have to sit here, I might as well eat.

'He said, "Do this" – break the bread, eat it . . . ' Ollie paused to check if he and the vicar were agreed on that.

The vicar nodded. '"In remembrance of me", yes.'

Ollie mumbled a paraphrase: 'When I'm gone, eat the bread and remember me, because it'll be like I'm here.'

'"I *am* here",' corrected the vicar, easily. '"This *is* my body",' he repeated.

Ollie nodded as if taking that in, or trying his best. But what he said – slowly, struggling – was 'It wasn't, though, was it. When he said, "This is my body", it wasn't.'

The vicar frowned, lost, and he wasn't the only one. I stifled a yawn.

'Because there he was,' said Ollie, 'in his body. Sitting there in the chair or whatever. And the bread was separate.'

'Chair?'

Bel cut in – 'Ollie' – and indicated the fire, which he then attended to. But unfortunately that didn't stop him talking. 'So he must've meant "This bread will be my stand-in when I'm gone."'

I tried but failed to catch Bel's eye; she should be bringing the evening to a close.

The vicar said, 'Well, he meant what he said, Oliver. And what he said – as you know, because you've read it – was "This *is* my body."'

'Yeah, but I'm not sure.'

I assumed we were going to suffer an explanation, but there was no more.

The vicar leaned forward. 'You're not sure that he meant what he said? I can't imagine you're claiming that Our Lord was lying.' He sounded genuinely puzzled.

Ollie swallowed. 'Well ...' but again, nothing more, and through the fug of my weariness I was beginning to recognise that this wasn't good. Bel's gaze eluded mine once more.

The vicar did a fair job of not looking scandalised, and repeated the quotation for him, his enunciation slow and gentle: '"This is my body."' Not complicated, I took him to mean. Beautifully simple, in fact. *Black's white*, I thought, distantly.

And Ollie almost laughed, exasperated. 'I know, but it was a bit of bread. So, I mean ...' but he didn't elucidate, just gawped at the vicar.

Thankfully, the vicar didn't seem worried, trotting out the usual – *ours not to reason why*, *all part of the wonder* – before turning, chattily expansive. 'Well, I'll tell you how I always see it. See Miss Jones, here.'

Intriguingly, Ollie wouldn't acknowledge that he did; he wouldn't quite look at her, staring eagerly at the priest instead. Bel overcompensated, making a little show of offering herself up for whatever it would be, although not without some unease, I sensed.

242

'See Miss Jones?' The vicar was pleased with himself; he had said it with something of a showman's flourish.

Ollie now conceded that he did.

'She's wearing a dress, of course, and is there a colour to this dress?'

Ollie's pause said, *You have to ask?* But apparently the vicar did. 'Yes,' Ollie allowed, with a hint of snippiness at being treated again as a five-year-old.

Delighted, the vicar asked, 'What colour is this dress?'

No reply.

'Oliver? The colour: it's . . . ?'

Ollie shrugged a refusal to play along, but then did. 'Brown.'

I wondered what he was playing at, but Bel laughed. 'We have this problem with him, Father. He often can't see green, sees it as brown, and that's not ideal for a tailor, and, well, if we had known . . . '

If they had known, then what? They wouldn't have taken him on? Did Ollie know that?

'Green, then,' Ollie snapped. Either he hadn't known, or he didn't appreciate it being broadcast.

Bel held up her hands, huffy in return: *I'm merely saying.* 'He's always going to need help,' she told the vicar. Rather cruelly, I thought.

The vicar seemed unperturbed, and continued. 'But it *has* a colour, yes? It's a dress, but it also has a colour. There's more to it than being just a dress. It can't ever be just a dress: it is also, at the same time, *more* than that, *other* than that. It's one thing, but it's also something else.'

Ollie looked nonplussed, as did Bel and no doubt I. Faintly, as if he didn't believe he had to, he said, 'But that's different.'

'Is it?' Evidently the vicar didn't think so. He sounded triumphant.

With reluctance, Ollie said, 'Well, yes, because the colour isn't separate. You can't hold the colour – alone – in your hand. But Jesus could hold that bread.'

To me, that seemed fair enough, but after a pause the vicar said, brightly, 'I shouldn't worry. It's often the simplest thing that confounds us. I wonder whether some instruction would be advisable. You leave it with me' – as if Ollie had requested it – 'and I'll see what I can do.'

For the rest of the evening we were back to small talk, Bel's and the vicar's. Ollie and I sat it out, until at long last it was all over. I had never been so glad to head to bed. I was in a truckle beside Bel's, on the understanding that the following day I would leave and find lodgings. I had fully expected to lie there wallowing in dejection, but in the event I was out like a light.

21

Nice and Neat

In the morning, she flounced off to work, leaving me to see myself out, which stung but was also at the same time something of a relief.

I needed to get to Whitehall, to try to return to the laundry as if for good. I had been told to see myself back and now I was going to attempt it, almost a year later, hoping and praying that no one in the laundry would ask awkward questions. Even if I had been replaced, the imminent royal birth could well mean that the laundry would welcome yet another pair of hands; and if Mrs Fox could find work for me, she'd find the wages.

First, though, I had to find a bed somewhere, because however it might turn out with Mrs Fox, I would need somewhere to lay my head that night. From the river, Whitehall looked to be filling up fast. When the barge eventually reached the head of the queue and managed to moor, I set off with no great hope to the Wiltons', shouldering my way through a festive gathering at the Kings Street gatehouse. Dozens of well-wishers were awaiting news of the arrival of the first royal baby in a generation; there had been none since the king, who had grown up – mostly – and already been dead for well over a year.

At the Wiltons', it was as I had feared: no joy – my place in the bed taken, no doubt by a laundress to some visiting lady or other; but as luck would have it, another had unexpectedly just been vacated next door at the widow Horenbolt's, and the Wiltons were happy to vouch for me.

That done, it was time to face the laundry, where Mrs Fox crowed, 'Well, look who it isn't!' to which I gave a quick rendition of the tale of the sick relative, embellished with children who had needed looking after. I made it clear that I was throwing myself on her mercy: was my position still open? She said it was, and asked me nothing, instead telling me, hands on hips, what had happened while I had been away. Kay had lost her two girls. 'St Swithun's, last.' Almost a year back. 'The sweat.' The sweat: *Bonny at breakfast, dead by dinner.* Horribly, this was just as Kay appeared in the doorway, oblivious as far as I could tell to what had just been said and on the cusp of greeting me, so that this was no moment to offer my condolences.

But when would be? That first day back, I barely paused for breath let alone for a quiet moment with Kay; and by the end of it, I felt as if I had been there for a month. The laundry was besieged. Visitors to whom royal favour was extended – or so they claimed – were sending their servants scurrying to hover on our threshold, each in his own distinctive fug of some faraway house built of brick or stone or timber, near woodland, water or scrub. They tried to make light of their various requests: could we laundresses just soak this, scrub that, dry this, press that? It wasn't their fault; however well prepared, not everything travels well or stores well in damp riverside rooms, and anyway, disasters happen – spillages and leaks – so that with the best will in the world the odd spot wash or dunking is needed.

Mrs Fox dealt with each of them either damningly (*We're up to our eyes*) or grudgingly (*Put it over there and don't come back before Friday*) or bountifully (*Leave it with me and I'll see what I can do*). These brush-offs and favours were meted out according to no measure that I could fathom. What was clear was that she was loving every minute. 'This past year,' she chirped to me, 'it's been one thing after another: coronation, wedding, a big Christmas, and now this . . . ' Court was bursting at the seams not just because of the visitors, she said, but the new staff, the nurserymaids and cradle-rockers, 'And because they're privy staff' – a jerk of her head towards the queen's apartment – 'their laundry falls to us, and there's a lot of it.' She gave me a dark look. 'Wouldn't surprise me if they've been storing it up for us. News comes that the queen's expecting, and for months on end every nurserymaid in the land is stuffing away her dirty laundry in the hope it'll end up in our tubs.' She got her own back by displaying items for our derision – 'Just look at this!' – and the pourer of cold water that she was, she had an eye for the most incriminating piece. The maligned garment might be too fancy – bristling with self-regarding stitches – or drab, faded, uncared-for: either too good or not good enough, but sometimes – better still, worst still, best of all, the real finds – committing both sins at once.

Even though the baby had yet to arrive, the laundry resounded with the patter of tiny feet – those of Mr Hobbes, scurrying around crates and boxes of gifts, cramming and stacking them into nooks and crannies as they kept on coming. Ballast, it looked like: the laundry like a hold. We were setting sail into the future and Mr Hobbes was fastidiously protecting us against a rough passage. Whenever I turned around, more had arrived: candles close-packed, nun-like in their conformity; lotions and potions separating in stoppered jars and pots; soaps silk-wrapped, ribbon-tied, stippled with lavender heads. And of course baby clothes, made of cambric and wrapped in holland: soft packages that we laundresses would tease open with a laundress-clean touch, to find lying there with the repose of a closed eyelid a baby garment stitched with sea horses and starfish, perhaps, or daisies and poppies. Bats and balls, owls and robins, towers and ladders, swans and sailboats, piglets and lambs, beetles and butterflies, all in silks of blackberry, rose, sage, white willow. Anything and everything you would find in England if you were giant enough to stretch out across the country and roll up woodlands, pick up windmills, flick drawbridges with your fingertips.

There was already more clothing than any baby could ever need. Enough to clothe all the infants of England. Most of those garments would never go near the royal baby, I thought: this royal baby wouldn't know it was born, and most of these clothes would never see the light of day.

So many people in and out of the laundry, but no Bel. I bided my time, but after three or four days I asked after her, making sure to sound casual, and Mrs Fox said she was due on some errand that remained unspecified. 'Needs to get her skates on, because we'll be waking up to bells if not tomorrow then any day now. By all accounts that little mite was kicking up a storm at Christmas, revelling with the best of 'em; he won't be hanging on in there much longer.'

The queen had already been in her confinement for some time; she had gone early, which Mrs Fox and Kay agreed had been for the best. *At her age*, no one said. But Mrs Fox did say, 'May the Good Lord be gentle with her,' adding, 'She's a good size,' which I took to mean big until she specified, 'Nice and neat.' She said, 'It's always a bit of a business, isn't it, but small helps and it'll be no problem because this little prince will be a toughie, just like Mum.'

And Dad? Dad, it seemed, was off on some kingly business somewhere or other in the Low Countries: good job, too, said Mrs Fox, because he'd done his bit and was best off out from under our feet. Ladies' business, said Mrs Fox, should be left to the ladies.

Then came the usual old story of the queen having been blessed, of it having been a bumpy ride but having turned out for the best. Her time had come. She had kept the faith and the good Lord had rewarded her.

Remiss of him, though, I thought, not to have rewarded Kay for all the years she'd worked her fingers to the bone to provide for her little girls' keep.

The talk of Mum and Dad gave me the opportunity to ask about the aunt: did they think the princess would be coming to court? But my fellow laundresses were barely able to remember that she existed – *Oh! The princess* – and it was clear this was no affectation. She had become an irrelevance, it seemed. Or, worse, she had become ridiculous, to judge from Mrs Fox's heavenward flick of the eyes. Ridiculous that she had ever been regarded as a princess? Or ridiculous that she had ever been regarded as a threat? Anyway, to them she was far away, and the trouble in which she might have had some involvement was long over. Ridiculous, then, perhaps, to have feared a girl of dubious lineage and her raggle-taggle of ill-favoured, sour-grapes servants somewhere out in the sodden west.

Another week, and still no Bel: no baby, and no Bel. Was it anger with me that was keeping her away, or indifference? And which would be worse? But it might be neither: I might well be neither here nor there, as far as she was concerned. I had to hold my nerve, and it wasn't as if I hadn't had practice at that, of late: me, Woodstock-trained in waiting. But her absence was a constant presence for me, and I jumped with every opening of the laundry door.

Doors all over Whitehall were busy. It wasn't only the unborn prince who was revelling. People were coming and going at all hours and, from the look of them, getting up to all sorts. The three girls in my room – whoever they were; I never did find out – were coming back in the small hours, merry, tripping over themselves and one another; and then, well before dawn, carts were trundling up Kings Street, supplies struggling to keep up with demand for firewood and candles. Everywhere I went at Whitehall, staircases and passageways rang with high jinks. Whilst the cat was away – in her confinement – the mice would play. In fact, real mice were becoming a problem: in the mornings on my way into work I had to pick my way around the boxes and cases of people awaiting adjudication of disputes over rooms, and squatting and scratching among all that luggage were lapdogs, which sent the palace cats into sulks.

In the laundry, I was on my guard against telltale flashes across the floor. Kay, too, I tiptoed around, desperate to acknowledge her loss but cringing from ambushing her with sentiment that could only fail to measure up. Then one day when we were working side by side, pressing tablecloths, I took the plunge, spoke her name to open up a moment in which she turned unsuspectingly to me and I made myself do it: said Mrs Fox had told me about the girls and I was so sorry. She smiled sadly, as she must have learned to do, and, turning back to her work, simply remarked that God gives and God takes away.

2 2

Bowls of This and That

There was no word of Bel for twelve long days, until Mrs Fox despaired, 'Where on earth is our Bel?' and Kay said she had glimpsed her, some days back, having dealings with the Lennoxes. The following afternoon, when I was busy scrubbing a collar, Mrs Fox exclaimed, 'Look who's graced us with her presence,' and I glanced up to see that she had been addressing Bel. Bel's eyes met mine, and she mustered a dutiful smile, a dignified nod, and my heart lurched towards her of its own animal accord even as I was thinking she would be a hard nut to crack.

She did whatever she had come to do — I kept myself to myself — and then she left for the riverside steps. I hurried to do the same under the guise of heading to the kitchen garden for some rosemary. As soon as we were outside, I ventured a remark on the weather — so cold for April — but was slapped down by a faint hitch of her eyebrows: *If you say so.* There were to be no pleasantries, then — not that mention of a howling east wind was exactly that. I shouldn't lose heart, I told myself. Chin up. Because here she was, and at least we were speaking, after a fashion. It was a start.

Keeping pace with her across the courtyard, buoyed up to

be in her company, I went instead for something innocuous, merely repeating what everyone else was saying. 'It's hard, all this waiting, isn't it.' For the birth of the prince, I meant, and she knew it but she answered back, 'Waiting's fine if you know it'll all turn out all right in the end,' and really, I should have seen that one coming.

It annoyed me, though, because even if we were in fact talking about what we were pretending to talk about, the safe delivery of the prince was far from a given. So I braved it, with my voice lowered. '*Will* it be all right, do you think?' A fair question, I thought, of an ageing queen, delicate in health at the best of times and with hips that were by no stretch of the imagination child-bearing; surely it was no disloyalty to admit to concern.

But no, she would admit nothing: her look said, *Oh ye of little faith*, and so there we were again with me as naysayer, shrivelled of heart and narrow of mind. Which had me retaliate, overstepping the mark and alluding to her own mother. 'Yes, but, well, you more than most would know . . .' Her own mother, dead in childbed; she would know this was what I meant.

Even that, though, was water off a duck's back. 'This is a queen,' she said.

But a queen is as mortal as any other woman, as we both knew, having spent months sifting the dresses of dead queens. And anyway, our last king, the boy-king, had been christened as his mother lay dying.

But it had come to this: whatever I said, she would claim the contrary. Black's white. Already, I felt exhausted; I might as well give up before I started. But that was what she wanted, so I persisted as we headed down the cloister. 'And when we have our new little heir,' I kept it conversational, 'what happens, I wonder, to the old one?'

'Which old one?'

For a second, my nerve failed me and I didn't dare mention the princess, instead gesticulating nowhere in particular: back where I had been, the gesture might have meant. Woodstock. Then she did get it – 'Oh!' – but she was dismissive. 'Married off.'

Was that why the princess was being summoned? Carefully does it, I warned myself. 'You think so?' As if I were curious only in passing.

'Well, I imagine so.'

She didn't actually know. I swallowed my disappointment.

'It's what they usually do, isn't it.' She was determinedly offhand.

I made a non-committal sound. If she didn't actually know, I wasn't interested in discussing it.

'It's what princesses are for. Marrying off.'

'This one, though?' And I meant it: half-princess, suspected traitor and heretic; who in the world would have her?

She tutted. 'Oh, but there'll be someone, abroad somewhere, won't there.'

'How awful,' and that, too, was genuine, spoken before I could stop myself. I didn't think of myself as caring that much about the princess – I had never warmed to her – but nor did I like to think of her living out her days in a diplomatic liaison in some distant principality.

Bel shrugged – this new wised-up little Bel, as she wanted me to see her – as if to say this was the price of being a princess. 'They're only ever half married anyway, aren't they. They can just live in some other palace, or the other half of it.'

I wasn't having that, and reminded her, 'Princesses have to have heirs, and they can't half do that.'

Even that, though, she wanted to belittle, giving me an arch look that said: *Oh, I don't know* . . . And I should have seen that coming (*Some things just have to be done, don't they*). I'd had enough, so I gave up and asked her how Ollie was doing, and she could make of that what she would. Inadvertently, though, it seemed, I had hit on something: she did have something to say about Ollie. She halted and, with an indulgent light to her eye, told me, 'He's at the bishop's.'

I couldn't for the life of me think what she meant: was this some London expression, some court expression? But she was saying how the new vicar – good as his word – had been to the bishop with the business about the bread, and the bishop had offered to help Ollie understand, and a couple of days ago he had been invited to the bishop's palace.

'Ollie?' I couldn't hide my astonishment.

'I know!' She was tickled by the incongruity of it. Her father had gone along with him, she said.

And thank goodness for that, because Ollie unsupervised in a bishop's palace, glaring tongue-tied from beneath his fringe? Not that her funny little father at the bishop's was all that much more imaginable.

She was enjoying telling the tale: man and boy waited on hand and foot, servants in and out with bowls of this and that, to which she did a kind of dance, a sway from side to side to depict those bowls being proffered left and right, and for a moment she was the Bel of a year ago and my heart lightened. 'Treated like royalty,' she said.

Ollie favoured, and not for the first time. But by the sound of it, her pride in this particular favouring was as if for a little brother.

'And did he?' I asked her.

She was nonplussed.

'The bishop, help.'

'Oh.' She turned pensive. 'Well, you know Ollie.'

Not half as well as you do.

He was staying on, she said, for a few days, as a guest of the bishop: in the bishop's gatehouse, in some style. The bishop had taken him under his wing, she said: he had told her father that Ollie was really bright.

'Ollie?' That was low, for a cheap laugh – which, to my surprise, it got me. But in truth, what did I know of Ollie? He had certainly done a lot better against that vicar than I could ever have managed.

She said, 'Likes a debate, the bishop.'

Yes, but probably only one that he can win.

'And it's a kind of schooling, I suppose, for Ollie, at the bishop's, which has always been his dream.'

She knew his dreams.

Her father wasn't best pleased, though, she told me, to have one fewer pair of hands at such a busy time. 'But, well, you don't argue with a bishop, do you.'

I remembered what I was here for, and took my chance, took a run at it. 'And you? Still go up to the queen, these days?' Ollie to a bishop, Bel to a queen: much of a muchness, or so I had hoped, but she shut down on me, shrugged me off. What did that shrug mean? Sometimes? Soon?

Scrabbling to fill the chasm that had opened between us, I burbled again about how I'd gone to see the princess most days, but this was met with a deliberately blank look – *Bully for you* – to make clear there would be no talk between us of my Woodstock days. Like a headless chicken I kept going, although swerving and backtracking to offer up that the princess had been hard to warm to, that I hadn't quite trusted her. Which got me another hard stare – *Goes without saying* – and crushingly we were back where we had started. She turned into the passage to the riverside with a cursory goodbye.

Had she not turned up at the widow Horenbolt's door the following morning, I don't know how I would have tried to patch things up between us. Not that she seemed to have come to make amends: she declined to join me inside the house, stayed outside the porch under a gull-coloured sky. It was eye-wateringly early; I had had to wrap up in a nightgown when called to the door. She was barely better dressed – I glimpsed mere chamlet beneath her cloak – and said she had come to tell me something: Ollie was in the gatehouse. But I already knew that. Ollie, guest of the bishop. Then I realised she had said *Newgate*, not 'gatehouse'. Her mistake, though, because only days ago he had been the bishop's guest and the bishop had liked a debate so why would Ollie now be in prison? Then I recalled that a bishop had been burned. Perhaps Ollie's bishop had been carted off and, in the mayhem, his household and guests along with him. She was saying something about a crowd, and used the word *frighteners*. When she paused, hugging herself against the chill, I doubled back over what she had said, to try to piece it together. The bishop was putting the frighteners on Ollie because Ollie was in with the wrong crowd. But, '*Ollie*? What crowd?'

She frowned at me. 'There *is* no crowd. You know Ollie.'

I tried again. 'But the bishop thinks there's a crowd?'

She snapped, 'How do I know? How do I know what the bishop thinks?'

Not only did I not understand, but I didn't even know what I was allowed to ask. My head was swimming.

In a small climbdown she admitted, 'He probably is a bit impressionable,' specifying, 'Ollie, not the bishop.'

Best, I decided, to start again at the beginning. '*Newgate?*'

Silence, which I took as reluctant confirmation.

I couldn't fathom it. 'But you said he liked him. The bishop, Ollie.'

'Did I?' She looked dazed.

'You said he thinks he's really bright.'

'They'd been debating.'

'So what has Ollie said?'

She was affronted. 'Nothing. He wouldn't say anything. Not to upset anyone. It's *Ollie*,' she insisted, so that I held up my hands, *I hear you*, struck that perhaps we didn't feel so differently about him. He was a sweet lad.

And this problem with the bishop was indeed nothing, I thought, or nothing much, merely some misunderstanding: must be, because it made no sense.

It had her rattled, though. I had never seen her like this, and I truly wanted to help, though what could I do? But no one need do anything, I told myself, because surely it would sort itself out. A tailor's apprentice wouldn't stay in prison for losing an argument with a bishop. Because who cared what apprentices thought? Least of all, surely, a bishop.

As if she had read my thoughts, she said, 'The bishop's just trying to make him see.'

Stupidly, I asked, 'See what?'

'Well *I* don't know!' Calmer, she said, 'To see that he shouldn't just follow the crowd.'

I didn't remind her that there was no crowd. I didn't have to. She concurred. 'He never goes anywhere, you know what he's like,' and then, as if she were appealing to me, 'He's shy. Homesick. Never wanted to be a tailor, wanted to be a lawyer, but . . . ' No money for that. 'Works hard, goes to church, keeps himself to himself. Nothing else. Sits around at home with the dog, and' – she shrugged – '*thinks*.'

Yes, I thought, that was indeed Ollie, and suddenly it was unbearable that he was in Newgate.

I wanted to talk more about it, but she wouldn't be detained; she declined an offer of beer, saying that her father had gone to the bishop and she wanted to be home when he arrived back.

For several days I didn't know if the awful business with Ollie had blown over. I had no idea if Bel's father had had any luck with the bishop; if he had been able to pour oil on troubled water, nor if Ollie had apologised – if that was what was needed – and the bishop was mollified, his mood lifted and attention shifted elsewhere. Bel's agitation stayed with me, though, clawing at my gut.

The long, wet, cold days were dispiriting; even in the drying room, nothing dried. After a week, I went into the laundry at first meagre light and worked until just before dinner, when I packed up without a word to anyone and took a barge through the rain down to St Paul's wharf.

Bel was at home, although not for dinner: there didn't seem to be any dinner, no scent of cooking nor even sight or sound of anyone else in the house save the dog, who heaved himself to his paws to give me a warmer welcome than that from his mistress. Bel looked dreadful; when I exclaimed that I was worried about her, I was speaking the truth. Unconvincingly, she claimed to be fine. We crouched too close for comfort on the cushions at a cold hearth – no offer of any refreshment – with Kit wobbling well-meaningly between us, prevaricating as how best to collapse his old bones to the floor. I asked what I had come to ask: was Ollie home? The answer was that his parents had arrived in the city and were at the jail talking some sense into him.

In the silence that followed, I repeated that I was worried about her, which was easier than saying that I was worried about Ollie, and again came her cheerless claim to be fine. With a lift of her chin, she added, 'I'm always fine,' and my heart sank at an inkling of where this was going. 'Fine before you came along, fine now you've gone. And, you know, before you came along I never dreamt of ... '

A woman. She stopped short, but that was what I took her to mean. This was new. I knocked it back with a tilt of my head worthy of Bluebell. 'So when *did* you dream of it?'

She was taken aback, perhaps not so much to be asked but, I sensed, because she had an answer: I saw it strike her, and I was intrigued. So there was indeed an instance that she held close to her heart. Would she share it with me? Me, of all people. But Bel liked to share treasure – hauling the coronation robe from its heavy bag, proffering the wedding kirtle – or at least with me she did.

258

She might also be tempted to rub my nose in what, in her view, I'd ruined.

I held my breath, and she went ahead: one day that autumn, she said, when we were at the Wardrobe and ready for a break, I had gone out onto the steps a few minutes ahead of her. 'And when I joined you, there you were, hanging about with a couple of the pages, telling them one of your stories,' and despite everything, she smiled at the memory. I was careful to take this exactly in the spirit it was offered, down to the fond if rueful smile, even if I couldn't stop myself from going on to ask, 'What story?'

'Oh, I don't know' — it didn't matter — 'but there you were. And it was then.'

Again I reflected her smile as if this were the essentially rec-ognisable me, regaling lads with stories, when all I could think was that I had never told a story in my life.

There was no invitation to stay to supper, and mindful of the turn of the tide, I left before too long, but not before she had relented to permit a chat. I was grateful for the chance for us to sit together and lose ourselves for a while in innocuous conversation about the state of her father's business, and the dog's increasingly poorly hips and potential remedies.

On my way back to Whitehall, gazing over sullen green water that was no single entity but a truculent congregation of eddies, I thought how I had no particular memory to match hers. All I recalled from that time, back at the beginning, was the sen-sation of my heart in my mouth. Back then, it seemed to me, I had forever been on tenterhooks for the next invitation from her. What had happened with Bel had been my choice — I would never pretend otherwise — but it was she, I felt, who had given me that choice.

And now she made it loud and clear that she didn't trust me: she suspected me, it seemed, of coming back in the hope that we could take up where we had left off. Presumably she thought I had lowered my sights, was prepared to be second best. It was true that our encounters had my heart thrashing like a fish on a hook. I had been naïve to think I could swan back, dip my toe in and feel little or nothing; and, yes, there were moments when I feared I was in over my head. Mere moments, though: they passed, I reminded myself. I knew very well that I had been right to leave. I wouldn't live the lie of being her best friend. And anyway, she herself had said it: I had been gone for almost a year. If I had wanted to come back, wouldn't I have done it sooner? Still, although I hated to admit it, I knew that my purpose was best served if she did think that was what was behind my return.

23

Wash

Another week passed and I had been a whole month away from Woodstock with nothing to show for it: I was no nearer to knowing what, if anything, was planned for the princess, nor even how I might find out.

The royal baby was a month overdue. A miscalculation of dates, apparently. The new due date was end of May.

Spring was similarly elusive: nothing raising its head, or not in expectation of anything good.

Laundry, though, kept on coming. In my half-dreams in the early hours I inhabited some hitherto unknown state whereby if we laundresses failed to keep pace, we would have to lever grime off collars with our fingernails.

The kitchen staff had it worse, though: I heard it said that meals were taking so long to serve to the crowds at the palace that they were running into one another. And rumour had it that throughout Whitehall servants were sleeping in shifts, rolling off one side of a pallet bed as someone else rolled on from the other. Making my way to and from my own bed, I skirted the Kings Street gatehouse, where in place of the gaggle of well-wishers of previous weeks – pleasant ladies with sweet-faced children, and students larking about – there was now an ever-growing crowd dazzled by acrobats and preyed upon by hawkers.

It had been a week since I had seen Bel; by now, surely, Ollie would be back at St Thomas Apostle Street. I went to the kitchens and begged some duck eggs for the dog, then – skipping Mass – travelled downriver on a Sunday, not least because that was when I was more likely to find Bel at home, and if not home then on her way back from church.

She was indeed home: the others were dining at Mrs Wilkinson's, she said, but she had cried off. She accepted Kit's eggs with mumbled thanks, and I realised to my dismay that there had in fact been no progress: Ollie still wasn't back home.

Showing me indoors, she said blankly and as if mid-conversation, 'He'll come to his senses,' which I took to refer to the bishop until she added, 'Because why argue with a bishop?'

Debate was the word she had previously used.

'Did he?' I followed her down the passage to the kitchen. 'Argue?'

'Must have done.'

Perhaps it had been the bishop who had argued with Ollie; but why? What would it matter to a bishop what Ollie thought?

At the kitchen door, she turned to me. 'The bishop says he'll make him a freeman. Says he'll give him forty pounds and set him up in business.'

'Jesus.' Forty pounds would set him up for life. He would be a good prospect.

'City needs men like Ollie: thinkers, keen to learn.' This was quoted with even less enthusiasm than that with which she had received the eggs. 'That forty pounds is there for him when he's ready to leave here, if he keeps out of trouble.' She went ahead into the kitchen. 'Why would you throw that away over a bit of bread?'

'It's not still the business about the bread, surely.'

She put one of the eggs in a pot. 'Well, it's all just words, isn't it, but yes, it's the bread, the' – she cast around – 'the body, the dress or whatever it was.' She was wide-eyed and tremulous in the gloom. 'I mean, why wouldn't you just say it?'

I shivered; it was freezing in there. 'Say what?'

'Whatever it is that he has to say. Forty pounds, if he recants.'

'Recants?'

She was lighting a brazier; I said it again, to her back: 'Recants?' and then, when she didn't respond, 'Since when has Ollie been going around . . . canting?' It was an absurd notion; I almost laughed.

Still nothing.

I paced to shake off the chill but also to try to think, and to right myself, because it was as if I had taken a wrong turn some-where, come through the wrong door. Then it struck me. 'You should take this to the queen.' Me, for once, with a bright idea. What had we been doing, mooching about, perplexed and help-less, when she had the chance of approaching the queen? Because if there was anyone who could go to the queen, it was Bel. And although I couldn't quite see how it would help me if she did, I had a sense it might. Any contact with the queen or her ladies, however vicarious, should be of help to me.

She didn't look up, spoke to the taper. 'I can't broach this with the queen.'

I tamped down the excitement in my throat. 'Yes you can.' There would be a way around it, for her.

She turned to me, but only to explain, as if to a child, 'The queen is in her confinement. She has to stay untouched by' – she considered how best to phrase it – 'the business of the world.'

But she was busy signing death warrants, and what was that if not worldly business? Moreover, she'd want to know about one of her bishops behaving bizarrely. *Cat's away.* 'And anyway, it's you,' I urged. 'You're you,' and there was no one who didn't love Bel, who didn't trust her and want the best for her.

And she's her, I could've said: the queen of gestures. The princess was as given to gestures as was her half-sister, but the princess's were calculated, calibrated, as if she were billing the recipients, whereas the queen's had something of the bold colours in which she decked herself. The queen's life story was the time-honoured one of riches to rags to riches, if without the actual rags. I could have said to Bel, Think of when she first came into London as queen and rode to the tower, knelt to that long-captive boy and raised him up. Think of her in Guildhall speaking to the people of London, telling them she was as a mother to them, while on the opposite bank Wyatt's men were calling for her to give up and stand down. Think of the plain gold band on her finger. She was Queen of England and Molly Milkmaid and everything in between, her timeless story coloured bright and deep like a book of hours, peopled with ladies and knights and stern but kindly confessors, and although the execution of the little cousin was, admittedly, a blot, it was part of the same picture of heroes and villains to which the ending was always the same: a happy one, a triumph, the dragon slain and peace coming full circle to reign over the land. This was a queen who would love a little-boy-lost returned to the fold. It seemed to me that this was a queen, if ever there was one, to whom to plead.

I stayed that afternoon and over bread and pickles we decided Bel would write a letter to Mrs Clarencieux to explain what was happening to Ollie and ask for her intercession. Bel was reluctant, but I got her to see that it was the best we could do.

There was no way for the letter to be given directly to Mrs C; it would have to be slid beneath the door to the chamberers' room, to be found by her or discreetly passed in her direction by one of the other ladies. From then on, the matter would be in her hands:

it would be her decision as to whether to raise it with the queen. If she chose to lose the letter, then so be it. Regrettable though that would be, the worst Bel would incur was Mrs C's displeasure.

I didn't know what Bel was going to write, and didn't dare ask. Perhaps she herself didn't know – she would never have written anything like that before. I left her to it, took Kit down to the gardens at the Vintners' Hall – open on Sundays – where it wasn't hard to idle away the best part of an hour, and when I arrived back at the house, Bel emerged pale-faced from her father's office with the letter written, sealed, addressed. From years of writing bills to Mrs C, she knew how to write that name I barely knew how to say.

On our journey together to Whitehall, Bel was apprehensive and weary. By the time we arrived at the laundry, only Mr Hobbes was there, on his way into the final supper service in hall and promising to have something sent in to us ('Asparagus this evening, a little bird told me'). We settled in the drying room to warm up, and in no time the asparagus was delivered, along with potted meats and good white bread.

We kept to small talk as we ate, then busied ourselves clearing away, rinsing and stacking the various dishes. When there was nothing more to do, we sank companionably enough into cushions at the hearth and stared into the embers.

By the strike of nine, the daily life of the palace had subsided, but Bel was slumped on those cushions and looked unequal to the task, so I volunteered to take the letter up to the door. It made no odds if I were the one to do it; I was as light-footed as she, and if by any chance I was found on that staircase, I had a more plausible excuse for being there. The queen's premature retreat into her confinement meant that her laundry supplies were running low, and we laundresses had been at the ready for a week or two; I could simply say that I'd thought I'd heard a call. I was happy to do it; and we were so nearly there.

So it was me who crept up there to discover the flaw in our plan: the letter wouldn't fit under the door. There I was, quiet as a mouse in a palace riotous with them, scrabbling about on my knees, jabbing the letter at the gap, scratching at the seal in the hope of flattening it. After a minute or two of that, the door opened without warning, sending me sprawling.

In the doorway were a lady's skirts, and at a distance was the voice of another: 'Suse? What is it?'

Too rapidly back onto my feet, I saw stars. The voice came again, 'Is everything all right?' and the figure in front of me drew breath to express doubt, but perhaps remembered something of me – laundress, pinholder – and anyway more pressing was my buckling there on the threshold. Behind her came a run of footsteps and more utterances of concern, and I was being taken hold of and supported.

Lost in the fuss was the matter of who exactly I was and what I was doing there. Perhaps each lady assumed the other had established the fact, and anyway I was only some girl, and a faintly recognisable one at that, a servant who might well have been crouching at the door in the hope of the sound of the miracle that was this child-bearing queen.

I was hauled up and taken along by those ladies, my mind blank; I would have to explain why I had been there, but at that point there was nothing inside me except the hiss of blood in my ears. The matting of the chamberers' room streamed away beneath my feet, and then we were through a doorway I knew to be the queen's.

The smell of all those bodies shut up for so long in that over-heated and tight-shuttered room came swarming around my head, funnelling up my nose and down my throat so that again I was sinking to my knees; but a lady swooped as if to break my fall, her own particular odour blurting from beneath her skirts and arms as she hunkered there and reached for me. Taking

266

my hands in hers, on which were jewels as globular as beasts' eyes, she spoke soothing words, which was when I knew this was the queen. 'Look at you, green around the gills,' said that croaky voice.

I braved a sip of a breath, and already the stink was diminished by acquaintance and less able to revolt me. The queen was saying she had been lucky, because she had suffered no faintness or sickness. 'Nothing, thank the Lord,' was directed over my head to the ladies, who murmured appreciatively, and for me came a tender admonishment: 'You shouldn't be working this late. You all work so hard for me, but did our Holy Mother have servants? If it were up to me, I'd creep off to some stable to do God's work. But no one's going to let me do that.'

Murmurs of amusement from the ladies.

She rocked back onto her haunches, which gave me space in which to tip forward properly onto my knees.

'I'm not afraid,' she told me, and she didn't sound it, 'of this extraordinary work that God gives we ladies so that we can know His love.' With a squeeze of my limp hand, she added, 'He blessed me with a baby in the first month of my marriage and sent me word then and there, pity my dear patient husband.' Her husband had been banished from the conjugal bed, she meant, a mere month into the marriage, and on the word, she would have us believe, of some visiting angel. 'Let's get you a drink,' she said, insisting to the ladies that she herself fetch the beer, and then she was up and off across the room, which gave me the opportunity for a furtive glance at those who had helped me. I wanted to offer my gratitude but couldn't catch an eye among the six or seven ladies who stood with hands folded and heads lowered as if to flatten themselves into the walls on which the buxom figures in the tapestries looked by comparison more alive.

Somewhere across the room, beyond the reach of my averted gaze, the queen poured the beer, and what I saw of her as she returned was bare feet scuttling over the matting towards me like a pair of creatures. Those feet, kicking up her hem, made her more naked to me than if she were entirely unclothed. Recoiling, shifting my gaze, I remembered only just in time to focus not on her but on the cup that she handed me. That hand: what a mess those clustered gemstones could make of a lip. Dutifully, I drank, but down in the malt darkness of the cup I was struck that although my gaze had risen as far as her belly, I had seen nothing of note: no bump. My own stomach somersaulted: was it all over and done with, then? But no, because she had been speaking hopefully of the labour to come. This baby hadn't yet been born. I despaired of myself to have been granted a glimpse of the heavily pregnant queen yet having failed to see that bump, and tried again from under my lowered lids, willing her to turn to a more revealing angle, which she then did, but to no avail, and I had a dizzying sense of the palace beneath me, all those nobles bloated by the endless meals, and the crowds at the gates too close around their campfires. The baby for whom they had already waited more than a month, and whom they were expecting tonight or tomorrow and certainly by the end of the week, was, I now understood, still months away.

The queen was saying kindly that I should go back down, and the soft gloved hands of the ladies were relieving me of the cup and helping me to my feet to send me on my way. Hold steady, I told myself, and stay calm, because as soon as I was down the stairs to Bel, all would be revealed. Bel would put me straight: there would be a simple explanation (*Oh, but queens always ...* and didn't I know?). Obviously there was something I had failed to grasp but which for Bel would be so commonplace that she hadn't thought to mention it. She would be sympathetic, apologetic for my needless confusion.

Back downstairs, though, Bel jumped up at the sight of me, alarmed, and I was ashamed that I hadn't thought how she had been left sitting there while I had been gone for so long, and then it was me doing the explaining and soothing: yes, I had been discovered, and yes, I had been taken into the queen's room, but – truly, honestly – everything was fine. So there we were, she and I, a respectful pace apart, trilling at each other – *What happened, what happened? It's fine, it's fine* – before she asked after the letter: that was fine too, yes? I had smuggled it in there?

I forced a smile to my face as my insides burned, because how on earth had I forgotten about the letter? The whole purpose of my going up there: how could I possibly have forgotten that? My heart skidded to a halt, but some other part stepped into the breach and covered for me as I floundered. A voice in my throat came up with the necessary assurances to keep her at bay while I snatched at tatters of memory and tried to piece it together: *What had I done with the letter?* It was no more credible to me that I had discarded that letter than if I had left a steaming pile of my own guts up there on the floor.

I didn't have it with me, though, which meant it was up there somewhere, almost certainly on the wrong side of the door: the door that had opened outwards and sent me several steps backwards, no doubt treading it underfoot. I could sneak back up there when Bel had gone and retrieve it, and try again, try harder, try something different to get it beneath that door. I would salvage it, I told myself, I definitely would, and my smiles and assurances had Bel backing off, accepting what I had told her, under the illusion that it was all falling into place as we had planned.

But then from nowhere came a memory of the letter in the hand of one of those ladies, and I could have wept with relief. Shakes began, cascading through me from head to toe and making it so that I couldn't even see straight. I heard, though, Bel's heartfelt apologies: how sorry she was for having put me in a position whereby I had been uncovered. Taking me by the arm, she coaxed me towards the fireside. Lowering myself onto the cushions, I looked into her eyes for the first time since I had come into the room, and with a jolt recalled what I had expected to find there: some acknowledgement of what I had – or hadn't – seen in the royal apartment. I had expected a knowing look from her, allowing me to broach the subject so that she could explain that conspicuous lack of bump (*Oh, that: you don't need to worry about that . . .*).

But she settled across the hearth from me and wondered aloud how long it might be until we heard anything from Mrs C.

Then she touched my forearm. 'You all right?'

I said nothing, because I had no idea how to start. She closed her eyes, said she was tired and would soon make up her bed, and then I understood that I would have to be the one to raise the subject. She detected something of my resolve, though, because, marginally more alert, she asked, 'What?' and then, with mild concern, 'Is everything all right up there?'

What on earth was I to say to that? *Well, you tell me, Bel.*

Her eyes were clear: a blue tint to the whites. She didn't look to be hiding anything.

'Alys?' Her concern was up a notch.

Tentatively, I asked her when she had last seen the queen.

She mused, 'When did I last see her?' and answered in the same tone, 'Couple of weeks ago,' the slight questioning note persisting: why would I want to know?

But if she had to ask, then she had seen nothing to worry her. How could that be? I wouldn't even have known the queen was pregnant had I not already been told.

My mouth dry, I managed, 'To me, she looks a long way off.'

The palace all around us was splitting at the seams, and crowds surging at the gates, but to judge from what I had seen – or hadn't – there would be no royal baby for months, and just what did Bel imagine was going to happen? Incredulous to recall it,

270

awkward at having to raise it, pretending to laugh it off even as I dared to voice it, I reminded her, 'You said everything would be all right.'

This is a queen had been her actual words, and there had been that look: *Oh ye of little faith.*

For a heartbeat, she seemed not to remember, but then she did and, almost bashful, reconsidered; I watched her wonder whether to say – how to say – whatever was coming next.

So here it is, I thought: the explanation. Here it came.

What she said was 'I would have made it all right,' as an admission of some kind, gently said, regretful, and it took me a moment to realise that she had misunderstood. She had thought I was talking about us and what could have been between us, and as remarkable to me as the misunderstanding was the tenderness with which she had spoken. She wanted me to know that had I stayed with her, she – maker and mender – would have done her utmost best by me.

There was a time when I had longed for a life with her, but we would have had to become a pair of spinster silkwomen, living a lie and not a particularly good one, the butt of the odd off-colour joke or remark because nothing was notably amiss in our looks or prospects to account for our lacking husbands. She would have weathered it. Everything was always all right for her, with her family and her house and all the goodwill she was gifted. She had never been on the sharp end of curiosity. If she had chosen to live like that, she would have got away with it, because she could get away with anything. She was always the exception, allowances made for her. But me? I doubted, now, that I would have braved it. For me, a single raised eyebrow was one too many. I could never allow anyone to assume they had the measure of me. I came from nowhere, and could give no one any reason to send me back there. Once an outsider, always an outsider, living life at one remove, watching my own back. There at the hearth with Bel I felt the crushing weariness of what it had taken for me to survive and how down the years it had hardened my heart to bone. She never saw that in me, I knew, and I had loved her for it; but now I understood that she only ever saw what she wanted to see, and for a moment I was more lonely than I had imagined possible.

She said she was going to bed, and I understood it was time for me to head off; we both knew that I wouldn't stay alongside her in the laundry nor invite her back to the widow Horenbolt's. I helped her fetch her eiderdown and together we shook it out, careful all the while not to catch each other's eye, and it was as I was shaking that eiderdown free of its folds that I remembered the queen's coy admission that her husband hadn't shared her bed after their first month of marriage. But the wedding had been almost a year back, I remembered, in the July that had been nothing like a July. If that was when the queen had last slept with her husband, I realised, she could only be a good nine months pregnant or not at all.

Early the next morning, the weather looked as if it would be kind for my journey to Woodstock: the river basted with sunlight, the sky succulent, the air billowing like a laundered tablecloth. Boarding that barge, I was tempted to sit tight, keep going ever further upstream and give the world the slip. No one would know. All anyone would see was a girl at the back of the boat, with a smile whenever a smile was called for. I could turn my face to the sun and let it happen. My dream come true. All I would be leaving was my bag, at Woodstock, stuffed with oddments and cast-offs that had come to me down the years, anything and everything a girl would need to make herself a wife. Someone else might make better use of it, I thought. Damascin, perhaps, who already had my ring: that bag would be a lucky find for her, if she knew to take advantage, although I doubted that. Still, she was young: she'd learn.

In a way, it was neither here nor there if I told what I had or hadn't seen in the queen's apartment, because it would all come out in the wash. No pregnancy, not even an imaginary one, can last forever. But the princess had to know, so that she could be ahead when the queen fell, and could step clear.

That the queen would fall I was certain – her word would never again be trusted – but what I couldn't have known, that morning, was how much longer that would take. She was way off course, but for another couple of years she would drift, her nobles and subjects jumping ship one by one, until she ended up a scuttled husk, a stump, a stone.

I didn't know either – and wouldn't, for several more weeks – that it was already too late for Ollie.

And I don't think it occurred to me that although the flow of the Thames is always one way or the other, there has to be an instant at the point of turn when it is neither. And it was into that instant that I stepped, from bank to barge, with my news that the queen merely imagined herself pregnant while no one dared disbelieve her. I didn't know what Mr Parry would make of it, but I was sure I'd cross that bridge when I came to it.

Historical Note

Charged with conspiracy and about to be escorted to the Tower of London, Elizabeth begged to be allowed to write to the Queen. In what has become known as the 'Tide Letter', she protested her innocence and implored her half-sister to hear her out in person. In this, she was ultimately unsuccessful, but the letter-writing did buy her a little time. The tide had turned before she had finished, so she couldn't be taken to the Tower until the following day.

Elizabeth's prospects were bleak. From the day of the Tide Letter, and for the rest of her sister's reign, staying alive would be pretty much all that she could do. Throughout England, too, it seems to me, there was a collective holding of breath, a praying for the tide of history to turn.

Mere months earlier, it had all started so well. Mary had come unexpectedly to the throne on a wave of popular goodwill. It is said that England likes an underdog, and Mary Tudor had taken a couple of decades of very public kickings. Now, against all the odds, this persecuted and disparaged middle-aged spinster ascended the throne that was, in the eyes of the people, rightfully hers as Henry VIII's elder daughter. All was right with the world after twenty years of strife, it seemed, and England rejoiced. Mary's fundamental mistake was to interpret this goodwill as a mandate to turn back time twenty years and return England to Catholicism.

It has always baffled me that Mary's catastrophic five-year reign and her relentless persecution of the half-sister who then became Elizabeth I has barely stirred the public imagination. It strikes me as a tale ripe for telling. Mary Tudor was England's first-ever ruling queen; and her heir, too, was an unmarried woman. There were conspiracies and rebellions, and the burning of 'heretics' on a scale unprecedented in England. Elizabeth was imprisoned in the Tower, then – when the charge couldn't be made to stick – held in rather bizarre circumstances under house arrest in Oxfordshire. Then came Mary's pitifully protracted delusion that she was pregnant, and the widespread complicity in what could never have been other than a doomed deception. Yet for all the high drama, there is a sense in which time stopped during Mary's reign, and England was suspended – hanging on by her fingernails is how I think of it – because all anyone could do, in the end, was wait for Mary Tudor to die. It seems to me that what Elizabeth endured in this peculiar period, and how she endured it, made her the queen she then became.

The main character in my novel is a fiction, as are her companions and the situation in which they become involved. The sequence and much of the substance of the events depicted in the book, though, are a matter of historical record. Elizabeth did retreat to Ashridge for Christmas 1553; she was ordered back down to Whitehall in February 1554 and then taken to the Tower; from there she was taken to Woodstock and held in a gatehouse under the supervision of the hapless Sir Henry Bedingfield, while her own household, directed by wily Thomas Parry, commandeered the nearby Bull Inn.

As regards the working life of my fictional heroine, it was from Janet Arnold's seminal *Queen Elizabeth's Wardrobe Unlock'd* that I gleaned the following, although of course any errors or inaccuracies are my own: the Pigeons – father and son – kept the Wardrobe of Robe's records during Mary's reign; the Yeoman of the Wardrobe of Robes at this time was a Mr Hobbes; Mary's tailor was a Mr Jones and her silkwoman a Mrs Wilkinson, and fine Spanish needles were indeed made by a black man in Cheapside; Elizabeth at the time of her coronation had a laundress named Elizabeth Smith in her service, and later in her reign employed a laundress named Mistress Twist.

From the same work I learned about the location and organisation of the Wardrobe. The site remains tucked away in the City of London as the enchanting 'Wardrobe Place', although the original buildings were lost in the Great Fire. For other topographical details of London and Whitehall Palace I consulted the Agas map, which is believed to have been created in the early 1560s, just a few years after the period covered in this novel. Huggin Lane, Maidenhead Lane, Blunderbuss Alley, Budge Row and Pissing Alley or Lane are all gone from the City of London but the other streets mentioned in the novel still exist, although all are now lined by modern office blocks. The churches featuring in the novel still stand, with the exception of All Hallows on Bread Street, which was demolished in the nineteenth century.

Laurence/Lawrence Saunders did work for a while at All Hallows on Bread Street, although in actuality he had moved on from there before his death and he was burned in Coventry. His wife and son are my invention. Coincidentally, he was brother to Sabine Johnson of Barbara Winchester's *Tudor Family Portrait* (1955). What happens to Ollie in this novel is based closely on the case of nineteen-year-old apprentice William Hunter, as detailed in *Foxe's Book of Martyrs*.

My invention of Alys and her story arose in part from several intriguing details and comments that I came across during my reading. First, the often-quoted claim by the Venetian ambassador at Mary's court: 'No one comes or goes and nothing is spoken or done [in Elizabeth's household] without the Queen's knowledge.' Then Janet Arnold's observation, in *Queen Elizabeth's Wardrobe Unlock'd*: 'Tailors might be employed in espionage.' She cites a confession regarding the stitching of notes

277

into hosiery, although she states there is no evidence that any tailors working in Mary's Wardrobe of Robes were involved in any such subterfuge. Next, David Starkey's remark in *Elizabeth: Apprenticeship*, his vivid account of Elizabeth's life before her ascent to the throne: 'Women [of Elizabeth's household] schemed and plotted with the best, and the ones who took the most risks were those who had already thrown over the restraints of marriage and family respectability.' He quotes, too, Sir Henry Bedingfield, despairing of Francis Verney that 'if there be a practice of ill, within all England, this Verney is privy to it'. And Starkey is one of several historians to make reference to the mysterious visit(s) of one of Elizabeth's ladies to the French ambassador (in 1556, a little later than I have it); he suggests that these clandestine meetings were to explore the possibility of Elizabeth's escape to France. England's history would no doubt have been very different had she gone.

In the writing of this novel, I found the following publications particularly valuable, although any errors and inaccuracies are my own:

Queen Elizabeth's Wardrobe Unlock'd by Janet Arnold (Leeds, 1988)

'Of Crymsen Tissue: The Construction of a Queen. Identity, Legitimacy and the Wardrobe of Mary Tudor' by Hilary Doda (MA thesis, Dalhousie University, 2011)

'"Ye Shall Have It Clene": Textile cleaning techniques in Renaissance Europe' by Drea Leed, in *Medieval Clothing and Textiles 2*, edited by Robin Netherton and Gale R. Owen-Crocker (Woodbridge, 2006)

'Dressed to Impress' by Maria Hayward, in *Tudor Queenship: The Reigns of Mary and Elizabeth*, edited by Alice Hunt and Anna Whitelock (New York, 2010)

Tudor London Visited by Norman Lloyd Williams (London, 1991)

The A to Z of Elizabethan London, compiled by Adrian Prockter and Robert Taylor with introductory notes by John Fisher (Lympne and London, 1979)

Elizabeth: Apprenticeship by David Starkey (London, 2000)

If any euer did try this olde sayinge that a kinges worde was more than
a nother mans othe I most humbly beseche your. M. to verefie it in
me and to remeber your last promis and my last demaunde that I
be not codemned without answer wiche it semes that now I am for
that without cause proued I am by your counsel frome you comaunded
to go vnto the tower a place more wonted for a false traitor, than a tru
subiect wiche thogh I knowe I deserue it not, yet in the face of
al this realme apperes that it is proued Wiche I pray god I may dye
the shamefullist dethe that euer any died afore I may mene any suche
thinge and to this present hower I protest afor God (who shal iuge
my trueth whatsoeuer malice shal denis) that I neuer practised
conciled nor cosented to any thinge that mioth be preiudicial
to your parson any way or daungerous to the state by any
mene and therfor I humbly beseche your maiestie to let
me answer afore your selfe and not suffer me to trust your
counselors yea and that afore I go to the tower (if it
be possible) if not afor I be further codemned howbeit I
trust assuredly your highnes wyl giue me leue to do it afor
I go for that thus shamfully I may not be cried out on as now I shal
be yea and without cause let coscienc moue your hithnes to
take some bettar way with me than to make me be codemned
in al mens sigth afor my desert knowen. Also I most humbly
beseche your higtnes to pardon this my boldnes wiche
innocecy procures me to do together with hope of your natural
kindnes wiche I trust wyl not se me cast away without deserte
Wiche what it is I wold desier no more of God but that you
truly knewe. Wiche thinge I thinke and beleue you shal
neuer by report knowe vnles by your selfe you hire. I haue
harde in my time of many cast away for want of comminge
to the presence of ther prince and in late days I harde my
lorde of Somerset say that if his brother had bine suffered
to speke with him he had neuer suffered but the
perswasions wer made to him so gret that he was brogth
in belefe that he coulde not liue safely if the admiral liued
and that made him giue his consent to his dethe thogh
thes parsons ar not to be copared to your maiestie yet I
pray god as euil perswatios persuade not one sistar again
the other and al for that the haue harde false report and
not harkene to the trueth knowen

theyfor ons agam with humblenes of my hart, bicause I am not
suffern to bow the knees of my body I humbly crave to speke
with your highthms wiche I wolde not be so bold to desier
if I knewe not my selfe most clere as I knowe my selfe most
tru. and as for the traitor Wia: he might parauentur writ
me a lettar but on my faithe I neuer receued any from him and
as for the copie of my lettar sent to the freche kinge I pray
God confonud me eternally if euer I sent him word message
take or lettar by any menes, and to this my truth
I wil stande til my dethe

I humbly crane but only one worde
of answer fro your selfe

your highnes most faithful subiect that
hathe bine from the beginninge and wylbe
to my ende Elzabeth

The Tide Letter,
noon, 17 March 1554

If any ever did try this olde sayinge that a kinges worde was more
than a nother mans othe I most humbly beseche your Majestie
to verefie it in me and to remember your last promis and my last
demaunde that I be not condemned without answer and due profe
wiche it semes that now I am for that without cause provid I am
by your counsel from you commanded to go unto the tower a
place more wonted for a false traitor, than a tru subject wiche
thogth I knowe I deserve it not, yet in the face of al this realme
aperes that it is provid. wiche I pray god I may dye the shameful-
lyst dethe that ever any died afore I may mene any suche thynge;
and to this present hower I protest afor God (Who shall judge
my trueth, whatsoever malice shall devis) that I neither practiced,
conciled nor consented to any thinge that might be prejudicial
to your parson any way or daungerous to the state by any mene.
And therefor I humbly beseche your majestie to let me answer
afore your selfe and not suffer me to trust your counselors yea
and that afore I go to the tower (if it be possible) if not afor I be
further condemned, howbeit I trust assuredly your highnes wyl
give me leve to do it afor I goe, for that thus shamfully I may
not be cried out on as now I shall be, yea and without cause. Let
consciens move your highness to take some bettar way with me
than to make me be condemned in al mens sigth afor my desert
knowen. Also, I most humbly beseche your higthnes to pardon

this my boldnes wiche innocency procures me to do togither with hope of your natural kindnis wiche I trust wyl not se me cast away without desert, wiche what it is I wold desire no more of God but that you truly knewe. Wiche thinges I thinke and believe you shal never by report knowe unles by your selfe you hire. I have harde in my time of many cast away for want of comminge to the presence of ther prince and in late days I harde my lorde of Somerset say that if his brother had hime suffer'd to speke with him he had never suffer'd, but the perswasions wer made to him so gret that he was brogth in belefe that he coulde not live safely if the admiral lived and that made him give his consent to his dethe. Thogth thes parsons ar not to be compared to your majestie yet I pray god that evil perswations perswade not one sistar agaynst the other and al for that they have harde false report and not harkened to the trueth.

Therefor ons again kneling with humblenes of my hart, bicause I am not suffer'd to bow the knees of my body I humbly crave to speke with your higthnis wiche I wolde not be so bold to desire if I knewe not my selfe most clere as I knowe my selfe most tru, and as for the traitor Wiat he migth paraventur writ me a lettar but on my faithe I never receved any from him and as for the copie of my lettar sent to the frenche kinge I pray God confound me eternally if ever I sent him word, message, token or lettar by any menes, and to this my truth I wil stande in to my dethe.

I humbly crave but only one worde of answer from your selfe.

Your hignes most faithful subject that hathe bine from the beginninge, and wylbe to my ende. Elizabeth.

Acknowledgements

Many thanks for patience, wise counsel, opportunities, expertise etc: David Kendall, Vincent Kendall Dunn, and Jean Harlow; Antony Topping, at Greene and Heaton; Clare Smith, Zoe Gullen, Charlotte Stroomer, Susan de Soissons, Hayley Camis, and Celeste Ward-Best at Little, Brown; Anna Davis, Jack Hadley, Katie Smart, and Jennifer Kerslake at Curtis Brown Creative; Brendan McLoughlin; Paul Hogan; The Royal Literary Fund fellowship scheme.

ALSO BY SUZANNAH DUNN

The Lady of Misrule

Elizabeth Tilney surprised even herself by volunteering for the job of companion to Lady Jane Grey, imprisoned in the Tower of London after only nine days as queen. All Elizabeth knows is that she's keen to be away from home. And anyway, it won't be for long: everyone knows Jane Grey will go free as soon as the victorious new queen is crowned.

The two sixteen-year-olds, however, couldn't be less compatible. Protestant Jane is an icily self-composed idealist, and Catholic Elizabeth is … anything but. They are only united by their disdain for Jane's seventeen-year-old husband, Guildford Dudley, kept prisoner in a neighbouring tower.

But Elizabeth finds herself drawn into the difficult relationship between the young couple, and when events take an unexpected and dangerous direction, her new-found loyalties are put to the test.

Continue reading for an extract from

The Lady of Misrule

A good Catholic girl was what they'd said they needed, and, seeing as no one knew otherwise, I was trying my hand at being exactly that. And so far – on that first, mid-July, swift-sweet day – I was getting away with it, scurrying behind the Lady Lieutenant through the Tower of London. We were on our way to some lodgings, I thought: somewhere for me to kick off my shoes and lay down my head, fasten some shutters against the belting of London's bells. After two long days on the road, that was as far as I could think, it was all I wanted, and at seventeen I was naïve enough to think that whatever I wanted, I'd get.

Nothing about the unguarded door to which she led me was any different from all the others we'd passed in passageways and courtyards. Not that I'd had time to see much; she wasn't hanging around. Tight-lipped and bustling, she acted as if England's unequivocal proclaiming of the wrong queen, thirteen days before, had been an oversight for which she, with a hasty rejig of household arrangements, could make amends.

Follow me, she'd said at the gatehouse, and diligently I'd done so, almost tripping over myself to keep up, but as far as I was concerned I was under no one's orders. I'd chosen to come, surprising myself as much as anyone else, the evening before, by raising my hand. Me, who usually kept my head well down. Me, who, if truth be told, couldn't have cared less who had been or should be Queen.

The Lady Lieutenant knocked on that unguarded door cursorily before opening it and drawing back, leaving me to go ahead. The walls were silk-hung, the ceiling looked gem-worked and the floor was a welter of honey-coloured carpets, each and every one of the thousands of brush-touches and knots of silk there to honour the occupant of the centrepiece, which was a throne. It was empty, though, and its gold-cloth canopy was being dismantled by a man who was overdressed for the task, the close-stitched pearls of his doublet squeaking against one another as he strained this way and that. His foreshortened steps around the obstacle of the throne gave him a fractious air, and he snatched at the canopy as if it were a prop and the show was over. His every move was thwarted by that expanse of thread-thin gold, which slipped and slid, making him cower and cringe as it threatened to swipe off his jewelled cap.

It was quite a spectacle, but the others in that room weren't paying him the slightest attention. All four of them were standing around a table on which was a leather chest, lid open. Two richly dressed gentlemen, stiff with self-regard, faced a girl of twelve or thirteen and – to judge from the protective hand on her shoulder – her older brother or cousin. So stunningly dressed were the younger pair – she in her deep, glossy greens and he from top to toe in gold-embroidered white – that I didn't, at first, think of them as real. They were players, I supposed, on their way to or from something ceremonial.

I too was in borrowed clothes, although mine were notably less glamorous and also too big for me. My sudden, belated awareness of how bad I must look gave rise to my first misgiving: what was I doing here? This was no place for me. But the Lady Lieutenant was ushering me forward – *Get on with you* – as she pushed past me to claim attention from one of the men: a touch to his elbow, a whisper which I overheard. 'The Tilney girl', she called me.

'Right,' was all the man said. I'd do, presumably, whoever I was: the catch-all Catholic girl that – in his eyes – I was. If he spared me a glance, I didn't spy it.

That green-dressed girl did, though: she regarded me briefly, and although there was nothing in particular to the look, there was light in it. And that was when I saw that she wasn't anything like twelve or thirteen, just small. The man who hadn't bothered to look at me continued his business: 'And the purse,' indicating the little drawstring bag that hung from the girl's girdle.

'Oh——' *of course*, and she obliged, unfastening it while the boy huffed and muttered on her behalf at the indignity, the pettiness of it. As soon as the man had hold of the purse, he stuck two fingers into its neck to stretch it, then upturned it over the table and shook it to release its cache. Two vigorous shakes yielded a splash of small coins, at which he jabbed with an interrogative fingertip.

That was when it occurred to me who that girl might be. But here, behind an unguarded door in the company of a couple of plume-crested, linen-spry dandies, along with that canopy-draped incompetent and a six-foot sulk? If she was who I thought she was, then the blond at her side – half as tall again – was no brother but a husband. Baby of the Dudley family, married off six weeks ago to the Grey heiress. Just in time, as his family would've seen it: just before she was bundled on to the throne. Mummy's boy, people were saying. What a pair they made.